*Make time for friends. Make time for **Debbie Macomber**.*

CEDAR COVE
16 Lighthouse Road
204 Rosewood Lane
311 Pelican Court
44 Cranberry Point
50 Harbor Street
6 Rainier Drive
74 Seaside Avenue
8 Sandpiper Way
92 Pacific Boulevard
1022 Evergreen Place
1105 Yakima Street
1225 Christmas Tree Lane

BLOSSOM STREET
The Shop on Blossom Street
A Good Yarn
Susannah's Garden
(previously published as Old Boyfriends)
Back on Blossom Street
(previously published as Wednesdays at Four)
Twenty Wishes
Summer on Blossom Street
Hannah's List
A Turn in the Road

Thursdays at Eight

Christmas in Seattle
Falling for Christmas
A Mother's Gift
Angels at Christmas
A Mother's Wish

The Manning Sisters
The Manning Brides

D1146858

Debbie Macomber

A Turn in the Road

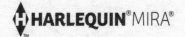

Harlequin MIRA is a registered trademark of Harlequin Enterprises Limited, used under licence.

Published in Great Britain 2011
Harlequin MIRA, an imprint of Harlequin (UK) Limited,
Eton House, 18-24 Paradise Road,
Richmond, Surrey, TW9 1SR

© Debbie Macomber 2011

ISBN 978 0 7783 0462 3

58-0811

Harlequin's policy is to use papers that are natural, renewable and recyclable products and made from wood grown in sustainable forests. The logging and manufacturing processes conform to the legal environmental regulations of the country of origin.

Printed and bound by
CPI Group (UK) Ltd, Croydon, CR0 4YY

With heartfelt appreciation to Nancy Berland
who has helped me navigate every turn in the road
in my publishing career

Dear Friends,

My husband, Wayne, and I love road trips. Because we have two homes, one in Washington State and the other in Florida, we drive back and forth twice a year. In case you're interested, that's 3,323 miles, door to door. Wayne plans the route and we've visited nearly every state between Washington and Florida. Perhaps because of that, I've always wanted to write a book that involved a cross-country drive.

Since I first wrote *A Good Yarn*, which introduced the character Bethanne Hamlin, she's been on my mind. When her husband left her and their family for a younger woman, Bethanne was devastated and eventually joined a knitting class as a kind of therapy. The friends she made in Lydia's yarn store helped her deal with the abrupt change in her life.

The idea for Bethanne's party business actually came from my daughter, Jenny Adele, who held a wonderfully creative party for our oldest grandson when he turned eight. They were living on a one-family income, so money was tight. Using her imagination and playing on Cameron's interest in the army, she mailed out draft notices as party invitations. Then my son-in-law designed an obstacle course on their property. Adding to the fun, my oldest son, Ted, a former Army Ranger, provided camouflage makeup and MREs. The boys had the time of their lives and the entire party cost little more than a cake mix and a few stamps.

I was proud of Bethanne and the success of her business and I wanted to do more with this character. I didn't like Grant, her ex-husband, the first time around, but when he reappeared in *A Turn in the Road* he was much more sympathetic. He's recognised his mistake and wants his family back. This is a difficult decision for Bethanne. As it happens, she has an opportunity to travel across the country with her daughter and her ex-mother-in-law. Three generations of women each facing…a turn in the road. By the way, if you're a committed film buff, you may notice that I've moved the release date of *Breakfast at Tiffany's* forward by a few months. I took this liberty because—well, frankly, it worked for the story.

As always, I'm eager to hear from my readers. You can reach me in two ways: either by logging on to my website at www.DebbieMacomber.com and signing the guestbook, or by contacting me at PO Box 1458, Port Orchard, WA 98366, USA.

Warmly,

Debbie Macomber

One

"I think Dad wants to get back together." Bethanne's daughter, Annie, spoke with studied nonchalance. "He still loves you, Mom."

Bethanne's spoon hovered over her bowl of soup as they sat at a window table in their favorite café. This wasn't actually news and shouldn't have come as any surprise. *Didn't* come as any surprise. She'd seen the signs, as recently as this morning. These days Grant was inventing excuses to call her.

Six years ago her world had imploded when her husband confessed that he'd fallen in love with another woman. With barely a backward glance, Grant had walked out—out of their home, their marriage, their lives. And now he wanted back in.

"Don't you have anything to say?" Annie asked, toying with her fork. She watched her mother intently.

"Not really." She swallowed the soup and lowered her spoon for another taste.

Annie, it seemed, had forgotten. But not Bethanne.

The morning Grant told her he wanted a divorce would stay in her mind forever. He couldn't seem to get away from her fast enough. He'd retained a lawyer and advised her to do the same, then coldly informed her that all future communication would be through their lawyers. The less contact with her and their children, the better, he'd said. A clean break was best.

Grant's decision had struck Bethanne with the force and unpredictability of a hurricane. She'd stumbled blindly through the next few months, trying to hold her family together, clinging to the semblance of normality while her world disintegrated around her. "You really don't have anything to say?" Annie prodded.

"No," Bethanne said shortly. She swallowed another spoonful of soup and reached for the herb scone. "What disturbs me is that your father would let you do his talking for him."

Annie had the grace to look chastened, but she pushed her food away as if she'd suddenly lost her appetite.

At one time Bethanne had dreamed Grant would regret what he'd done, that he'd seek her forgiveness and come crawling back to her. She'd wanted him to suffer for the way he'd treated her, for the hurt he'd inflicted when he'd turned his back on their children.

But in the years since the divorce, Bethanne had gradually found her footing and, in the process, discovered a self she didn't know existed—a stronger, independent Bethanne, a woman forged in the fire of despair. Now her two children were on their own; her oldest, Andrew, was engaged to be married in a few weeks, following his graduation from law school. As for her daughter, Annie was a year from obtaining her MBA. She worked part-time with Bethanne on the creative end of the party business Bethanne had established in the wake of her divorce.

During her twenty years of marriage, Bethanne had become known for her lavish and inventive parties. She'd taken pride in making Grant look good by hosting unforgettable events for clients and potential clients—an invitation to Grant's home became a sought-after privilege in certain circles. Her birthday parties for Andrew and Annie were legendary. But never once had she dreamed that her party-giving skills would eventually be parlayed into such a success.

She'd started the business, which she called simply Parties, as a way of making enough money to continue living in their family home, although she'd had to take out a substantial second mortgage to get Parties off the ground. Grant had paid the required support, but depending on that would've meant moving to a smaller house in a different neighborhood. If ever her children needed stability, she knew, it was in the period after the divorce. She'd since paid off both mortgages.

To Bethanne's astonishment, the business had taken off immediately. She'd started small, with themed birthday parties for children. The Alice in Wonderland Tea Party had been the most popular of the dozens of concepts she'd created. With busy schedules, parents were looking for an easy, economical way to make birthday parties special. Bethanne's company had filled that need.

Currently, there were five Parties stores in the Seattle area, including the original location, and she was considering a deal that offered national franchising opportunities. The key was to keep the ideas fresh and the prices reasonable. This past winter she'd added a "birthday party in a box"—more scaled-down, do-it-yourself versions of her trademarked theme parties.

A year earlier Bethanne had hired Julia Hayden as her corporate operations manager. Julia was efficient, dedicated and gifted. She loved the job and had begun overseeing the company's day-to-day activities, freeing Bethanne to focus on creative development. Annie worked with her, and the two of them had recently developed birthday party ideas for cats and dogs, which was now a popular trend, especially among childless, affluent professionals. They'd expanded into other types of parties, too—anniversary and retirement celebrations, Christmas and even Halloween events.

Bethanne signaled for the check, and they went their separate ways with a quick hug and a wave. Annie was walking back to the office, while Bethanne headed for Blossom Street and A Good Yarn. Knitting had become one of her favourite activities. When she needed to think, nothing helped more than sitting down with a knitting project. She felt a sense of happy anticipation as she parked in front of the yarn store, which was owned by her dear friend Lydia Goetz.

With the wedding only six weeks away, she'd wanted to knit something for Courtney, her almost-daughter-in-law, to wear during the wedding.

The wedding. It was why Grant had called her two weeks ago—their son's marriage had given him a legitimate excuse—and he'd called twice since then, including this morning.

Other than the occasional joint decisions they'd made regarding their children, they'd had little personal contact since the divorce. Then Grant had phoned her with a question about a wedding gift for Andrew and Courtney. He'd been friendly and relaxed. And this week, he'd asked her to dinner.

Dinner. She and Grant. After six years?

She'd heard from Annie that his marriage to Tiffany had ended in divorce the previous year—after a brief separation—and felt genuinely sorry for him. This was a second divorce for Tiffany, as well. In fact, Bethanne had briefly dated Paul, Tiffany's first husband, shortly after the divorce, although *date* wasn't exactly the right word. They'd been more of a two-person support group, helping each other grapple with their betrayal by the people they loved.

Unfortunately, Andrew's relationship with his father remained cool. Her son had met his father's desertion with a bitter resolve that only seemed to harden as he grew older. Andrew was polite but kept an emotional distance from Grant.

For Annie, sixteen at the time, the divorce had been nothing short of devastating. Always a "daddy's girl," she'd acted out her shock and pain as only a willful teenager can. Annie blamed Tiffany for stealing her father away and had done everything she could to sabotage the marriage. But Bethanne was also a target for her rage during those early months. Annie had railed at her for being too "boring" and "clueless" to keep her father happy. Bethanne had never responded to Annie's accusations about her failures as a wife, afraid to reveal how close to home her words had hit. Eventually, Annie had adjusted to the new reality, although she still referred to Grant's second wife in sarcastic tones as "the *lovely* Tiffany."

Bethanne thought about her conversation with him that

morning. His excuse for calling this time was so flimsy Bethanne couldn't even remember what it was. He'd kept her on the line, relating office gossip as if she was still intimately familiar with the goings-on at his workplace. After several minutes of chatter, he reminded her that she hadn't given him a definite answer regarding his dinner invitation.

"Grant," she'd said bluntly. "Why are you doing this?"

For a moment there was silence on the other end. When he spoke, any hints of lightheartedness were gone. "I made a mistake, Bethanne." His voice caught, and for once he seemed at a loss for words. "A major one." He left the rest unsaid, but she knew what he meant. He wanted things back the way they used to be.

Well, good luck with that. Bethanne wasn't the same naive woman he'd divorced, and she wasn't interested in retracing her steps.

After six years on her own, she'd discovered she didn't want or need a man complicating her life. Years ago she'd read somewhere that "it takes a hell of a man to replace no man." At first, that remark had seemed merely humorous; she hadn't completely understood what it meant. She did now.

While she was flattered that Grant wanted to reconcile, the situation wasn't that simple. He'd had his chance. *He* was the one who'd deserted *her*, who'd left her floundering and shaken. Without ever thinking about the consequences of his actions, he'd ripped apart their family, betrayed her and their children, robbed them all of their security.

Now he was sorry. Fine. He'd seen the error of his ways and realized what a terrible mistake he'd made.

So of course he wanted her back. She was a successful businesswoman with a growing company that received lots of media and corporate interest. In six short years she'd made a name for herself. She'd been interviewed by *Forbes* and the *Wall Street Journal*. A piece had been written about her in *USA Today*. Her ex had his nerve.

Contrition was all well and good. Bethanne felt a certain vindication in hearing Grant admit how wrong he'd been, a certain sense of righteousness. She'd forgiven him to the best of her ability, refusing to let herself be trapped in the mire of resentment. He had a new life and so did she. But forgiveness, she'd learned, was tricky. Just when she felt sure she was beyond rancor, she'd find herself wallowing in indignation. Like the night three years ago when the pipe burst in the basement and she couldn't figure out where to turn off the water. If Grant had been there he would've known what to do. By the time she found the tap she'd been shaking with anger, and as unreasonable as it seemed, she'd blamed Grant. This was all *his* fault. He should've been there. How dared he do this to her and, worse, to their children!

She should reject his invitation, she told herself now. Laugh in his face. Tell him to take a hike.

To her astonishment she couldn't.

It had taken courage for Grant to approach her, courage and, yes, nerve. She'd give him that. Crazy though it might be, Bethanne realized she still had feelings for Grant, feelings she'd pushed aside for the past few years. She didn't love him, not in the all-consuming way she had when they were married. Back then, she'd been blind to his flaws and his weaknesses, blind to what should've been obvious, especially after he'd started the affair. His betrayal had revealed that the man she'd married was selfish and shallow. And yet he hadn't *always* been like that. She couldn't forget the companionship—and the passion—of their early years together....

She loved him.

She hated him.

Both emotions warred within her.

"Dinner for old times' sake," he'd almost pleaded. "Besides, we need to talk about Andrew's wedding."

Six years ago Bethanne had been desperate for him to come home. Her pride was gone. What she'd craved was exactly what Grant wanted now—for everything to go back to the way it had been. At the time she'd believed she could fix whatever was wrong. They'd been happy, and could be again.

When it became apparent that his affair with Tiffany wasn't a fling and Grant fully intended to go through with the divorce, an all-consuming rage had taken root. She couldn't sleep, couldn't eat. At night she lay awake plotting revenge. One day Grant would be sorry. He'd beg her to take him back and she'd laugh in his face. He would pay for what he'd done.

Then, several months after the divorce was finalized, she woke with that familiar ugly feeling in the pit of her stomach and realized this corrosive, soul-destroying bitterness couldn't continue. As the saying had it, the best revenge was living well—living a successful, independent life. So Bethanne had dedicated herself to her business.

Gradually, she'd stopped thinking about Grant. She embraced her new life, her new identity. Indirectly, she had Grant to thank for her flourishing business, her circle of loyal new friends, for the strength and confidence she'd never known she had. It felt odd to her now that she'd once been content to be simply Grant's wife, looking after his social affairs and staying in the background.

Dinner for old times' sake? Just the two of them?

In the years since the divorce, Bethanne had dated a number of men. Besides Tiffany's ex, a couple of them stood out in her mind. But she'd been so focused on building her business that neither relationship had lasted more than six months. She wasn't ready or willing to make a serious commitment to anyone. Those relationships, albeit short, had boosted her depleted ego. She'd enjoyed them but she wasn't looking for a long-term commitment.

Bethanne had concluded their phone call without giving Grant an answer. She needed to ponder her ex-husband's newfound contrition, and there was no more effective way of doing that than knitting. It was both productive and contemplative; you created something while you meditated on your problems. That was why she'd stopped at Lydia's—to pick up yarn for the elegant fingerless gloves she'd make for Courtney's wedding.

Lydia glanced up from the display she was working on and smiled when Bethanne entered the store. "You got my message! The cashmere yarn's in."

Bethanne smiled back. "I can hardly wait to get started." Knitting had seen her through the darkest days of her life. Annie was the one who'd signed her up for classes, because even dialing the phone number for the yarn store was more than she could manage back then; the smallest tasks had seemed insurmountable. In retrospect, Bethanne knew she'd fallen into a dangerous depression.

Annie had enrolled Bethanne in a beginners' sock-knitting class. Meeting the other women had been a turning point for her. Her new friends gave her courage and the determination to emerge from her ordeal a stronger woman. Not only that, it was through the knitting class that she'd met Elise, and through Elise, Maverick. He'd ended up being the "angel" who'd helped her launch Parties. Her classmates had reminded Bethanne that she wasn't alone, rebuilding her confidence one stitch at a time.

That class was the beginning of Bethanne's new life. And Part Two turned out to be better than Part One had ever been. Was it possible to knit the two halves together again? Did she want to?

"The pattern isn't difficult," Lydia told her as she brought the yarn to the cash register. "Once you do a couple of repeats, I'm sure you won't have a problem, but if you do, just stop by and I'll help you figure it out."

Bethanne paid for the purchase, grateful that Lydia had wound the yarn, saving her the effort. At first, she'd considered knitting Courtney's veil, but there wasn't time. Although a bit disappointed, she knew fingerless gloves were a far more manageable project. Her hope was that the gloves would be beautiful enough to become a family heirloom, passed down from one generation to the next.

"Alix was in this week and brought Tommy with her," Lydia said as she handed Bethanne the yarn. "You wouldn't believe how much he's grown. It's hard to believe he's nearly a year old."

Alix, a friend of theirs, was employed as a baker at the French Café across the street. "She's gone back to work?"

Lydia nodded. "Just part-time. Now with Winter preg-

nant…there must be something in the water over there."
Lydia grinned. "Or the coffee."

So many changes on Blossom Street, and all of them
good.

"How's Casey?" Bethanne asked about Lydia's adopted
daughter. A couple of months before, when Casey turned
thirteen, Bethanne had planned her birthday party.

"Casey's fine," Lydia assured her. "She had a few aca-
demic challenges and will be attending summer school
again. It's not the end of the world but Casey tends to get
down on herself. We're working on that." Lydia leaned
against the counter. "The poor kid came to us with a lot
of baggage."

"No doubt about that." Bethanne had to admire Brad
and Lydia for opening their hearts and their home to the
troubled girl.

"It helps that she's so close to my mother…. My biggest
fear is what'll happen once Mom is gone," Lydia said, her
voice subdued.

"Is your mother doing okay?"

Lydia rubbed her eyes. "Not really." She gave a small,
hopeless shrug. "She's declining, and that's so hard to
watch. You know, she sometimes forgets who I am but
she always remembers Casey. I think it's one of those
small miracles. It makes Casey feel important and loved,
which she is. Everyone at the assisted-living complex
adores Casey. I wouldn't be surprised if they hired her
once she's old enough to have a job. Her patience with
Mom and Mom's friends is amazing. She loves hearing
their stories."

Bethanne nodded sympathetically.

"No one seems to have enough time for the elderly

anymore...." Lydia shook her head. "I'm guilty of rushing visits myself, but not Casey. She sits and listens for hours and never seems to get impatient, even when Mom repeats the same story over and over again."

"And Margaret?" Bethanne noticed that Lydia's older sister, who often worked with her, wasn't in the store.

"She took the day off. Wednesdays are slow, and she had a dentist's appointment at eleven. I told her to enjoy the afternoon."

Margaret was a store fixture and so different from Lydia that new customers often didn't realize they were sisters. Margaret was good-hearted but tended to be gruff and opinionated, and took a bit of getting used to. "How's business going?" she ventured, aware that she was the only person in the store at the moment.

"Surprisingly well." Lydia cheered visibly. "People turn to domestic pursuits during recessions, and lots of people want to knit these days."

"Have you talked to Anne Marie and Ellen since they moved?"

Lydia returned to arranging the yarn display. "Practically every day. Ellen didn't want to leave Blossom Street but I see her as much as ever. She has plenty of friends in her new neighborhood and has definitely made the adjustment."

"I'm so happy for her." A young widow, Anne Marie had adopted the girl after volunteering at a local grade school. Although Lydia had never said so, Bethanne knew that Ellen's adoption had influenced her and Brad to make Casey part of their family.

"Do you have a few minutes for tea?" Lydia asked.

Bethanne checked her watch. "Sorry, no, I'm on my way to the office. I'm supposed to meet with Julia."

"Soon, then." Lydia waved as Bethanne opened the door.

"Soon," Bethanne promised.

"Stop by if you have any trouble with that pattern," she called over her shoulder.

"I will."

As she unlocked her car, Bethanne looked over at the French Café and was startled to see her ex-mother-in-law, Ruth Hamlin, sitting at an outside table eating her lunch.

Despite the divorce, Bethanne had a warm relationship with Ruth. For her children's sake she'd kept in touch with Grant's mother and his younger sister, Robin. But as Lydia had so recently reminded her, no one had enough time for older people anymore. Bethanne felt guilty as charged. She rarely saw Ruth these days, and it had been several weeks since they'd talked.

Ruth had been horrified by Grant's decision to walk away from his family. She hadn't been shy about letting her son know her feelings, either. She'd always been generous and supportive to Bethanne, making her feel like a beloved daughter in every way. Ruth had stood at Bethanne's side through the divorce proceedings, convinced that Grant would one day realize his mistake.

Bethanne rushed impulsively across the street. She really didn't have time and the ever-punctual Julia would be waiting. As it was, Bethanne had spent far longer with Lydia than she'd intended. In addition, she had a tight afternoon schedule that included a meeting with her managers. But Bethanne was determined to make time for the

woman who'd once been such an enormous encouragement to her.

"Ruth?"

Her mother-in-law looked up from her soup and sandwich plate and instantly broke into a smile. "Bethanne,
my goodness, I never expected to see you here."

The two women hugged. "I was picking up some yarn
I ordered. What are you doing in this neighborhood?"
Bethanne pulled out the chair opposite Ruth's and sat
down.

Her mother-in-law placed both hands in her lap.
"Robin suggested we meet here for lunch. It's not that far
from the courthouse, but you know Robin…"

"Has she left already?" Bethanne looked around, then
down at Ruth's barely touched plate.

"She didn't show up," Ruth said, coloring slightly.
"I'm sure she got stuck in court…." Robin was with the
Prosecuting Attorney's office in Seattle, and frequently
dealt with violent crime.

Bethanne frowned. "Did you call her?"

Ruth shook her head. "I refuse to carry a cell phone.
They're an intrusion on people's privacy and—well, never
mind. Although I will admit that at times like this a cell
would come in handy."

"Would you like me to phone?"

"Oh, would you, dear?" Ruth squeezed her hand gratefully. "I'd appreciate it."

Digging in her purse, Bethanne found her cell. She had
Robin's number in her contacts and, holding the phone
to her ear, waited for the call to connect. Robin's phone
went directly to voice mail, which meant she was probably still in court.

"I think you must be right," Bethanne told Ruth.

The older woman exhaled. "I was afraid of that. I don't know when we'll have a chance to meet again before I leave." Ruth straightened and picked up her sandwich. "But it doesn't really matter, because my daughter is *not* going to change my mind."

"Change your mind about what?"

Ruth lifted her chin. "Robin wants to talk me out of attending my fifty-year class reunion." She took a determined bite of her turkey-and-bacon sandwich.

Why would her sister-in-law do such a thing? "I hope you go," Bethanne said.

"I am, and nothing she says will convince me otherwise." Bethanne had never seen Ruth so fired up.

"Good for you." She watched in amusement as her ex-mother-in-law chewed with righteous resolve.

Swallowing, Ruth relaxed and sent Bethanne a grateful smile. "And I intend to drive to Florida by myself. That's all there is to it."

Two

"Florida?" Bethanne repeated slowly. Her mother-in-law wanted to drive across the entire country? *Alone?*

"Oh, Bethanne, not you, too." Ruth groaned. "I'm perfectly capable of making the trip."

"Can't you fly?" As far as she knew, Ruth didn't have any fear of air travel.

"Of course I could, but what fun is that?" Ruth tossed her napkin on the table. "For years Richard promised me a cross-country trip. I'd spend days planning the route, and I'd write all my friends to tell them we were coming. Then invariably something would come up at Richard's work." Her lips tightened at the memory. "He canceled the trip three times until I finally gave up."

Richard was a workaholic who hardly ever took vacations. He spent most weekends in the office of his engineering firm, missing countless baseball games and piano recitals. In fact, he died in that very same office. How long had he been gone now? Seven years, maybe eight, by Bethanne's calculations.

Grant had taken his father's death especially hard. They weren't close but Grant had looked up to his father and respected his work ethic. As for Robin—well, she'd been cut from the same cloth as Richard. She'd married right out of law school, but divorced three years later. Robin was wedded to her job; there wasn't room for anything or anyone else. Even her desire for a family had faded next to the demands and rewards of her meteoric career. The only time Bethanne actually saw her sister-in-law was at Christmas and that hadn't happened in years, not since before the divorce. They did chat by phone every now and then, and Robin remembered to send cards and checks on Andrew's and Annie's birthdays. But she wasn't involved in their lives—or anyone else's, it seemed, except her colleagues'.

"I'm not getting any younger, you know," Ruth went on, interrupting Bethanne's musings. "If I'm going to see the country, I don't feel I can delay it anymore. I wanted to ask Robin to accompany me but we both know *that* would be a waste of breath. I don't think she's taken more than a week off in the past ten years."

Bethanne had nothing to add. Ruth was right; Robin would never go on a road trip with her mother, would never devote two or three weeks to family.

"In all these years, I've only been back to my home-town three times." Ruth's words were tinged with long-ing. "For my parents' funerals and then once for a brief vacation. But I've kept in touch with several of my high school friends. Diane and Jane both came out to Seattle with their families to visit. When we were together, it was like we were teenagers all over again! I enjoyed it so much, and the reunion's the perfect opportunity to see them. I'm determined to go." She leaned back in her chair and crossed her arms.

Bethanne could tell that she wasn't going to dissuade her. "Then you should do it," she said mildly.

"I am," Ruth insisted. "I'm leaving the first of June."

"So soon?" Bethanne raised her eyebrows.

"Yes, the reunion's on the seventeenth and that gives me plenty of time to see the sights. I've always wanted to visit Mount Rushmore and the Badlands. My grandparents originally settled in the Dakotas, you know."

Bethanne didn't want to discourage Ruth, but she did feel a twinge of anxiety about her traveling that distance by herself. She'd be an easy mark, especially alone.

Ruth fixed her with a stubborn glare. "Before you say anything, I want you to know I've rented a car since I'm planning to fly back, and I've already booked my flight from Florida to Seattle. So don't even try to talk me out of this."

Bethanne gave up the idea of arguing with her and instead patted the older woman on the arm.

"No one takes the time to travel by car anymore," Ruth said plaintively. "Life is 'rush here' and 'rush there.' My children are grown, and I'm sorry to say they're both a disappointment to me. I hardly ever see either Robin or Grant. I'm sixty-eight years old and—" Her voice cracked. "I am *not* old and I refuse to be treated like I'm too fragile to know my own mind."

Bethanne reached across the table and clasped Ruth's hand. She thought of Casey Goetz and the close relationship she had with Lydia's mother. In a few years it might be difficult for Ruth to drive cross-country. It was either take this trip now or give up her long-held dream.

"I'll go with you," Bethanne said in a soft voice.

Ruth's head shot up. "You?"

"I haven't taken a vacation in years." Aside from a few trips with the kids to visit relatives, her last real vacation had been with Grant. They'd gone to Italy to celebrate their tenth anniversary.

Ruth continued to stare at her, obviously at a loss for words.

"It would do me good to get away for a few weeks," Bethanne said. "I have some decisions to make that I'd like to mull over. Getting away will give me a chance to do that."

"You're serious? You'd drive with me?"

"Of course." Bethanne smiled at Ruth's excitement.

"I want to see New Orleans!"

"I'd love that," Bethanne said.

"And Branson, Missouri…"

"You, me and the Oak Ridge Boys," Bethanne said, laughing now and feeling energized by her spur-of-the-moment decision.

"And Andy Williams," Ruth moaned, crossing her hands over her heart.

"Fine, Andy Williams, it is." Bethanne was gratified by Ruth's reaction. "It might take me a couple of days to clear my desk," she warned. Thankfully, Julia was more than capable of filling in for her.

"I don't plan to leave until after Memorial Day," Ruth said, eyes bright with unshed tears. "Oh, Bethanne, you don't know how happy this makes me."

"I'm happy, too," she said, and she was. This spontaneous decision felt incredibly right. She needed time away to think about Grant's recent overtures. She didn't know if it was possible or even desirable for them to reconnect; after everything she'd been through, she could hardly imagine him in her life again. And yet... She couldn't help wondering whether her feelings for Grant, the love that had survived the divorce, would be enough to sustain a second attempt at marriage. Could the woman she'd become find a place for him in the very different life she'd created?

"You're sure about this?" Ruth pressed.

"Positive."

Ruth studied her, frowning slightly. "You aren't doing it out of pity, are you?"

"No." Bethanne tried to hold back a smile.

"Well, I don't care if it's pity or not. I'm just grateful to have you along."

And then she clapped her hands like a schoolgirl.

"Mom," Annie cried the instant Bethanne walked into Parties' Queen Ann Hill headquarters. The retail store was her very first location, and she'd quickly taken over the offices on the second floor. "Where have you *been?* Julia's been waiting for half an hour, and the other managers are arriving in fifteen minutes!"

"Sorry, sorry..." Bethanne mumbled.

"You didn't answer your cell." Annie was pacing Bethanne's office like a fretful cat.

"I was with Grandma Hamlin."

Annie stopped pacing. "She's okay, isn't she?"

"Never better." Bethanne went into the supply cabinet and grabbed a yellow pad. Although Julia was already in the conference room, she picked up the messages on her desk and shuffled through them. She paused when she saw Grant's name.

"Dad phoned," Annie said from behind her. "I talked to him."

Bethanne turned to face her daughter. To her relief, Annie and Grant had mended fences in the past couple of years; their once-close relationship had reemerged. Father and daughter had always been so much alike, both of them charmers, both of them stubborn to the point of inflexibility. Their reconciliation had really begun when Tiffany left Grant. Annie certainly hadn't shed any tears over the breakup of *that* marriage. In fact, she'd had difficulty hiding her joy.

"I feel like Dad's himself again these days," Annie said earnestly.

"I'm glad," Bethanne responded, returning her attention to the stack of phone messages.

"He's working really hard to make it up to Andrew and me."

Bethanne met her daughter's gaze squarely. "He's your father, and you two are the most precious things on earth to him." She doubted Grant understood how close he'd come to losing his children during the years he'd made Tiffany his priority.

"Are you going to call him back?" Annie asked.

The slip was at the bottom of her pile. "I'll do it when I have time," Bethanne said firmly. "Now, I can't keep Julia waiting any longer."

As they hurried down the hallway, Annie said breathlessly, "Vance called this afternoon."

Vance was her daughter's college boyfriend. They'd dated on and off for almost three years. Bethanne knew Annie was serious about him, but she felt they were both too immature to even think about marriage. Despite her age and accomplishments, Annie still seemed so young to Bethanne. Perhaps it was a result of the divorce, but Annie's attachment to both her and Grant struck her as a bit excessive—seeking them out for advice and approval at every turn. Bethanne wondered if *she'd* been that dependent on her parents when she was Annie's age. She didn't think so. However, she hadn't had to cope with the disintegration of her family or the anger and grief it caused.

"Vance calls or texts at least six times a day," Bethanne said. That might be an exaggeration but they seemed to be in constant communication.

"He asked me to dinner at the Space Needle!" Annie was practically vibrating with excitement.

Bethanne arched an eyebrow. "Are you two celebrating a special anniversary?"

"Not that I remember. And trust me, if anyone would remember, it's me."

Bethanne agreed. Like her father, Annie had extraordinary recall when it came to dates, facts and figures; she'd always been a top student in math and history. Bethanne thought of the endless memory games Annie and Grant loved to play on long car trips, egging each other on to greater and greater feats of recall.

"Then what's the occasion?"

Her daughter's eyes were wide. "I'm pretty sure he's going to ask me to marry him," she whispered.

Bethanne did an admirable job of hiding her dismay. "Really?"

Annie nodded. "When I mentioned something last week about Andrew and Courtney's wedding, he told me he's a big believer in marriage and family."

"Family is important," Bethanne said noncommittally.

"Yes, and we agree on practically everything—family, church, politics. Those are the important subjects, don't you think?" Annie searched Bethanne's face for confirmation.

"I do, but a single comment on the subject doesn't mean Vance is ready to propose, Annie." Bethanne's voice was gentle, but inside she marveled at her daughter's naiveté. She didn't want Annie to set herself up for disappointment. A mother never outgrew her protective instincts, she realized.

"Oh, I know, but Nicole saw him at a jewelry store in the University District. It only makes sense that he was looking at engagement rings. Why else does a guy go to a jeweler?"

For any number of reasons, but Bethanne couldn't bring herself to burst her daughter's bubble. "When's the hot date?"

"Friday night."

"Fabulous. I hope everything works out." Either way—engagement or not—she had concerns, but this wasn't the time to discuss them.

"Thanks, Mom." Annie just about skipped down the hall toward her own office.

"Annie," Bethanne called out, stopping her. "I have a bit of news myself."

Her daughter turned back, anxiety clouding her eyes.

"When I saw your grandma, she told me she's planning to drive to Florida next week. I've decided to go with her."

Annie's mouth sagged open. "You and Grandma are driving to *Florida?*"

Bethanne laughed. "Don't say it like that. We're two mature women who can look after ourselves. Your grandmother's wanted to make a road trip across the country nearly her entire adult life, and for one reason or another it's always been put off. She's determined to go—and I can't let her go alone."

"What about Aunt Robin?" As soon as the words were out, Annie shook her head. "Never mind. Aunt Robin wouldn't take the time for that."

Bethanne nodded. "It was a…sudden decision."

"What about the business?" Annie nodded in the direction of the conference room, where the various store managers would soon be gathering.

"Julia can handle whatever comes up in the next few weeks," Bethanne said calmly. "I'll be accessible by phone and email, if she really needs me."

Annie stared at Bethanne. "Wow, Mom, taking off on the spur of the moment—that isn't like you."

"True, but I've got a lot to think about right now, and this will give me a chance to weigh my options."

"Does Dad know?"

"Not yet," Bethanne said, waving as she hurried to the conference room. "I'm sure your grandmother will tell him when the time is right."

The meeting with Julia was abbreviated due to the arrival of the managers. Afterward, Julia and Bethanne parted with a promise to catch up the following day. When she finally made it back to her office to return phone calls, Bethanne saved Grant's for last. The commercial real estate market was still depressed across the country, but it had recently started to pick up in the Seattle area. As the broker in charge of one of his company's most successful offices, Grant had significant responsibilities.

His assistant connected her immediately. "Bethanne," he said, sounding grateful to hear from her.

"Hello, Grant. Annie told me you called." She got right to the point; they were both busy people.

"Tell me, when did our little girl become such a dynamic young businesswoman?"

Bethanne smiled. "I believe she inherited her talent from you."

"I don't know about that," Grant countered. "You're the business powerhouse these days."

Grant had always been skilled at making everyone feel special—like the most important person in the room—and it had served him well in his career. Now he was turning that charm on her, something he hadn't done in years.

"I called about dinner on Friday. You never did say if you were available."

She didn't need a reminder; his invitation had been on her mind for the past three days.

"I thought we'd go to that little Mexican restaurant we used to like so much," he went on, obviously—and correctly—interpreting her silence as hesitation.

"They're still at the same location, can you believe it?" He laughed nervously. "What do you say? You and me, for old times' sake?"

Bethanne closed her eyes, her knuckles white around the receiver. She was decidedly tired of that expression. "Not all our old times were that happy, Grant."

"I know," he was quick to admit. "But we do need to discuss Andrew's wedding."

"We can do that just as easily over the phone."

"We could…" Grant conceded. "But I'd much rather do it over a margarita." She heard him sigh. "You used to like yours on the rocks. Do you still prefer them that way?"

Bethanne couldn't recall the last time she'd even had a margarita. Too many hours in the office and not nearly enough fun. "I suppose."

"So, will you have dinner with me Friday night?" He wasn't pleading, but she thought she detected a note of yearning in his voice.

She exhaled and, with her arm hugged tight around her middle, finally said, "All right."

"I'll pick you up—"

"I'll meet you at the restaurant at seven," she interjected, far more comfortable providing her own transportation.

"Seven," he repeated, not bothering to hide his enthusiasm. "See you then."

Three

Bethanne sat at her desk late Friday afternoon and reviewed the latest figures Julia had given her on the other five stores. She was fortunate that in a struggling economy, Parties continued to thrive. Julia had various suggestions she wanted Bethanne to consider, and in the past months Bethanne had come to rely on her more and more. If it wasn't for her operations manager, she wouldn't be able to take time off to travel with her mother-in-law.

In the years since the start-up of Parties, her business had experienced steady growth and, according to Julia, there was huge potential for the future as long as they were judicious about their finances and their expansion plans.

One of the benefits of her success was the knowledge that she could travel anyplace in the world she desired, something she'd long dreamed about. This was heady for Bethanne. She had good business instincts, as well as basic skills she'd learned watching her husband and his colleagues. Because her ideas were so innovative, she'd received more than her share of attention from the press. She kept copies of the articles written about her novel approach to parties.

Reaching for the folder, she leafed through it, scanning each news clipping and magazine article with a sense of pride and accomplishment. She paused at last year's photograph of herself smiling at the camera, standing outside this building, which housed the original Parties. The photo was flattering. She was at her leanest, her shoulder-length brown hair turned up slightly at the ends. Not bad for forty-seven.

When she'd seen the picture, her thought had been that she looked happy. It was at that moment that she'd realized she was over Grant. Life did go on.

Soon after that photo was published with a profile of her in *USA Today,* Annie told her that Tiffany had left Grant and filed for divorce. A few days later, Grant had called to give Bethanne the news himself; it was the first time they'd spoken in months. He'd sounded depressed, and Bethanne had felt sympathetic. After all, she'd been there....

Grant. Her thoughts had turned to him often since his call earlier in the week. After years of forcing him from her mind, she found it uncomfortable to be entertaining memories of him now.

Bethanne checked her watch. If she was going to be on time to meet her ex-husband at Zapata's, she needed to leave the office now. Because it was the start of the Memorial Day weekend, she was caught in heavy traffic and arrived at the restaurant ten minutes late.

As she entered the dining room, the scent of fried tortilla chips and spicy salsa triggered a wave of nostalgia.

When they were first married, this hole-in-the-wall restaurant had been their favorite. They could order a bean
burrito, plus two tacos with rice and beans, and split the
dinner for $5.50, including tip. If they had extra money,
they bought a single margarita with two straws.

It had been important to them both that Bethanne
stay home with the children until they were in school.
Once Annie went into first grade, Bethanne had been
prepared to finish her degree and rejoin the workforce,
but Grant had asked her not to. She was his partner, his
support—and he liked having her available to manage
the day-to-day tasks that allowed him to focus on his
career. Bethanne had agreed; by then he was doing well
financially and he always let her know how much he appreciated her support.

Seeing her across the room, Grant stood and waved.
The small restaurant was crowded. Almost every seat was
taken and the waitstaff angled between tables, carrying
trays of drinks with chips and salsa. Mariachi music blared
from the speakers.

Bethanne made her way over to Grant, who'd remained
standing. He immediately helped her remove her jacket.
He'd always been attentive about those gentlemanly details. He would open a door for her or pull out her chair
as a matter of course—but he didn't hesitate to rip out her
heart.

Stop.

She refused to let the old bitterness overtake her. She'd
never been the vindictive type, and she'd worked hard to
put the past behind her.

"I ordered you a margarita," Grant said as he slid her

chair under her. She felt his hand graze her shoulder, lingering just a second beyond casual.

The warm chips and salsa were already there. Bethanne's stomach growled as she reached for one, wondering if the salsa was still as spicy as she remembered. One bite assured her it was.

"The menu's almost unchanged after all these years," Grant said as he sat down across from her. He held her look for a moment before opening his menu again.

Obviously, this place brought back memories for him, too.

"I see the prices have changed," she remarked, scanning her own menu. A picture of the Mexican general adorned the plastic front.

He smiled. "Well, I guess we can afford it now."

Bethanne didn't recognize any of the staff. The waitress brought two margaritas over ice, each with a thick ring of salt around the rim of the glass.

"At least we can have two drinks this time around," Grant said, watching her lick the salt off her glass and take a sip.

His familiar use of *we* made it sound as if they were a couple again, but she didn't react. "I hope the same holds true for dinner," she said mildly.

"I believe anything you order will fit into my budget," Grant murmured, still studying the selections.

"I don't think I ever told you I don't like bean burritos," she blurted out.

"You don't?" He sent her a shocked look over the top of his menu. "But...but we ordered it every time we came here."

Bethanne said nothing. In their dozens of meals at

Zapata's, not once had he asked why she never ate her half of the burrito.

"I thought you were just being generous," he said. "You know—saving more for me, the way you did for the kids." He set down the menu, genuinely crestfallen. "I'm sorry, Bethanne, for being so oblivious."

Bethanne was relieved that the waitress returned at that moment for their order. She chose the Tex-Mex salad, while Grant ordered chicken enchiladas and a bean burrito combination plate.

As soon as the waitress left the table, Bethanne took a long drink of her margarita, savoring the warmth spreading through her. She sat back in her chair and waited. Grant had asked for this meeting. She was curious to hear what he had to say.

"I've met Courtney a couple of times now," he began, referring to their son's fiancée. "I like her a great deal. She's very down-to-earth, a good match for Andrew, I think."

"I think so, too," Bethanne murmured.

"I understand that Andrew and Courtney are planning the wedding themselves, and that you're helping them, which makes sense." It was rare to see Grant visibly nervous, but he seemed to be so now, fiddling with his silverware and avoiding eye contact. He cleared his throat. "I'd like to contribute."

"You'll need to take that up with Andrew and Courtney," Bethanne said.

He nodded absently. They both knew that Andrew had ambivalent feelings toward his father. Bethanne felt a pang of sorrow for Grant. She knew he hoped the wedding would provide him with a means of getting closer to Andrew.

"So, *is* there anything I can do?" Grant asked.

"I'm not sure…. I've given Andrew and Courtney contact information and steered them toward people I trust." The couple had made their own decisions, and while Bethanne had offered suggestions, this was their wedding. She'd walked a fine line, trying to advise them without being controlling.

"Weddings are expensive," Grant observed.

"True enough." Bethanne had seen people spend upward of thirty thousand dollars.

"I'd like to help financially." He rested his hands on the table.

She sipped her margarita. "That's kind of you, Grant, but you should be telling Andrew and Courtney this, not me."

"I wanted you to know."

"You've always been generous with the children," Bethanne conceded. A slight exaggeration, but close enough to the truth.

"I almost lost them," Grant muttered, staring at his hands. "I wasn't sure, you know, if it was a good idea to tell Andrew I wanted to help financially… I thought it might be better coming from you."

Bethanne waited until he met her eyes. "No, you tell Andrew," she said. "He loves you, Grant. You're his father."

Grant bowed his head in a gesture of agreement or maybe just avoidance.

"Is that the reason you asked me to dinner?" she asked.

Might as well be blunt—it would've saved her a lot of angst if he'd come right out and said so.

He didn't answer for a moment. "I have something else I'd like to discuss," he said quietly. She strained to hear him over the raucous mariachi music.

"What is it?"

"At the wedding…do you think—" He hesitated. "Would you object if the two of us sat together at the church? As Andrew's parents?"

"Sat together?" Bethanne kept her expression neutral.

"Most divorced couples don't," he acknowledged.

"True."

"I'd like to present a united front to our guests and, more importantly, to our families and our children."

She tried not to grimace. He hadn't been concerned about this "united front" when he'd abandoned them. Oh, why was it so hard to truly forgive? She was shocked by how easily her anger still surfaced, when she'd assumed that she'd moved past the pain.

"It won't be awkward, if you think about it," Grant reasoned. "You haven't remarried and I'm single again. Wouldn't it feel a bit odd for the two of us to sit separately?"

"You're single now, but you haven't always been," she said tartly.

Grant stiffened. "All I'm asking is that you consider it. We'd sit together during the ceremony and stand together in the receiving line. If you agree, I'd appreciate it, but if not…" He took a deep breath, as if to calm himself. "Well, if not—I'll understand. I guess what I'm trying to say, and doing a rather poor job of it, is that I'll accept whatever you decide."

Bethanne couldn't suppress her retort. "In other words, you want the world to know all is forgiven? That we're still friends? That's a noble thought, but I'm not sure it sends the right message."

He looked down at his drink. "I know it may not be possible for you to ever completely forgive me."

Bethanne felt a twinge of shame. She sighed heavily. "I apologize, Grant," she said. "I don't hate you. Really." She'd given him twenty years of her life. He was the father of her children. And there *was* a part of her that still loved him.

Grant's eyes flickered with hope. "Can we do that? The two of us together for Andrew's sake on the most important day of his life?"

"I'll think about it," she promised.

"That's all I ask," he said, and didn't raise the subject again.

Their meals arrived shortly afterward. Grant spooned salsa over his enchiladas. Bethanne remained silent as she waited for him to hand her the bowl.

"I understand Annie's got a hot date tonight," he said.

Although Annie rarely mentioned her conversations with her father, Bethanne knew the two of them spoke regularly these days.

"What's your impression of Vance?" Grant asked, sliding his fork under the steaming enchilada.

Bethanne finished spooning salsa over her own dish as she gathered her thoughts. "He's a good kid...a bit immature, I'd say." She paused. "But then, so is Annie." She took another sip of her drink. "He's an archaeology major and graduated this year. As far as I know, he's going to graduate school."

"Annie seems to think he's about to pop the question."

"So she said." Bethanne set her fork down. "Frankly, I feel they're both too young for marriage. If they do become engaged, I hope they decide on a lengthy engagement."

Grant frowned. "You don't feel Vance is a good choice for our daughter?"

"I didn't say that."

"It's what you implied."

Bethanne's gaze was direct. "No, what I said is that I hope she'd have the sense to wait before making that kind of commitment."

Grant took a bite of his enchilada. "Were *we* too young?"

She shrugged, uncertain how to answer. Like Annie and Vance, Bethanne and Grant had attended the same college. He was a business major and she'd been pursuing a degree in education. They'd met over the summer between her junior and senior year. From their first date, Grant Hamlin had become her entire world. They were engaged by Christmas, and while her parents liked Grant, they'd wanted them to delay the wedding until after Bethanne graduated.

Waiting, however, felt impossible. Grant was out of school and job-hunting. He was hired by Boeing in their corporate office, and with his first paycheck bought her an engagement ring.

Against her parents' wishes, Bethanne dropped out of school just six months shy of graduation. From that point forward she'd dedicated her life to being a good wife and mother. She'd worked briefly in a department store, but only until Andrew's birth.

"Too young?" she repeated his question. "Perhaps…"

They finished their meal quickly after that, avoiding awkward subjects. When they left the restaurant, Grant walked her to her car.

"I enjoyed dinner," he said, standing beside her. "Did you?" The driver's side door was open and she'd already thrown her purse on the passenger seat.

"I did."

"And your dinner companion?"

She gave him a warning look: *don't push it.* "Tonight brought back a lot of memories," was all she said.

"It did for me, too." He touched her car, tracing patterns in the dust. "We were happy, Bethanne," he said, so softly she almost missed it.

She nodded, suddenly sad. "We were," she agreed. "At one time."

He tentatively raised his hands to touch the curve of her shoulders. "I'd give anything to take back the past six years," he said, staring down at her.

"Make that seven," she added. His affair with Tiffany had been going on long before he'd asked for the divorce.

"Seven," he amended, and exhaled slowly. Then something in him seemed to deflate, and she read the regret in his eyes. "Tell me…is there any hope for us?"

As she considered his question, she saw him tense, as if anticipating a blow.

"I don't know," she said, shaking her head. Everything was just so confusing….

"Would it be possible to put the past behind us—forget about the divorce and pretend the past seven years never happened?"

"But they did."

"I know," he whispered brokenly. "If I could take away what I did to you and the kids, I would. I'd pay whatever it cost. If you wanted blood, I'd bleed. I'm miserable without you, Bethanne." His words were heartbreaking in their sincerity. "Tell me you'd be willing to let me have a second chance. All I need is a sliver of hope."

He wanted an answer…but as hard as she tried, Bethanne couldn't give him one.

A lump formed in her throat. She had loved Grant… still did in certain ways that were tied to their shared past, to the memories of their marriage, the years of struggle and sacrifice, the happiness of companionship. And despite everything, they were linked forever through their children.

"Maybe," she breathed.

He smiled then, and his shoulders relaxed. "That's enough for now."

Four

Annie rummaged around inside her mother's closet looking for the silver chain belt that would go perfectly with her Mexican-style skirt. When Vance came by to pick her up for dinner, she wanted him to be awestruck by her beauty. It wasn't every day of the week that a girl got a marriage proposal—if that *was* what he intended. Annie thought so; all the evidence pointed to exactly that. Dinner at an expensive restaurant, being seen in a high-end jewelry store. What else was she to think?

She located the belt and wrapped it around her waist, checking her reflection in the full-length mirror that hung on her mother's bathroom door. The mirror also reflected the queen-size bed her parents had once shared. Even after six years of living alone, her mother still slept on the right-hand side. Not in the middle.

Silly as it sounded, this gave Annie hope that her parents would one day reunite. It was what her father wanted most in the world. What Annie wanted, too. Her parents were meant to be together. Her father had made a terrible mistake, but he was sorry. More than anything he wanted to make it up to the family, and in Annie's opinion they should let him.

It felt good to be close to her dad again. Now that the *lovely* Tiffany was gone, Annie felt there was real hope for a reconciliation between her parents. It just seemed wrong for them to live apart. The problem was getting her mother to recognize how sincere he was and take him back. Annie loved them both so much, and all she wanted was for them to be happy. What they did with their lives wasn't really up to her, as Andrew pointed out with annoying regularity, but sometimes she felt she understood them better than they understood themselves.

The security alarm beeped, indicating that someone had entered the house. "Is that you, Mom?" Annie called down from the second-story hallway.

"Annie? What are you doing here?"

Annie had her own apartment near the University of Washington campus. "I came to borrow your silver belt. You don't mind, do you?"

"Of course not."

"Are you and Dad finished with dinner already?" she asked as she walked down the stairs.

"Yes, it didn't take long." Bethanne hung her jacket in the hall closet and smiled over at Annie. "You look fabulous."

"You think so?" Confirmation from her mother meant everything.

"What time is Vance picking you up for dinner?" her mother asked, glancing at her watch.

"Eight-thirty. Our reservation isn't until nine."

"That's a little late for dinner, isn't it?"

Annie nodded. "Vance said that was the earliest he could get us a table. Every tourist visiting Seattle wants to eat at the Space Needle. Vance must have pulled a few strings to even get a reservation."

Her mother considered the comment. "I didn't realize Vance knew anyone with strings to pull."

"Mom," she protested. "Vance had classes with Matt, remember? And Matt buses tables at the Space Needle. Matt must've put in a word for Vance."

"He must have." Her mother walked into the living room, where she kept her knitting.

"How're Courtney's wedding gloves coming along?"

"So far so good." Bethanne settled into her favorite chair. She had the pattern on a clipboard, held there by a magnet that marked her row. Her mother picked up her glasses, perching them on the end of her nose, and her knitting, which only had a few rows completed.

This was a far more complicated project than anything Annie would ever undertake. "I want you to knit something for my wedding, too, you know."

"I wouldn't dream of doing anything else—when the time comes. If you want, you can take a look at the dress and veil I wore when I married your father. It's yours should you choose to wear it."

"Oh. Mom, could I really wear your wedding dress?"

"We're about the same size, so I don't see why not."

Her parents' wedding picture used to hang on the stairway wall. Annie had seen it practically every day of her life until after their divorce. She didn't know where the photograph was anymore. The last time she'd noticed it, the glass had been cracked. She assumed her mother had broken it the morning her father announced he was in love with the *lovely* Tiffany.

Annie couldn't quite remember what the wedding dress looked like. What she did recall was the joy on her mother's face. She'd been such a young woman— younger than Annie—and a beautiful bride. Her father had been young, too, and so handsome. Annie had loved that photograph.

"It would make me happy if you decided to wear my wedding dress when you do get married." Then, as if her mother wanted to change the subject, she said, "Oh, and thank you."

"For what?"

"For not mentioning to your father that Grandma Hamlin and I are taking this road trip."

Annie felt uneasy about the whole plan. The thought of her mother and grandmother traveling unescorted across the entire country, from Washington to Florida, sent chills down her spine. "I still don't think this is a good idea."

"Nonsense." Her mother leaned forward and, using a yellow pen, marked off the row she'd just finished.

"You told Dad, didn't you?" Annie asked. She hadn't said anything about it because she was sure her mother would.

"Actually, no."

"Mom!" Annie couldn't believe her mother would keep this a secret. "Dad has a right to know what you're doing."

Bethanne glanced up from her knitting. "And why is that?"

"Because...because he might object."

"Annie, sweetheart, I stopped listening to your father's objections a long time ago."

"But you're going with Grandma!"

"Then she can tell him."

What her mother said made sense, but Annie had the feeling her grandmother wasn't going to let Grant or Aunt Robin know what she intended, either.

"If you aren't going to say anything, then *someone* needs to let him know."

Her mother heaved an exasperated sigh. "Do what you want, but as far as I'm concerned it isn't any of his business."

"Honestly, Mom, how can you say that?" Annie grabbed her sweater. "I've got to go. Wish me luck." She held up her left hand and wiggled her ring finger, then rushed out the door.

Vance picked her up right on time and looked great in his slacks and plaid shirt with a button-down collar. He didn't have a tie—he hated them—but that was fine. He'd wear a tuxedo for the wedding.

Annie had narrowed her bridesmaid choices down to five. She'd ask Courtney, her sister-in-law-to-be, and Libby, Belle, Jazmine and Maddy. Ideally, she'd like six or seven bridesmaids, but that would require the same number of groomsmen and make for an impossibly large wedding party. In any case, with everything she knew about organizing social gatherings, their wedding would be the event of the year.

Vance seemed unusually quiet as they drove to the Space Needle. He didn't use valet parking, so they walked the short distance from the closest lot.

"Oh, Vance, this is a lovely idea," she said, clutching his hand. He could be such a romantic.

He responded with a weak smile.

His hand was sweaty, and Annie realized Vance was nervous. She longed to hold on to every detail of this special night and keep them close to her heart. One day she'd tell their children about the evening their father proposed. These were the moments of which family stories were made.

After the elevator ride to the top of the Space Needle, they were seated at a table overlooking the city. The restaurant did a slow rotation, so that during the course of the meal, they'd be treated to a full view of Puget Sound, the Cascades to the east and the Olympics to the west, along with the Seattle city lights.

Staring at her menu, Annie was convinced she wouldn't be able to eat a single bite until Vance got up the courage to propose. From the way he kept looking uneasily around and drinking from his water glass, she figured he might need some help.

"Tonight's special, isn't it, Vance?" she said as she set aside her menu.

"Very." He smiled, but his eyes refused to meet hers.

"Are you…nervous about something?" This part would make a great addition to the story when she repeated it to their children.

"A little."

"Vance, there's no need. We know each other so well, there isn't anything we can't say."

He glanced at her as if to gauge the truth of her words. "You're sure about that?"

"Positively sure." She offered him one of her brightest, most encouraging smiles.

"Maybe we should have dinner first."

"Will you enjoy the meal if you put this off?" she asked gently.

He shook his head and his shoulders sagged. "Probably not."

"Then why don't we discuss what's on your mind?" Maybe it would help if she told him she knew what he intended, but she decided not to ruin his moment. "I believe I know why you're trying to make this night so special," she said instead, hoping she didn't sound coy. "Please, Vance, don't be intimidated. Just ask me."

"Okay, if you're sure." He braced his forearms on the edge of the table. "First, you know you're the one for me, right?"

Annie's heart beat just a little faster. "And you're the man for me." She stretched her arm across the table and Vance took her hand. His thumb stroked her wrist.

Thankfully, the waiter seemed to recognize that now was not the time to take their drink order. He started toward their table, then did a quick about-face.

"That's why this decision has been so difficult," Vance continued.

"Difficult?" Annie didn't understand why giving her an engagement ring would be the slightest bit *difficult*.

"I've decided to go to Europe for a year." The words came out in a rush as if he were gasping for air.

"Europe? A year?" she repeated in confusion.

"With Matt," Vance elaborated.

"Matt? The same Matt who got you the reservation for tonight? *That* Matt?"

Vance nodded. "We've been talking about it for months," he said excitedly, "and we both felt that if we were ever going to do it, this is the time. I've got my graduation money and Matt's been saving up what's left over from his paycheck. We plan on staying in hostels and traveling from country to country by train. There's even a chance we might be able to work on a dig near Ephesus. That's in Turkey."

"I know where Ephesus is," she said through gritted teeth.

"Right...sorry. You're not upset, are you?"

This was a joke. It had to be. Only, she wasn't laughing and Vance seemed about to bolt.

"I wanted to make sure you know I love you," Vance went on. "And...and I didn't want you to hear from anyone else that Jessie Olivarez is going with us. She's Matt's girlfriend and an archaeology major, too, but I didn't want there to be any misunderstanding. Like, I don't want you to think I'm dating Jessie because I'm not. I'm in love with you."

"Jessie?" Vance and Matt were taking a girl with them. "Jessie Olivarez is traveling with you?" They'd met twice, and Annie found her clingy and immature.

"I knew you couldn't take that much time out of your life," Vance said. "You've got your brother's wedding and another year of school. Besides, you're working with your mom, and that would make it hard to leave for so long."

"You could have asked!"

"I was going to, but...well, you know, you've got responsibilities and you'd constantly be on the phone checking in with your mother."

"Are you suggesting my mother and I are joined at the hip?" Talk about adding insult to injury!

"No…no. Annie, please, there's no need to raise your voice." He glanced nervously around them.

Seething on the inside, Annie closed her eyes in an effort to control her raging emotions. "I can't believe this is happening," she finally muttered.

"I know it's a shock and everything," Vance responded, sounding calm now, "but I brought you here because I wanted our goodbye dinner to be special." After what was obviously meant to be a significant pause, he said, "I feel our love is strong enough to wait a year, don't you?"

She didn't answer right away. She could barely take in that he didn't have an engagement ring in his pocket, let alone the fact that he planned to travel in Europe with his friend and another woman.

"You went to University Jewelers," she mumbled. She'd assumed that meant he was going to propose. She'd assumed—

"I did?" He frowned and then relaxed. "Oh, yeah. My mom asked me to drop off her watch for repair. It was still under warranty."

Annie wadded up the linen napkin on her lap. "When do you leave?" She would be adult about this. Okay, fine, he wasn't asking her to marry him. Instead, he wanted her to twiddle her thumbs for a year while he explored Europe with Matt and Jessie Olivarez. Jessie Olivarez!

"Actually…the three of us are flying out tomorrow night. Do you think you could drop us off at the airport?"

He was out of his mind.

"Matt's father was going to do it, but he forget and made other plans."

"You want *me* to drive you and another *girl* to the airport?" The insensitive jerk!

"If you could. It'd be a big help and that way you can see me off."

She'd see him off, all right. "I don't think so," she said, then leaned down and reached for her purse.

"You're upset, aren't you?"

Clearly Vance had talents she never knew. Now he was a mind reader as well as a jerk. "What was your first clue?" she asked sweetly.

"But you said there wasn't anything we couldn't discuss! Come on, Annie, it's only a year."

"It's more than the fact that you're going to Europe, Vance. You've been planning this for a long time. Didn't you even *think* to mention it to me?" By his own admission, this trip had been in the works for months.

He did look slightly guilty. "I wanted to tell you, but Matt said it would just cause problems. I can see he was right."

Annie stood and threw her napkin on the table. "Have a great time, and when you get back, don't bother to call. We're done."

"Annie," he cried, "you don't mean that!"

"Wanna bet?" They had the attention of half the restaurant. The entire room seemed to go quiet. Not wanting to be the subject of anyone's dinner conversation, Annie ran toward the elevator. A line had formed, waiting to be taken down to street level.

Vance hurried after her. "I was afraid you were going to be upset. I wanted to tell you, I really did, but Matt said—"

"I already know what Matt said." Annie crossed her arms and stared fixedly at the elevator door, willing it to open. Pressing her lips together, she did her best to ignore him. There was nothing Vance had to say that she wanted to hear.

"Come on, Annie. I hate leaving when you're upset with me."

She turned her back and looked in the opposite direction.

"Annie, please."

What was taking the elevator so long? All she could think about was escaping Vance as quickly as possible.

"Okay, fine, be mad."

She didn't need any encouragement from him.

"Give me the silent treatment. See if I care."

She pretended not to hear.

"All I want to know is if this means you won't be driving us to the airport."

She whirled around, shocked that he could even ask.

"Well?" He spoke with an air of defiance.

She shook her head. "No, Vance, I won't be driving you to the airport, but have a nice trip. In fact, have the time of your life because that's certainly what I intend to do."

The elevator arrived and, after it emptied, the line moved forward. Annie stepped inside and, just before the doors closed, she took one last look at Vance, standing in front of her, still holding the black linen napkin in his hand. She gave him a short, sarcastic wave.

"Ta-ta," she said as the door glided shut.

Five

The phone rang, waking Bethanne from a sound sleep. No one called in the middle of the night unless it was an emergency. Caller ID indicated her daughter's name. With nervous, uncooperative fingers Bethanne answered. "Hello?"

"Mom!" Annie wailed.

Shifting into a sitting position, Bethanne rubbed her eyes. "Annie, what's wrong?"

Annie tried to speak but Bethanne couldn't understand a word she said. And what she did grasp made no sense. "Vance is going away?" Bethanne asked.

"To Europe with Jessie."

This came out in a screech, which led Bethanne to believe Jessie was most likely a girl. So tonight's dinner at the Space Needle wasn't the marriage proposal Annie had so eagerly anticipated. While Bethanne was grateful, she hurt for her daughter.

"Oh, baby, I'm so sorry."

"I… He actually wanted me to drive them to the airport. Can you believe that?" The anger was coming through loud and clear. "He said he couldn't ask me to go to Europe with him because I had another year of school and…and responsibilities."

"Everyone has responsibilities," Bethanne said, stifling a yawn.

"I… Mom?"

"Yes, sweetheart?"

"This is what it was like when Daddy told you about… the *lovely* Tiffany, isn't it? You didn't know, you didn't even suspect. You were completely oblivious to what was going on right in front of you. Well, so was I." She sniffed loudly. "I feel so stupid."

"Oh, Annie."

"How could Vance be so insensitive?"

Bethanne remembered the shocked, numb sensation that had come over her when Grant left. Unlike her, Annie didn't have a twenty-year marriage; still, she'd just been given a small taste of what Bethanne had experienced.

"Mom?"

"Yes, honey?"

"Can I go to Florida with you and Grandma Hamlin?"

"Uh…"

"I can't bear to stay here alone."

Bethanne resisted the urge to remind her that Grant and her brother would be in town. And she had lots of friends. Annie was far from being alone. On the other hand, having her accompany them wasn't a bad idea. "I'm sure your grandmother will be fine with it, and I'd love to have you."

"Thanks, Mom," she said, still sniffling.

"Do you want to come home and sleep in your old

room?" Bethanne asked, thinking that what Annie really needed was to feel loved and protected.

"No...I'll be okay now."

"If I could, I'd give you a big hug."

"I know. You're the best mom in the world."

Bethanne smiled sleepily.

"Thanks, Mom... Would you call Grandma in the morning and ask her?"

"Of course."

"And I'm telling Dad, too."

"If that's what you want, go ahead." Bethanne had no objection to Grant's knowing her plans but she felt no obligation to tell him herself.

They spoke for a few more minutes and then Bethanne replaced the phone. Resting her head on the pillow, she closed her eyes, trying to go back to sleep.

This would be a fascinating trip across the country now that both her ex-mother-in-law and her daughter were coming.... Well, interesting at any rate. Bethanne drifted off as she began to make mental lists of the clothes she needed to pack and the people she needed to call.

Saturday morning she woke later than usual. Although it was a holiday weekend, she had a hundred things to take care of at work if they were going to head out early Wednesday morning.

After showering and dressing, she set off for the office. She'd wait until after ten to call Ruth regarding Annie.

While she was driving in Seattle traffic, her cell phone rang. The readout on her dashboard showed Ruth's name and number.

Bethanne pushed a button on her steering wheel to answer the phone, and Ruth's voice came through.

"Bethanne, where are you?"

"I'm in my car. What can I do for you, Ruth?"

"Would it be too much trouble to stop by the house this morning sometime…soon? I really hate to bother you."

"It's no bother. I'll leave now."

"How long will that take you?"

"Oh, about ten minutes, fifteen at the most. Is everything all right?"

"Yes, I…think so." Her voice wavered slightly, indicating that everything *wasn't* all right.

"I'll be there as soon as I can."

"Thank you," Ruth whispered gratefully.

When Bethanne pulled up to the Hamlin family home, she saw two cars in the driveway. The first belonged to Grant, and the second she guessed was Robin's. Brother and sister were double-teaming their mother. The poor woman needed backup.

Bethanne rang the doorbell, then let herself into the house. "Hello, anyone home?" she called out.

Ruth appeared immediately, and the relief that spread over her features the instant she saw Bethanne was almost comical. The older woman rushed across the room to grab Bethanne's elbow. "Thank goodness you're here," she whispered.

"Bethanne," Robin said in the tone she probably used to intimidate witnesses in the courtroom. "Tell me you aren't serious about driving cross-country on some ludicrous scheme of my mother's."

At one time Robin might have intimidated her, too,

but no longer. With a cool smile, Bethanne faced her. "Personally, I don't think attending a fifty-year class reunion is all that ludicrous."

Grant stood by the fireplace and seemed content to let his sister do the talking.

Robin didn't give up. "You two don't have a clue what you could be getting yourselves into. It isn't safe out there. You're both much too trusting. I simply can't allow my mother—"

"I didn't ask your permission," Ruth told her daughter stiffly. She raised her chin to signal that she wouldn't be browbeaten, nor would she change her mind. Robin could disapprove all she liked.

"Mother, for once be sensible."

"Sensible?" Ruth repeated. "I've been nothing *but* sensible. It's my life, and at sixty-eight I should be able to do what I want, when I want. If I choose to drive to Florida, then I will."

"And I'm accompanying her." Now might not be the best time to mention that Annie was tagging along, so she held back that information. "You don't have a thing to worry about. We'll be fine."

Robin looked up at the ceiling as though her patience had reached its limit. "I can't believe I'm hearing this." Then, turning to Grant, she added, "A little help from you certainly wouldn't hurt."

"I figured you were doing well enough without me," he said, grinning at Bethanne and his mother.

Ruth and Bethanne stood side by side, with their arms linked.

Ruth looked at her children. "Really, there's no reason to worry. I have the route planned out, I joined AAA and

I've made hotel reservations. I've rented a car, which I'm dropping off in Florida, and we're flying back. I'm sure I've thought of everything."

"Do you have a list of your medications?"

Ruth frowned. "I take one blood-pressure pill and that's it—oh, and I have eyedrops. It isn't like I need a permission slip from my physician to travel. You're grasping at straws. Furthermore, you're treating me like a child. I can take care of myself."

"The roads aren't safe," Robin insisted, "especially for two women traveling alone."

Again Ruth frowned. "If someone does kidnap and murder me, as you seem to expect, you can rest assured that I died happy."

"Oh, honestly, Mother."

"What about Bethanne?" Grant asked. "If she's kidnapped and murdered, how would you feel then?"

"I've had three karate lessons," Ruth said facetiously. "I'll defend her."

Grant burst out laughing. Robin, however, didn't seem to find anything her mother said the least bit amusing.

"Fine." Robin pointed an accusing finger at Bethanne. "Just know that if anything happens to my mother because you were foolish enough to fall in with this crazy scheme of hers, I'm holding you directly responsible."

Bethanne tightened her hold on Ruth's arm. "I accept full responsibility for your mother."

"No, you don't," Ruth protested. "I'm responsible for myself. Besides, if anything did happen, it would be just like my daughter to file a lawsuit against you."

"No, she won't," Grant said, glaring across the room at his sister.

"Don't count on it," Robin said, glaring right back. She crossed her arms as if waiting for them to capitulate. In that case, Bethanne hoped Robin was a patient woman because she had no intention of backing down. And she was sure Ruth wouldn't, either.

After a tense moment, Robin dropped her arms. "Okay, fine. Risk your life. Grant, if you weren't going to support me in this, you should never have come."

"Actually, I think I should be the one to drive them," he said.

"No way." If Ruth agreed to that, Bethanne was counting herself out right then and there. She wanted to get away, reflect, consider the possibility of a future with Grant. She could only do that if he wasn't trying to influence her. Having him along was out of the question.

Ruth looked from one to the other. "You'd do that, son?"

"I'd need to make arrangements with the office and I might have to change the dates, but if this is important to you, Mom, I'd make it work."

"Then you won't need me," Bethanne said, starting to withdraw her arm from Ruth's.

Her mother-in-law held her tight. "Check that computer phone thing you always have with you," Ruth said. "Tell me when you'd be free for two entire weeks to drive me all the way across the country."

Grant took out his iPhone and scrolled down the screen. "Like I said, I'd need to make a few phone calls, rearrange some appointments..." he said slowly. "The second and third weeks of August would be manageable."

"That's too late," Ruth told him. "The class reunion is June 17 and I'm going to be there." She looked pointedly at Robin. "It doesn't matter what scare tactics you use. I won't let tales of renegade truckers and biker gangs intimidate me. Bethanne and I are leaving on schedule and nothing you say is going to change that."

"Now, Mom, you can fly out for the reunion and we can drive back again in August," Grant suggested. "That way—"

Ruth shook her head. "I heard all those promises from your father. Year after year he said we'd drive across the country, but something always interfered. It did with Richard and it will with you. No, Grant, my mind is made up."

"And so is mine," Bethanne added for emphasis.

"Then I say—" Grant turned to his sister with a shrug "—that we let them go."

"Like either of them could stop us," Ruth muttered.

Bethanne grinned and, leaning close, whispered, "Annie wants to join us."

"Annie," Ruth said aloud. "Why, that's a wonderful idea!"

His daughter's name instantly caught Grant's attention. "What's this about Annie?"

"She phoned last night and asked to come with us."

Instead of objecting, as she'd half expected, Grant broke into a wide smile. "I agree with Mom. Bringing Annie with you is a good idea."

This was an interesting development. Bethanne had assumed that once he learned Annie intended to accompany them, it would be all the excuse he needed to demand they fly.

Robin stared at her brother as though he'd taken leave of his senses. "I give up," she said, grabbing her briefcase and her purse. "I can see I'm fighting a losing battle. I have a meeting, so I won't waste any more time here." She stalked toward the door.

"Robin," Bethanne said, halting her progress.

"Yes?" she snapped, whirling around.

"You might want to wish your mother and me a good trip."

But Robin just rolled her eyes and left the house, slamming the screen door on her way out.

As soon as his sister was gone, Grant started laughing. "Well, she was in rare form, wasn't she?"

Bethanne hugged Ruth, who had begun to tremble. "Everything's okay, Ruth. We're going on the trip of a lifetime."

Grant waited until they'd finished hugging before he spoke. "You didn't mention this last night when we had dinner." The comment was filled with accusation.

"Was there any reason I should?"

"You're planning to drive across the country with *my* mother," he said. "Didn't you think Robin and I were entitled to know?"

This was a repeat of the conversation she'd had with Annie. "It was up to Ruth to mention it, not me," she told him, unwilling to be chastised by her ex-husband.

Grant's response was a raised eyebrow, but he didn't say anything else.

"I was afraid Robin would make a fuss," Ruth said. "I wish now I'd kept my mouth shut."

Bethanne agreed it would've been preferable had Ruth waited until they were on the road, but that seemed a bit underhanded.

"If I can, I'd like to ask one thing of you," Grant said,

obviously deciding on a more conciliatory approach. "I'd feel better about the three of you being on the road if you'd call me at least once a day."

"We could do that," Ruth said, eager to make peace with her family.

"Will *you?*" Grant posed the question to Bethanne.

"I'm sure Ruth and Annie would be happy to keep in touch," she said curtly, reluctant to add her name to the list. The idea of calling her ex-husband didn't sit well with her, despite his unexpected support.

Grant held her look. "I won't be able to relax if I don't know that the three most important women in my life are safe."

"We'll check in," Bethanne eventually promised.

"Thank you."

Bethanne drove to the office a few minutes later, but for the rest of that day, she couldn't get Grant out of her mind. She had to appreciate the fact that he hadn't joined forces with his sister against them. His concern for Ruth, Annie and her seemed genuine. She'd given him a glimmer of hope that a reconciliation was possible; the idea didn't seem as repugnant to her as it once had and that, she guessed, was a good sign.

At her desk, she made all the necessary arrangements to leave the office for a few weeks. She went home at five that afternoon, slightly depressed at the prospect of an empty house, and wondered what it would've been like if Grant had been there waiting for her with a glass of wine and a welcoming smile.

Six

"Finally! We're actually on the road," Ruth marveled as they reached the summit of Snoqualmie Pass, crossing the Cascade Mountains. They were a little more than an hour outside Seattle, heading due east.

Ruth had the map supplied by AAA spread out on her lap and acted as navigator while Bethanne drove. Annie had claimed the backseat; she'd been suspiciously quiet since they'd left Seattle. Bethanne knew Vance had deeply hurt and disappointed her daughter. The fact that he'd decided to travel in Europe for a year—and hadn't bothered to tell her—could only feel like a betrayal. Bethanne hoped that spending these weeks with her grandmother and with her would help. Annie was still young. In time she'd recognize that Vance's leaving was the best thing that could have happened.

She remembered when she'd told her parents she wanted to marry Grant. Her family, especially her father, had urged Bethanne to complete her education first. With just one semester to go before she obtained her degree, he'd argued that it made sense to put off the wedding. Bethanne, however, had been unwilling to listen, unwilling to wait a day longer than necessary to be Grant's wife. And she'd refused to be separated from him; the university was in the town of Pullman in eastern Washington, while he was working in Seattle. She'd finish school later—only she never had.

In retrospect, it had all worked out, but if she'd had her teaching degree who knows how different her life might have been. One thing was sure; with a career of her own, or at least the qualifications for one, she wouldn't have felt so completely vulnerable when Grant asked for a divorce.

Annie's situation was different to that extent, anyway. She'd graduate the following year with a business degree. She'd gotten practical experience working at Parties and that would serve her well.

Annie stirred in the backseat, sitting up and yawning. She removed the iPod earbuds and stretched her arms to the side, arching her back. "Where are we?"

"Just over the pass," Bethanne told her.

"Already?"

"Have you been asleep?"

"I think I was," Annie murmured sadly. "I haven't had much sleep the past few nights."

"Oh, sweetie, I'm sorry."

"Vance, Matt and Jessie got off okay," she muttered with no degree of pleasure. "They ended up getting a cab. He sent me a text from the airport and said he'd keep in touch."

Bethanne suspected Vance's effort to communicate wouldn't last long. If the tone of Annie's voice was any indication, she'd figured that out, too. Vance would stay in touch for the first few weeks, and then all his good intentions and promises would fall by the wayside. Frankly, Bethanne was just as glad, although she'd never tell Annie that.

"Where are we spending the night?" Annie asked, leaning forward and thrusting her head between Bethanne and Ruth in the front seat.

"I have a reservation in Spokane," Ruth answered.

"Spokane?" Annie repeated. "That's only five hours from Seattle. Can't we drive farther than that?"

Ruth looked over at Bethanne. "When I made these arrangements I intended to travel alone. I estimated that between four and six hours on the road would be my limit. I wanted to make it a leisurely trip."

"We've been to Spokane at least a dozen times," Annie complained. "I've seen everything there is to see."

Bethanne had, as well. "This is your grandmother's trip, Annie," she reminded her daughter. "If Grandma Hamlin wants to spend the night in Spokane, then that's what we'll do."

"Okay." Annie slumped back and folded her arms. "Does the hotel have a swimming pool?"

"I don't know." Ruth flipped open her itinerary.

"Tell me the name of the hotel and I'll look it up on my phone."

"You can do that?" Ruth sounded impressed.

"As long as they have a website I can."

Ruth gave Annie the hotel name, and Annie immediately started clicking away. Judging by her sigh, the hotel was pool-less.

"We'll have lunch, and then check out the local attractions. There's a mall close by, isn't there, and a movie theater? No reason we have to stay in the room." Bethanne offered what she hoped were helpful suggestions.

She assumed they'd reach Spokane a little after one. The truth was, Bethanne agreed with Annie. She was certainly willing to drive beyond Spokane. However, this was Ruth's trip, as she'd pointed out, and she was reluctant to do anything that would diminish her mother-in-law's enjoyment. Ruth had waited years for this opportunity, so Bethanne refused to cheat her out of even one second of her carefully planned adventure.

"I...I suppose we could go a bit farther," Ruth murmured after a while. "I'm anxious to get to Florida."

"Have you heard from anyone there?" Bethanne asked.

"Just Jane and Diane."

"Wow, fifty years," Annie said. "That's a long time."

"It is." Ruth nodded slowly. "The funny thing is, it doesn't seem that long ago—it really doesn't."

"How many years has it been for you, Mom?"

"Let me see. I graduated in..." Bethanne quickly calculated the years, astonished that it'd been twenty-nine years since she'd left high school. "Twenty-nine years," she whispered, hardly able to believe it.

"Did you ever go to your reunions?"

Annie certainly seemed to be in an inquisitive mood. "No. Your father—" Bethanne paused, about to lay the blame at Grant's feet. While it was true that Grant hadn't been enthusiastic about attending her high school functions—or, for that matter, his own—she'd consented. She could've gone by herself, and hadn't. It wasn't like Eugene, Oregon, was all that far from Seattle. "No, I never did," she said.

Her father, an English professor now retired, had taught at the University of Oregon. Her mother had died a couple of years ago. Bethanne was proud of the way her father coped with being a widower. Despite his grief he hadn't given up on life; in fact, he was currently in England with a group of students on a Shakespearean tour.

They spoke and emailed regularly, and she'd recently learned that he was dating. Her father had a more active social life than she did, which actually made her smile.

"Wasn't Dad born in Oregon?" Annie asked.

"Yes, in Pendleton," Ruth confirmed. "Richard and I were newlyweds, and he was working on a big engineering project there. I don't remember exactly what it was now. We moved around quite a bit the first few years we were married."

"How far is Pendleton from here?"

"Oh, dear, I wouldn't know."

"I'd like to see the town where Dad was born," Annie said. "Couldn't we spend the night there instead?" She reached for her phone again. "It would mean we'd need to change our route, but it wouldn't be that much out of our way."

"We were only in Pendleton for the first year of his life," Ruth said.

"Do you have any friends living there?" Annie pressed, but before Ruth could answer, she asked another question. "I'll bet it's been ages since you connected with them, isn't it?"

"Well, that was forty-nine years ago. I'm sure they've moved on."

"What are their names?" Annie's fingers were primed

and ready as she held her cell phone. "I'll look them up and find out for you."

"Annie," Bethanne warned. Her daughter seemed to be taking control of the trip.

"Okay, okay, I'll shut up and we can spend the night in Spokane and sit around the hotel room all afternoon."

Bethanne cast Ruth an apologetic look.

"I had a friend by the name of Marie Philips." Ruth's voice was tentative, uncertain. "She was married and a young mother herself. Her parents owned a small café on the outskirts of town. I'm sure it's long gone by now."

"We need to eat, don't we?" Annie said triumphantly.

"The café might not even be in business anymore," Bethanne felt obliged to remind her.

"Is her name listed on that computer phone of yours?" Ruth asked, sounding more interested by the minute.

Bethanne could hear Annie typing away.

"P-h-i-l-i-p-s?" Annie spelled it out. "With one *L*?"

"Yes. The café was where the bus stopped, too. They served the most wonderful home cooking. Marie was a real friend to me, but we lost contact after Richard and I moved."

"What was the name of the café?"

"Oh, dear." Ruth shook her head. "I don't remember, but I do know where it is…or was."

"So, can I see the town where Dad was born?" Annie asked eagerly. "Even if we spend the night in Spokane, I'd still like to visit Pendleton."

"I don't see why we couldn't," Ruth said, apparently catching Annie's enthusiasm. "My goodness, I haven't thought of Marie in years. She had a son around the same age as Grant. I wonder what became of him. Marie had an older boy, as well. Like I said, she was so helpful to me. She's one of those salt-of-the-earth people." Ruth seemed immersed in her memories.

Bethanne continued driving in silence. They passed Ellensburg and were headed toward the bridge that spanned the mighty Columbia River, on the way to Moses Lake. All of this was familiar territory. If they made the decision to go to Pendleton, they'd need to change course after crossing the bridge.

Annie was still typing. "The Pendleton directory lists a Marie Philips."

"It does?" Ruth's voice rose excitedly. "Let's call her."

Annie called and left a message on the woman's voice mail. When she'd finished, she asked, "Do you want me to see about changing our hotel reservations?"

"I've already made a deposit at the hotel in Spokane," Ruth lamented.

Bethanne hated to admit it, but even she was disappointed. She was enjoying the drive and it did seem a waste of time to arrive in Spokane for lunch and call it a day.

"It's a chain hotel," Annie said. "If there's one in Pendleton, I bet they can switch reservations without a penalty."

Ruth was quiet for a moment. "Okay, call and see if the hotel is willing to do that."

"When you're ready, give me the phone number."

Ruth rattled it off. Annie got through right away and made the arrangements. She disconnected, saying, "Done. The manager told me it wasn't a problem."

"That's great," Bethanne said, pleased her daughter was so technologically savvy. She had the same phone as Annie and Grant but couldn't do nearly as much with it.

The problem was that she hadn't made the effort to learn. It seemed that whenever she got comfortable with her phone, it was time to upgrade and she'd have to learn a whole new process.

"I wonder what Marie's doing these days," Ruth said thoughtfully.

"Well, we'll find out," Annie responded.

"We can have a light lunch when we hit the Tri-cities," Bethanne suggested, "and once we reach Pendleton we can look for the café your friend's family owned."

"I'd like that," Ruth said, "but we all know there's no guarantee the café will still be there."

"Right, but we can look, can't we?" Annie said. "Then, after we eat, can you show me the house you lived in when Dad was born?"

"Sure thing," Ruth said, "but again you have to remember that was a long time ago."

Bethanne didn't understand Annie's sudden interest in her father's birthplace. Ruth, however, seemed happy to stroll down memory lane. Annie was encouraging her, and this exchange of questions and anecdotes was probably good for both of them.

Annie's cell phone rang when they stopped for lunch in Richland. They found a chain restaurant off the freeway and each ordered soup.

"Oh, hi, Dad," Annie said, and her gaze immediately went to Bethanne. "Yeah, we're in Richland." She smiled and added, "We made good time. Mom's driving—and guess what?"

Bethanne was determined not to listen, but she couldn't avoid hearing Annie's side of the conversation.

"Mom's right here. Do you want to talk to her?"

Bethanne shook her head vigorously. Annie ignored her reaction and handed over the cell.

Reluctantly, Bethanne accepted it. "Hello, Grant," she said without enthusiasm.

"You turned your cell phone off," he said, although his words lacked any real censure.

"I'm driving," she pointed out. The rental car didn't have a Bluetooth connection.

"That's what Annie said."

Silence.

"How's it going so far?"

"Fine." She resisted telling him that they'd left just that morning and were only about two hundred miles from Seattle.

"What's this I hear about you spending the night in Pendleton? Did you know I was born there?"

If she'd forgotten, she'd received plenty of reminders in the past few hours. "Annie mentioned it." Bethanne wondered if Grant had put their daughter up to this. She was well aware that Annie had her own agenda. But then, perhaps she was becoming paranoid.

"I hoped you'd call and check in every now and then," he said in a hurt-little-boy voice that was meant to elicit sympathy.

"You should talk to Annie or your mother," she told him. "If you'd like, I'll remind Ruth to check in with you or Robin every day so you can rest assured that all is well."

"Yes, please do."

"Here's your mother." She passed the phone across the booth to her mother-in-law.

Annie waited until their soup arrived before she spoke. "Honestly, Mom, you could be a bit friendlier to Dad."

"Oh?"

"Yes. You know how he feels."

Bethanne did. "This is about more than feelings, Annie."

"At least let him prove himself. You don't need to be so…" She couldn't seem to find the right word. "Unfriendly," she said, repeating herself.

"Did I sound short with your father?" she asked.

"A little."

Bethanne looked at Ruth, who shrugged. "Just a tad, honey."

Bethanne exhaled and forced herself to remember that she was traveling with two of his staunchest advocates.

"Is there any possibility the two of you might reconcile?" her ex-mother-in-law asked, eyes wide and hopeful.

"Of course there's a chance," Annie answered on Bethanne's behalf. "There's always a chance, right, Mom?"

Bethanne took her time answering, apparently longer than Annie liked, because both her daughter and Ruth stopped eating and stared at her intently. "Yes, I suppose there is," she finally agreed.

Seven

"Look, the café's still there!" Ruth called from the backseat. Annie had been driving since Richland, with Bethanne knitting beside her. Ruth leaned forward, thrilled about the opportunity to see her old friend again. When she'd met Marie, she'd been pregnant, away from family and friends, and in a marriage that hadn't started out in the most positive way.

They'd moved to Pendleton because that was where Richard's first job was. He'd wanted to make a good impression on his employer; he'd been young, ambitious and eager to prove his worth. Her husband of less than a year had worked long days, abandoning Ruth to countless hours alone in a rental house in this town where she didn't know a single soul. Meeting her neighbor, Marie, had been a lifesaver. Ruth had needed a friend, a connection with someone. She hadn't really been prepared for the pregnancy, and she suffered from violent bouts of nausea that lasted through most of the day.

Not only did Marie become her friend, she'd taken

Ruth under her wing, recommended her own obstetrician and driven Ruth to and from her first few appointments. She'd shared baby clothes and maternity outfits with her. Best of all, she'd taken time for long afternoon chats, despite the fact that she had children of her own and often helped her parents at the roadside restaurant.

Ruth had lived in Pendleton for only a couple of years, but she never forgot Marie, even though her own life had changed—and improved—soon after. The effort to stay in touch lasted several Christmases but eventually they'd lost contact. Still, Marie's friendship had brought her comfort and support all those years ago.

The café sat back from the road, surrounded by a gravel parking lot, just outside the Pendleton city limits. The white paint had long since grown dingy, and the windows looked like they hadn't been cleaned in months. A sign out front announced Home Cooking.

"Looks like it's still in business," Ruth said, unable to keep the excitement out of her voice.

"I *told* you this was a good idea," Annie said. "You're glad we came this way, aren't you, Grandma?"

"Very glad," she said, and it was true.

"The sign on the building says it's Marie's Café," Annie pointed out.

"She must've taken over from her parents," Ruth commented. She grabbed her purse and was practically out of the car before Annie had pulled to a complete stop. She didn't wait for the others.

The café door creaked as she opened it—and then came to an abrupt halt. It was as if she'd stepped back fifty years. The café was the same as she remembered, right down to the aluminum paper napkin dispensers and the tabletop jukeboxes. The booths had the identical red vinyl upholstery, but surely the seats had been recovered, probably more than once. The plastic-covered menus were tucked behind the ketchup and mustard containers, which stood next to the salt and pepper shakers.

More afternoons than she could recall, Ruth had sat in one of these very booths with her infant son at her side as she drank a cherry soda and talked over life's challenges with her friend.

At one stage, soon after Grant's birth, Ruth had been ready to admit her marriage was a huge mistake. She wanted to end it. Marie had listened and been sympathetic to her tales of woe. Richard spent so little time with her and their son that Ruth was convinced he didn't love her, that he never really had. Their marriage was a sham, she'd told her friend, and it was better to own up to her mistake and get out now before their lives became even more complicated.

Marie didn't attempt to talk her out of her decision; all she'd really done was ask Ruth a few questions. As she answered, Ruth realized how important it was to do whatever she could to make this marriage work. Not only because of their son, but because marriage was supposed to be a partnership and that required something from her, too. An honest commitment, a genuine effort… In the back of her mind, and it embarrassed her now to admit this, she'd felt she could always go home, back to Florida….

Back to Royce Jameson. She suspected Bethanne had picked up on the fact that there was more involved in this reunion than meeting her high school friends, much as she looked forward to that. Royce would be there, too;

Jane had written her with the news. The possibility of seeing him again had everything to do with wanting to return to Florida. They'd been high school sweethearts—an old-fashioned term, perhaps, one Annie might have scoffed at, but it was true. They'd been so young and so deeply in love. But she'd hurt him terribly and even after all these years she wasn't sure he'd forgiven her.

The last time they'd stood face-to-face was the summer after their high school graduation. They'd held each other and they'd kissed, vowing that nothing would ever come between them. He was leaving for boot camp and she was heading off to college. They'd promised to love each other forever and ever. Six months later she was engaged to Richard.

Their final conversation had been horrific. Ugly. She'd taken the coward's way out and written him from college that she was marrying Richard. Back then Royce was in the marines and stationed in California before being deployed. When he received her letter he'd phoned her at her college dorm, angry and hurt. She'd listened while he accused her of terrible things. The conversation was one of the most painful of her life, and she'd sobbed for hours afterward.

All she knew of Royce's life in recent years was that, like her, he hadn't attended any of the previous reunions. And, like her, he'd lost his spouse.

In the end, of course, Ruth had stayed with Richard and later given birth to Robin. She'd heard from Diane, her high school friend, when Royce had married. It'd been a good time in her own marriage and she was happy for him. She wished him well.

"Can I help you?" A woman in her late sixties or early

seventies hurried out from the kitchen, wearing a white apron. Yellow rubber gloves covered her hands; she appeared to be the dishwasher.

"Marie?" Ruth asked tentatively. "Is that you?"

Marie came a step closer. "Ruth? Ruth Hamlin?"

They both gave a shout of recognition and advanced toward each other, arms outstretched, laughing and talking at the same time.

"I'd recognize you anywhere," Marie claimed.

"You look *wonderful*."

"I'm an old bat," Marie countered, still laughing.

"Me, too."

They embraced like long-lost sisters, hugging each other and clinging hard.

Bethanne followed Ruth into the café and watched the two women embrace. When Annie had suggested they spend the night in Pendleton, Bethanne had her doubts. She was loath to disrupt Ruth's careful plans. Yet from the moment they'd crossed the Columbia River, her mother-in-law had been animated, reminiscing about the early years of her marriage, the cities in which she and Richard had lived and the friends she'd made.

"Bethanne, Annie," Ruth said, turning to them, her face aglow. "Meet Marie. She was one of my dearest, dearest friends all those years ago." She shook her head, then hugged Marie again. "Annie's my granddaughter and Bethanne, her mom, was married to Grant." She lowered her voice but Bethanne could hear every word. "Officially, they're divorced, but I have high hopes of a reunion now that my son has come to his senses."

"Hi," Annie said, and raised her hand in greeting.

Bethanne decided to pretend she hadn't heard Ruth's comment and smiled at the other woman, who seemed five or ten years older than Ruth. Marie's hair had gone completely white and her face was heavily wrinkled. The years hadn't been nearly as kind to her as they had to Ruth.

"Where is everyone?" Ruth asked, looking around the café. Many of the tables had yet to be bused. The counter was cleared, but a couple of syrup bottles remained, standing in sticky puddles.

"When Richard and I lived here, there wasn't a seat to be had, day or night. Don't you remember we used to quote Yogi Berra? We said the place had gotten so popular, no one went there anymore." She giggled like a schoolgirl and so did Marie.

"Everyone wants to stay close to the freeway these days," Marie lamented. "Thank goodness the bus still stops here. Otherwise, I'd be out of business for sure."

"Your mom's chicken-fried steak was the best I ever ate," Ruth said. "I don't think I've ever tasted gravy that good, before or since."

"It's still on the menu. A heart attack on a plate, as they say, but it's my bestseller."

"No wonder."

"I was about to close up shop," Marie said, drying her hands on her apron. "Maggie phoned in with the flu and my dishwasher's out sick, too. I don't have any choice."

"I thought the bus stopped by every day."

"It does, but I can't cook, wait tables and wash dishes all by myself." She frowned, shaking her head helplessly.

"Has the bus come by today?" Ruth asked.

"Not yet." Marie glanced at her watch. "It's due in another forty minutes."

Annie tugged at Bethanne's sleeve and whispered, "We could pitch in."

Marie stared at them. "Could you? I mean, I'd be willing to pay you. I'm afraid if I close for even one day, the bus company might not renew my contract and then I'd be flat out of business."

Ruth shoved her sweater sleeves up past her elbows. "I'm a champion dishwasher, at your service."

"I can bus tables," Annie offered.

"Uh." Bethanne hesitated. She was thinking *she* should wash dishes.

"Come on, Mom, you'd make a great waitress."

"Nothing like a pretty girl to build up business," Marie told her, grinning as she said it. "And I could certainly use the help."

"Then I'd be delighted." The last time Bethanne waited tables had been the summer after she graduated from high school. She'd gotten a job working at the local Denny's. The experience had convinced her that she wasn't waitress material. It'd been hard work, lifting heavy platters and busing tables. In addition, she'd discovered that people could be demanding, rude and insensitive. But she'd be able to manage for a few hours.

"I've got another apron in back. Let me get it for you." And Marie bustled into the kitchen, with Ruth close behind.

"I hope I don't spill coffee on anyone," Bethanne worried. "Or mix up all the orders."

"Mom, like Grandma always says, don't borrow trouble. We'll do great."

As little as ten minutes ago, Bethanne had been sitting quietly in the car knitting a wedding gift for her future daughter-in-law. Now she wore a pink apron with a frilly starched border. She looked like a character in some movie about a diner, and since she wore the uniform, she might as well play the role. She purposely tucked the pencil behind her ear, then reached for the order pad and slipped it in her apron pocket.

"The specials are listed on the chalkboard outside," Marie explained. "It might be a good idea to memorize them."

"Gotcha," Bethanne said, and walked outside. She studied the blackboard. Ham and redeye gravy was first, followed by macaroni and cheese. The third special was pot roast with mashed potatoes and gravy. Apparently, Marie was fond of smothering food in sauce.

She'd finished familiarizing herself with the specials when she heard the roar of motorcycles in the distance. The sound was deafening as it drew closer. "What is it about men and motorcycles?" she muttered as she went back inside.

"How long before the bus gets here?" Annie asked. She wore her own apron and carried a cleaning rag and a gray plastic tub piled high with dirty dishes.

"About twenty minutes," Marie called from the kitchen. "Listen, you might fill the water glasses now. It'll save you time later."

"I'll do that," Bethanne said. She found a pitcher and set about pouring water into each glass. While she was at it, she figured out how to work the coffee machine. Meanwhile, Annie washed the counter, cleaned the tables and put out silverware.

The roar of engines thundered to a stop just outside the café and, shortly after, four burly men dressed in leather vests and calf-high boots walked in as if they owned the place.

Bethanne stared at them. They paused by the door and looked around. Bethanne wasn't easily intimidated, or so she'd always thought, but these men seemed like the real thing. Road warriors. They were everything Grant's sister had warned them about. Not that Bethanne knew *anything* about biker culture, but to her inexperienced eye, two of them looked halfway decent and the other two looked suspicious. She certainly wouldn't trust any one of them with her daughter. Come to think of it, they were four women alone…

A prickle of fear went down her spine and she stood there paralyzed, unable to move or even breathe. She could imagine the headlines now. Four Women Raped and Murdered. Biker Gang Suspected. If anything happened, Robin would blame *her*. Not that it mattered, seeing as she'd most likely be dead.

Annie's eyes connected with hers. Deciding not to give in to her overactive imagination, Bethanne straightened. "You gentlemen can sit anywhere you want."

The older one, with the short, skinny ponytail, said, "We generally do."

The others laughed. The four of them slid into a booth and studied her as though she were a fresh piece of meat and they were hungry wolves.

"I'll take your order in just a minute," she said, pretending to ignore their menacing demeanor.

Annie held her mother's gaze and then scurried into

the kitchen. Bethanne trailed her at a more leisurely pace, unwilling to show how intimidated she actually felt.

"Do you know those men?" Ruth asked her friend, peering into the café from the kitchen entrance. "They look like they belong to some rough-and-tumble gang."

"Bikers stop by here all the time. Don't let them scare you," Marie said. "They all like to act tough, but underneath they're pussycats." She was busy stirring a pan of gravy and didn't even glance out. "Besides, their money is as green as anyone else's."

"Right." Trying not to reveal her fear, Bethanne removed the order pad she'd stuck in her apron pocket, took the pencil from behind her ear and headed back out.

"What can I get you boys?" she asked, forcing herself to act as if she was in a theater production. Or one of those diner movies. All she needed was a wad of gum to go with the attitude.

"Boys?" Again it was the older man with the ponytail who responded. "Do I look like a boy to you?"

"It's a figure of speech," she said, holding her ground. "Would you like separate checks?"

"Please." The one who answered was the most tanned of the group, which suggested he'd been on the road the longest. He had intense brown eyes and wore a leather bandanna tied at the base of his neck. His leather vest looked well-worn and he had on fingerless gloves. She almost mentioned that she was knitting a similar pattern for her son's fiancée—but she didn't. It was a good bet that he wouldn't be interested in her latest knitting project.

"Cheeseburger, with double pickles and no onion," the man sitting across from Ponytail told her.

Bethanne wrote that down. She looked over at the biker

next to him, who ordered macaroni and cheese. Leather Bandanna ordered a bowl of chili and Ponytail wanted the pot roast special.

"I'll have those out for you in a few minutes." It wasn't until she gave Marie the order that she realized she hadn't asked if they wanted anything to drink. The coffeepot was full, so she carried it over to the table, and when they all righted their cups, she did her best to fill them without letting her hand shake. She didn't want these men to know how nervous they made her.

Bethanne started to turn away when Ponytail stopped her. "Where's your name tag?"

"Ah…I left it at home. I'm Bethanne." As soon as she said it, she regretted not giving him a fake name.

"Bethanne," he repeated, then nodded as though he approved.

"What's yours?"

"I go by Rooster."

"Rooster?"

"After the John Wayne movie," one of the other bikers explained.

"Oh, okay," Bethanne murmured. "*True Grit,* right? The original version."

"Right."

The biker pointed across the booth at the two other men. "That's Willie and the good-looking one is Skunk. This here is Max," he said, nudging the man beside him.

"Bethanne," she repeated.

The two men across from Rooster nodded. Ignoring her, Max looked out the window. The two other bikers were adding cream to their coffee. Rather than encourage further conversation, Bethanne retreated behind the counter. Her hand trembled slightly as she returned the coffeepot to the burner.

The door opened again, and a steady stream of customers filed into the café. Bethanne glanced outside, seeing that the bus had arrived ahead of schedule. She'd been too distracted by the bikers to notice. She grabbed the coffeepot again and moved toward the counter, which had filled up first. Annie had taken on waitress duty, as well, and the two of them were running from one end of the café to the other. In no time the two coffeepots were empty.

"I need coffee down here," an ill-tempered man shouted from the rear of the café.

"Coming right up," Bethanne promised. She started taking orders and shuffled them to Marie as fast as she could. Once the coffee had finished brewing, she hurried to the grouch by the window. He had an entire booth to himself.

"Is this decaf?" he demanded.

"No…I don't believe so."

"Get me some decaf."

"I'll need to brew that. It'll be a few minutes."

"What kind of joint is this?" he complained loudly.

"Would you like me to take your order?" she asked, thinking charitably that he was probably hungry and tired.

"No, I want my decaf coffee."

"Is that all?"

"No," he said pointedly, "and the longer you stand here arguing with me, the longer I'm going to have to wait for my coffee. I have to get back on that bus, you know."

Bethanne realized she should have automatically brewed a pot of decaffeinated coffee. There was simply too much to remember.

"I'll get it," Annie called out, and hurried toward the coffee machine.

Bethanne was still taking orders when she noticed the decaffeinated coffee was ready. Dropping off more orders with Marie, she picked up the coffeepot and rushed over to the complainer. He sat with his arms crossed, scowling. He didn't bother to right his cup so she did it for him, and filled it to the brim.

"You overfilled it," he snarled. "Now there's no room for cream."

"Sorry." She reached for a second cup and poured again, leaving it three-quarters full.

"That's only half a cup!" he nearly shouted. "I suppose you intend to charge me for a full one?"

Bethanne started to add more coffee when she felt a hand on her shoulder. Rooster, the older biker, stood directly behind her.

"Listen, buddy," he said, and the threat in his voice made her shiver. She couldn't see his face but she saw the reaction of the man with the coffee and he seemed to cower in the booth.

"I'm real hungry, and when I get hungry I get cranky. You're delaying my meal. Trust me, you don't want to see what happens when I get cranky."

The other man didn't move. In fact, it looked as if he'd stopped breathing. The rattle of dishes died down and conversation fell to a soft hush. Soon the whole café had gone silent as Rooster bent over the man in the booth.

"That coffee's just fine now, isn't it?" Rooster asked.

The other man nearly jerked his head off in his eagerness to assure Rooster it was.

"That's what I thought." Rooster gently patted Bethanne's arm as he returned to his friends.

"I think your order's up now," she said. He winked as he passed by, and Bethanne did her best to disguise a smile but knew she hadn't succeeded.

Still grinning she walked back to the kitchen and placed the orders for the four bikers on a large tray and delivered them to the table.

"Thanks," she whispered.

"I didn't do that for you," Rooster said, fork in hand. "I like my mashed potatoes and gravy hot."

She was about to turn away when she became aware of Max, the man who sat beside Rooster, watching her. His eyes, dark and sober, met hers for a long moment. His look seemed to go straight through her and Bethanne felt herself flush. Her reaction embarrassed her but she didn't know how to explain it. She wasn't seeking any connection, romantic or otherwise. She was there to do a job—help Ruth's friend—and that was it. Glancing away, Bethanne hurried back to the kitchen.

Eight

"Mom," Annie said from the backseat of the car. "Have you ever been to Vegas?" This trip was turning out better than she'd hoped. But then, her expectations hadn't been that high.

When her grandmother announced the day before that they were going to spend the night in Spokane, Annie had wanted to scream with frustration. Spokane? It was an all-right town, but it sure wasn't exciting.

Well, visiting Pendleton, Oregon, wasn't exactly like being in Paris. To be fair, they'd had a decent afternoon. She'd actually had fun waiting tables at the café, which wasn't nearly as easy as it looked. The next time she ate in a restaurant, Annie knew she'd see the waitress in an entirely different light.

She'd suggested Pendleton because of her father. A little while ago, he'd mentioned that he'd been born there, although Annie couldn't remember why they'd even been talking about it. That part wasn't important, anyway. The one thing that did matter was getting a feel for what her mother was thinking about her father. Driving to Pendleton was Annie's way of casually bringing him into the conversation. She *wanted* her mother to be thinking about him, to miss him and to consider reuniting the family.

Unfortunately, Annie hadn't been able to figure out how her mother really felt. Of course, they'd been too busy at the café to discuss much of anything. Then, after Marie closed for the night, they'd toured the town. There'd been a lot of talk about her grandparents' early years. Annie had listened politely and so had her mother. Bethanne seemed interested but Annie noticed she didn't ask many questions.

The first place Marie took them was the old neighborhood. Annie saw the house where her grandparents had lived when Grant was born. It was small and drab and nothing like she'd expected. True, it was nearly fifty years older now, but she could hardly imagine her father living in such a tiny house. The yard was overrun with grass and thick with weeds. The sidewalk leading to the front porch was cracked. Someone had left a red wagon outside, along with a tricycle, so another young family occupied the house these days.

While Annie loved her grandmother's stories, her attention was repeatedly drawn back to her cell phone.

Vance had texted her twice. His first message said he'd landed safely in Rome. Well, good for him.

She didn't text back.

Then, less than three hours later, he sent her another message.

Miss you.

As far as she was concerned, he didn't miss her nearly enough—or he wouldn't have left. She didn't answer that one, either, although it boosted her ego considerably that he'd attempted to contact her.

Nevertheless, Vance was out of her life. He'd taught her a valuable lesson and she was determined to learn from it. She was hurt by what he'd done and embarrassed by how oblivious she'd been. He'd lied to her, keeping his plans a secret. She should've known, though. In retrospect, there'd been clues, like his lack of interest in doing anything with her this summer and his frequent visits to Matt's place—without her. What was that cliché about hindsight being twenty-twenty? She understood it now.

This thing with Vance was kind of eerie because it reminded Annie of when her father moved out. She'd commented on that to her mother, who'd agreed. Bethanne had been shocked when it happened; even Andrew hadn't seen it coming.

Annie had been shocked at first, too, but when she thought about it, the signs had been there. Just like with Vance, but more obvious. Her father often got home late from the office and always seemed in a hurry to leave again. He'd bought her a new computer, too, for no reason. It wasn't until much later that she'd realized his gifts were motivated by guilt, which proved he did have a conscience. Later, Annie had purposely ruined the computer, but that was beside the point.

Her mother had been totally blind to what her father was doing. That had infuriated Annie, who thought Bethanne should have recognized that her marriage was in trouble. A woman who'd been married for twenty years, who supposedly *knew* her husband…

Back then it'd been easy to blame Bethanne. Annie got over that fast enough, but some of her residual anger had lingered.

Until the night Vance dumped her.

Well, he didn't *officially* dump her, but that was how it felt. Actually, she almost wished he'd ended the relationship completely. A clean break and all that.

Well, it didn't matter because she was finished with Vance. He could send her all the text messages he wanted but she had no intention of responding. What she needed now was to have fun. A *lot* of fun.

She looked down at the map a second time. Vegas wasn't that far, but she'd have to convince her mother and grandmother to head toward Nevada instead of South Dakota. Mount Rushmore wasn't going anywhere. She'd let all her friends know where she was and eventually the news would reach Vance and then he'd regret what he'd done.

The taste of this small revenge was sweet on her tongue. Vance might think Rome was fun, but Annie could guarantee Vegas was a whole lot more exciting than touring some museum.

Annie's question caught Bethanne by surprise. Vegas?

"Have you ever been to Vegas?" Annie asked again.

Where was this coming from? Bethanne was driving while Ruth napped beside her and her daughter sat in the backseat.

"Well, yes, your father and I were in Vegas years ago." Grant had taken Bethanne to a Realtors' convention. They'd stayed at one of the gigantic hotels on the Strip, and she remembered those three days fondly. Because of the divorce it was sometimes difficult to recall the good times she'd had with Grant. Like all married couples, they'd experienced ups and downs through the years. Every marriage did. It was easy to forget the laughter they'd once shared when her memories were tainted by Grant's betrayal.

"You awake, Grandma?" Annie leaned forward to peer around Ruth's seat.

"Mmm."

"Have *you* been to Vegas?"

"No, never," Ruth admitted. "Richard went there on business any number of times but I was always busy with the children."

"We should go to Vegas!" Annie said, as if this was the idea of the century. "The three of us. We'd have a hoot."

"We can do that one day," Bethanne agreed. Their second day on the road, and so far, everything had gone well. They'd deviated from their plans once already, but this was Ruth's trip, not Annie's. Or Bethanne's.

"I mean we should go *now*," Annie said. "Really, how many road trips do the three of us expect to take together?"

"Now?" Bethanne asked. "You mean today?"

"Not exactly today. It's a ways yet. I've got the map here, and if we head south on Highway 93 at Twin Falls we can reach Vegas tomorrow afternoon."

"Honey," Bethanne reminded her daughter for probably the fifth time. "Your grandmother has carefully planned our route and we're going to South Dakota to see Mount Rushmore."

"I know, but wouldn't it be more fun in Vegas?"

Ruth didn't comment one way or the other.

"It's boring on the freeway," Annie continued. "If we're going to drive all the way across the United States, it'd be a lot more interesting on the highways and byways than the interstate."

"Vegas," Ruth murmured.

"Remember, you specifically mentioned Mount Rushmore," Bethanne said mildly, not wanting to put pressure on her former mother-in-law, but not wanting her to be disappointed, either.

"I know I did," Ruth said. "But that old mountain will be there until the end of time. Annie's right. It isn't every day that I have the opportunity to visit Las Vegas—and with two of my favorite people."

"You mean we can actually go to Vegas?" Annie didn't seem capable of containing her excitement.

"We're going to Vegas!" Ruth shouted.

"And what happens in Vegas stays in Vegas," Annie returned, laughing.

Bethanne had to smile, too. Vegas did sound like a lot more fun than elbowing her way through the tourist crowds anxious for a better view of Rushmore.

"Just promise me," Ruth said, "that you won't say a word about this to Grant or Robin. I promised them we'd stick to the freeway the entire trip, but Annie's got a point. This is pretty dull driving. If we're going to see the country, we need to get off the interstate. We should explore a little."

"Look at the map and tell me where you want me to go," Bethanne said. This was turning into far more of an adventure than she'd ever anticipated. Her stint as a waitress at Marie's café yesterday had been quite an experience. Bethanne had nearly forty dollars, her share of the money they'd made in tips. Gambling money. The biggest surprise had been Max, the biker who sat next to the older man who called himself Rooster. It was Max whose eyes had connected with hers, Max who'd looked at her so…knowingly.

After the busload of customers left, Marie had prepared dinner for them all. Ruth said the chicken-fried steak was even better than she remembered. The two older women sat, chatting over coffee, while Annie and Bethanne finished the cleanup. Later that night, after Marie had given them a quick tour of town, Bethanne had crawled into the hotel bed, exhausted and oddly exhilarated as she closed her eyes. As soon as she did, the image of the biker filled her mind. Max. He hadn't spoken a word to her, other than to place his order. It'd been that brief look they'd exchanged. A couple of times Bethanne had tried to shake the memory and found she couldn't.

She was getting fanciful, she'd thought. Downright silly. She had absolutely nothing in common with this biker, and it was highly unlikely she'd ever run into him again, which was just as well. She'd mumbled a prayer for him—there was something about the sadness in his eyes—and then she'd fallen almost immediately into a deep and peaceful sleep.

"We're about an hour away from Twin Falls," Ruth said, breaking into Bethanne's musings. She glanced up from the map, which Annie had handed over to her. "I'll need to cancel my hotel reservation again."

"We should probably cancel them all," Annie advised. "I mean, we've already changed Grandma's plans once, and now we're doing it again. It's way more fun making plans as we go along, don't you think?"

"It is," Ruth said. "I'm so grateful to have the two of you with me. This is much better than driving alone."

Bethanne smiled. Annie had added spontaneity and adventure to the trip. If it'd just been Ruth and Bethanne, she would've gladly followed her mother-in-law's itinerary.

"Where should we spend the night?" Ruth asked, unfolding the map on her knees.

"Where do you suggest?" Bethanne asked.

"Hmm. There aren't too many big towns on the way into Vegas. I think our best bet is Ely. Maybe Annie could check the internet for a hotel and make a reservation."

"Good idea," Bethanne inserted.

"How far is Ely from Twin Falls?" Annie asked.

"Oh…" Ruth paused, as though calculating the distance. "I'd say about three or four hours."

"That'll make nine hours in the car, Ruth," Bethanne said, a bit concerned. "Is that too long for you?"

"It's fine," Ruth insisted.

"Let's stop in Wells and pick up lunch and find somewhere to eat along the way," Annie suggested. "There's all kinds of small lakes, but I heard someone mention one called Snow Water Lake. I don't remember who, but they said it was absolutely pristine. We could have a picnic there."

"Sounds like a great plan," Ruth concurred. "I'd like to stretch my legs and be somewhere cool and refreshing."

Bethanne agreed, content to let Annie handle the details.

They purchased sandwiches, sodas and chips in Wells,

Nevada, and turned off the interstate onto Highway 93. They gassed up there, too. Bethanne decided to continue driving. The car turned over a couple of times before starting, which worried her, but she didn't have a problem after that.

The two-lane highway was far more relaxing; it was a relief not to have to deal with so much traffic. She drove at a moderate speed and absorbed what she could of the scenery.

"I do prefer highway travel over the interstate," Ruth said after a while. "There's more character along the high-way." She gave an exaggerated shudder. "I can only imagine the lecture we'd get if Grant or Robin ever heard about this."

"I'm not going to tell them," Bethanne reassured her.

"We're gonna have to tell Dad we're in Vegas, though," Annie said.

Despite the thought of Grant's disapproval, Bethanne smiled. She could guess what he'd say once he learned that they were visiting Sin City. And while she was there, Bethanne fully intended to have fun. She wasn't much of a gambler, but there'd be shows to see and casinos to visit. She'd heard so much about them. The Wynn, Mandalay Bay, the Venetian...

"Can we spend more than one night in Vegas?" Annie asked.

"We can take as long as we like with one stipula-tion," Ruth told her. "I have to be in Florida before my reunion."

"No problem, Grandma. I'll make sure we're exactly where you need to be with time to spare."

Bethanne wasn't quite sure how Annie had taken over

their itinerary, but she didn't object. And apparently neither did Ruth. Although she'd hoped to have a chance to think, consider her options, decide what she really wanted, it felt good to simply enjoy this time with her daughter and mother-in-law. *Ex*-mother-in-law—but who cared?

There was nothing pressing on either the home front or at the office. She'd talked to Julia and been assured that all was well at Parties.

As for Grant... Reuniting with him wasn't a decision she had to make this week or the next. That, too, could wait. She'd give them six months to become reacquainted. In six months she'd see how the relationship had progressed. What she found most difficult was how badly her family—well, Annie and Ruth—wanted her to go back to Grant. In a perfect world she'd fall in love with her ex-husband again and they'd all return to being the ideal family they'd once been. Except maybe it hadn't been so ideal... Besides, this was far from a perfect world and there was more to consider than making Annie and Ruth happy.

She wasn't sure how long they drove; she didn't look at the dashboard clock or her watch. The scenery was engaging and kept her attention. Thankfully, the rental car was air-conditioned because the Nevada heat was brutal, even in the mountains.

"Okay, Mom, slow down," Annie eventually said, studying the map. "The turnoff for Snow Water Lake should be coming up soon."

Bethanne would have missed the arrow if Ruth hadn't pointed it out. "How far is the lake from the road?" she asked Annie, turning off the highway onto the narrow paved road.

"It's hard to tell on the map, but it can't be more than a few miles. Five at the most."

That seemed reasonable, although she had to wonder if they were heading toward a designated picnic area or invading personal property. Well, they'd find out soon enough.

Minutes later, they reached the lake. There wasn't a picnic table—or a picnicker—in sight. They saw the remains of a campfire someone had made some time ago, but no other evidence of anyone's presence. Using the hood of the car as a table, Ruth spread out their feast and they stood in the shade and ate their sandwiches and chips. Lingering over sodas, Annie and Bethanne walked along the lakeshore.

Annie removed her shoes and waded in the water. "Wow, this is cold."

"It isn't called Snow Water Lake for nothing," Bethanne teased.

"Come on in, Mom," Annie said, and kicked her feet at the water's edge, splashing onto the shore.

Although they'd been out of the car for less than thirty minutes, Bethanne roasted in the early-afternoon heat. Sitting on the sand at the lake's edge, she slipped off her shoes and waded ankle-deep into the chilly water. After the initial shock she quickly grew accustomed to the cold.

She got up and, with her arm around Annie's waist, ambled through the water.

"I should probably call Dad," Annie said. "He'll want to know we've changed our plans."

Bethanne didn't comment.

"Dad talked to you about Andrew's wedding, didn't he?" Annie asked. "We can sit together as a family, can't we?"

Bethanne hadn't given Grant her final answer. "I suppose."

"Good." Annie rested her head on Bethanne's shoulder. "I want us to be a family again."

"I know you do, honey," Bethanne said in a soothing voice. "Annie, you have your *own* life now. Your own place, a promising future... And your dad and I both love you."

"Yeah. But nothing's been the same since Dad moved out."

Moved out, divorced her, remarried and gone through a second divorce, Bethanne added to herself. The man who'd walked out the door wasn't the same person anymore, nor was she. A lot had changed, and Bethanne wasn't sure either of them could return to the past. Perhaps that was a good thing; she didn't know.

"Dad's different," Annie continued, almost as if she'd been reading Bethanne's thoughts.

"We both are."

"Dad's learned his lesson. He's humbled. You know that can't be easy for him."

What Annie said was true. With Grant's pride, it had taken a great deal for him to admit he'd made a mistake and seek a reconciliation.

"You don't mind if I call him, do you?"

"Not at all."

Annie reached for her cell and punched a couple of buttons. After a moment, she muttered in frustration. "We don't have coverage here."

"It can wait. In fact, if you call him now he'll only worry. Why don't we call once we're in Vegas?"

"Okay."

By the time they returned to the car, Ruth had cleaned up their leftovers and they were ready to go back to the highway.

"I'll drive," Annie said.

Bethanne was happy to relinquish the wheel. If she was going to finish the wedding gloves, she'd need time to knit. She'd made progress their first day on the road, but none today. She was counting on the trip to afford her knitting time she didn't generally have.

Ruth climbed into the back, while Bethanne sat in the passenger seat next to her daughter. Annie inserted the key and the engine turned over once and then quit.

Frowning, Annie looked at Bethanne. "What's wrong?"

Bethanne's heart slowed as she remembered what had happened at the gas station in Wells. "Try again."

Annie did, and the engine caught right away. Bethanne relaxed, giving her daughter a reassuring smile. The last thing they needed now was to get stuck in the middle of nowhere with a broken-down vehicle and no cell coverage.

The car lurched forward and died again.

"Is there a problem?" Ruth asked anxiously from the backseat.

"I'm not sure," Bethanne said.

Annie tried again. Nothing. When it became apparent that no amount of cranking was going to start the engine, Bethanne placed her hand over her daughter's.

"Now what?" Annie asked.

Bethanne's head was spinning. They didn't have a lot of options. "How far are we from the main road? Isn't it about five miles?"

"Yup. Farther than I'd want to walk," Annie said, "especially in this heat."

"I agree. It's too far to walk in this heat," Ruth said emphatically.

"Then we're stuck until someone comes along." Annie dropped her hands from the steering wheel. "Does anyone know anything about fixing cars?"

Bethanne shook her head.

"Not me," Ruth said. "I left all that to Richard. After he died I had to learn how to fill my own gas tank. But that's about all I can do."

"We could be here for days," Annie moaned.

"Why don't we wait until it cools down and then walk to the highway."

"This is all my fault," Ruth wailed. "I was so eager for adventure that I put us in danger."

"*I* was the one who suggested we eat lunch by the lake," Annie said.

"Stop," Bethanne told them both. "This isn't anyone's fault. We'll be fine. There's nothing to worry about. Besides, there are worse things than being stuck by a beautiful lake on a summer afternoon."

"Right," Annie said, instantly perking up. "Let's go swimming. We have our swimsuits, don't we?"

"Uh, I didn't bring one," Ruth confessed. "I didn't want anyone to see my fat thighs."

"Ruth," Bethanne said, rolling her eyes. She was on her way to Florida and some of the most beautiful beaches in the world—and she was worried about showing her thighs. "Who'll even notice?"

"What about you, Mom?" Annie asked.

Bethanne's smile faded. "I don't own a suit."

"You've got to be kidding me," Annie said, staring up at the car ceiling. "Okay, you two, I don't care if you have your bathing suits or not, we're going swimming."

"You can," Ruth said, "but I'm staying out of the water."

"Suit yourself, Grandma, but Mom and I are getting in the water."

Bethanne hesitated. "You go on and I'll join you later."

"Mo-om," Annie groaned. "Okay, if it'll make you both feel better, I'll swim in my underwear."

Annie shucked off her shorts and cotton top, leaving them at the water's edge, and walked into the lake with her arms raised. "Oh, boy, this is cold."

Bethanne kept a keen eye on her daughter. The cool water lapped at her bare toes, and she felt the sweat roll down her neck. The sun was even fiercer now. Annie, meanwhile, was floating on her back.

"Are you coming in or not?" she shouted to Bethanne.

"Coming in." Bethanne carefully removed her own clothes and waded into the water in her bra and underpants. The lake seemed even colder than before and shock made her gasp.

Ruth strolled down to the shore, watching them more intently than a lifeguard at the baby pool.

"Come on, Ruth," Bethanne said. "You wanted adventure. Well, this is it!"

Her mother-in-law paced the shoreline. "I've never done anything like this in my life."

"Don't be shy," Annie said. "We could be here for hours. We might as well enjoy ourselves."

Ruth cast them an anxious look. "You won't tell anyone, will you?"

"Cross my heart," Annie said, standing up to make the motions.

"Come on," Bethanne encouraged her again, waving her in. "The water's fabulous."

Ruth took off her clothes and folded them in a neat pile. Then she walked straight into the water. Unlike Annie and Bethanne, who took time to adjust to the cold, Ruth plunged ahead. Maybe she feared one of them would comment on her thighs, Bethanne thought with amusement.

The three frolicked and played like schoolchildren splashing one another and diving under the water. Bethanne couldn't remember the last time she'd swum in a lake. She was enjoying herself so much, she didn't immediately hear the noise that attracted Ruth and Annie's attention.

Both of them got to their feet and stood there, unmoving.

Bethanne turned around and was instantly overwhelmed by the sound of motorcycles moving toward them.

"Mom," Annie said, grabbing Bethanne's arm. "I remember where I heard about this lake," she cried. "It was from the bikers at the restaurant."

Nine

The motorcycles roared right to the edge of the lake, and lined up side by side.

Shivering in the water Bethanne huddled close to Ruth and Annie. No one seemed to know exactly what to do or how to react. The water suddenly went from comfortable to below freezing. All three of them crossed their arms, although Bethanne realized their efforts to hide themselves were futile.

"Didn't Robin say something like this would happen?" Ruth wailed. "We're goners for sure."

"Over my dead body," Bethanne said from between clenched teeth.

"That's what I'm afraid of," Ruth muttered. "How will I ever explain this to Grant? This is all my fault."

"It's no one's fault," Bethanne said. She wasn't about to let these men intimidate her *or* her family. Squaring her shoulders, she began marching toward the shore, her legs making rippling, splashing movements in the water.

Annie tried to grab her arm. "Mom, what are you doing?"

"I'm going to ask them for help," she said. If she treated them with respect, then they'd do the same. She hoped.

"Mom!" came Annie's plaintive cry as Bethanne pulled her arm free.

With her back straight, Bethanne ignored Annie and Ruth's pleas and the teasing catcalls from the bikers. She was all too aware that her wet underwear concealed nothing. Scooping up her capris, she tried to pull them on, slipping one leg in. Because she was wet, the fabric stuck and she lost her balance. She would've tumbled to the ground if not for one of the bikers who reached out and caught her.

"Thanks," she said breathlessly.

The biker removed his helmet.

Bethanne blinked twice. It was the same man she'd served in the café less than twenty-four hours earlier. The one who'd stayed in her mind, the biker named Max. Their eyes met again, his dark gaze unreadable.

Rooster removed his helmet next; so did the other two bikers, Willie and Skunk, if she remembered correctly.

By then Bethanne was fully dressed, although her clothing clung to her, soaked as it was from her underwear.

Annie stepped out of the water and quickly dressed, too. That left Ruth, who stubbornly remained in the water. She squatted down so only her head was above the waterline and refused to budge.

"Grandma, it's all right," Annie told her. "You can come out. We know these guys."

"I'll stay where I am until those...those men turn around and stop gawking at me."

Rooster threw back his head and howled. "I don't think you've got anything I haven't seen before, Grandma."

"Turn around," Ruth barked. "All of you. I don't need any Peeping Toms staring at me."

To Bethanne's amazement, all four bikers did as Ruth demanded.

"We'd appreciate your help. Our car won't start," Bethanne said, as much to distract the four men as to secure their assistance.

"We didn't flood the engine, either," Annie added.

"I had a problem starting it earlier." Bethanne led them to the rental vehicle. "This is a relatively new car, so I'm surprised we're having trouble," she said.

"I don't know that much about cars," the guy she remembered as Willie said with a shrug. "I can fix a motorcycle with a bobby pin but cars baffle me."

"Same here," Skunk chimed in.

Rooster and Max exchanged glances. "I'll take a look at it for you," Rooster offered.

Bethanne didn't immediately find the hood release. "Like I said, this is a rental car...or I'd be more familiar with it." As soon as she managed to release the hood, both Rooster and Max bent over the engine.

It didn't take long to detect the problem, which according to them was something to do with the carburetor. "You're gonna need a tow truck," Rooster said. "With a bike any of us could lend a hand, but these engines aren't what they used to be."

"We don't have cell coverage out here," Annie told him. "We'd have phoned for help earlier if it was that easy."

"Do any of you ride?" Willie asked.

"No...afraid not," Bethanne said, answering for all three.

"Then one of us will need to take you into Wells."

"Hold on just a minute here," Ruth said, wagging her index finger at them. She'd dressed, putting her blouse on inside out, although Bethanne wasn't about to tell her that.

"Before we do any such thing, the three of us need to talk." Ruth steered Bethanne and Annie away from the bikers. They stood several feet away, forming a tight circle. Ruth glanced over her shoulder and lowered her voice. "I don't like the idea of one of us leaving with a biker."

"But, Grandma, what else are we going to do?" Annie asked.

"Do you honestly think we can trust these men?" Ruth pinched her mouth into a thin line and frowned. "They're…riffraff."

In normal circumstances Bethanne wouldn't have considered riding with any of them, but at the moment their options were few. "Do we have a choice?" she asked.

"We could always stay right here and stick to our original plan," Annie suggested. "Only…"

"Only *what?*" Ruth whispered.

"Well, I heard them talking at the café yesterday…and I'm afraid this might be a biker hangout. At least we've met these guys before, and even though they might *look* a bit intimidating, they seem decent enough."

Ruth shook her head. "I still don't like it."

"I'll go," Bethanne said.

"No, you won't," Ruth insisted. "If anyone goes, it'll be me."

"You'll have to ride on the back of a motorcycle," Bethanne reminded her.

Ruth paled. "I…I can do it."

"Mom, it makes far more sense for me to go," Annie said, as if it meant nothing.

"No." Bethanne refused to even discuss it. She wasn't about to put her daughter in any additional danger.

Cutting off further argument, Bethanne broke away from the others and approached the bikers. They stood with their arms crossed, waiting. "Okay," she said, walking toward them, hands held out. "If one of you would take me into Wells, we'd deeply appreciate it."

"That's real big of you." Willie's voice was sharp with sarcasm.

"I'll take her." This came from Max.

His offer appeared to surprise Rooster, who shrugged and stepped back. "Your call."

Max started toward his Harley and Bethanne followed. "You ever ridden in the—" he hesitated "—buddy seat?"

Willie and the other two bikers broke into hoots of laughter.

Bethanne turned back, not understanding what they considered so humorous.

Max silenced them with a single look. He was an intense man who rarely spoke, she'd noticed, and never seemed to smile. He wasn't especially big. About six feet, with broad shoulders. He seemed to be her age, possibly older.

Rooster handed Bethanne his helmet.

"Mom, are you sure about this?" Annie asked anxiously.

Bethanne nodded, although she wasn't sure of anything. She set the helmet on her head and draped her purse crossways over one shoulder. Max climbed onto the bike. Apparently, it was up to her to find her own way onto the Harley. She managed, but it wasn't pretty.

"Oh, Bethanne," Ruth cried, covering her mouth with her hand. "Be careful."

"I will," she promised. She didn't like this any better than Annie and Ruth did, but someone had to ride into town and she was the logical choice.

The only instruction Max gave her was to hold on. It wasn't like there was an extra pair of handlebars for her to grab. Her one option was Max and, not knowing what else to do, she slipped her arms around his middle—and clung for dear life.

The first turn nearly unseated her. She cried out in alarm, but if Max heard, he gave no indication. Even with the helmet, the noise was deafening; the roar sounded as if she were next to a jet engine. It seemed to take forever to reach the town of Wells. By then she was so tense and stiff she found it difficult to breathe. Thankfully, Max knew where he was going. He pulled into a garage and turned off the engine, then braced his feet on the pavement and set the kickstand in place.

Bethanne didn't dare move. She pried her fingers loose, one by one. It occurred to her that her stranglehold might have been uncomfortable for him.

Max took off his helmet and climbed down; she did, too, with a lot less grace. "Were you able to breathe?" she asked.

The merest hint of a smile touched his mouth. "Barely. I think I might have a couple of cracked ribs."

Bethanne didn't know if this was a joke or if he was serious. "Sorry."

He entered the garage and she trailed after him. The

mechanic brightened the instant he saw Max, came forward and thrust out his hand. "Max! Good to see you again. I got that widow's car running and—"

"Hey, Marv, I need a favor," Max said, cutting him off.

"You got it," the other man said without hesitation. "I owe you. I didn't need even half the money you gave me to fix that old Ford."

"You don't owe me a thing."

The mechanic obviously knew and trusted Max. That was a good sign as far as Bethanne was concerned.

He nodded at Bethanne. "Name's Marvin Green."

"Bethanne," she said. "Bethanne Hamlin."

"Can you send a tow truck out to Snow Water Lake?" Max asked his friend.

"Sure." Marvin went into a small windowed office and picked up a phone. Max and Bethanne waited outside.

"Is there a rental car place in town?" Bethanne asked, since they'd need to exchange vehicles.

"I only ride," he said, which she guessed was his shortcut way of telling her he didn't know.

"You don't talk much, do you?"

"No."

"Any particular reason?"

He shrugged. "I generally don't have a lot to say."

Bethanne didn't believe him but didn't respond, either.

Max walked over to the soda machine, inserted a couple of dollar bills and bought two sodas, bringing her one.

"Thanks," she said, accepting it gratefully. Her throat was parched. They wandered over to a row of plastic chairs and sat quietly, side by side, while Marvin made phone calls.

After several minutes of discomfort, Bethanne found herself breaking the silence. "I thought about you last night." The confession popped out before she could censure it. She had no idea what had prompted the comment and instantly regretted it.

His gaze shot to hers. She could tell she'd surprised him.

Instead of dropping it the way she should have, she made matters worse. "Actually, I said a prayer for you.... I didn't used to pray," she added awkwardly, feeling she needed to explain herself. "Not until recently." The words just kept coming. Normally Bethanne would never have blurted out something this personal. She hardly ever talked about politics or religion and never with someone who was basically a stranger.

He stared at her as if he didn't know how to take her admission.

She'd started down this road, so she might as well continue. "I always believed in God. I went to church and all that, but, well...after my husband left me, I backed off for a while. I feel differently now...."

"You're divorced?"

She nodded. "Six years now. Annie's my daughter and Ruth's my—mother-in-law."

"Ex-mother-in-law."

"Technically, you're right. But I don't think of her in those terms. Grant divorced me, but I chose to keep Ruth."

"Your husband's an idiot," Max said.

"*Ex*-husband," she corrected, and to her astonishment, Max laughed.

Marvin glanced their way and lifted his chin. Max stood, joining the mechanic in his office. The two men spoke for a while; she finished her soda before Max returned.

"Marvin found a tow truck willing to drive out to the lake."

That was a relief. "Would it be okay if I rode back with the driver rather than on the Harley? No slight intended, but I think we'd both be more comfortable."

"That's fine."

Once again they sat in silence. Finally, Max leaned forward, his forearms resting on his thighs. "Why did you feel you needed to say a prayer for me?" he asked.

Bethanne wasn't sure what to tell him. She couldn't very well admit he'd remained in her thoughts—and that she didn't understand why. "I…asked God to keep you and your friends safe on the road. Of course, at the time, I didn't know I was going to be riding, uh, buddy with you in the very near future." She tried to make light of it and realized she was saying far more than necessary. Maybe it was because *he* didn't speak much that she felt this compulsion to fill the void with chatter.

"Why?" he asked again after she'd stopped talking.

Bethanne closed her eyes and settled back against the hard chair. "I don't exactly know." She wasn't being completely honest. At the café she'd been aware that he was watching her as she moved about, waiting tables, delivering meals, doing her best to keep up with customers' demands. A couple of times their eyes had met. She'd smiled, but he hadn't. His lack of response hadn't intimidated her; instead, she saw something in him... something she recognized in herself. Pain. She sensed that he'd suffered the same kind of wrenching emotional pain she had. Ultimately that was what had prompted her to pray for him.

"Would you mind if I asked you a question?" She looked up at him.

"That depends. You can ask, but I might not answer."

"Fair enough."

Max walked over to the vending machine as if he needed to put distance between them.

Bethanne stood and followed him. "Did your wife leave you?" she asked in a low voice.

He turned and faced her and seemed to be studying her intently. Bethanne held his gaze.

"No," he said after a lengthy moment.

"Oh." She couldn't keep her foot out of her mouth with this man.

"Kate died three years ago."

Bethanne wanted to tell him how sorry she was but instinctively knew he'd find no comfort in her condolences. "You've been on the bike ever since, haven't you?"

He frowned and then nodded.

Bethanne wasn't sure how she knew it, but she did. Living the life of a drifter probably meant he didn't have children. No roots. No ties. Free to roam wherever the wind took him.

"Grant married Tiffany," she said.

"Good for him."

"Then she left him."

Max smiled. So did Bethanne.

"You're supposed to say it served him right."

"Served him right," Max echoed.

"He's divorced now and—"

"He wants you back."

Bethanne gaped at him. "How'd you know?"

"Makes sense. Are you going to take him back?"

That was the million-dollar question. "I don't know...I just don't know." Bethanne wasn't an indecisive woman; she'd learned not to be in the six years since Grant had walked out. This question, however, left her stomach in knots and her mind in a state of confusion. Fortunately, an answer wasn't immediately required. She had time.

Before she could say more, the tow truck rounded the corner. "Max?" she whispered. "Listen, I might not get a chance later but I wanted to thank you."

He lifted one shoulder. "You're welcome."

Unable to stop herself, she briefly, gently, touched his hand. Despite their physical contact on the bike, this was different. More intentional, more...personal. She felt the urge to at least *try* to comfort him, to show him how sorry she was about his wife's death.

From the look on his face she could see that her gesture had jolted him. He stared down at her and frowned.

Then, just as she removed her hand from his, Max stepped toward her.

Tentatively, he circled her waist with his arms and she returned his embrace. His pulse thundered in her ear. Slowly, ever so slowly, his hold tightened. She felt him inhale deeply and closed her eyes at his touch. She wanted to weep; she didn't understand why.

Max's hands moved over her back, caressing her.

"It gets easier," she whispered. "I promise you it does."

Max brushed his lips against her hair, then dropped his arms and stepped back.

"Thank you," she said, feeling foolish and sentimental.

The tow truck driver climbed out of his rig and walked toward them but before she left, Bethanne had one last thing to say. She couldn't meet Max's eyes. "Your Kate must have been very special," she said softly.

Max reached for his helmet. He didn't speak for a long time and then murmured, "She was."

Ten

"I don't like this. I don't like this one bit," Ruth told her granddaughter as Bethanne left riding behind that biker. For all they knew, Max could be some kind of…hoodlum. She'd read about motorcycle gangs, and while she doubted that these four belonged to any organized group, she was sure they couldn't be trusted.

"What alternative do we have?" Annie asked.

Ruth feared they'd been far too quick to let Bethanne leave with Max. They knew absolutely nothing about these men, other than the fact that they weren't capable of fixing a carburetor. "We should've done what we originally planned—waited until dusk and then walked to the highway." In retrospect, Ruth regretted not insisting they do exactly that.

"And take our chances hitchhiking into Wells?" Annie shook her head. "I doubt that people who pick up hitchhikers can be trusted, either, Grandma. At least we've seen these men before."

Annie could be right. Hitchhiking into town didn't

sound too appealing and it could make them even more vulnerable. She tapped her fingers nervously on the car's hood while she worried about Bethanne alone with that biker.

"Why didn't I listen to Robin?" Ruth muttered. She'd assumed Robin was being overprotective. Because of her experience in court, dealing with criminals day in and day out, Robin had a polluted view of humanity. She trusted no one and seemed to look for the bad in people, to expect it. All with good reason; Ruth understood that, but it saddened her.

Ruth's job now, she felt, was to protect Annie in case these men decided to take advantage of her granddaughter. She drew Annie away from them to stand beneath the shade of the only tree, which happened to be several feet off.

"We should make contingency plans," she whispered, although there was little chance the men could overhear their conversation.

"How?"

"In case…" Ruth didn't want to say it. "You know."

Annie gave her an odd look. "You mean we should dismantle their motorcycles so they couldn't come after us if we ran away?"

Ruth hadn't thought of that, but it was an excellent idea. "Good plan," she said approvingly.

Annie rolled her eyes. "Grandma, I was only joking!"

"That would be our insurance."

Annie frowned. "I don't think—"

"It's what Robin would suggest."

"Yes, but Aunt Robin—"

Ruth already knew what her granddaughter was about

to say. She agreed, but they didn't have time to discuss Robin. If they were going to act, they had to do it now. "I'll distract the men and then you do whatever one does to make motorcycles refuse to start."

"Do you know what that is?" Annie asked.

"No. Don't you?"

"Nope."

"Oh, dear." So much for that. Ruth bit her lip as she searched for another idea. "There's got to be a way to protect ourselves." Her gaze fell to the ground as she began pacing. "And your mother—"

"I think Mom's safe."

"I certainly hope so," Ruth said, her mind whirling. "What would we tell the police? These bikers don't even have real names! Who ever heard of men named Rooster and Skunk? If something *did* happen, God forbid, how could we tell the police we let your mother drive off with someone named Rooster?"

"She's with Max, not Rooster. Nothing's going to happen, Grandma. You're getting yourself worked up for no reason."

"Forget the police," Ruth continued. "What am I going to tell your *father?*"

"Grandma, repeat after me. *Nothing is going to happen.*"

Ruth ignored that. "Grant will be so upset with me," she went on. "He'll say it's all my fault and I can't blame him. I'm responsible for this mess. I should've insisted I be the one to go. I've lived my life. You and your mother are young."

"You want to see your high school friends again, don't you?"

"Of course." Ruth sighed. She desperately wanted to

see Royce, too. Just once, so she could tell him how sorry she was, how deeply she regretted having hurt him. But if she had to give up her life in order to save her daughter-in-law and granddaughter, Ruth wouldn't think twice. A small part of her wondered if she was overreacting, but she decided she simply couldn't take the risk.

"Do you have any ideas?" she asked her granddaughter. Annie was smart and sensible like Bethanne. The girl would come up with something.

"In my opinion, we should just wait this out. If Mom isn't back in, say, another hour—"

"Another *hour?*" Ruth interrupted. That seemed far too long.

"Grandma," Annie said, "it'll take time to get into Wells and then more time to arrange for a tow truck. We should wait a minimum of ninety minutes."

"Then what?"

"Then we…I don't know, regroup, I guess."

"Okay." However, Ruth didn't like it. She checked her watch so she'd know exactly when those ninety minutes were up and prepared to wait.

To distract themselves they discussed Las Vegas and what they'd do when they got there.

After ten interminable minutes, Ruth chanced a look at the bikers and to her shock saw the three of them swimming. Their clothes, all of them, were piled along the shoreline and…oh, my goodness, they'd gone in the water nude. She felt herself flush. While she'd been talking to Annie, those men had stripped naked.

"We don't have a thing to worry about," she told Annie. Ruth had the perfect plan. "I've got everything under control."

"What do you mean?"

"You'll see." As casually as possible, Ruth strolled toward the lake.

"Grandma," Annie called after her. "What are you going to do?"

She whirled around and pressed her finger to her lips, shushing Annie.

"Grandma," her granddaughter called again, this time in a harsh whisper. "Don't do anything…silly."

Ruth waved off her concern. As fast as she could, she gathered up the men's clothes. Clasping them to her chest, she ran toward Annie.

"What are you doing?" Rooster shouted.

Facing them, Ruth said loudly, "I'm taking your clothes and I'm not giving them back until Bethanne is returned safe and sound." She clutched the clothes even tighter, unwilling to surrender a single item.

All three men laughed as though they thought her hilarious.

Without another word, Rooster started walking to shore and the other two followed. Soon vital body parts were fully exposed. Ruth gasped and backed away. Clearly the threat of not having their clothes meant nothing to them.

"That scares us, Grandma. That really scares us."

Ruth dropped the clothes and, feeling more than a little ridiculous, hurried over to Annie.

They heard the roar of a motorcycle in the distance.

"Mom's back!" Annie cried.

The weight of worry and responsibility instantly lifted from Ruth's shoulders—until Max rode into view.

He was alone.

Ruth grabbed Annie's arm. "Your mother isn't with him," she hissed.

"She's probably with the tow truck driver," Annie said, not revealing the slightest alarm.

"And where *is* the tow truck?" she asked. A chill went down her spine. Hands on her hips, Ruth marched up to Max and waited until he'd turned off that blasted ear-splitting engine. "What have you done with my daughter-in-law?" she demanded.

Max slowly removed his helmet.

"I want to know right this minute where Bethanne is," she yelled.

"Grandma, Grandma," Annie hollered. "The tow truck is here."

Ruth wagged her finger under Max's nose. "You're fortunate Bethanne is safe. Otherwise...otherwise, you would've been sorry."

"Ooh, he's shaking in his boots," Rooster said, then practically collapsed with laughter.

Ruth was pleased to know she was such a source of amusement. The tow truck parked, the passenger door opened and Bethanne climbed down. Ruth ran over to her.

"I was so worried," she blurted as she pulled Bethanne into her arms and hugged her hard.

"I'm fine, Ruth, just fine."

Bethanne stretched out one arm to Annie and they held hands. "I talked to a mechanic who's going to fix the car. We'll need to spend the night in Wells, but we should be able to leave sometime tomorrow."

Annie nodded. "As soon as we're somewhere with cell

coverage, I'll find us a hotel room and cancel our reservations in Ely."

"Now I'm thinking we shouldn't go to Vegas," Ruth said. "We went off course and look what happened."

"Not go to Vegas?" Annie wailed. "Oh, Grandma, we can't change our plans now."

"Why can't we?"

"I—" Annie turned to Bethanne. "Mom…"

"I was looking forward to seeing Vegas and so was Annie," Bethanne said. "I'm sure everything will be fine now. We'll pick up a new rental car while we're there and continue on our trip."

Ruth seemed unconvinced. "I don't know…."

"Please, Grandma," Annie begged. "Vegas will be fun, and after today that's what we need."

"Oh, all right." She felt she'd succumbed far too easily, but it wasn't in her to disappoint Annie or Bethanne.

"Good." Bethanne returned to the tow truck and removed a large white bag.

"What's that?" Annie asked.

"I got the driver to take me to a fast food place so I could pick up burger-and-fry combos for the guys," she said. "I can hardly imagine what we would've done if they hadn't stopped by the lake when they did."

"You bought them burgers?" These were the men who'd frightened her out of several years of her life, and her daughter-in-law wanted to feed them?

Bethanne brought the bag over to the bikers who were, thankfully, dressed by now. At least Bethanne had been spared *that* sight.

"You should know Grandma there tried to abscond with our clothes," Rooster said as he helped himself to a burger and a bag of fries. His eyes twinkled with merriment. "She assumed that was a major threat."

"We showed her," Willie said.

"That's just it," Ruth snapped, unwilling to be the butt of their jokes. "You *did* show me—you exposed yourselves. There's laws against that. I should've made a citizen's arrest."

Bethanne grinned, and Ruth decided it would be best to simply drop the matter.

Annie distributed the rest of the food, and the men sat together while the three women went off to relax under the tree.

Ruth hadn't realized how thirsty she was until she drank a bottle of the water Bethanne had brought back. They'd already eaten lunch, but even if she'd been ravenous, she couldn't have managed a bite—and the thought of a greasy burger was singularly unappealing. Not so with the bikers and the tow truck driver, who wolfed down their food so fast it made her feel nauseous.

Bethanne and Annie thanked everyone for their help. Although the men on bikes hadn't turned out to be ax murderers, Ruth let the other two women do the talking.

Fortunately, the tow truck had a backseat so they could all fit inside. During the ride into town Bethanne seemed unusually quiet and Ruth could only speculate on what she was thinking.

"Those bikers weren't so bad, now, were they?" Annie said.

Ruth nodded reluctantly. "They weren't as bad as I feared."

"Oh, Grandma, admit it. They were cool guys, helping us like that."

"Cool guys?" Ruth glanced at Bethanne. She could do with some reinforcement in case her daughter-in-law hadn't noticed.

"Actually, Max was a real gentleman," Bethanne said.

"A gentleman?" Well, okay, maybe she'd been wrong, but Ruth always figured it was better to be prepared.

Eleven

There wasn't much to recommend Wells, Nevada, as a tourist destination. The entire town consisted of two casinos, gas stations, a fast-food joint and a few watering holes. After the vehicle was repaired, with the promise of a replacement once they reached Las Vegas, Bethanne, Ruth and Annie found a room for the night.

"I think we should call Dad," Annie said, sitting cross-legged on one of the two queen-size beds. "He should know where we are."

"You can if you want," Bethanne told her daughter. She propped her suitcase up on the luggage holder, unzipped it and took out what she needed for the night.

"He's not going to be too happy with us," Annie murmured, looking thoughtful. She nibbled on her lower lip. "Maybe I should wait until we're in Vegas."

Bethanne made a noncommittal sound.

"We might as well face the music," Ruth said. "Get it over with." She sat on the edge of the bed, obviously worn-out from their unexpected adventure. "Guaranteed,

Grant will mention it to Robin and then we'll all get read the riot act."

"The riot act, Grandma? What's that?"

"Oh, it's an expression based on an old English law. It just means Robin's going to be furious—and she's going to let us know it. I don't care. She can say what she wants. We're safe now and that's all that matters." Ruth set her pajamas on the second bed and sank into the mattress. "I don't mind telling you, after a day like this, I'm completely exhausted."

"Me, too," Bethanne said. Both Ruth and Annie had questioned her repeatedly about the time she'd spent with Max. It wasn't that she didn't have an answer, because she did. Her thoughts, however, were ones she wanted to keep to herself. Although she was unlikely to see Max again, she couldn't help being curious about him. She'd wanted to ask about his wife, Kate, and what had compelled him to take to the road three years ago—and stay there.

Annie glanced from one to the other and frowned, disappointment flashing from her eyes. "You're going to bed? Now? Don't you want to go downstairs and gamble?"

"Tonight?" Ruth asked. "Not me."

"Me, neither," Bethanne concurred.

"You mean we're spending the night in a casino hotel and no one wants to play the slot machines?"

"Not tonight, sweetie," Ruth said again, and yawned.

"I'll wait until Vegas," Bethanne added. She was tired; besides, she'd already promised herself a forty-dollar limit, the money she'd earned in tips, and didn't want to start spending it yet. "But, Annie, if you want to check out the casino, go ahead."

"Okay," her daughter muttered, but she didn't sound enthusiastic. In fact, she stayed where she was, her expression perplexed and a bit glum.

Ruth took the first shower and Bethanne went next, brushing her teeth and changing into her pajamas. When she came out of the bathroom, Annie was on the phone, talking to Grant.

With her cell against her ear, Annie paced the room, looking guilty as soon as she saw Bethanne.

"Mom's here now. Do you want to talk to her?"

Apparently, Grant did, because Annie thrust the phone at her. Bethanne hesitated, then reluctantly took it. She didn't owe Grant any explanations and she didn't plan on listening to his complaints, either.

"Hello, Grant."

"It seems the three of you had quite an adventure," he said. Although his comment was mild enough, Bethanne sensed his concern, mingled with irritation.

"We're fine."

"Bethanne, don't you realize what a crazy risk you took?"

"Like I said, we're fine. Nothing happened." She didn't want or need a lecture from him.

"You rode off with a biker? A *biker?*"

"His name is Max, and like I told your mother and Annie, he was a perfect gentleman."

Grant was silent for a moment, as though weighing how best to continue. "Annie suggested they might be Wild Hogs. You remember the movie? Businessmen escaping the corporate world? She even said they went skinny-dipping, just like in the movie."

"I...don't know about that. What I do know is that they came to our rescue and I'm grateful."

Again he paused. "Promise me you won't do anything that foolish again."

"Grant, I'm not a child." She appreciated his concern but at the same time found his reaction condescending. She hadn't been in any danger; her instincts told her as much. Grant still didn't seem to grasp that she was an independent woman now. While she understood his feelings, she wasn't about to let him scold her.

"I know that, and it's your business if you want to take those kinds of risks. But don't drag Annie and my mother into it."

The tightness of his words told Bethanne that he was struggling to hold on to his temper.

"I think we should change the subject," she said, unwilling to get into an argument. He was right; she'd probably been far too trusting. Still, she didn't feel she'd had any choice.

"Fine," he snapped. "We'll change the subject." But he didn't introduce a different topic; neither did she.

"Would you like to speak to Annie again?" she asked a few seconds later.

"Please."

Bethanne handed her daughter the cell.

Turning her back on both her mother and grandmother, Annie walked to the window. "All right, Daddy, I will. I know." This was followed by a short silence. "I know. Okay. Goodbye. I'll check in tomorrow night, I promise." She closed the cell, then turned around and stared at Bethanne.

"What?" Bethanne asked. She'd crawled under the

sheets and opened her book. Ruth had turned off her light and was asleep, or pretending to be.

"You upset Dad," Annie said. "All he cares about is our safety. There was no need to get huffy with him."

Rather than argue, Bethanne shrugged. "Did I?"

"Yes, you did," her daughter challenged. "Can't you see how hard he's trying?"

"I know he is," Bethanne conceded. Annie had a point; she'd been short-tempered with Grant. In theory she'd moved past the divorce, past the pain, and yet every now and then, when she least expected it, those old resentments would rear up, taking her by surprise.

"He's doing everything he can to make up for what he did," Annie said. "All he wants is for the two of you to get back together."

"Annie—" She wasn't allowed to finish.

"Maybe you think I shouldn't have told him about you riding off with Max, but…I felt he has a right to know."

"If you feel it's important to keep your father updated, then do so," Bethanne told her daughter. She stopped herself from saying that she'd prefer it if Annie omitted any details pertaining to her.

"Daddy loves you," Annie added. "You can't expect him to deny his feelings."

Bethanne didn't doubt that Grant had loved her in the past, especially when they were first married. At the births of their children he'd wept tears of joy as he held her hand and thanked her for making him a father. She remembered the good years they'd shared, the career he'd built and the comfortable lifestyle he'd provided. However, those happy reminiscences were tainted by everything that had led up to and followed the divorce. Did he love her when he checked into a hotel room with Tiffany and then came home at night, all smiles? Did he love her the day he announced he wanted a divorce? He'd been heartless the morning he walked out the door. Bethanne had worked hard to forgive him, but she wasn't sure she could ever forget the devastating pain Grant had brought into her life and her children's. Or could she? If they were to reunite, that was the question she'd need to confront—and answer.

"I think I'll settle down for the night," Bethanne said, closing her book.

"Mom?"

"Yes?" Bethanne rearranged her pillows and looked up at her daughter.

"Say something!"

"About what, sweetie?"

"The fact that Daddy still loves you." Annie's eyes widened as she waited for Bethanne's response.

"I know he does, and I love him, too…. I always will." That love had altered but the flame hadn't completely burned out. She didn't *want* to feel anything for Grant and yet she did. How could she not? They were married for twenty years. She'd given birth to his children. Those were facts she couldn't ignore or forget. But love, she'd discovered, had many sides, many angles, and some were sharper than others.

"Then there really is hope that you might reconcile?" Her daughter's face filled with anticipation.

This was the same question that had been rattling around her head for the past few weeks—and the past few minutes. "I can't answer that yet."

"But you're thinking about it?"

Bethanne smiled at her. "I'm giving it…consideration."

"If you don't mind my saying so…" Ruth levered herself up on one elbow. She hadn't been sleeping, after all. "Grant's learned from his mistake. He's paid the price. We all do sooner or later," she said, looking tired and sad. "For myself, I appreciate that he's man enough to admit it. Not many would, you realize?"

"You're right."

Annie and Ruth exchanged warm smiles.

"I guess I'll wait until we get to Vegas to check out a casino," Annie said, and swallowed a wide yawn. "We've had quite a day."

"Indeed," Ruth murmured.

Grinning to herself, Bethanne reached for her novel again, while Annie changed clothes and slid into bed beside her. Within minutes, her daughter's even breathing told Bethanne she was asleep. Ruth was, too. As soon as she finished her chapter, she closed the book and turned off her light. With her head nestled in the pillow, she shut her eyes, confident that sleep would soon overtake her despite the relentless glow from the casino's blinking sign. On, off. On, off…

To her surprise, she found her thoughts drifting to Max and what he'd told her about losing his wife. It'd been three years, he'd said. He'd grieved for three years. This man loved deeply. The possibility of that kind of unwavering love brought her solace, and she fell instantly asleep.

Annie woke when she heard her mother flick off the bedside lamp. The hotel room was bathed in muted shades of red and green from the casino's neon lights, which shone outside their window. They flashed off and on in Christmas colors and flickered through the slit between the drapes.

Rolling onto her side, Annie pulled the sheet over her shoulder and tucked it securely around her. She wished now that she hadn't called her father. She'd tried Andrew, but he hadn't been home and apparently hadn't checked his text messages, either. Otherwise, he would've called her back.

Mainly Annie had wanted to tell someone about their adventure. In retrospect, the afternoon had been amusing. A great anecdote that the three of them would repeat for years. Until recently, she would've immediately called Vance and regaled him with it, too. Only, he was out of her life.

Her ego was gratified by the fact that he'd made several efforts to contact her, all of which she'd ignored. He was not to be trusted. Annie had never hidden anything from him and yet he'd— Well, it didn't serve any useful purpose to review the list of wrongs Vance had committed against her.

Because her brother was clearly preoccupied, and she wasn't talking to Vance, and her friends were all off in various places this summer, Annie had phoned her father. She thought her grandmother had been hilarious, taking the bikers' clothes. Even now, just thinking about it made her smile.

Except that her dad hadn't been nearly as amused. When he learned Bethanne had ridden into town with Max, he'd been upset. Justifiably so. She could see his point and, again, wished she'd squelched the urge to call.

Another mistake she'd made was giving her mother the

phone. That hadn't gone nearly as well as she'd hoped. Before long, her parents were snapping at each other, and it was all Annie could do not to grab the phone out of her mother's hand.

More than anything, Annie wanted her parents back together. They belonged with each other; at least her father could see that now. Lots of men made mistakes. Women, too. Annie knew that from watching her friends' parents.

Men, in particular, supposedly went through this middle-age form of adolescence, where they behaved badly. According to what she'd heard, sooner or later they came to their senses. Some were smart enough to do whatever it took to get their families back. The lucky ones did. They reconciled with their wives and kids and started fresh, with a new appreciation of what they'd lost.

Annie wanted her father to be one of the lucky ones. He had to be impressed by everything her mother had accomplished since the divorce. Annie would admit that even she was surprised by the success of the party business. She wasn't the only one, either.

Annie suspected that the attention her mother received had become an issue between Tiffany and her father. Grant didn't openly acknowledge that but Annie could read between the lines. The *lovely* Tiffany's career wasn't exactly going gangbusters these days, not that Annie was sorry to hear it. Frankly, she'd be just as glad never to hear the other woman's name again. Fortunately, the *lovely* Tiffany was out of the picture.

She'd given her own motivations some serious thought when Andrew had challenged her. He'd accused her of wanting to revert to a perfect past that hadn't been as perfect as she'd chosen to believe. Not true. This was more about instinct and love than any childhood fantasy.

Her parents needed each other, and Annie considered it her duty as their daughter to encourage their reconciliation. Now all she had to do was pave the way for her mother and father to meet in the middle and resolve this.

Come to think of it, she might offer her father a suggestion or two. Flowers for when they arrived in Vegas might help her mother forget their little argument that evening.

Hmm... She set her cell phone to wake her early so she could call her dad. Roses, she told herself sleepily. Red ones...

Bethanne's next conscious thought was that Annie was awake and moving about the hotel room. Although she was obviously making an effort to be quiet, she didn't succeed. She dropped her cosmetics case with a clatter.

"Annie," Bethanne groaned. "What time is it?"

"Six. The way I figure it, we could get to Vegas this afternoon if we leave early."

"Is your grandmother awake?" Bethanne asked, her eyes still closed.

"I am now," Ruth muttered.

Bethanne opened her eyes and noticed Ruth sitting up in bed, stretching her arms as she arched her back. "Get me coffee and I'll do my morning exercises, then we can hit the road."

"Vegas, here we come!" Annie cried. She was already dressed, with her suitcase packed and waiting by the door.

"I'll jump in the shower," Bethanne said, and tossed

aside the covers as she climbed out of bed. Retrieving her clothes, she stepped into the bathroom. By the time she finished, Annie had prepared coffee and Ruth had done her stretching exercises and was dressed.

"Ready, Mom?" Annie asked as Bethanne repacked her suitcase and slipped her book into her purse.

"I'm ready. But the question should be…is Vegas ready for us?"

Annie laughed. "I sure hope so."

They were on the road by seven-fifteen, and rolled into Vegas seven and a half hours later. Annie had booked them into the Hard Rock Casino just off the Strip. It wouldn't have been either Ruth's or Bethanne's first choice, but one casino was probably as good as another.

While Annie and Ruth checked in, Bethanne found the rental car location and swapped cars, more for peace of mind than anything else. Marvin back in Wells had done an excellent job, but they still had a long way to travel. Bethanne didn't dare risk another breakdown.

When she returned to the casino, both Annie and Ruth were playing the slot machines. The sights and sounds of the casino were everywhere. Instead of being annoyed by the din, Bethanne discovered that it added to the excitement.

"Sit down and play with us," Annie urged, intent on a game named after the television show *Wheel of Fortune*.

"Okay." Bethanne wasn't keen on giving her hard-earned forty dollars to a slot, but it did look like fun. The thought of turning that fun into winnings was too tempting to ignore.

She found a machine with a cartoon Texas oilman

called Texas Tea, pulled out a stool and plopped herself down. Twenty dollars went quickly, although it was a nickel machine. At $2.25 with every push of the button, her twenty bucks vanished almost before she knew it. She wondered whether to feed it her last twenty, but hesitated, then decided she'd reached her limit for that day.

"Have you been up to the room yet?" Ruth asked when Bethanne sat next to her mother-in-law.

"Not yet." Annie had taken up Bethanne's suitcase and given her the room key earlier.

"You need to see the room," Annie said, smiling broadly. "If you wait a minute, I'll go up with you."

"Is anyone hungry yet?" Ruth asked. She removed the receipt for her winnings and stuffed it inside her purse.

"I'm starving," Annie said. "Lunch was hours ago. But let's go to the room first."

Bethanne couldn't imagine why seeing their room was so important. Hotel rooms were pretty much alike. Beds, a television, sometimes a desk, and, of course, a small and generally cramped bathroom, and that was about it.

What awaited her was a large bouquet of red roses. Dozens of beautiful red buds in a crystal vase. "Roses?" Bethanne breathed as she stepped into the room.

Ruth and Annie looked positively delighted. "The card says they're for you," Annie crowed. Her eyes gleamed as if she was personally responsible.

"Me?"

"Well, all of us. Read the card and see."

Bethanne unpinned the envelope from the pink ribbon and stared down at it for a moment while a strange thought went through her mind. Could they have come from Max? But that was impossible. He had no idea where she was. Or did he? Roses were extravagant. Special. She loved roses, always had. Max didn't know that—but Grant did.

"Read the card, Mom," Annie said a second time.

Bethanne ripped open the tiny envelope and removed the card. "For my three favorite women." It was signed "Grant." "They're from your father," she said as a warm feeling settled over her. A feeling of being cherished.

"I told you Dad was trying," Annie said. She seemed really pleased by the gesture.

"You father knows how much I love roses." Bethanne glanced at the card again.

Ruth reached for the card and read it, too. "I'm sure Grant felt bad about your conversation last night and wants to clear the air."

"I'm sure that's it," Bethanne agreed.

"Still, roses are pretty special." That comment came from Annie.

"I'll call your father and thank him." And she would… later. It was a lovely thing to do and Bethanne did appreciate his effort. Grant was trying to win her back. Now it was up to her to decide if that was what *she* wanted.

"Shall we think about dinner?" Ruth asked.

It was still a bit early, but Annie was right; they'd eaten hours ago. Because they were so eager to get to Vegas, they'd had a skimpy lunch. Breakfast had consisted of coffee and the bottled orange juice Bethanne picked up at a filling station on the way out of Wells. After some discussion they had dinner at the hotel's buffet.

Bethanne ate until she was stuffed. At only seven-thirty, it seemed a shame to go back to their room so early. They were planning to spend the next day exploring the Strip. For tonight, that left the slots.

"I've got forty dollars burning a hole in my purse." Ruth was grinning like a five-year-old at her own birthday party. "Let me at those *Wheel of Fortune* machines."

"I guess I'll give that Texas oilman another chance to show me what he's got," Bethanne said.

"I don't know what I want to do just yet," Annie told them.

They set a time to reconvene and then split up. Two hours later, Bethanne arrived at the designated area. Ruth was already there.

"I'll never think of Vanna White the same way again," her mother-in-law muttered. "She took all my money."

Bethanne laughed. She, on the other hand, had struck oil and was up more than a hundred dollars.

"Tell Annie good-night for me, will you?" Ruth asked. "I'm going to the room. I'll read for a while and turn in for the night."

"Okay. Good night. I'll probably be joining you myself in an hour or so."

Annie showed up a couple of minutes later with a young man in tow. "Mom, meet Jason. Jason, my mom. We're going to hang for a while," Annie announced, then kissed Bethanne's cheek and was off.

Bethanne had barely managed a word. "Well," she said with a sigh, "I suppose I'll sit down with that oilman again." She found the area where she'd been earlier and slid onto the stool. After inserting a twenty-dollar bill, she pushed the button and waited.

"Any luck?" a familiar voice asked.

Bethanne swiveled the chair around as Max claimed the empty seat beside her.

Twelve

Bethanne was speechless. As casually as could be, Max fed a twenty-dollar bill into the machine next to hers, glanced over and smiled.

A smile. He'd actually smiled. "Hi," he said.

"Hi." Her tongue felt as if it had twisted itself into knots. "How did you know where to find me?"

He spoke as he played the slot machine. "Rooster heard Annie and Grandma talking about Vegas. I figured if I was Annie's age I'd head for the Hard Rock Casino, so I took a chance you'd be here."

Out of all the casinos in Vegas, he'd found the one she was in, although it was Friday night and the city was crammed with people and cars. The clang of the slots, music, laughter—the sounds of excitement were all around. Even if he'd guessed the right hotel, it was pure luck that he'd happened upon her.

"I've been winning," she said, imitating his casual tone.

"How much?"

"Not enough to set the casino back any."

The music pounded in the background and seemed ten times louder than before. Bethanne had lost track of popular tunes and musicians years ago; she couldn't have identified the singers' names or the song titles. In fact, she was aware of nothing except the man sitting next to her.

After several minutes Max sent her a pained look. "Do you like this music?"

"Not particularly."

"Wanna take a ride on my bike?"

She nodded. She wanted to get away, too. With him. It was difficult to think, but she couldn't blame that entirely on the music. "Have your ribs healed?" she asked.

"Not quite, but I'm willing to risk it again."

"You're a brave man."

They stepped outside and the contrast to the ear-splitting music was almost shocking. She started to tell him how much she appreciated the fact that he'd found her, but he shook his head.

"What did you say?" he asked. "My ears are still ringing."

"Just that I'm glad you're here." Bethanne hadn't intended to admit that. Yet it was true. She hadn't expected to see him again, hadn't believed it was even possible. The explosion of surprise mingled with joy gave her pause. Bethanne had planned to use these weeks away to consider her future with Grant. This wasn't the time to confuse the issue by indulging some romantic fantasy about a man on a motorcycle.

Max studied her with those intense brown eyes. "I'm glad I'm here, too." He clasped her hand and intertwined their fingers. Bethanne's heart raced like that of a teenage girl on her first date. *Get a grip,* she told herself. As they walked out of the casino she kept reminding herself how ridiculous being with Max was. This was a dead-end relationship. A dead-end everything.

Although it wasn't nine o'clock yet, it remained light out. "Any place you'd like to go?" he asked.

Being unfamiliar with Las Vegas, Bethanne didn't know what to suggest. "Not really."

"Okay, I'll choose."

They reached his bike in the parking lot and he removed Rooster's helmet from the older man's Harley, which was parked beside his, and handed it to her. She climbed on the back of Max's bike and set her feet where he'd shown her before. Max took his seat, started the engine with a roar and turned out of the parking lot.

Bethanne slipped her arms around his waist and held on, although less tightly than the first time she'd ridden with him. Closing her eyes, she felt the breeze rush past and after a few minutes she relaxed. She wasn't sure where Max was going. It didn't matter.

When he slowed the bike, Bethanne realized they were completely out of the city, on a hill that overlooked the valley. Night had settled in and the casino lights lit up the sky.

"It's beautiful, isn't it?" he said, after they'd parked and taken off their helmets. He looked down at the city, and Bethanne joined him.

"I used to sit up here and just stare at the lights," Max continued. "It's so crazy down there and so peaceful up here." He stood beside her in silence for a few minutes. "Tell me about your ex-husband," he suddenly said.

"Grant?" she asked, uncertain what to say.

"You have more than one?"

"No. Your question surprised me, that's all."

"Is it difficult to talk about your divorce?"

She shook her head. "Not anymore. I guess it comes down to a case of the two of us growing apart. He found someone else and the sad part is, I was so involved with his career, with our children and friends, that I didn't notice. I mean, a wife's supposed to sense these things, right?"

"I wouldn't know."

"Did you…did you ever cheat on your wife?"

"Never." His answer was quick and decisive. "I wasn't even tempted."

"At the time, Grant and I had been married nearly twenty years. We'd grown comfortable with each other. Complacent, I guess. He wanted me to be a stay-at-home mother and I enjoyed that role. I hosted dinners, arranged all his travel… I considered myself a full partner in his life and his career—and yet I didn't know about Tiffany. I honestly didn't have a clue. If someone had told me, I swear I wouldn't have believed my husband was capable of betraying me that way."

"Were you unhappy?"

"No, not in the least. But after Grant moved out, I was an emotional mess. I felt lost, bewildered, defeated. As if I'd suddenly been blinded, with no idea where I was or how to find my way out. It took weeks—no, months—to come to grips with the situation. I'm a different person now. The years have given me perspective. I can understand better what happened and why Grant was attracted to Tiffany."

"Sounds as if you're making excuses for him."

"Does it?"

"Yes."

She looked down at the ground and moved the dirt around with the toe of her shoe. Maybe she *was* making excuses for Grant; if so, it was probably because he'd recognized how wrong he'd been and told her so, over and over. "Grant's sorry about it now…. I mentioned before that he wants us to get back together. He had roses delivered to the hotel."

"Here in Vegas?"

She nodded. "They were in the room waiting for us. He wanted to apologize because we had a small argument over the phone last night."

"About me, I suspect."

"If you must know, he was horrified that I'd taken off with you."

"He's right. It was a risky thing to do."

"Are you dangerous, Max?"

He didn't answer.

"Is Max your real name?"

"It is. Max Scranton. My friends find it ironic—the Mad Max thing. But I've been Max my whole life." He hesitated and leaned back against the bike, stretched out his legs and crossed his arms. "Kate used to call me—" He didn't finish the sentence.

"Does it hurt to talk about her?"

He looked away. "What you told me yesterday is true. It does get easier. I didn't think that was possible."

"How much longer will you continue to run?" she asked. She wouldn't have been nearly as forward if he hadn't been curious about her and Grant.

"Is that what I'm doing? Running away from the pain?" The question didn't appear to offend him.

She nodded. "Actually, I think I would've pulled up roots and left Seattle if not for Andrew and Annie." It occurred to her that he might have children. "Did you and Kate have a family?"

Anguish came and went in his eyes so quickly that Bethanne wondered if she'd imagined it. "A daughter. Katherine was born with a rare genetic disease. She died when she was eleven. Since we both carried the gene, we decided not to have any more children. After Katherine it was just the two of us. Then…Kate was gone, too. I didn't deal well with that. I blamed myself for a long time." He spoke with his gaze on the lights of the city below. "I buried myself in a bottle for the first year. I don't know what would've happened to me if it wasn't for Rooster and my brother. Fortunately, Luke stepped in to take over the business. Otherwise, I would've lost it, along with everything else. In a way I think that's what I wanted. Maybe what I deserved. Death robbed me of the two people I loved most. Nothing else mattered. I think I wanted to die myself. Death would be easier than living with the pain." He paused and inhaled deeply. "Then Rooster took control. He refused to let me slowly kill myself. I'm grateful now, but, trust me, at the time I much preferred the idea of drinking myself to death."

Max had lost so much. His daughter and then his wife.

"I don't talk about Katherine," he murmured, staring into the night sky. "Not with anyone." He looked decidedly uncomfortable. "You…unnerve me, Bethanne. I don't know how else to describe it—and I don't like it.

Feeling vulnerable is something I avoid. I don't understand what makes you different."

Bethanne didn't understand it, either. She placed her hand on his forearm and felt him tense. "Why did you come looking for me?" she asked.

He snorted softly as if he wished he knew the answer himself. "The thing is, I'm not sure why I wanted to see you again. All I knew was that I...needed to."

Still sitting, he held out his arms, and she leaned into his embrace. He held her close. Bethanne tucked her head beneath his chin and released a slow, thoughtful sigh.

A hundred questions chased one another in her mind, but she couldn't ask a single one. After what seemed like a very long time, he reluctantly let her go.

"You feel like you belong in my arms," he whispered.

Bethanne wanted to tell him she felt the same way, but she couldn't afford to encourage this relationship. Over the past six years she'd dated, but no one had affected her the way this man did. Instead, she looked up at him, and his dark eyes held hers.

She shook her head. "No, don't..."

"Don't?"

"You're going to kiss me. Aren't you?"

He frowned.

"I'm flattered, don't get me wrong—but my life's complicated. I took this trip with my mother-in-law and Annie because I needed time to sort through some things."

"Whether to reunite with your ex-husband."

"Like I said, my life's complicated...and I can't...I won't get involved with you."

He grinned.

"This isn't funny! My life is—"

"Complicated," he finished for her. "Yeah, I know. It's just a kiss, Bethanne."

"I know." She felt foolish for acting as though it was something more. "But the way I feel…" She didn't finish, wasn't even sure she should. She'd just told him how attractive she found him.

He seemed to realize what she meant. "Got it. It's time I took you back to the hotel."

"Right." She didn't want to leave, but it was for the best and clearly he recognized that, too.

He placed the helmet on his head and climbed on the bike. Bethanne did the same. Instead of circling her arms around him the way she had previously, she simply gripped the sides of his leather jacket. If he noticed, he didn't mention it. In her two times on the bike, she'd learned quite a bit about motorcycles. As they rode, her body automatically adjusted to the curves and turns.

The reverse journey, back into the city, seemed to take ten times longer. When they reached the Hard Rock Hotel and Casino, he pulled into the parking area, where the valets assisted drivers. He waited for her to climb off first.

She removed the helmet and handed it to him. Her throat clogged with tears as she struggled to speak. She wouldn't see him again, and while she knew that was the only responsible option, it saddened her. Finally, she decided on a simple "Thank you."

He nodded without looking at her.

Turning away, she entered the casino and was startled by the surge of loud music.

Tired now and discouraged, Bethanne hurried toward

the elevator. She was standing in the lobby when she saw Rooster making his way toward her.

"Where's Max?" he asked, obviously surprised to find her alone. He held a beer bottle in one hand.

She shrugged. "I don't know. He dropped me off and left."

Rooster frowned and took a swallow of his beer. "He just dropped you off?"

She hoped Max's friend would give her some insight into him. "We went up to a hill where we could look at the city and talked for a while."

Rooster led her away from the crowd and into one of the bars. "Let me buy you a beer."

"Thanks, but I'm not much of a beer drinker."

"Order whatever you want," he said. He found them a table and raised his hand to get the attention of the waitress.

"I prefer red wine."

He grinned at that.

"There's nothing wrong with red wine," she said.

"Nothing whatsoever. You might ask Max about that the next time you see him."

Bethanne doubted she'd have the opportunity.

The waitress came for their order and quickly returned with another beer for Rooster and a glass of merlot for Bethanne. Actually, she was glad she'd run into Max's friend.

"He nearly tore this town apart looking for you," Rooster commented. He leaned toward her, his elbows propped on the table.

By contrast Max had made it sound as if he'd tracked

her down without much effort. "Did he tell you why it was so important to find me?"

"No."

"Where are Willie and Skunk?" She shouldn't ask questions. What she should do was drink her wine, thank Rooster and go up to bed.

"They took off on their own when they got tired of racing from one casino to the next. Can't say I blame them."

"I don't think Max is all that pleased he found me."

"Don't be so sure."

"Frankly, I'm not sure of anything, including how I feel." She thought for a moment. "I guess I'm sad, mostly." Still, she felt honored that their brief time together had such a strong impact on him. It'd been the same for her, but the timing was all wrong. The situation, too. She tasted her wine, then held the glass by its stem. For some reason, she felt an urge to explain. "I can't get involved with Max," she said. "I just can't. Not right now. I have responsibilities, decisions to make, and I need a clear mind."

"You sound like Max."

"How?"

"At every casino he said he didn't need a woman messing with his mind. He said he wasn't going to let a woman make him stupid."

"What does that mean?"

"Hell if I know. You'll have to ask him. All day, casino after casino, he kept saying he needed his head examined and yet he kept searching. I asked him what was so special about you, and he wouldn't answer. He didn't stop until he found you and I don't think he would have, either."

Despite herself, she smiled. "When he hugged me, he said I...belonged in his arms."

"You hugged? That's all?" Rooster sounded incredulous.

"That's all."

"He hasn't touched another woman since Kate died. You've obviously had a powerful effect on him."

She sipped her wine while she tried to make sense of all this. "He'll be fine." Taking her business card from her purse, she handed it to Rooster. "Give this to him and tell him to call me when he's ready." By then she would have reached her own decision regarding Grant. She'd know what she wanted. With time and distance she'd be able to think, to put her history with Grant and this new attraction in perspective. If she went back to Grant, she'd inform Max—provided she even heard from him again. If not...

Rooster put the card in his pocket and frowned at her. "You sure you want to do this?"

She nodded. "I'm sure."

And she was.

Thirteen

Bethanne was putting on eye makeup when Annie, dressed in her pj's, stumbled into the bathroom bleary-eyed, her hair a tangled mess.

"Did you have fun last night?" Bethanne asked. She'd lain awake a long time and heard Annie tiptoe into the room around three that morning. In fact, Bethanne doubted she'd slept more than a couple of hours the entire night. She'd been thinking of Max and their conversation. She couldn't help wondering what might have happened if she'd let him kiss her. Well, it was too late to question that now.

"I had a blast," Annie said as she ran a brush through her hair. "Would it be all right if you and Grandma did your own thing today?"

"Are you seeing Jason again?'

"That's okay, isn't it? I met his parents. They're with him and his sister is, too. Apparently, a cousin of his got married yesterday afternoon. We hung out with his sister most of the night."

"Sure. That's fine."

"I'm meeting his parents for breakfast. Why don't you come with us?"

"Thanks, I will. But I don't want you to stay out as late tonight, okay? We're leaving in the morning."

"I won't, I promise."

Annie dressed quickly in cotton capris and a tank top, and put on minimal makeup. Oh, the benefits of being in your twenties! Not that middle age didn't have its compensations...

When Bethanne had finished her own makeup, her mother-in-law was sitting on the end of the bed waiting. "You ready for breakfast, Ruth?" she asked. "We've been invited to join Annie's friend Jason and his family."

"More than ready." Ruth reached for her purse and together they left the room. They spent a delightful hour with Jason and his extended family, all of them friendly and outgoing people, then walked the Strip, visiting one casino after another. They rode the gondola at the Venetian and shopped at Caesars Palace, then ate lunch at Wolfgang Puck's restaurant. Ruth's energy surpassed Bethanne's. Her mother-in-law might be attending her fiftieth class reunion, but she was physically fit and mentally alert. *And* she'd had a good night's sleep, unlike Bethanne.

"I have to admit I'm enjoying this more than I would Mount Rushmore," Ruth told her as she set her fork down. "I'm feeling lucky. Would you mind if I went back to the hotel and gave Vanna a chance to return my money?"

"Of course. You do what you want. This is your trip."

Ruth looked unsure. "But I want you to enjoy yourself,

too." She paused. "Annie certainly seems to be having a good time."

"I am, too. A wonderful time," Bethanne assured her and, truthfully, she was.

"What will you do?" Ruth asked.

"Well, that Texas oilman and I have struck up a friendly relationship. I think I'll go visit that slot machine again and see if he's willing to hand over any more of those oil residuals."

Her plans for the afternoon seemed to appease Ruth. Bethanne walked her mother-in-law back to the Hard Rock casino and sent her off to find the *Wheel of Fortune* slot machines. Then she strolled around until she came across the Texas Tea slots. Yesterday's machine was available and she grabbed it. Once seated and comfortable, she opened her purse to take out her wallet. She wouldn't have heard her cell phone if not for the fact that her purse was open. Automatically she pulled it out. She didn't recognize the number.

"Hello," she said breathlessly.

"Why did you give your business card to Rooster?"

"Max?"

"I'm asking why you gave Rooster your cell phone number," he repeated.

"I don't know," she murmured, shocked to hear from him and equally pleased. Last night she'd reviewed their conversation over and over, and each time she'd felt a sense of loss. She needed to consider her relationship with Grant, but that didn't mean she had to shut herself off from a new one, did it? Well, yes, it did if she and Grant were going to reconcile. She'd finally fallen into a troubled sleep and woke with no clear understanding of what her ultimate decision would be. What it *should* be.

"Yes, you do."

He was right; she did know why she'd done it. Even as she handed Rooster the business card with that vague comment about how Max should call when he was "ready," she knew. "I wanted to see you again."

"Where are you?"

"Same casino. Same machine."

"Are you alone?"

"Yes."

"I'll be there in ten minutes."

Bethanne's hand trembled as she dropped her phone back inside her purse. She told herself she should get up and walk away that very minute. But she couldn't do it.

Max seemed to recognize her indecision the moment he approached her. She started to talk, but he stopped her by pressing his finger against her lips. Taking her by the shoulders, he smiled down at her. "Haven't you heard that what happens in Vegas stays in Vegas?"

She nodded.

"I respect what you told me. I appreciate that you've got a weighty decision to make. All I ask is that you give me today. I won't ask for anything more. Can you agree to that?"

Again she nodded.

He smiled and slipped his arms around her, and they hugged.

His embrace felt warm and familiar as if this was where she belonged. Wasn't that what he'd said—that she belonged in his arms? It was exactly how she felt, too. Why, oh, why did *he* have to be the one who made her heart flutter? Why, oh, why did it have to be *now?* If she was confused and uncertain when it came to Grant, meeting Max only complicated that situation.

"I could hold you like this all day," he whispered into her hair.

She wanted that, too. Maybe, she mused, she was using Max as a distraction to avoid thinking about Grant.

"I have no intention of wasting what's left of today," Max said, clasping her hand. "Let's get out of here."

"Okay."

When they went outside, the summer sun beat down on them. The heat hadn't reached its zenith and wouldn't for several hours, but the sun shone with a brilliant intensity. Bethanne put on her sunglasses as they walked. "Where are we going?" she asked.

"A place I know not far from here."

It turned out to be an ice cream shop a couple of blocks off the Strip. Bethanne slid into the booth and Max took the seat across from her. He ordered a vanilla ice cream soda, while Bethanne had coffee.

They talked for four hours straight. Four hours. The conversation drifted naturally from one subject to another. They discussed music, politics, books and friends. She learned he was in the wine distribution business. That was the reason Rooster had commented on her preference for wine over beer. Rooster owned an advertising agency and had worked with Max on his company's account.

He asked her plenty of questions, too. He wanted to know about her children and she described Andrew and Annie with pride. In fact, they talked about everything—except Grant or Kate or his daughter. It was as though the subject of the people they'd once loved was strictly taboo.

About halfway through their conversation, Ruth phoned to say she was feeling a bit under the weather. Too much sun, too much food and her dismay that Vanna was a lot greedier than she'd expected. Bethanne was concerned, but Ruth claimed she'd feel better if she didn't interrupt Bethanne's fun with her Texas oilman. Bethanne didn't enlighten her mother-in-law about where she really was or who she was with.

"Tell me more about your business," Max said after she'd put away her cell. He held her card in his hand and turned it over two or three times as if there was some invisible message scrawled across the back.

"I never dreamed Parties would be as successful as it is. All I set out to do was make enough money to take care of my children and keep our home. The shock was how timely this idea turned out to be." She smiled. "There was an article about me in the *Wall Street Journal* when we added birthday parties for cats and dogs."

"You're joking, right? Parties for dogs?"

"Cats, too, and the idea's really caught on. Baby boomers love their pets and are willing to spend hundreds of dollars to throw them birthday parties."

"That I don't understand."

"You don't need to, but trust me, it's big business. I've had offers to franchise, but it doesn't feel right. Not yet. The problem with so many companies is that they expand too quickly. I don't want to do that. Once the five stores are all operating at a comfortable profit margin, I'll look into it again, but for the moment, I'm content."

"It sounds as if you have a good head for business."

"I like to think so." She didn't mention that most of what she'd learned had been gleaned from her years with Grant. She'd often remained in the background, but she'd absorbed a lot of business strategy and financial wisdom.

"So the divorce is actually responsible for your starting up the business?"

She nodded. "I had help." She told him the story of the knitting class she'd joined and the friends she'd made, including Elise Beaumont. "Elise's husband, Maverick, was a professional gambler—and he took a gamble on me."

"One that paid off."

"Yes, thankfully. So you're right. Grant was indirectly responsible for my decision to start this business."

"And now he wants to get back together with you?"

She cradled her mug with both hands and looked down into the cooling coffee. "He does, and I'm having a hard time deciding. I was with him for twenty years. We have a long, shared history, two children and a lot of happy memories. He realized he made a mistake and will do anything he can to rectify it…. I just don't know if it's possible to go back. I've changed and so has he."

"Have you forgiven him?"

"I hope so." She paused, then resumed, speaking slowly. "About a year after the divorce I woke up feeling miserable and depressed. Annie had let it slip that Grant and Tiffany were in Paris. Paris. I'd longed to visit Paris, and Grant knew that.

"All I could think about was how unfair it was that I should be alone, while Grant and Tiffany were off having the time of their lives. I buried my face in the pillow and just sobbed." The memory of her grief and her tears that bleak morning was fresh in her mind even now. "I realized then that I had to forgive him."

"What made you decide right *then* that you had to forgive him? And how did you manage it?"

"At first, I thought it would be impossible. I thought no one could forgive what Grant had done to me and our children. But then…" She bit her lip.

Max reached for her hand, gripping her fingers hard, silently encouraging her to continue.

"Then I understood that unless I freed my heart of the bitterness and resentment I felt toward Grant, I'd be incapable of ever loving again. I had to unclench my fist of anger in order to fill my palm with happiness, with joy… with love."

"And you've done that?"

"Max," she whispered, unsure how to respond. "I've done my best but I've discovered forgiveness is a lot harder than it looks. Just when I think I'm completely over what he did, something will happen that shows me how far I still have to go."

"Like what?"

"I told you he was upset with me because I took a risk and rode off with you. That angered me and I let him know it. Later, I felt bad because all Grant was really doing was telling me he was concerned about me and that he loves me. I was shocked by how quickly those old resentments returned."

Max circled the straw around his empty soda glass. "How's Grant's relationship with his children?"

"Better." Bethanne carefully chose the appropriate word. "Andrew's had a hard time trusting his father. When we were first divorced, Annie acted out her anger but eventually she calmed down and now they're as close as they used to be. I'm pretty sure he's keeping tabs on me during this trip through Annie." In other words, Grant had more than likely heard an earful about Max already.

"No doubt," he mumbled.

"Andrew's wedding complicates matters even more," she said. "Grant wants us to stand together, united as a family, as we celebrate our son's marriage. In theory it sounds like a good idea."

"And you'd like that, too?"

"Yes, I suppose I would. Grant and I love our son and we adore Courtney. But…"

"But?"

She was astonished by how easily she could voice her feelings to him. "Grant and me together sends a message to our family and friends that isn't accurate. We aren't a couple and haven't been for six years."

Bethanne was grateful that Max didn't share his opinions or offer advice. His willingness to remain silent told her that he trusted her judgment and her ability to make difficult choices. To make the decisions that were best for her and her children.

As the afternoon progressed, she saw that the ice cream parlor had started to fill up. Max looked around and noticed it, too. They were taking up spaces paying customers could use.

"Can I take you to dinner tonight?" he asked.

"Ice cream? Dinner? Apparently, what happens in Vegas is really pretty tame." She smiled as she said it.

Max smiled, too. "The night isn't over yet."

They set a time and place to meet, and Bethanne went up to her room to change clothes and check on Ruth. Her mother-in-law sat on the bed, leaning against some pillows she'd stacked behind her, feet crossed at the ankles. She was knitting and watching television.

She looked up when Bethanne walked into their room. "I called Jane in Florida," she said, blushing a little. "I used the hotel phone, which probably cost me more than I lost at the slots, but I wanted my friends to know where we were. Jane asked how soon we'd be in Florida." She beamed with pleasure over the phone call.

"What did you tell her?"

Ruth's grin seemed to brighten her entire face. "I told her we have a long way to drive, but we'll get there. Jane said that since we're in the area, it would be a shame not to see the Grand Canyon. We should go, don't you think?"

"We really should," Bethanne agreed. She opened her suitcase and unpacked the only dress she'd brought. "Have you heard from Annie?"

"Not a peep."

Bethanne nodded and called her daughter's cell. Annie explained that she and Jason had tickets for a show that evening; she was definitely amenable to visiting the Grand Canyon. "Might as well," she said cheerfully. "Bye, Mom!"

Bethanne shook out her dress and hung it in the closet. While her back was to Ruth, she said, "Max invited me to dinner. Will you be all right by yourself?"

"You're going out?" Ruth sounded surprised. "With that biker?"

"It's Vegas." Bethanne shrugged, but she did feel guilty about deserting her mother-in-law.

Ruth frowned. "Are you sure that's wise?"

"I'll be fine, although I hate the thought of you spending all your time in the room. You should go out, explore the town, enjoy yourself." She took her dress into the bathroom to change into and set out a pair of strappy heels to wear.

Ruth didn't seem keen on the idea of going out on her own. "I suppose I could find something to do," she muttered when Bethanne reappeared. "But I wonder whether you should be having dinner with another man..." She left the rest unsaid.

"Ruth, don't worry, I know what I'm doing."

Ruth glowered. "I hope you haven't taken leave of your senses."

Despite her effort not to, Bethanne laughed. She wasn't going to argue with Ruth, wasn't even going to point out that this was *her* business. "I won't be late," she said as she breezed out of the room. One day was all Max had asked of her and she couldn't refuse him—or herself.

Max met her in the lobby and did a double-take when he saw her. He'd changed, too, and wore slacks and a crisp cotton shirt, one she suspected from the crease marks was brand-new. It occurred to Bethanne that it hadn't been practical to wear a dress if he planned on taking his bike. Rooster was with him and straightened when he saw her.

"Wow, you clean up nice," the older man said.

"Thanks." She ran her hand down the front of her pale pink sheath.

"What's Ruth up to tonight?" he asked.

"She's threatening to order room service." Bethanne rolled her eyes at that. Ruth could pitch guilt with the best of them, but Bethanne refused to cancel her evening with Max.

Both men chuckled and Rooster sauntered over to the elevators. "Shall we?" Max said, offering her his arm. Once they were outside the hotel, the doorman got them a taxi. The restaurant Max took her to turned out to be a high-end steak house. Everything was delicious, from her salad to the rich dessert they shared. Max selected the wine, a rich cabernet sauvignon from France, and they discussed various Old and New World wines.

Max paid the bill, and when they left, he waved down a taxi. He gave the driver an address, and Bethanne asked, "Where are we going?" as he held her door.

He smiled, eyebrows raised. "To a biker bar."

"Oh." She'd feel terribly out of place.

"Don't worry," he said as he got in beside her. "It isn't what you think."

A few minutes later, they arrived at what appeared to be a honky-tonk tavern, where the band was loud and the crowd boisterous. Max found them a table in a shadowy corner and ordered drinks—pints of beer from a micro-brewery she'd never heard of. Several couples were dancing, and before the waitress returned, Max led Bethanne onto the floor.

They danced until they were breathless. The live music was energetic, the atmosphere festive. Several men cast her questioning looks but she doubted their curiosity was due to her or the way she'd dressed. The men seemed surprised to see Max with a woman, which made Bethanne feel even more special.

When she was convinced she couldn't dance another step, they went back to the table and collapsed into their chairs. Bethanne hadn't spent that much time on the dance floor in years. Max dragged his chair next to hers and picked up his beer mug, draining half of it. Then he set the mug aside, slipped his hand around her shoulder and drew her mouth to his.

This time Bethanne didn't hesitate. She closed her eyes and met him halfway. Winding her arms around his neck, she leaned into the kiss, which was gentle and soft. In the beginning. That quickly changed as passion flared between them. It'd been so long since she'd experienced desire, real physical need, that it rocked her. The kiss became so intense, she nearly slid off her chair.

Max seemed to feel just as shaken. He broke off the kiss and slumped back. His eyes met hers; he had the look of a man who was dazed, stunned. Bethanne understood, because she felt that same mixture of astonishment and wonder.

Neither seemed to know what to say. After a moment, Max touched her face. "You taste nice," he whispered, sounding unlike himself.

She lowered her lashes. "So do you."

He leaned forward and kissed her again as though testing his own observation. She clung to him. His kiss was urgent, needy, and once again desire sparked between them, scorching Bethanne's senses. She turned her head away and buried her face in his shoulder, trying to understand what was happening to them. Max ran his fingers through her hair and continued kissing the side of her face.

Anywhere else Bethanne would have been embarrassed. Thankfully, no one here seemed to notice or care.

They danced and kissed and became so involved with

each other that it was after two in the morning before she was aware of the time. Resting her forehead against his, Bethanne sighed. "I have to go."

His hold on her briefly tightened. "Okay."

"Don't think that's what I want," she said. "I'd like nothing better than to spend the rest of my time in Vegas with you."

"But you can't."

"No, we're leaving for the Grand Canyon tomorrow morning."

"It's spectacular. You'll love it."

"Thank you," she whispered. "I'm so glad you called."

"I am, too. Can I call you again?"

She didn't know how to respond.

"Tell you what," Max said. "You call me. You should have my cell number in your phone index. If I don't hear from you...let's say by August first, after your son's wedding, then I'll know you've decided to go back to Grant."

She nodded.

Max escorted her to the hotel and kissed her one last time. He was wrong about one thing, she thought. What happened in Vegas *wouldn't* stay here. It would always be with her.

Fourteen

By the time Ruth, Annie and Bethanne left Las Vegas, it was almost noon. They'd slept in until after ten, eaten a late breakfast, packed up the car and were now on their way. This was the new rental and once again they'd opted to do without a navigational device. They had their map and an atlas; that should be enough.

No one seemed to be talking much, and the tension inside the car remained high as Bethanne headed toward Henderson, Nevada, and then over Hoover Dam south on Highway 93. It went without saying that Annie and Ruth were upset with her for staying out so late with Max, but neither commented. Just as well. Her relationship with Max was none of their business, regardless of what they might think. Soon the map directed them toward the cutoff for Grand Canyon National Park.

Finally, Annie broke the ice. "Will you be seeing Max again?" she asked from the backseat. Although the question was thrown out casually, Bethanne could see that both her daughter and Ruth were keenly interested in her answer.

Would she see him again? That depended on what she decided about Grant—a decision that was hers alone. She'd told Max she'd contact him after Andrew's wedding. The beginning of August, he'd suggested, but that seemed so long to wait. Even after she'd slipped into bed beside Annie, all Bethanne could think about was the kisses she'd shared with Max. No man had affected her the way he did, not since she was in college and first met Grant.

"Mom?" Annie prompted.

"I...I don't know," she said. "Will you be seeing Jason again?"

"Probably not," Annie admitted reluctantly, "but he has my cell number."

Max had hers, too, but he wouldn't use it, wouldn't phone until she'd called him. That was how they'd left it.

"We're in a different time zone," Ruth announced, changing the subject as they crossed the state line. "Arizona isn't on daylight savings."

Bethanne knew that her mother-in-law had always been uncomfortable with conflict and tried to avoid it whenever possible. Bethanne had been much the same for most of her married life. But that had gradually changed; she'd reinvented herself as a businesswoman, which had required her to negotiate, to compete and to promote her services. A woman who lacked confidence couldn't do those things.

The tension in the car eased, and the silence became companionable. Bethanne turned on the radio, filling the car with ABBA and the Fifth Dimension. It wasn't long before Ruth and Bethanne were singing along and Annie's voice harmonized with theirs.

"That's just plain good music," her daughter said, apparently surprised that she'd be enjoying the same songs as her mother and grandmother.

They drove out of range and lost that station after half an hour or so. Bethanne snapped off the radio, and they lapsed back into silence.

"How are the wedding gloves progressing?" Ruth asked after another lengthy period when no one seemed inclined to talk.

"When has Mom had time to knit?" Annie joked. "Frankly, I never imagined I'd see my mother on a Harley."

Her daughter didn't know her nearly as well as she thought, but Bethanne didn't say anything. Annie's vision of her was a contradictory one—including both the independent businesswoman of today and the complacent wife of years past.

"This is all too weird for me," Annie was saying. "My mom and Mad Max? It's just…odd, you know."

"Odd?"

"Don't get me wrong, Mom. I realize this is your life and everything, but a guy on a bike? Really? My *mother*?"

"I don't find it odd at all," Bethanne muttered. But it was a moot point, since she likely wouldn't see Max again, although the prospect saddened her.

Ruth broke into a half smile.

"That reminds me of my family's opinion of Royce and me."

"Who's Royce?" Annie immediately asked.

"I think he's another friend your grandmother hopes to see in Florida."

"Oh-h-h," Annie said, dragging out the word in a meaningful way.

Bethanne could only assume her mother-in-law *wanted* to discuss this man—or else why bring him up?—but she had to grin at Ruth's blush.

"So, tell us about Royce," Bethanne said, taking advantage of the change in subject so she wouldn't have to answer questions about Max. She wasn't so different from Ruth, after all, trying to maintain the peace and avoid discord. Perhaps she hadn't changed as much as she thought....

"Oh..." Ruth stared down at her hands. "As you've already guessed, we dated during our senior year. We broke up after I went to college and he became a marine."

"So he's attending the reunion, too?"

"Yes."

"And you're hoping to reconnect with him?" Bethanne asked.

Ruth nodded. "We had a...nasty falling-out, so I'm a bit apprehensive."

"Oh, Grandma, he's probably just as excited about getting together as you are."

"Do you really think so?"

Ruth's question was so sincere and charming that Bethanne wished she could lean over and hug her.

"So it's been years and years since you last saw him?" Annie asked.

"Oh, yes...so many that I can hardly believe it. I heard he lost his wife a few years back, and Richard's gone, and, well, I hoped... Oh, I don't know, other than that this would give me the opportunity to resolve things between us. We parted on such bitter terms."

"Does he realize you're coming to the reunion?"

"I...I don't know."

"Are you going to fall in love all over again and marry him, Grandma?" Annie teased.

"Annie," Bethanne chastised. "Come on. Don't put your grandmother on the spot like that."

Ruth twisted around to look at Annie. "Honey, remember we haven't seen each other in over fifty years and—and there's a lot we have to say."

"Can't you say it on the phone?" Annie asked. "You should call him."

"Call him? When?"

"Now. Or before you show up at the reunion, anyway."

"I don't think I can do it," Ruth murmured, pressing her palms against her cheeks. "What I need to tell him— well, it's the sort of thing I'd rather do face-to-face."

"Oh," Annie said as though she understood. "You loved him, right?"

"Yes. Very much. And then I met your grandfather and...everything changed."

"Do you still love Royce?"

"How could I possibly know? I was eighteen when we dated. He came from a poor family, and my father never really approved of our relationship. In retrospect, I know Daddy only wanted the best for me. He liked Richard and, well, it was such a long time ago...."

Ruth was so quiet all of a sudden that Bethanne glanced in her direction, shocked to see tears making wet tracks down her cheeks.

"Ruth," she whispered. "What is it?"

Shaking her head, Ruth buried her face in her hands and started to weep in earnest.

"Grandma?" Annie leaned forward, touching her grandmother's shoulder.

"What is it, Ruth?" Bethanne asked softly. Whatever it was must have to do with Royce.

"You don't understand," Ruth managed between sobs.

"We will if you explain it to us," Annie said in a gentle voice.

Ruth shook her head again. "I don't know if I can face Royce after what I did to him." Ruth's hands trembled and she took a gasping breath. "I hurt him deeply."

"Ruth, you were young. I'm sure he's gotten over it."

Ruth refused to make eye contact. "He might have, but I'm not sure I ever can."

Annie handed Ruth a tissue, which she clenched as if it were a lifeline.

"We promised to love each other and be true..." she choked out. "That's what we called it back then—being true." She closed her eyes.

"And...you weren't?" Bethanne probed.

Ruth looked down at her purse, winding the strap around her hand. "I went to a party with friends soon after I got to college. I'd never drunk anything stronger than beer. Someone brought vodka and mixed it with orange juice and gave me a glass. I remember how good it tasted and I had more of them...and the next thing I knew, I was necking with this boy and I didn't even know his name." She tried to stem the tears, swiping at them with the crumpled tissue. "I told him I needed to get back to my dorm and he offered to walk me there.

He seemed friendly and nice, and when we arrived, I let him kiss me again."

"Ruth, you were on your own for the first time," Bethanne said. She found it painful that after all the years, her mother-in-law still couldn't forgive herself for a youthful indiscretion.

"Grandma, so what if you let a boy kiss you?" Annie said. She rubbed her grandmother's shoulder with soothing strokes.

Ruth continued in a ragged voice. "I told him I already had a boyfriend and…and he said that was fine."

"Did you see him again?" Annie asked.

"I couldn't help it. We were in the same history class. We talked after the lecture a couple of times and went for a Coke. He was always nice to me. I wouldn't let him kiss me again and he respected that. I wrote Royce every single day but I never told him about Richard."

"Richard?" Bethanne repeated, stunned. That was Grant's father.

"Yes. Then one night we attended another party. He and I went together. I thought I'd be all right because I was with Richard, but someone gave me a spiked drink and we…we—" She paused and once more hid her face in her hands. "We made love in the backseat of his car and a few weeks later I realized I was pregnant."

"Oh, Ruth." Bethanne looked away from the road long enough to reassure her mother-in-law that she was the last person who'd think badly of her. How strange that they should be having this conversation, which was probably the most serious and honest of their entire relationship, while driving down the freeway.

"Richard took the news like a gentleman.… He said he

loved me and would marry me. But we hardly knew each other and I hadn't even told Royce I'd met anyone else... and then I had to tell him I was marrying another man and that I was pregnant—and all of this happened while he was still in basic training!"

"Ruth, my poor Ruth..."

"Oh, Grandma, how awful for you."

"I broke his heart," Ruth said with finality. She gazed at Bethanne, her tears drying as she resumed her story. "He said if I could be unfaithful so soon after leaving home, I wasn't the person he thought I was. He said he was happy to be rid of me."

Again Bethanne looked away from the road. "I'm sure he didn't mean that. He was speaking from his pain."

Ruth went on as if she hadn't heard. "Richard was a good husband. We were both determined to make the best of the marriage, and we did, but through the years..." She hesitated. "I often wondered what might've happened if I'd stayed home that night instead of going to the party. I wonder if Royce and I would eventually have married."

"It's only natural to wonder," Bethanne said.

"You were pregnant with Dad when you married Grandpa?" Annie said. "Wow. I never added up the dates before."

"Annie."

"Grandma." Annie ignored Bethanne. "I meant what I said—I bet Royce is just as anxious to see you again. You're probably the reason he's attending this reunion."

"I hope so, but I can't be sure."

"You should call him and at least let him know you'll be there."

"I can't," she said adamantly.

"Why not?"

"For one thing, I wouldn't know what to say. Besides," she said as though this was a more convincing excuse, "I don't have his number."

"That's easy." Annie pulled out her cell phone. "Tell me his full name and I'll get it for you."

Frowning, Ruth turned to Bethanne, her face creased with doubt and indecision. "Do *you* think contacting Royce before I arrive is a good idea?"

"I don't think it would hurt," Bethanne said. "If you chatted briefly, then your mind would be at rest. You'd know what to expect."

Ruth's shoulders sagged. "Maybe later. Okay?"

"Of course it's okay," Bethanne assured her.

"You do what you feel is best," Annie echoed. "But I'll look up his number for you, anyway."

"Okay," Ruth said. "I'd like to have it…in case I do decide to call. In case I can figure out what to say," she added under her breath.

It was afternoon when they entered the national park. The sights were as spectacular as Max had promised. They walked across the Grand Canyon Skywalk and marveled at the twisting, curving Colorado River far below.

Later, Ruth was in the gift shop and Annie was speaking to one of the park rangers, a young woman who didn't look much older than her daughter, when Bethanne's cell phone rang.

Digging in her purse, she located it just before it went to voice mail.

"Hello."

"Bethanne, where are you?"

She groaned inwardly. "Hello, Grant." She almost wished she hadn't answered—or that she'd taken the time to check call display. "We're at the Grand Canyon."

"Sounds like you got a late start."

"We did, but we drove straight here. Your mother's eager to get to Florida."

The words were barely past her lips when Grant asked, "What's this about you taking off with that biker?"

Apparently, Annie had told Grant, which Bethanne didn't appreciate. "Is that what Annie said?"

"Well, some variation of it. I'm sure she's exaggerating."

"I'm sure," Bethanne echoed, unwilling to discuss Max with her ex-husband.

"So what happened?"

"What do you mean?"

"You took off with this biker and according to our daughter you spent the night with him."

"What?" Bethanne nearly exploded with outrage—and then laughter. "You've got to be joking!"

"Okay, well, I hear you were gone until three."

Bethanne neither confirmed nor denied the report. Let Grant think whatever he wanted. She didn't owe him an explanation *or* an excuse.

"Did you have a good time?"

"The best." And she meant it. The night with Max was one she would long cherish. He made her feel more alive, more feminine, and he'd brought back the thrill of newly discovered passion. Yet he hadn't done anything other than kiss her and hold her. The desire was there; the need had felt urgent.

"You sound like you're falling for this guy."

"Do I?" She turned the question around, wanting him to form his own opinion.

"Yes." The amusement was gone from his voice. "We've already had one rather unpleasant discussion about this man. I'd hate to have a repeat of that."

"So would I." She had no intention of defending herself to Grant.

"Do you plan on seeing him again?"

She didn't answer.

"Bethanne?"

"I don't believe that's any of your business," she said. "I don't mean to be rude, Grant, but my relationship with Max has nothing to do with you."

His silence spoke volumes. "True, but you have to know I'm working as hard as I can to rebuild *our* relationship. It doesn't help that every time I turn around, I hear about you and this biker."

"His name is Max."

"I don't care what his name is."

Bethanne sighed, unwilling to get into an argument with her ex-husband over a man she'd dated once. Arguing put her on the defensive and she wasn't going to allow that.

She heard Grant exhale as though struggling with himself. "I imagine women are easily enthralled with that kind of guy."

"You mean the way middle-age men fall for younger women?" That small dig apparently went right over Grant's head.

"True enough," he agreed, and his voice was back to that cajoling tone she knew so well. "On a completely different subject, how's my mother holding up?"

Bethanne was grateful to talk about something other than Max. "She's doing great."

"And you?"

"Annie and I are fine."

"Good. Listen, I have some news I thought I'd pass along."

"What is it?"

"I found out there's a real estate conference in Orlando the same week as Mom's class reunion."

"Oh." She already knew what Grant was going to say. "You've decided to go."

"What could be more perfect?" Grant asked.

Indeed, Bethanne mused. What could be more perfect?

Fifteen

They spent the night in Flagstaff, Arizona, and were up early Monday morning, waking to sunshine. By seven, Annie had dragged the suitcases out to the car, while Bethanne dealt with the hotel.

"I'll drive so you can knit," Ruth volunteered.

Bethanne let her take the wheel, sitting beside her, while Annie climbed into the backseat. A little more than two hours later, they were in Albuquerque, New Mexico. They stopped for breakfast at a restaurant just off Interstate 40.

They were seated in a booth and reading over the menus when Annie said, "Dad told me he called while we were at the Grand Canyon." The comment was directed at Bethanne.

"He did," she confirmed without adding any details.

Annie set her menu aside. "Did he say anything about the Realtors' convention?"

In response, Bethanne looked at Ruth. "Grant will be in Orlando next weekend, the same time as your reunion."

"How far is Vero Beach from Orlando?" Annie asked.

Bethanne referred the question to her mother-in-law, who was far more familiar with Florida than she was. Ruth glanced over her menu. "About two hours, I think—but it's been a long time since I made the drive."

"So Dad will be only two hours away," Annie said, sounding downright gleeful.

"Do you think he'll come to Vero Beach?" Ruth asked hopefully.

"I'm sure he will." Bethanne kept her feelings well under control. Actually, she'd be happy to see Grant. Maybe she could finally come to some conclusion, some decision; maybe she could finally say yes to a reconciliation. She'd been giving their situation a great deal of thought. Grant had been persistent, determined to regain her love and trust. The problem—and this had only recently become a problem—was the way Bethanne felt about Max. Every time she considered what her life would be like if she and Grant were to reunite, Max was there, competing with those visions, those possibilities.

Max of the rare smiles, grinning at her. Memories of riding on his Harley, her arms hugging his waist. Memories of dancing and kissing. With Grant it was expensive champagne, classical music, two children and a twenty-year history. With Max it was cold beer, loud country music and one night in Vegas. No, it was time to put him out of her mind. He was little more than a drifter running from life. Deep down she suspected that her fascination with him was prompted by her fear of facing the issues she needed to confront regarding her ex-husband. She'd forgiven Grant—hadn't she? Forgiveness, as she'd discovered, could be deceptive.

She didn't know if it was possible to trust him again.

Grant was sorry. He'd admitted he'd been wrong and accepted full responsibility for the pain he'd inflicted on her and their children. Ruth had a point; that couldn't have been easy, especially for a proud man like Grant.

If only she could forgive wholeheartedly and forget the past...

And then there was Max. Gentle, loving Max, devoted to his wife. He'd never cheated on Kate. He loved beyond the grave. Instinctively, she knew she could trust him.

"You ladies ready to order?" asked the waitress, who appeared to be somewhere between Ruth's age and Bethanne's. She stepped up to their table, pad and pen in hand.

"I'd like French toast," Annie said, and gave the woman her menu.

"One poached egg on dry wheat," Ruth said.

"Max." Bethanne closed the menu and held it out to the waitress—and found three women staring at her. "What?" she asked, not understanding why her scrambled eggs had elicited all this attention.

"There's no Max on the menu," the waitress said, grinning.

"I said *Max*?" Bethanne asked, startled to realize she deserved the looks Annie and Ruth were sending her.

The waitress continued to grin. "I guess one of you ladies is missing her man."

"My mother is not missing that...biker," Annie snapped.

Ruth refused to meet her eyes.

Bethanne's hand tightened on the menu. "Would you both feel better if I said Grant's name?" The answer was obvious. Then, glancing at the waitress, she said, "Grant is my ex-husband."

"But he wants to get back together with my mom," Annie explained.

"My son was an idiot, but he's regained his sanity just in time for my daughter-in-law to lose hers," Ruth said in a disgruntled voice.

The waitress stood there, holding the pad and pen, her gaze wandering from one to the other. "Ladies, I'm no Dr. Laura. All I do around here is take orders and fill coffee cups. If you want advice, I suggest you turn on the radio."

"I'll have a latte." Bethanne decided to forgo the scrambled eggs, as her appetite was gone.

The waitress wrote down the order, hesitated a moment and then slid into the booth next to Bethanne. "You really should have some protein for breakfast."

"All I want is a latte."

"You got man problems, don't you, sweetie?" she said, ignoring both Ruth and Annie. "I don't normally get involved with customers but I've been married a time or two myself, and it seems to me it takes a real man to admit when he's wrong." She shook her head. "It doesn't happen often."

"I keep trying to tell Mom that," Annie insisted.

"Did this ex-husband of yours drink too much?" she asked.

"No," Bethanne said.

"He didn't slap you around, did he?"

"No!"

"Chase skirts?"

"Just the once." It was Annie who answered. "And that was a big mistake."

"It always is," the waitress said. "Half the time men's

brains are located below their belt buckles. Eventually they come to their senses but by then it's usually too late."

"Eunice." The cook stuck his head out of the kitchen. "Are you fraternizing with the customers again?"

Eunice rolled her eyes. "If I don't watch myself I'm going to lose this job." She hurried toward the kitchen and put their order on a hanging circular device for the cook to grab.

"What a sweetheart," Ruth murmured.

"Wise, too," Annie said pointedly.

"I can tell Eunice has been around the block a couple of times and found her way home," Ruth said. "I'm leaving her an extra-big tip."

Bethanne felt embarrassed about having her personal situation aired in front of a stranger, no matter how sympathetic, and furious at her daughter and mother-in-law. And yet... She'd begun to think they were right. Regardless of her infatuation with Max, she felt she had to give her ex-husband an honest chance. She had to give their *relationship* an honest chance, and she couldn't do that with Max hovering in the background.

Five minutes later, Eunice returned with their breakfast order. Lost in her thoughts, Bethanne sipped her latte. Thankfully, neither Annie nor Ruth appeared to notice how distracted she was.

When she saw Max the night before last, she'd told him she'd call after the wedding. But it wouldn't be fair to keep him waiting and guessing. The only decent thing to do was call him now and explain that she wouldn't be contacting him in the future.

Bethanne slid out of her booth and headed for the door.

"Mom?" her daughter asked. "Where are you going?"

"I need to make a phone call" was all she was willing to tell either Annie or Ruth.

Standing in the parking lot, Bethanne took out her cell phone. Max had programmed in his number and she hit speed dial, knowing she was about to do something irrevocable. She felt regretful, but relieved, too. Closing her eyes, she leaned against the rental car and silently prayed he'd answer.

He picked up on the third ring, but at the sound of his voice, she suddenly couldn't speak.

"Hello," he said again.

After a long moment, his voice softened. "Is that you, Bethanne?"

"Yes."

He waited for her to continue.

"I won't be calling you." Then, because she owed him an explanation, she rushed to say, "I'm truly sorry, but I've made my decision."

Her announcement was met with stark silence.

"Did you hear me?" she asked.

"I heard you."

Silence again.

"Don't you have anything to say?" she demanded.

"You're going back to Grant?"

"Yes…"

"Your final decision?"

"Yes…" It was her final decision—to give a new relationship with her ex-husband every opportunity to succeed. That didn't guarantee success, of course, but she could only go into this with an open heart. Without reservations. She couldn't have one eye on the exit as she and Grant tried out their new roles.

"You don't sound convinced."

"I am completely convinced that this is the right thing to do."

"Then why did you call me now?"

"I didn't want you waiting to hear from me."

"Did you assume I was waiting?"

"You were, weren't you?" That was the way she remembered their discussion when they'd parted in Vegas.

"What happened? You only left Vegas two days ago."

"Grant phoned and he's coming to Florida and…and I can't stop thinking about you and it's causing all kinds of problems." She hadn't intended to admit all that, but it slipped out. "To top everything, we went for breakfast and instead of ordering scrambled eggs, I ordered you." She could sense his smile. "This isn't funny, Max."

"I've been thinking a lot about you, too. Kate would've liked you."

"I can't do this, Max. I mean it."

"I know."

"You don't believe me, do you?"

"No."

He didn't even bother to pretend otherwise, which frustrated her. "You won't be hearing from me again," she said, trying to sound firm.

"Okay. If that's what you want."

She felt like stamping her foot. "Why don't you believe me?"

"Are you really going back to your ex-husband?"

She didn't respond for a moment. Then she said in a low voice, "I don't know yet."

"That's what I thought."

"He loves me," she insisted.

"And you love him," Max said. "I understand that. But do you love him enough?"

"We have children together, a twenty-year history as husband and wife. I already told you all this."

"That doesn't answer the question."

"I don't know how I feel. I can't deal with this," she whispered, and her voice cracked.

"Bethanne, listen," Max said, speaking softly now. "This doesn't have to be decided this very minute. I thought we were going to connect after your son's wedding. It's in July, right?"

"July 16."

"You have lots of time. We both do."

Despite what he'd said about understanding, he really didn't. No one did. "I want this over *now*. I can't be seriously considering getting back with Grant and dreaming about you. Why you? Oh, Max, why does it have to be *you?* Of all the men I've dated in the past six years, none of them made me feel the way you do."

"Me, too," he whispered, his voice husky. "No one. Not ever. I loved Kate, adored her, but that was…different."

Neither spoke for what seemed like a long time. Then Bethanne saw Annie and Ruth walking out of the restaurant. "I need to get off the phone."

"Where are you?"

"Albuquerque." Fearing he might try to find her, she added, "Don't come. Please don't try to follow me."

"I won't."

"Goodbye, Max."

"Goodbye."

Annie was staring intently at her and so was Ruth.

Rather than say anything more, Bethanne snapped her cell shut and dropped it in her purse.

"Who was that?" Ruth asked.

Bethanne felt incredibly guilty and guessed she must look it, too. But she didn't respond. She had a right to her private conversations, dammit! Ironically, she'd been trying to do something that should please them.

"You were talking to Max, weren't you?" Annie said.

Not waiting for a reply, both women turned toward the parking lot. Bethanne went back inside the restaurant, to the ladies' room. Her nerves were a mess.

Instead of feeling better after talking to Max, she felt worse. She hadn't settled a thing. Quite the contrary; she'd muddled her thoughts and emotions even more.

Washing her hands in the empty room, Bethanne looked at herself in the mirror and announced, "I am my own woman. I will not let the dictates of my family influence my decisions." Then she dried her hands carefully with a paper towel and left the bathroom.

When she got to the car, Annie was in the driver's seat with Ruth in the back. Bethanne climbed into the front passenger seat and closed the door. She automatically reached for her knitting.

Without a word, Annie backed out of the parking space.

"I have to tell you that I'm worried about you," Ruth said, leaning forward. She apparently felt obliged to impart her misgivings.

"I appreciate your concern, Ruth, but you don't need to worry. I know what I'm doing."

"What about Dad?" Annie cried.

"What about him?" Bethanne asked. She continued

to work the white cashmere wool, knitting faster than she'd thought possible. Thankfully, the pattern wasn't so complicated that she had to study every row.

"He loves you! Doesn't that matter?"

"Of course it does," Ruth answered for her. "I think we should leave your mother alone. She's right. This is her decision."

"I'm not sure I can keep quiet," Annie said, completely ignoring the fact that Bethanne was sitting beside her and could hear every word.

"Your mother wants to return to Grant on an even playing field," Ruth said stiffly.

"What does *that* mean?" Bethanne asked, twisting around in her seat.

Ruth wouldn't look at her. "It means," she said, glancing at Annie, "that Bethanne wants to have an affair with this biker before she takes your father back. It's tit for tat."

"Ruth!" Bethanne could hardly believe she'd said that. "How can you even suggest such a thing?" After all these years she'd assumed her mother-in-law knew her better. "If it'll help either of you, I'll let you know that Max and I have done nothing more than kiss." She instantly regretted telling them even that much.

"Mom," Annie said in the same voice she'd used as a little girl when she wanted something important. "I promise I won't bring up Max's name again if you'll do just one thing."

"What's that?"

"Give Dad a chance. It isn't fair when Dad's in Seattle."

What do you think I'm doing? she wanted to shout. *This is all about giving him a chance.*

"It isn't like Max is trailing behind our car on his motorcycle," she said tartly.

"Just don't do anything foolish, okay?"

"I'm not a foolish woman," she told her daughter.

"I didn't used to think so," Ruth muttered under her breath but loudly enough for Bethanne to hear.

"I am *not* a foolish woman," Bethanne repeated, and then suddenly realized her purse wasn't within sight. "Did either of you pick up my purse?"

"I didn't," Annie said.

"Why would I take your purse?" Ruth asked.

Oh, my goodness. Bethanne remembered that she'd left her purse in the restroom at the Albuquerque diner. "Annie," she said, trying not to panic. "I left my purse at the restaurant." She'd been upset and walked off without it.

"Mom, we're on a freeway! I can't just turn around. I have to wait for the next exit."

Ruth leaned forward. "Now, what were you saying about not being a foolish woman?"

Sixteen

"I've always wanted to see the Alamo," Annie said once they were back on the road after collecting Bethanne's purse. Her forgetfulness had cost them over an hour.

"I have a reservation in Branson for tomorrow night," Ruth said. "Remember what happened the last time we went off course?"

"Oh, come on, Grandma, Vegas was fun."

"More fun for some than others," Ruth said sharply.

Bethanne was getting used to the verbal darts and disregarded the comment.

"Personally, I'm looking forward to Branson," Ruth continued. "My friends tell me Andy Williams gives a terrific performance."

Annie glanced over at Bethanne. "Just who is this Andy Williams?"

"My goodness, Annie, he's one of the best singers ever," Ruth said enthusiastically. "Well, in my opinion, anyway. He's like Perry Como, Frank Sinatra and Steve Lawrence all rolled into one."

"I've never heard of Perry or Steve, either, Grandma. Were they part of a group?"

"Heavens, no! Bethanne, this girl needs a musical education."

Bethanne laughed, glad that good humor had been restored.

"Does this mean we're going to bypass the Alamo?" Annie asked, sounding disappointed.

"It does," Ruth said. "The next time your mother drives, I want you to get on that phone of yours and buy the three of us tickets for Andy Williams. This is something I don't want you girls to miss."

"Yes, Grandma," Annie murmured, but she didn't sound happy about it.

Bethanne took over driving just outside Texas. Studying the map, she saw that their little venture to Las Vegas had taken them even farther off course than she'd realized. Fortunately, Branson was in the southern part of Missouri.

Once Bethanne was behind the wheel, both Ruth and Annie took naps. She welcomed the silence because it gave her a chance to think. Each day on the road, she'd chatted with Julia Hayden about the business and received an update. The company hardly needed her anymore; Julia was efficient and had good judgment.

She regretted the phone call to Max earlier that morning. At the time she'd been serious—clearing her mind of him was the only sensible option. What she'd told him was true. She couldn't make a decision about Grant if all she could think about was Max. The best thing was to sever the tie quickly. Yet the moment she'd heard Max's voice, Bethanne knew she couldn't do it, couldn't walk away as if he was nothing more than a Vegas fling.

Maybe she just needed to get him out of her system. Really, what could possibly come of a relationship with someone like Max? It wasn't as if she could climb on the back of his Harley and travel across the country without a care in the world. Bethanne had responsibilities, a thriving company. Max had taken a sabbatical from his wine distribution company but he'd been away for three years. He hadn't said when he planned to return, if ever.

He rode from one end of the country to the other with no destination, stopping here or there on a whim. What kind of life was that? He'd lost his wife and daughter. That was hard, grief was hard, but it'd been three years and he gave no indication that he was ever going to relinquish this lifestyle. The thought of any long-term relationship with Max was irrational. Out of the question.

If Max was a tumbleweed, drifting with the wind, Grant was like a rock. Solid. Hardworking. A family man. Even if he'd stumbled badly when he married Tiffany. For a short time, his world had revolved around the young woman and he'd turned a blind eye to everything he'd once considered a priority, including his own children.

But his infatuation with his new wife hadn't lasted long. Only a few months after they'd married, there'd been trouble in that relationship.

Bethanne knew nothing about Grant and Tiffany's divorce settlement, but she did know that Grant had paid dearly—and not just financially. Soon after he left her he'd been passed over for a huge promotion and changed companies as a result. She assumed he was doing well, since he never seemed to be strapped for money whenever the children needed it, although that wasn't often these days, other than their college expenses.

"Mom?" Annie said, straightening and rubbing her eyes. "Where are we?"

"We're near Amarillo, Texas," Bethanne told her.

"Texas? We can't be that far from the Alamo, then. It would just be a short side trip, wouldn't it?"

"A short side trip like Vegas?" Ruth said, obviously awake now. "There's a lot of miles between Amarillo and San Antonio, and this time I'm not giving in. We're going to Branson, and that's it."

"Okay." Annie sighed. "But I really don't think the Alamo is that much out of our way."

Bethanne handed her daughter the map. "You might want to take a look to get an idea of how big Texas is."

"Mo-om, I know my geography."

"How far is Amarillo from Branson?"

"According to MapQuest," Annie said a few minutes later, studying her phone, "it's almost nine hours." She groaned with frustration.

"We'll need to find a place for the night," Ruth said, arching her back. "I'm beginning to go stir-crazy in this car."

"We should spend a couple of days in Branson," Bethanne suggested. "Shake off the road dust and let down our hair."

"*Two* days." Annie flopped back in her seat.

"I've always dreamed of seeing Andy Williams in concert," Ruth said wistfully. "And now it's about to become a reality."

"That's always been my dream, too," Annie muttered sarcastically.

"Annie," Bethanne said. "This is your grandmother's trip." Those words were a now-familiar refrain.

"I suppose I'll have to wait until I'm in my sixties before I see the Alamo?"

Bethanne smothered a laugh. "Then you'll appreciate it all the more, the same way your grandmother's looking forward to seeing her teenage idol."

"Whatever." Annie slouched down in the seat. "I wrote an essay on it, you know," she said righteously. "I got an A." She closed her eyes, apparently picturing Davy Crockett and Jim Bowie making their last stand.

Just before they left the state of Texas, Bethanne stopped at a Dairy Queen for ice cream, which made for a small break. Several police and fire department vehicles were parked outside. Long ago Bethanne had read a comment that Dairy Queen restaurants were like city halls in Texas—the one establishment where everyone convened.

For reasons she didn't even want to consider, she removed her cell from her purse and typed a text message to Max. She didn't know if he'd receive it or if he'd respond. All she said was:

Spending two nights in Branson, MO.

She hesitated before she pushed the send button, but sent it, anyway.

What was she doing? She felt like a first-time shoplifter certain to be caught. Regardless of all her assertions that what she did was her own business, she didn't want Ruth or Annie to know.

"You okay?" Annie asked.

"Sure. Why wouldn't I be?" Bethanne realized that, once again, she must look guilty. Why else would Annie

question her? In fact, she *felt* guilty. She'd resolved to reconcile with Grant, or at least try, and yet she'd impulsively
contacted Max....

"Mom!" Annie nudged her. "Your ice cream's melting
all over your hand."

"Oh." She looked down to discover that Annie was
right. In the warm sun the soft-serve ice cream had melted
and dripped down her wrist.

"Here." Ruth passed her a wad of napkins.

Bethanne licked away at the cone but soon realized it
was a lost cause and tossed the entire mess into a nearby
garbage can.

Back on the road with Ruth driving, Bethanne
fidgeted, crossing and uncrossing her legs. She stared out
the window and chewed on her fingertip. Even knitting
didn't help.

"What's wrong with you?" Annie demanded.

"Why should anything be wrong?"

"How would I know?"

It wasn't until they stopped for the night that Bethanne
had a chance to look for Max's reply, if there was one. Her
eyes widened when she saw it. She held her breath. His
response was simple:

I'll meet you there.

Snapping the cell phone closed, she held it against
herself only to find both Ruth and Annie studying her
curiously. She exhaled and carefully set her phone aside.

Annie leaped off the bed, stalked over to the dresser
and grabbed Bethanne's cell. She opened it and frowned
at the screen. "Mother!"

"What did she do now?" Ruth asked.

"She's meeting Max in Branson."

"Now listen," Bethanne said. "First of all, Annie, what you've done is rude and it's an invasion of my privacy. Secondly, I make my own decisions and I'm telling you right now, the more you pressure me into going back to Grant the more attractive Max looks. Unless I figure out how I feel about Max, I'll never be happy with Grant."

Ruth shrugged and got her book from her economy-size purse. "What you decide is up to you. You're over twenty-one."

"Way over." Annie threw herself down on the bed.

"Thank you." Bethanne felt better for having spoken her mind, although she could have done without Annie's comment.

Her daughter plugged in the earbuds to her iPod and lay back, eyes closed.

Bethanne took a long, hot shower, crawled into bed beside Annie and opened her book. She read late. Both Annie and Ruth were asleep by the time she turned off her light.

Although it was past midnight and they had every intention of getting an early start in the morning, Bethanne couldn't sleep. Whenever she closed her eyes, all she could see was Max. Not Grant. Max.

He planned to meet her in Branson. She didn't know where he was when he got her message. Apparently, close enough to Missouri to get to Branson by the following afternoon. She wondered if Rooster was traveling with him. She didn't like the thought of him on the road alone, although she understood that was often the case.

The next day when they arrived in Branson, the traffic

was worse than Manhattan at rush hour. It took them forty-five minutes just to reach the hotel. Once they were in their room and unpacked, they went downstairs and ate a quick lunch in the hotel's coffee shop.

Ruth paid the tab and went to collect the show tickets Annie had ordered for her. While she was away from the table, Bethanne's cell phone rang. In her eagerness to answer, she dropped her purse and scrambled to retrieve it.

"Is that Max?" Annie asked.

"I don't know yet," she said as she bent down to get her cell from her bag. Caller ID revealed Grant's name. She pushed the button that would send him directly to voice mail. "It's your father."

"Why didn't you talk to him?"

"I will when I'm ready."

"You'd rather speak to *Max?*" Annie sounded like a hurt little girl.

Bethanne put the cell beside her on the table. "Annie, please try to understand. I don't know what I find so attractive about Max. I wish I did. I'm sorry I'm such a disappointment to you and your grandmother, but I need to do this."

"All right, Mom, have your fun. Dad and I will be waiting for you."

The call from Max came fifteen minutes later. She and Annie were just finishing their coffee.

"Hi," she said, keenly aware that Annie was listening.

"Hi. Where are you?"

She gave him the name of the hotel. "I'm not the most popular person at the moment."

"So you told Grandma and Annie I was meeting you?"

"I did," she admitted.

"I thought you didn't want to see me again," he commented, obviously amused.

"A sensitive man wouldn't remind me of that."

"I guess that tells you all you need to know about me."

Bethanne grinned but her smile faded when she saw Annie scowling at her.

"I'll meet you in the lobby in an hour," Max said.

"I'll be there." She closed her phone and then looked at her daughter. "Are you coming?"

"Where are you going?" Annie asked, following Bethanne out of the hotel.

"Shopping."

"For what?" Annie asked, hurrying to keep up with her. "And shouldn't we invite Grandma?"

"Sure. Give her a call."

Bethanne was on a mission. She had an hour to deck herself out in jeans, boots and a Western shirt. If she was going to be in Branson, she intended to look like she belonged here.

With Bethanne and Annie shopping, Ruth stayed in their hotel room alone. She'd made her excuses and was grateful for this time by herself. She sat on the bed and fingered the paper Annie had given her. The paper on which her granddaughter had written down Royce's phone number. She hadn't decided what to do.

Thankfully, neither Bethanne nor Annie had pressured her about contacting him, although both seemed to think she should. Bethanne had said something that made a lot of sense. If she called Royce now, she wouldn't have that confrontation awaiting her when she arrived and she'd be able to enjoy the rest of the trip.

Every mile that brought her closer to Florida, closer to Royce, increased her anxiety.

She needed to do this—and she didn't want Bethanne and Annie hearing her conversation. Although she sort of wished someone *was* with her now to hold her hand, to encourage her and to offer comfort if it went badly. This was really difficult, so much more difficult than she'd ever expected.

She took the hotel phone from the nightstand next to the bed, stretching the cord so she could set it beside her. She smoothed out the slip of paper, running her hand over it two or three times. Finally, she reached for the receiver, following the instructions in order to place a long-distance call.

A minute after that, the phone rang at the other end.

It rang again as she held her breath. Again.

Then Royce answered. "Hello."

Despite all the years since they'd spoken, she recognized his voice.

She couldn't speak.

"Hello?" he repeated.

"Royce?" Somehow she managed to whisper his name.

"Yes? Who is this?"

His own voice fell, and Ruth was fairly certain he already knew the answer.

"It's Ruth." The silence was terrible. "I heard you planned to attend the class reunion," she said.

"Yes."

"I…I thought it was only fair that you know I'll be there, too. Actually, my daughter-in-law and granddaughter felt

I should warn you." At first, she couldn't utter a word, and now she couldn't seem to shut up. "We're driving across the country…. We're in Branson and we— Oh, none of that's important."

The silence on his end of the line returned and Ruth was convinced she'd made a mistake.

"Would you rather I didn't attend the reunion?" he asked after another long moment.

"Oh, no…I mean, yes. I want you there. I'd really hoped we'd have a chance to talk first, though…if you agree."

More silence. Ruth couldn't stand the tension.

Eventually, he spoke. "I think that would be a good idea. Call me when you get into town, okay?"

"Yes…I'll do that." Her hand squeezed the phone so hard, she thought her fingers might leave indentations.

"Ruth?"

"Yes?"

"I'm glad you called."

The tension between her shoulders eased. "I am, too."

She replaced the receiver, but her hand lingered on it for several minutes as she considered their short conversation. Already she felt better. Setting the phone back on the nightstand, she nearly collapsed against the pillows.

Annie's sour mood improved fast, which was due, no doubt, to some old-fashioned retail therapy. Bethanne made her purchases in record time. The two of them returned to the hotel room, their arms loaded with packages.

Ruth talked to Annie about their shopping excursion as Bethanne hurriedly changed into her new outfit, complete with red cowboy boots. If her friend Anne Marie Roche, the local bookstore owner, could own a pair, then she could, too.

"How do I look?" she asked her mother-in-law, twirling around and modeling her new clothes.

Ruth frowned. "Like Dale Evans."

"Dale who?" Annie asked.

"Never mind." Ruth got her purse. "Come on, Annie, or we'll be late."

"Late? For what?"

"The show. I told you I wanted both of you to see it, and your mother obviously isn't coming with me. I've got three tickets, for heaven's sake. I have no intention of going alone." She frowned. "Maybe I can scalp one of them."

"Grandma!" Annie rolled her eyes. "Until yesterday I didn't even know who this Andy person was."

Bethanne didn't stick around to hear the rest of the conversation. She was out the door before either of them had time to protest. Entering the lobby, she looked around, disappointed to see that Max hadn't arrived yet. She found a vacant wingback chair by the fireplace, where she sat and waited—but not for long. A few minutes later, the elevator doors slid open and Max and Rooster stepped out.

Max looked even better than she remembered. For a moment all Bethanne could do was stare. He didn't immediately see her, but when he did, a slow smile crossed his face.

"Hi," she said, standing and walking toward him.

"Hi." He met her halfway.

Bethanne held out her hands to him, and Max took her fingers in his.

"I didn't ride all this way to hold hands," he said. "I'm desperate for one of those hugs of yours."

She was equally desperate to give him one, knowing the kisses would come later. As they embraced, she closed her eyes. His arms felt so good around her, so right.

"Twenty hours on the bike and all he wants is a hug?" Rooster laughed. "There's definitely something wrong."

"Twenty hours?" Bethanne asked, breaking away to study him.

"We took off the minute he got your message," Rooster elaborated.

"Where were you?"

"Doesn't matter. I'm here now," Max said, glaring at his friend.

"Vegas," Rooster supplied.

"Oh, Max." She held her palms against his face, wanting more than anything to kiss him. She couldn't. Not here in the hotel lobby, but soon. Very soon.

Seventeen

"Daddy," Annie said the minute she was in her assigned seat at the Moon River Theater. She didn't appreciate having to attend this show with her grandmother, especially since her mom got out of it. Fortunately, that meant the seat beside her wasn't occupied. "It's Annie," she said, leaning into the empty seat and doing her best to keep her voice down.

"Hi, sweetheart. Did you get to Branson okay?"

"We made it fine."

"What's that noise?"

Annie wouldn't have believed old people could make such a racket. The noise level was as high as a rock concert. Well, maybe not *quite* as high, but it was up there. She pressed one finger to her other ear.

"I'm sitting with Grandma, waiting for Andy Williams to come onstage, but I thought I should call you right away."

"Grandma dragged you with her to see Andy Williams?" He sounded far too amused, in her opinion.

"Don't go there, Dad. Grandma also got tickets for the Twelve Irish Tenors, and she expects me to go to that one, too." She leaned even farther into the empty seat so Grandma Hamlin wouldn't hear. This was ridiculous. If she wanted to listen to tenors, she'd attend church services more often.

Her father laughed outright.

"Dad, this isn't funny!"

"Sorry, sorry."

He wasn't nearly as apologetic as he should be.

"I'm glad you made it safely to Branson," he said. "Thanks for the updates on your travels. Otherwise, I'd be worried about the three of you on the road."

"That's not why I'm calling," Annie said. She didn't like being a tattletale, but someone had to tell him what was happening with her mother and Max.

"What's wrong?" Any amusement left his voice.

"It's Mom."

Her father went completely silent.

"Did you hear me, Dad?"

"Is she talking to Max again?"

"It's worse than that. He's here."

"In Branson?"

Although he couldn't see her, Annie nodded. "She sent him a text message sometime yesterday. I don't know when." On second thought, maybe she did. "Actually, I think it was while we were at a Dairy Queen in Texas. She started acting all weird."

"Do you have any idea what she said to Max?"

"Just that she'd be in Branson for the next two days."

"How do you know?"

"I, uh, read it. And I read his reply. She got really mad

at me. Max said he'd meet her here." She felt even more like a tattletale but her father needed to know.

"Annie," her father said, his voice solemn. "I appreciate you telling me this. However—and this is important—you have no right to be reading her private messages."

"I know," she mumbled. "But Mom was there in the room. And she didn't do anything to stop me. Maybe she *wanted* me to see it," she said mutinously.

"It doesn't matter. Don't do that again."

"Okay, okay."

"So—Max is in Branson?"

"Yup."

"Has your mother seen him yet?"

Her father obviously didn't understand the seriousness of the situation. "Daddy, she's with him right this minute. Why else do you think I'm the one with Grandma? Mom was supposed to go, too, but she and Max went off together and Grandma and I are at this…event. I don't think there's anyone under thirty except for me." In Annie's opinion, this was above and beyond her duty as a granddaughter.

"Where did they go?" her father asked.

It took Annie a moment to catch up with the conversation and realize he was asking about her mother and Max. "I don't know."

Her father went quiet again.

"That's not all, either." Annie felt a bit childish, but she couldn't stop herself.

Grant sighed. "Just don't tell me she's run off and married him."

"No, she'd never do that."

"Good."

"Mom and I went shopping, and she got a whole new outfit and red cowboy boots."

"Red?"

"Yes, Anne Marie Roche has a pair. She's the lady who owns the bookstore on Blossom Street, remember?"

"What have red boots got to do with anything?" He seemed confused.

"Nothing, I suppose, except that Mom always admired Anne Marie's, and when she saw a red pair she decided to get them for herself."

"It sounds like your mother's become a...free spirit."

"Oh, it's worse than that. All she thinks about is this biker. Yesterday morning at breakfast she—" Annie wished she hadn't said anything now. "Never mind. The thing is, Dad, Mom isn't acting like herself. Grandma and I don't know what to do."

"I love your mother," Grant said after a long pause.

"I know you do, and I'm afraid she's actually falling for this...this biker. As far as I can tell, he doesn't have a job. I can't believe it...I really can't. My mother and a *biker?*" Saying the words aloud made it seem even more unlikely.

"Maybe she *is* falling in love." Her father sounded sad, but not as disturbed as Annie had thought he'd be.

"Then we need to *do* something." Annie hoped her father had an idea because she didn't. Acting upset and giving her mother the silent treatment hadn't kept Bethanne away from Max. In fact, it seemed the harder Annie tried, the less effective her methods. Grandma disapproved, too, and that hadn't influenced her, either. She seemed bent on being with Max. Bent on throwing away the past and destroying the future. It wasn't that Annie didn't understand that sometimes divorce was the best option, but this one should never have happened. Her parents belonged together. Andrew called her arrogant for saying that; however, Annie didn't care. She was absolutely *convinced* she was right.

"Annie, listen to me, and when we finish speaking, let me talk to your grandmother."

"Okay, I'm listening." Annie pressed her cell even harder against her ear and held her finger against the other ear. She closed her eyes because that helped her concentrate.

"I hurt Bethanne badly. I betrayed her and the vows of our marriage. I realize now what a huge mistake I made. I'm praying it's not too late and that there's something left of our relationship to salvage."

"I want that, too, Daddy, more than anything."

"I know you do."

"So does Grandma." She didn't mention Andrew. Her brother wasn't willing to forgive and forget as easily as the rest of them. Annie got frustrated with him but Andrew had apparently divested himself of all feelings for their father. Their relationship was as minimal as he could make it. Well, her brother had an excuse. He had other things on his mind, like getting married. Still, she hoped his attitude would change with time.

Annie knew Andrew and their mom were close, the same way she was with their dad. Her brother was quick to defend their mother and blame their father. But Dad recognized that he'd been in the wrong, and in her opinion Andrew should take that into consideration.

"I gather my mother isn't a fan of Max's, either," her father continued.

"Dad, if you met him you'd wonder what Mom ever saw in him. He's…he looks just like a stereotypical biker." Okay, maybe he was attractive for an older guy, but muscles and lean good looks weren't everything.

"I understand your mother. We weren't married all those years without me knowing her…."

Annie couldn't figure out why her father wasn't more upset. "It sounds like you're happy Mom's chasing after him." That was a slight exaggeration. But she'd expected him to react more strongly to this latest update.

"I started to tell you, Annie, I hurt your mother."

"I know and she knows that, too, better than anyone. But it's different now. You're back and the *lovely* Tiffany is out of your life."

"Yes, thank God, but this isn't about Tiffany or me. It's about your mother and Max."

"You have a plan." Annie should've guessed her father wouldn't stand idly by and let some other man step into the place he belonged. "You're flying into Branson, aren't you?"

"No."

"No?" Annie echoed. "What do you mean?"

"Your mother's well aware of how I feel. If I could go back six years, trust me, I would."

"Oh, Daddy." Annie, too, would give anything to turn back time.

"Your mother and you and Andrew are my whole world and I was stupid enough to leave you. I've paid the price for being such an idiot, but I might still lose your mother."

"I want you and Mom to get back together," Annie said fervently.

"The thing is, Annie, it might be too late." His voice was bleak, as if he'd already given up. "If that's the case, then all I can do is accept it."

"*Accept* it?"

"I don't have any choice but to abide by your mother's wishes. I'll always love her, always. Even when I was married to Tiffany I loved your mother. I might not have shown my love the way I should have, but my feelings for her never went away. Tiffany sensed that, I think. My family was an issue between us from the beginning, which is why she tried so hard to keep us apart."

Annie felt her throat thicken. She didn't like to remember how it had been when her father left them. Those were dark days for all of them. Her brother was the one who'd held the three of them together those first few weeks. Meeting Courtney had helped him, and that was good, but at the time she'd had no one. Her mother was a basket case and Annie had floundered badly.

"Mom said that when I get upset about her seeing Max, that only makes him more appealing."

"She's right," her father agreed. "Don't you remember that plaque she has up in the kitchen?"

"The plaque," she repeated. "The one about setting a bird free?" That ceramic wall hanging had been in the kitchen for years, and while she'd seen it practically every day of her life, she didn't remember the exact words.

What it meant was that if someone was meant to return they would of their own accord.

"Annie, listen. You and I need to set your mother free. Let her enjoy her time with Max. Let's both give her that. I'll meet you in Florida in a few days and we'll see how things go. Until then, leave your mother alone. Tell your grandmother to do the same. Okay?"

"But, Dad—"

"I love your mother enough to want her happiness. If she finds that with Max, then all I can do is step aside."

Annie wanted to argue—but she couldn't. Her father was wise. "You're right," she said. Bethanne would choose for herself; that was her privilege and her responsibility. Annie just hoped she made the choice they wanted her to make.

"Now let me talk to your grandmother."

"Okay." Annie straightened and tapped her grandmother on the arm. "Grandma, it's my dad. He wants to talk to you."

Ruth looked concerned. "Did you tell him about you know who?" she asked in a loud whisper.

Annie nodded. "He's cool with it."

Her grandmother widened her eyes as she took the cell. "Hello," she said.

Annie listened hard but she could only make out bits and pieces of the conversation. Apparently, her father said the same thing to Ruth that he'd said to Annie, because her grandmother shook her head as if she had trouble accepting his advice.

After a few minutes she handed the phone back to Annie. "He wants us to let your mother have her fun."

"I know."

"I don't think this is a smart decision."

Annie was inclined to abide by her father's judgment. "He says he'll be in Florida next week and we should be patient."

"He loves your mother."

Annie nodded. Until then, she'd never realized how much.

Eighteen

Bethanne and Max sat on the hotel porch on an old-fashioned bench swing. They'd gone to dinner with Rooster. As soon as they'd finished the meal, Rooster excused himself and went inside the hotel, insisting he was on his way to bed.

"You must be exhausted," Bethanne said as they gently swayed. Max sat with his arm around her shoulders and her fingers tangled with his.

"I'm not so tired I can't appreciate time with you."

"Go to bed, too," she suggested. "We have all day tomorrow."

"Not yet," he said through a yawn.

Bethanne was just as glad. She rested her head against his shoulder. "Even though we've talked about a lot of things, I know almost nothing about you."

"I don't like to talk about myself," he said.

"So I've noticed."

"What would you like to ask?"

Of all the questions that buzzed around in her head, she

asked one of the least important. "How long have you and Rooster been friends?"

Max blinked, and Bethanne saw that he was struggling to stay alert. "For most of my life. He's my brother's age and we were neighbors growing up. You know we also have a business connection—he handles our advertising."

Bethanne nodded. "Is he married?"

"No. Well, he was at one time but it didn't last long. He's currently between…well, I hesitate to say *girlfriends*. *Companions* might be the better word."

"He only joins you on the road part of the time, right?"

"Right. A month every summer, and sometimes a few weeks in the spring and fall."

"Any family?"

"Who, Rooster or me?"

"You."

"A brother. Luke's ten years older. He's taken over the business since I've been away. His kids are raised and he travels to Australia and New Zealand every chance he gets. We connect three or four times a year when I'm in California."

"Are your parents alive?"

"They died a year apart back in the late nineties."

She already knew his only daughter had died at a young age.

"Have you ever been to Seattle?" she asked.

"Once. Rooster and I took a ride around the Kitsap Peninsula and into the rain forest a couple of summers ago. It's beautiful country."

"I love it there."

"You're still in the same house where you and Grant used to live?" he asked.

Bethanne found it a curious question. "Yes. It's the only home our children had ever known. There was enough upheaval in their lives without me pulling *that* rug out from under them, too."

"Have you ever considered moving?"

"No." That was the truth. She loved her home and had no intention of leaving.

"Anything else you want to know about me?" Max asked.

"Do you have a home?"

She felt his smile against her hair. "I don't need one. Wherever I am, that's home. However, I own a house in California."

"Do you visit often?"

"No."

"Friends other than Rooster?"

"A few here and there."

"How do you live?"

"You mean money? My needs are simple. I don't require much, don't want much."

Bethanne had guessed they had little in common, but that didn't dissuade her. The attraction she felt for him was as strong as ever. Stronger. He'd ridden twenty hours to see her. Even now, he was so exhausted he could barely keep his eyes open and yet he wanted to stay up so he could be with her. She couldn't imagine Grant being content to sit on a porch swing like this.

Oh, that wasn't fair. She couldn't compare them. They were as different as any two men—any two people—

she'd ever met. Grant would always be ambitious, driven to succeed. She knew that when she'd married him.

Max didn't seem to care about financial or career success, not anymore. And she could tell it had never been the be-all and end-all for him.

She instinctively recognized that he was a man who loved completely. Grant—well, he'd claimed to, but he'd deviated from his love, his vows, without caring how that affected her or their children.

After several minutes of silence, he said, "I know from what you told me that you had to find your way back to God after Grant left you."

"Yes." It'd been a small epiphany for her.

"You helped me see that I needed to do the same thing—make peace with Him."

"Oh?"

"We've been at odds ever since I lost Katherine. My daughter lived longer than any of her doctors expected. It was bad enough losing her, but then Kate…" He hesitated. "Losing my wife was too much, and frankly I've ignored anything spiritual ever since. Then, at a time when I least expected it, you plowed your way into my life."

"Plowed?" She raised her eyebrows. *"Plowed?"*

He laughed. "Okay, you appeared in my life. And for the first time since I buried Kate, I could *feel*. I could breathe without pain. I could face the future. I have to say it felt damn good and then…you were gone."

She tightened her hand around his, unsure what to say.

"I had a choice," Max went on. "I could get angry all over again or I could be thankful that you came when you did."

"And?"

"I chose to be thankful. Don't get me wrong, God and I aren't back on speaking terms but I'm getting there."

"Oh, Max." Not caring who saw them, she turned her head so their lips could meet. Early in their relationship, Grant had always been the romantic one. He'd written her poems and sent her flowers on the flimsiest of excuses. And yet no one, not even Grant, had said anything more beautiful to her than this.

"Whatever happens, whatever you decide—" he continued, after breaking off the kiss. He paused, then kissed her again. "—I'll accept it with gratitude."

Bethanne felt as if she might weep.

Max kissed the top of her head. "This probably isn't a good time for us to talk about serious matters."

"Why not?"

"I'm too tired to filter what I say."

"Tell me, anyway."

"I didn't think I could ever love again after I lost Kate. You've shown me it's possible."

She sighed, savoring his words, and snuggled closer. "I know what you mean. I thought it would be impossible to feel this way after Grant left me. I was sure I'd never be able to trust another man, let alone give him my heart."

"Could you give me your heart, Bethanne?" he asked.

"Yes, and it scares me to death."

He smiled. "It does me, too." He kissed the side of her neck and his lips against her skin felt like a mild electric shock.

"I...think it might be best if we both went to our rooms. You're tired, and I need time to sort all this out in my head."

Walking hand in hand, they approached the elevator.

Once inside—fortunately they were alone—Max punched their floor numbers. As soon as the door closed, he drew her into his arms and kissed her. The kiss was hot and urgent, and when he released her they were both breathless. His gaze held hers and she smiled at him.

He hugged her again and Bethanne stepped into the hallway that led to her room. Her mother-in-law and daughter were still out, to Bethanne's rather guilty relief.

She undressed and climbed into bed and sat there, mulling over the conversation with Max.

After Grant moved out, Bethanne had dated Tiffany's ex-husband. Paul was much younger. They'd bonded over the trauma of having loved an unfaithful spouse. Paul had since remarried and recently had a baby son. She was happy for him.

After Paul, Bethanne had dated off and on. Nothing had come of those relationships. And now she'd met Max... It seemed as though she'd been waiting for him all these years. Why now? Falling in love couldn't have come at a more inconvenient time.

Bethanne was still sitting up in bed, staring blankly at the wall, at about ten, when the door opened and the other two came in. Both were surprised to find her in the room.

"I thought you were with Max," Annie said.

"I was. We had dinner and then he went up to his room." She didn't mention that he'd spent twenty hours on his bike, riding through four states in order to meet her.

"Did you have a disagreement?" Ruth asked, sounding hopeful.

"No. He was tired and so was I." Preferring not to discuss Max, she asked, "How was the show?"

"Incredible," Ruth said on the end of a dreamy sigh. "I could fall in love with Andy Williams all over again. Oh, my, that boy can sing."

"He's hardly a boy, Grandma."

"Was it as dreadful as you feared?" Bethanne asked her daughter.

Annie set her purse on the dresser. "You know, it wasn't bad."

"Told you." Ruth couldn't keep from chortling.

"He isn't someone I'd purposely see again," Annie added, "but I have to admit he does have a decent singing voice. Even at his age."

"What about the songs?"

"They were all right." Annie shrugged as if to say she could take them or leave them.

"All right?" Ruth muttered. "'Moon River' is *all right?* It's brilliant!" After a moment she started to undress for bed.

Annie sat beside Bethanne, then tucked her feet up and rested her chin on her bent knees. "Dad and I had a long talk."

"Oh." No doubt she and Max were the main topic of that conversation.

"I told Dad how strange you've been acting." She grinned as she said it.

"I'm sure he had a lot to say." Bethanne let the acting-strange comment go unchallenged.

"I told Grant he should be more concerned than he is, but I'm afraid my son gave up listening to my advice a long time ago," Ruth said as she smoothed hand lotion over her upper arms and vigorously rubbed it in.

"Dad said we should leave you and Max alone," Annie astonished her by saying.

"He did?" That hardly sounded like the Grant she remembered.

"Yes. I know he's right." She looked steadily at Bethanne. "He also said he might've already lost you, and if so, it's what he deserved."

Grant said that?

"Dad told me you'd have to make up your own mind."

"Personally, I think my son has lost his," Ruth murmured as she capped the lotion. "The least he could do is show a little gumption and fight for you."

Unable to resist, Bethanne smiled. Ruth made it sound like the two men should choose their weapons and face off at dawn.

"This is Grant's business and yours," Ruth went on. "So I'll butt out. Besides, I have news."

Annie bounced on the bed. "You called Royce!"

As though embarrassed, Ruth lowered her head and nodded.

"When?"

"Earlier, when you were shopping."

"What did he say?" Again it was Annie who asked, leaning forward in her enthusiasm to hear. "I'll bet he was glad you called."

"I think so...I think he even recognized my voice. I certainly recognized his. It hasn't changed a bit. He sounded the same as he did at eighteen."

"How did the conversation go?" Bethanne didn't want to appear too eager, but judging by the look on Ruth's face, she already had her answer.

"We agreed to meet before the reunion to talk."

"Oh, Ruth, that's wonderful." Bethanne was pleased for her and grateful that the conversation had gone well. She'd wondered if Ruth would find the courage to contact Royce—and hoped she would.

"I talked to Jane, too."

"Is everyone excited about the reunion?" Annie sank back against the pillow and yawned.

"Yes, and everything seems to be coming together nicely," Ruth said, her eyes bright. "Jane told me they have the high school gym for the dinner and dance, just the way we did for the senior prom. She heard from Jim Maxwell and Alice Coan. They've been married for fifty years now, so it's a double celebration for them."

"Do you remember your senior prom?" Annie said, studying her grandmother.

Ruth laughed. "I doubt I'll ever forget it."

"Were you with Royce?"

"Oh, yes," she said dreamily.

"It must've been so romantic."

"Hardly." Ruth shook her head. "Actually, it was one of the worst nights of my life."

"Grandma, how can you say that? What happened?"

Ruth pulled down the covers and sat on the edge of the bed. "It's quite a story."

"Tell us," Bethanne urged.

"Well…I might have mentioned that Royce's parents didn't have a lot of money. The Jamesons sold everything they owned for the opportunity to purchase an orange grove. Unfortunately, for the first couple of years the crops didn't meet their expectations. Royce worked with his brothers and parents, but there never seemed to be enough money."

"Did purchasing the grove pay off over time?" Bethanne asked. She hated the thought of that kind of effort going unrewarded.

"I believe so, but not while Royce was living at home."

"What happened at the prom?" Annie asked again.

"Oh, yes, our senior prom." Ruth smiled as she said it. "Royce asked me, and naturally I said yes."

"Naturally," Annie echoed.

"He couldn't afford to buy me a corsage for the dance, so his mother did her best to make me one from orange blossoms, but it just wouldn't stay together. Not wanting to offend her, Royce took the corsage she'd made but when it fell apart he bought me a plastic rose."

"He bought you a *plastic* rose for the prom?" Annie sounded incredulous.

"Annie," Bethanne said, "that was all he could afford."

"Did he wear a tux?" her daughter asked, despite Bethanne's caution.

"A tux?" Ruth repeated. "My heavens, no. He had on his Sunday best, but it wouldn't have mattered to me if he'd been in his coveralls. He was still the handsomest boy in his class."

Annie stared at her, clearly fascinated by this glimpse into a life so different from her own.

"He picked me up in this vehicle they used in the groves. It didn't have a top, although it might have at one time."

"Oh, no," Annie gasped. "Can this get any worse?"

"I'm afraid so. It rained on our way to the prom."

"No!"

"Oh, yes, and until you see rain in Florida, you haven't seen rain. The drizzle we get in the Pacific Northwest can't compare."

"And you were in your prom dress?"

She nodded. "With my hair all done up and my new chiffon dress. I arrived at the prom looking like something that had crawled out of the Everglades."

"Oh, Grandma."

"Royce felt terrible."

"The poor boy," Bethanne said, picturing the nightmarish scene. She couldn't imagine anything else going wrong.

"And yet Royce was wonderful about everything. He wiped the streaming mascara from my face and kissed away my tears."

"He must have been drenched, too."

"Oh, for sure, but he didn't care about himself. All he wanted was to make the night special for me, and he'd tried so hard." She smiled wryly. "We didn't end up going to the prom, of course. He took me home and went back to his own place to change, then we spent the rest of the evening watching TV."

Bethanne hadn't met Royce yet, but she liked him already.

"Do you think he's changed much over the years?" Annie asked.

"I don't know about him," Ruth said, "but I have."

"We all change," Annie said, sounding mature. "Because of the things that happen to us."

Bethanne nodded. She'd changed since Grant had left

their marriage. Changed in many ways, some of which she was only beginning to understand.

Soon afterward they turned off the light. It wasn't long before Ruth's steady breathing told Bethanne her mother-in-law was asleep.

Annie lay on her back, then shifted onto one side; she seemed unable to find a comfortable position. Something was bothering her and Bethanne guessed it was directly related to Vance.

"Have you heard from Vance lately?" Bethanne whispered. Annie had mentioned him only once since he'd left for his European adventure.

"Sort of," Annie muttered, and bunched up her pillow with unnecessary force.

"How do you *sort of* hear from someone?"

"He sent me a text, which I ignored, and then he emailed me, but I haven't answered that, either," she said. "He told me he arrived safely and that he's having a wonderful time. Well, good for him. He doesn't need to rub it in."

"But you're having a good time, too," Bethanne reminded her. "And you met Jason in Vegas, didn't you?"

"Right." The word was full of enlightenment. "I should let him know I'm not sitting at home pining after him." She scrabbled for her cell phone on the nightstand, and although the room was dark, immediately started scrolling down her emails.

Annie paused and sent Bethanne a look of deep satisfaction. "There's another email from Vance."

"Oh? What did he say now?" Bethanne raised herself up on one elbow.

Annie seemed inordinately pleased. "That he's miserable, homesick and sorry he ever left Seattle."

"How does that make you feel?" Bethanne asked.

Annie's returning smile was answer enough.

Nineteen

Grant Hamlin sat in his recliner and stared at the television. If anyone had asked him about the program, he couldn't have said what he was watching. All he could think about was Bethanne.

He was losing her.

Even now, he couldn't believe he'd told their daughter to leave Bethanne to her own devices, to let her reach her own conclusions. He'd said what he knew he *had* to say, as a parent and as a man who loved his ex-wife. But the words left him feeling ill. Yes, he wanted Bethanne to make the choice that was right for her—but he wanted that choice to be him.

What he'd told Annie was true. He loved Bethanne. Tiffany had come between them, but he'd let her do that. He took complete responsibility for his mistake. He hadn't started out looking for an affair but he'd obviously been open to one. Tiffany had seemed vibrant, exciting, ambitious, and Bethanne, by comparison, had been… dull, mired in the tedium of domestic life. It appalled him that he'd been so blind, so selfish. He'd lost interest in their love life, too. Still, the affair had begun innocently enough. An office lunch that lasted nearly two hours. A simple kiss at a Christmas party. By Valentine's Day, they were meeting in hotel rooms and Grant had the sexual stamina of a teenager. Perhaps not surprisingly, that changed shortly after they were married.

In retrospect, he knew it was unconscionable that he'd abandoned his family; walked away without a qualm or a doubt. And yet, he'd done exactly that.

At the time Grant had convinced himself he was lucky to escape when he did. He'd told himself that because Andrew was about to graduate from high school and Annie would join her brother in college the following year, neither child needed him any longer. How wrong he'd been to underestimate his children's need for their father.

Grant rubbed the back of his neck. He'd quickly recognized his mistake in marrying Tiffany. And to compound the humiliation, she'd decided *he'd* been a mistake—too old, not successful enough, not as sexually adventurous as she wanted. The end of their marriage hadn't come soon enough. After Tiffany moved out—oh, what a godsend— he'd been too embarrassed to approach Bethanne.

By then she'd started her business and it had taken off. Watching from the sidelines, he'd been impressed and astonished by how well she'd done.

In the past couple of years, Grant had eased his way, carefully, cautiously, back into his family's life. Annie had accepted him without question. Andrew was a different story. His son wasn't as willing to put the past behind them. Eventually, Grant hoped, Andrew would see that he was genuinely contrite and trust him again.

At least Andrew wasn't openly antagonistic. He remained cool and withdrawn. Grant didn't blame his son for being wary; it was what he deserved and he knew it. Andrew was his mother's son for sure.

Thinking about him, Grant went into his small office in the sparsely decorated condo and reached for the phone. He checked his watch. It wasn't quite nine. A bit late, but not too late to call Andrew. He had to look up the number—a sad commentary all on its own.

Andrew answered as if he'd been holding his cell. "Hello."

"It's Dad."

"Anything wrong with Mom or Annie?" Andrew asked immediately. "Or Grandma?"

It hurt that Andrew assumed a phone call from Grant could only mean an emergency. "No. They're in Branson, Missouri."

"Last I heard they were in Vegas."

"Yes, they arrived in Missouri this afternoon. Your grandmother took Annie to see Andy Williams."

Andrew snickered. "I bet she loved that."

"Not so much, I'm afraid." He inhaled softly. "Listen, has anyone said anything to you about those bikers they met along the way?"

"Max and Rooster?"

He was shocked that his son knew their names. "What have you heard?" He felt guilty pumping Andrew for information. But what else could he do? He'd advised Annie not to spy on her mother or try to influence her. That nobility was costing him now. He felt at a real disadvantage, being miles away while this Max character was right there on the scene.

"Mom called a couple of days ago and told me about the car breaking down and how these bikers stopped to help her."

"How come you know their names?"

"Mom told me."

He wasn't exactly free with his information. "Did she mention that she met Max and Rooster in Vegas?"

"She might have."

"I see."

"Are you worried, Dad?"

Grant frowned. His son sounded pleased, almost gleeful, that Grant was concerned. "Yes, I guess I am," he said honestly. "I haven't made a secret of the fact that I'm hoping to get back with your mother." He paused, hoping his son would offer him a word of encouragement.

"Mom said something about that."

"Any advice you'd care to give me?" Grant asked.

"Not really. Mom's done well for herself."

As if he didn't know. "I'm proud of what she's accomplished," he said.

Andrew didn't appear to have anything to add.

"Is there some way I can help with the wedding?" His son hadn't asked a single thing of him from the moment Grant walked out of the house. Andrew hadn't even invited him to attend his high school graduation. Bethanne was the one who'd let Grant know the time of the ceremony. His son's graduation from college hadn't been much different. Annie had hand-delivered the invitation; Grant suspected that had she not done so, he wouldn't have been included. Bethanne was kind enough to invite Grant to the party she threw afterward. He felt out of place and miserable in the home he'd once shared with his family. Former friends seemed to avoid him. He did his best to socialize, but the situation was painfully awkward. Rather than ruin the day for Andrew or Bethanne, Grant had quietly slipped away.

That afternoon had been pivotal for Grant. It was then that he'd realized how badly he missed being part of the family. *His* family. He felt like an outsider and, with his son, an outcast.

"I don't need anything, Dad, but thanks for offering."

"What about money?" He'd never known a kid to turn down financial help.

"Thanks, no. Courtney and I have it covered."

"I'm happy to do what I can," Grant rushed to say, feeling the pain of his son's rejection. "Anything you ask."

"Actually, Dad, I think you've done enough."

The words stung and Grant was forced to swallow a retort.

They chatted a bit longer and then Grant disconnected. If anything, he felt worse than he did before he'd phoned.

Disheartened, Grant returned to his recliner and the TV. He had a lot of ground to recover with Andrew. His son wanted vindication, and the sad part was, Grant knew he was entitled to feel that way. Like his mother, Andrew was intensely loyal.

Leaning forward, Grant pressed his head into his hands. He wanted his family back and he wasn't sure how he was going to make that happen. All he could do, he figured, was show them, by whatever means possible, that he loved them and longed to be with them again.

If only Bethanne…

★ ★ ★

...Bethanne. Max couldn't get the image of her out of his mind. It used to be that he'd close his eyes and Kate's face would flash before him. For three years she'd been foremost in his thoughts.

The police had never determined whether the car accident was suicide or simply an error in judgment. Max knew. Kate, distraught over the death of their daughter, had fallen into a deep, lingering depression. She'd chosen to take her own life. He didn't know if he could ever accept that. He'd lost so much—his daughter, his wife... his reason for living.

The shock of her death had numbed him for the first few weeks. Then came the anger. Didn't she understand what her death would do to him? She'd deserted him, left him desolate and alone. The anger had been all-consuming. He couldn't sleep, couldn't eat. More than once he'd driven to the cemetery and raged at her.

Then his anger had been joined by guilt. A guilt so intense he couldn't function anymore. For days he'd stayed home, staring at the wall, unable to cope with even the most mundane tasks. He should've known Kate would do something like this. The signs had been there. Because he'd buried his own grief over the loss of their daughter in his work, he hadn't recognized those signs until it was too late. He should've gotten Kate the help she needed. He should have demanded she see a counselor, that they both see one. Nightmares had plagued him. He'd ignored what should have been obvious, convinced everything would get better with time.

But it hadn't. It'd gotten worse. Much worse.

After months of being unable to function, of drinking

too much and taking stupid risks, Max talked to his brother and asked for some time away. Originally, he'd thought all he'd need was three months, six at the most. But once he was on the road he found peace. Rooster, his lifelong friend, had come with him. They'd ridden bikes since Max was in his teens. Rooster had provided companionship when he'd needed it most. He hadn't tried to tell Max how he should feel but was there to listen when he wanted to talk. Best of all, life on the road was simple. Even though he moved from place to place, there was a predictability that calmed him and, surprisingly, friendships that gave him purpose. This solace was still shaky but at least he was able to sleep. At least the nightmares had stopped. Everything was going smoothly until this summer.

When he met Bethanne.

Now she was all he could think about. An hour after he'd returned to his room he still couldn't sleep. He'd ridden more than twenty hours with only short breaks for the opportunity to be with her again. It was a testament to Rooster's friendship that he'd traveled with him. Both Willie and Skunk had taken off, which was fine with him. Max had met them along the way. They'd traveled together for a week or so and they might meet up again sometime. If not, it wouldn't bother him.

Rooster seemed to enjoy watching him make a fool of himself over a woman. Max closed his eyes. Some nights he talked to Kate, relaying details of where he was and the people he'd met on the road. The people he'd helped or tried to help. He did that whenever he could. It was a penance of sorts, he supposed, for having failed his wife. These friendships, most of them brief, allowed him to make up for what he hadn't done. They silenced the accusations inside his head.

Instinctively, he knew Kate would have approved of Bethanne. He liked to think she'd approve of the fact that he was getting involved with life again.

Max didn't know what it was about Bethanne that appealed to him so strongly. He'd met other attractive women, but none had stirred him the way she did.

He'd been faithful to Kate from the moment they'd met and he'd been faithful since her death, too. Like Bethanne, he wasn't the type to fall in and out of bed, driven by hormones and the need for sexual satisfaction.

He'd sensed Bethanne was someone worth knowing the first time he'd laid eyes on her in that café near Pendleton, Oregon. They'd looked at each other when he placed his order and he'd experienced a strong physical reaction. Almost a feeling of *recognition*. He wasn't sure what else to call it. There was attraction, of course, but it was more than that.

She must've felt it, too, because when they met again at the lake, she told him she'd thought about him that night. The way she'd touched his hand... It was as if she'd identified the pain he carried inside and somehow known how to ease it. He usually tried to avoid being touched but with Bethanne it was different.

Yes, this woman belonged in his arms. In his life. He knew it then. He knew it now.

Apparently, he fell asleep soon after he'd decided that. What seemed like minutes later, Rooster was knocking at his door, waking him. Max had no idea how it could be morning already, but the clock radio in his room confirmed that it was. He staggered to the door and un-latched it to let him in.

Rooster had showered, shaved around his neatly trimmed white beard and changed clothes. "You look like hell," he said with a grin.

Max grumbled some meaningless reply and went into the bathroom. By the time he'd finished, Rooster had coffee brewing in the small pot provided by the hotel.

"What are you and Bethanne up to today?" he asked, making himself at home in the room's only chair.

"I don't know yet." They hadn't made plans to meet in the morning, although it was understood that they would. Maybe he'd take her to Al and Susie's place, which wasn't far away. When he'd learned Bethanne was in Branson, he'd called them.

"You mean you traveled all this way and you're not even going to see her again?"

Of course he was, but he didn't answer. He poured a cup of coffee and handed it to Rooster, then poured his own.

Sitting on the edge of the bed, Max sipped the hot liquid and hoped it would restore his composure.

"You've got it bad," Rooster commented.

No sense denying it. Max hadn't spent twenty hours on his bike for the fun of it. He'd come for Bethanne.

"What have you told her?"

"She knows about Kate, just not the suicide."

"She knows about the wine business, doesn't she?"

Max nodded. "Yeah."

Rooster braced his elbows on his knees. "You've told her more than I figured you would."

"Bethanne might go back to her husband," Max murmured. His stomach tensed at the thought. The possibility was real, and he needed to prepare himself for whatever she decided.

Rooster immediately shrugged off Max's concern. "You didn't see the way her face lit up the second she saw you. The girl's got it as bad as you." He drank his coffee. "It's a good thing she sent you that text message."

"Why?"

Rooster shook his head. "Honestly, Max, you moped around like a lost puppy dog from the moment she left Vegas. Her phone call didn't help, either."

"She called to say she didn't want to see me again."

"Obviously, you talked her out of that."

He hadn't even tried. "No."

"Listen, are you getting dressed or not? I'm hungry."

"Give me a few minutes."

"You got it." Rooster sat back, balancing his ankle on the opposite knee.

Max changed into jeans, the shirt he'd bought in Vegas and his leather vest. He didn't own much of anything else outside of his biking gear. Back at the house, he had a closet full of business suits. It'd been so long since he'd worn one, he wondered what it would feel like.

They headed for the elevator. "You going to call Bethanne?" Rooster asked.

"Later…" He couldn't forget that Grant was still a factor. Her ex wasn't going to simply remove himself from the picture.

The elevator finally came and they stepped inside, Rooster pushing the button for the lobby. The car stopped on the ninth floor. Bethanne's floor.

Annie's grandma was waiting in the hallway.

She hesitated when she saw them, then stiffened her shoulders and walked into the elevator, probably wishing there was someone else inside. Someone besides the two of them.

"Good morning, Grandma," Rooster said.

"I am not your grandmother," she snapped. Her back was as straight as a poker. "In fact, I'd venture to say you're older than I am."

That was patently untrue, but Rooster exchanged a smile with Max. "Are you going to let me buy you breakfast?" he asked, leaning forward and speaking into her ear.

"I should say not." She made it sound as if he'd propositioned her.

"Anyplace in town you want," Rooster said, not easily rejected.

His persistence appeared to fluster her. "Thank you for the invitation," she said formally, "but I'm having breakfast with my daughter-in-law and my granddaughter. They're in the lobby."

"Sleep in, did you?"

"Heavens, no. I forgot my tickets in the room. We're going to see the Twelve Irish Tenors and the Oak Ridge Boys."

"The Oak Ridge Boys are in town?" Rooster asked, not hiding his excitement.

"Annie and I are going to the afternoon show."

The elevator arrived at the lobby and the doors glided open. Max immediately saw Bethanne and Annie standing by the fireplace waiting. His gaze went directly to Bethanne. Without conscious thought, he started walking toward her and she toward him.

"How'd you sleep?" he asked in a low voice.

"Badly," she whispered, avoiding eye contact.

"Me, too."

"Are you going to breakfast or not?" her daughter demanded.

"*We're* going," Rooster said, and offered Annie and Ruth each an arm, elbows jutting out.

Max reached for Bethanne's hand, and every doubt he'd experienced instantly fled. They were together and that was enough. They would take this day by day.

"I don't know what you think you're doing," Ruth said to Rooster.

"Why, I'm taking two beauties out for breakfast, that's what."

"I believe that's our cue to slip off by ourselves," Max said. They walked out of the hotel, and when Rooster went left, they went right.

Max's heart lifted. He had twenty-four hours with Bethanne. It was going to be a good day.

Twenty

"How about a ride?" Max asked Bethanne after they'd finished breakfast. They'd returned to the hotel, strolling lazily down the busy sidewalks of Branson. Bethanne hadn't seen Ruth, Annie or Rooster since they'd parted ways about an hour earlier.

"I'd think after all that time on the bike, riding would be the last thing you'd want to do."

"There's a place I want to show you."

"Then I'm all for it." Twice now Bethanne had ridden with Max and each time she'd felt more relaxed, more comfortable. He must have planned this, because when he collected his Harley, he had Rooster's helmet.

When she was securely seated behind him, Max took off. He hadn't said where they were going, but it really didn't matter. She would've gone anywhere with him.

They rode for about forty minutes. He turned off the main road to a lake with a number of upscale modern homes built along the shoreline. Then he pulled into the driveway of one of those houses and climbed off the bike.

After removing his helmet, he said, "This belongs to a friend of mine. He said I can stop by anytime I want."

"Is he at home now?" she asked, removing her own helmet.

"I don't know. I left him a voice mail and said I'd like to take him up on his offer. I haven't heard back."

Bethanne dismounted and tucked her fingertips into the rear pockets of her jeans while Max walked over to the house. He dashed up the steps to the porch and rang the doorbell. When no one answered, he lifted a brick from beneath the window, thrust his hand in the hole and took out the key.

"Looks like we have the place to ourselves," he said, unlocking the front door.

Bethanne hesitated. "You're sure your friend won't mind?"

"I'm sure."

"You've done this before…stopped in like this."

"No."

"Max," she protested.

"It's okay, I promise." Without waiting for her, he walked inside.

Reluctantly, Bethanne followed. When she entered the house she noticed large, comfortable furniture. Max went over to the triple-wide sliding glass doors that led to the deck. He opened two, letting a clean breeze waft through the rooms.

He moved to the railing and looked out over the lake, which sparkled in the sunshine. It was alive with activity. The sounds of enjoyment—laughter and good-natured shouting—carried easily to the house. People were boating and fishing. A water-skier crossed the lake, and a couple of Jet-Skiers left huge rooster tails in their wake.

Bethanne joined him on the deck, and he slid his arm around her waist. "I had no idea this was so lovely," he said, almost as if he was speaking to himself.

"You haven't been here before?"

"Once. That was about two and a half years ago. Like I said, a friend of mine owns this. It was a little over a year after Kate died and I was consumed with grief. I was here, but I don't even remember looking at the lake."

"Grief takes over your life, doesn't it?" she said, growing thoughtful. "Years ago I read that grief is the place where love and pain converge. For whatever reason, that stayed in my mind. The truth of it hit me after Grant left. I grieved for my marriage." Like Max, she spoke in a whisper. "In the months after that, I discovered a number of things about myself, and they weren't necessarily things I liked. My husband had moved in with Tiffany. I wanted him back. I was willing to do anything, be anyone, if only Grant would come home again. I needed my husband. I'd never experienced that kind of emotional pain. Never understood how the man who'd vowed to love me could hurt me this badly."

Max's arm tightened around her.

"That first year forced me to reinvent my life," she said, "but a large part of who I am was formed by my love for Grant."

Max nodded. "Yes," he murmured. "And he tried to destroy that."

She didn't respond.

"I know how much you loved Kate," she said after a moment, leaning her head against his shoulder. "I wish I could tell you that the grief you're feeling will disappear and never return. But by now you've discovered it won't completely vanish."

He slowly exhaled.

"Because of Kate and Katherine, because you loved them, you're a different person. That love, and the love they had for you, will stay with you forever. Nothing can change the way you feel about them. They're part of you and always will be."

Max turned her to face him and whispered, "Thank you." Wrapping his arms around her, he held her close. For a long time they stood there and simply clung to each other. They didn't feel the need to kiss, and she believed that was because what they shared transcended the physical. This understanding—that they'd both lost what they'd treasured most—brought them together in a more profound way than mere attraction.

Eventually, they wandered down to the lake, took off their shoes and walked along the shore, holding hands. They smiled at a group of kids digging in the sand with colorful shovels and pails. After a while they found a private spot, where they sat and gazed out at the water.

"You're leaving in the morning?" Max asked, although he already knew the answer.

Bethanne splayed her fingers in the sand and nodded.

"Have you decided where you're going next?"

"Probably New Orleans." Bethanne remembered that was on Ruth's original route. "Ruth had everything worked out before Annie and I joined her."

"Ruth planned to drive cross-country alone?"

"We weren't about to let that happen."

"I'll be forever grateful you tagged along." He reached for her left hand and kissed the knuckles.

Bethanne would be forever grateful, too.

Her right hand continued to make circles in the sand. "Why did you want to know about our next stop?" she asked as casually as she could. She might appear relaxed, but she held her breath, torn between hope and dread. She hoped he'd follow but didn't dare ask if he would.

"Have you ever been to New Orleans?" Max asked.

"Never."

"It's a wild and crazy town."

"So I've heard."

Max squeezed her fingers. "I can't meet you there."

She blinked, trying to hide her disappointment. "What about Florida?"

"Probably not."

She blinked again. He hadn't offered any explanations or excuses. She could always ask but decided against it. If Max wanted her to know his reasons, he would volunteer the information. She wasn't a needy individual who craved constant reassurance.

"Then this is it?" she asked, swallowing hard.

Max's eyes immediately sought hers. "No…" He shook his head, then looked away. "The truth is, I don't think I can give you up."

The tension left Bethanne and she threw her arms around him and smiled. Max smiled, too, then leaned over and kissed her. She set her hand on his shoulder and kissed him back. After a moment, they drew apart.

Max lay in the sand and closed his eyes. "I never expected to feel this kind of peace again."

"I know. I'm six years out of my marriage and I'm

only beginning to feel content. Sometimes I'm amazed to realize I'm truly happy. At first, I didn't believe that was possible."

"Are you happy now?"

She closed her eyes, too, and felt the wind and the sun against her face, heard the excited sounds of children playing. Max was sprawled out at her side—a man she barely knew, yet was convinced she could love. "Yes," she whispered.

"I hardly ever tell anyone about Kate and never about Katherine."

She'd noticed more than once how infrequently he spoke of anything personal.

"Rooster was shocked that I told you."

Turning onto her side, she kissed him again and then lay back in the sand, nestling her head on his shoulder. "From New Orleans, we're only a day and a half from Vero Beach," she said. "That's where Ruth's class reunion is taking place."

"How long do you plan to stay in Florida?"

"A week. We'll return the rental car at the Orlando airport and fly back to Seattle on June 19."

He grew quiet.

"I should tell you that Grant will be in Florida at the same time. He says it's for a Realtors' convention in Orlando, but I know that's only an excuse."

"Grant loves you."

"So he claims—but he said that to me every morning when he went to work and was actually sneaking off with Tiffany to some hotel room." She sighed, a little disturbed by the surge of bitterness she felt. "The thing is, I don't know if I can ever trust him again...or if it's even possible to go back."

Grant had surprised her, giving Bethanne these days with Max. Andrew had left a message on her cell the night before, saying Grant had phoned and offered to help with the wedding. It seemed Grant was trying not only with her but with their children.

"I should stay away from Vero Beach," Max said. "If I showed up there, it might be awkward."

"I don't really care what Grant thinks," she insisted. She wanted Max with her. "Come to Florida," she urged.

"You're letting this—" he gestured around him at the beach "—influence you. Us, together, all by ourselves. But as you've pointed out, your life's a lot more complicated than that."

"I know, but..."

"Besides, I can't. I'm meeting my brother next week. I'd like to meet you there, but...it's not a good idea. Not now. You have things to discuss with Grant, and I need to get back to California."

"The only reason Grant decided to fly to Florida was to keep you away."

"I don't blame him," Max said. "In his shoes, I'd do the same thing. He and I both understand that you have to make your own decision. So, take this time with him. Celebrate your son's wedding, and when it's over, I'll be in touch."

"What if—"

He didn't allow her to finish, cutting her off with a deep, hungry kiss. "You can consider all the what-ifs later, but for now let's just enjoy being together."

By noon it was too warm to stay on the beach. They

walked back to the house and sat out on the shaded deck. After searching through the refrigerator and cupboards, Bethanne found frozen lemonade mix and a pitcher. She prepared it, then poured them each a tall glass and added ice.

Rejoining Max, she brought out the drinks.

He sat with his head bent forward, brushing sand from his hair.

As Bethanne set the drinks on a small table, she noticed that he was badly in need of a haircut.

"You could use a trim," she said.

"I know, but I've been chasing after this incredible woman and haven't had time."

"I used to cut Grant's hair. I could cut yours."

Max glanced up. "You cut your husband's hair?"

"Don't sound so shocked."

Max's eyes narrowed slightly. "From everything I've heard about Grant, he seems more like the type to pay for an expensive cut."

"I'm sure he is now. In the early years we were short of cash and looked for ways to save money. I discovered I had a knack for cutting hair. He actually preferred me to do it because I knew exactly how he liked it."

"You're a woman of many talents."

"So I've been told. I'm serious, Max, I'd be happy to give you a trim."

"You have scissors?"

"Not with me but I found a pair in the kitchen that would work nicely."

"Then, by all means, have at it."

It'd been several years since she'd cut anyone's hair but

she was confident in her skills. While Max wetted down his hair in the laundry room sink, Bethanne got a towel from the hall cupboard. Then she dragged a kitchen stool onto the deck.

Max returned a few minutes later. She took one look at him, at his hesitancy, and smiled. "You don't have a thing to worry about, so stop frowning."

"I was just asking myself how well I really know you."

"And how did you answer the question?" She patted the stool cushion, indicating he should sit.

"I decided I could trust you."

"Good decision."

She used the comb he supplied and started by cutting the small hairs that grew above the ears. Blowing the bits of hair away, she felt the tension leave his shoulders.

"I'm glad you've relaxed," she said.

"Actually, I've been dreaming about you blowing in my ear."

"I will as long as you whisper sweet nothings in mine."

He laughed.

Bethanne chatted as she worked. The more she engaged him in conversation, the more at ease he became. Standing in front of him she examined her work and was pleased with the result so far. As she stepped back, he took her hand, raised it to his lips and kissed her palm. Goose bumps shivered up and down her arms.

Before she was completely sure how it'd happened, she was sitting on his lap and they were deeply involved in a series of kisses. The scissors and comb were forgotten on the deck floor as she twined her arms around his neck.

"We'd better stop," he whispered.

"You're right."

"Personally, I'd rather find out where this will take us."

She hid her face in the side of his neck. "We already know that."

"Yes, and it's becoming more appealing by the minute." Then, as if drawing upon some inner reserve of strength, he gently pushed her away. "I never appreciated how sensuous it could be to have a woman cut my hair."

It hadn't been like this with Grant, she thought, even early in their marriage. She immediately felt guilty for making the comparison.

Resuming her work, she walked around to the back of his head and asked him to tuck in his chin while she clipped the hair at the base of his neck.

"How does it look?" Max asked once she'd finished.

"You'll have to tell me." She dug a small mirror out of her purse and handed it to him.

Max opened it and studied his reflection. He seemed surprised at what a good job she'd done. "Wow."

"Is it okay?"

"It's great."

She began to leave to get a broom from the kitchen when he caught her fingers and pulled her close. "I'm going to miss you," he whispered.

"I'll miss you, too." And she would, more than she dared admit.

Max was about to kiss her when the front door opened and a large man in Bermuda shorts walked in. His face instantly lit up in a huge grin. "Max!" he shouted, and started across the house toward the deck.

Max met him halfway and the two hugged and slapped each other on the back.

"Al, this is Bethanne. Bethanne, Al."

Al nodded at her. "I came as soon as I got the message that you were at the house."

Twenty-One

Al was a bear of a man, easily six-five or more. He engulfed Max in another hug and then turned to Bethanne.

"Hello," she said, hardly knowing what to think. "I hope you don't mind that we invaded your home."

"Not at all." He clasped her by the shoulders. "Now, let me take a good look at you." He smiled down at her, then glanced over his shoulder. "Hey, Max, you got yourself a cutie."

When he released her, Bethanne nearly stumbled backward.

"I hope you found everything you need," Al said as he walked into the kitchen. He removed a beer from the fridge and motioned to Max with it, silently offering him one.

Max declined with a shake of his head.

Al pulled back the tab and took a deep swallow. He returned to the living room and sat down on the sofa.

"How's Sherry?" Max asked.

"She's doing great," Al said.

Bethanne assumed the other woman must be Al's wife but didn't ask.

Obviously feeling the need to explain, Al looked over at her. "Sherry's our daughter. Max picked her up hitch-hiking three years ago—thank God—and managed to talk some sense into her. Our little girl got hooked on painkillers. We hardly knew her anymore. She stole her mother's jewelry and hocked it for drug money and was on a downward spiral."

"I'm glad to hear she's better," Bethanne whispered. This was every parent's nightmare.

"She did a complete turnaround," Al said. "If it wasn't for Max picking her up that night I don't know what would've happened to her. How he talked her into going to rehab I'll never know. Her mother and I begged her over and over but she wouldn't listen to us."

"You did that?" Bethanne stared at Max.

"He does that sort of thing," Al continued.

"Al," Max said under his breath. "Enough."

"I haven't known him long," Bethanne said, cutting Max off. "Tell me more."

"I think we should head out." Max stood and started for the door.

"We've got time," Bethanne countered, winking at Al.

"You don't know?" Al looked from Bethanne to Max and then back again.

"Bethanne, come on," Max said through clenched teeth.

"I'd like to hear what Al has to say," she told him. "Come back and sit down." When Max hesitated, she added, "Please?"

Max claimed the chair he'd recently vacated, but he didn't seem pleased about it.

"Max rides his motorcycle from one end of the country to the other, and along the way he helps people in need," Al explained. "If he comes across someone in trouble, Max lends a hand. Sometimes it's talking to them, like it was with our Sherry. Other times it's getting them something to eat and a place to live. All he asks in return is that whoever he helps pays it forward."

"He's definitely one of the good guys," Bethanne said. Now she understood what the mechanic in Wells, Nevada, had been talking about.

"I'm no saint," Max grumbled.

"He doesn't talk about it, either. As you might've noticed, he doesn't like people knowing what a soft heart he has."

"How'd *you* find out?" Bethanne asked. "Other than through Sherry, I mean."

"Rooster."

Max grunted in disapproval.

"Name's a bit odd. His real name's John Wayne Miller. John Wayne played a guy called Rooster in a movie called *True Grit* back in the sixties and apparently that's how Rooster picked up the nickname."

Bethanne nodded. "Yeah, I heard that."

"I wish you two'd stop talking about me as if I wasn't here," Max complained.

Al continued to ignore Max. "Max stops by to see Susie and me every now and then." He smiled at Max. "This is the first time he's ever brought a lady friend."

"Actually, Max helped me when our car broke down

in Nevada." She caught his eye. "I don't recall you asking me to pay it forward."

"Can we go yet?" Max asked pointedly.

"I was with my daughter and mother-in-law, and—"

"Ex-mother-in-law," Max corrected.

"Yes, I'm divorced. Max and I just sort of hit it off."

Al looked pleased as spiked punch. "I always wondered why he never had a woman in his life."

"I prefer my own company," Max said.

"Doesn't look like it to me." Al laughed. "You've found someone special, and you should be grateful. It's not much of a life, racing from one coast to the other, especially if you're alone."

"I like my life the way it is."

"Sure you do," Al muttered sarcastically.

"I do," Max said. He held his hand out to Bethanne; it was time to leave.

"No need to rush off. Susie's on her way home and I know she'd love to see you."

Bethanne agreed with Max's friend. "We should stay and say hello to Susie."

"She'd be real disappointed if you took off," Al said. "Besides, she's bringing lunch. I'll give her a quick call and tell her to pick up enough for five." He grinned. "I eat as much as two normal people, so she automatically buys two of everything when she's feeding me."

"Lunch," Bethanne said sweetly.

Max nodded reluctantly.

Sure enough, Susie arrived about ten minutes later and the men met her in the driveway. Al and Max brought in grocery bags and two six-packs of beer, plus an equal number of sodas.

Susie was a petite woman who stood a full foot and a half shorter than her husband. She had curly brown hair and big hazel eyes. Clearly she adored Max and welcomed Bethanne with a warm smile.

"I can't tell you how happy I am to meet you," she said, rushing inside. "Al and I were so thrilled to hear from Max, we immediately changed our plans and headed for the lake house."

Bethanne followed Susie into the kitchen and began unpacking groceries, setting the food on the kitchen counter.

"What else can I do to help?" Bethanne asked when she'd finished.

"Grab those bags over there," Susie said, pointing to the chips.

Bethanne was put to work opening bags of potato chips and emptying them into plastic bowls while Susie made a salad.

Al and Max moved onto the deck, where Al turned on the barbecue.

"How long have you and Max been together?" Susie asked as she sliced tomatoes.

Bethanne peeled a cucumber. "We aren't exactly together. We only met a few days ago." Although it felt as though she'd known him for a lot longer...

"Really? Well, you found yourself a gem of a guy. I don't know what happened to him. Max has never spoken about why he lives the way he does, but it's obvious there's some tragedy in his past."

If Max hadn't explained, then Bethanne didn't feel she could.

"He's done so much for others," Susie went on. "Rooster

told us that he helped a handicapped woman in Boston by replacing her roof. And a friend of ours told us about a family who was about to lose their home due to the husband's unemployment. When the bank threatened to repossess it, Max stepped in and made the late payments."

Just then Max appeared in the kitchen doorway. "What are you two talking about?" he asked suspiciously.

Susie rolled her eyes. "Why do men always assume we're talking about them?"

"Ego," Bethanne said, and they laughed. If any man *didn't* suffer from an outsize ego—in her opinion, anyway—it was Max.

"Hey, Max, I bought you chocolate ice cream," Susie said as she arranged silverware on the table on the deck. Smiling at Bethanne, she added, "He's got a weakness for chocolate ice cream."

Max snuck up behind Bethanne and slipped his arms around her. "What I have is a weakness for you," he said, kissing her cheek. He whispered, "Promise me you won't believe a word these people tell you."

"And why is that?"

"I already told you, Bethanne, I'm no saint."

"You make it sound as if you're ashamed of helping other people."

"I'm not, but I don't like to broadcast it."

"So, you're a lone wolf, a drifter who needs no one, riding off into the sunset."

He frowned and muttered, "You making fun of me?" in a mock-ferocious voice.

Bethanne laughed. "Guess so."

They ate hot-off-the-grill cheeseburgers around three o'clock. Bethanne liked his friends. Al and Susie carried the conversation, regaling her with stories about their children. Sherry was the youngest of three, and their problem child, although she'd successfully gone through rehab and had now returned to school. In large part due to Max, as the couple were quick to remind Bethanne. Max scowled every time they mentioned his name.

Bethanne helped with the cleanup and Max suggested they leave close to five. The afternoon had been perfect in every way. Al and his wife both hugged her before she went out to join Max on the Harley.

"He needs you," Susie whispered to her. "He's a lost soul."

Bethanne smiled and hugged the other woman back. "I'm so glad I met you and Al."

"Me, too. I hope we'll see you again."

She put the helmet on and climbed onto the bike. As they took off, engine roaring, Bethanne slipped her arms around Max's middle and relaxed against him. After a while she loosened her grip. Occasionally she even stretched her arms out at her sides, feeling free and un-encumbered. She sensed that she was finally getting to know him—that they'd breached some barrier.

The return to Branson seemed to take far less time than the trip to the lake.

Annie was sitting in the lobby waiting for Bethanne. "Mom!" she cried. "Where did you go? Why didn't you answer your phone?"

"When did you call?" Her purse had been near her most of the day, but she hadn't heard her cell.

"Half an hour ago."

That explained it. "What did you need?"

"Everybody left me," Annie complained.

Bethanne managed not to sigh—or say something sarcastic. "Where's Grandma?"

"She's still out with Rooster. They went to see the Oak Ridge Boys. At breakfast I said I didn't want to go and Rooster jumped at the chance. I haven't seen them since."

Ruth had gone with Rooster. That was a shock. "You spent the entire day on your own?"

Annie nodded, then shrugged. "I had fun shopping, though."

"That's my girl."

"So, where *were* you?"

Max stood beside her and they held hands. "I was with Max."

"Hi, Annie," he said, giving her a friendly smile.

"Well, duh, I figured that much," she told her mother. "Hi," she muttered grudgingly in Max's direction.

"We went to see some friends of his."

"Oh."

"Maybe we could all go to dinner tonight," Bethanne said.

Annie didn't show much enthusiasm. "We're leaving in the morning, right?"

"Yes, and according to your grandmother's schedule, we're headed for New Orleans."

"That sounds great."

"Max says it's a real party town. Should be lots of fun."

"More fun than Vegas?"

"A different kind of fun," Max said. "I wish I could go, but I'm headed somewhere else."

Annie didn't look at all disappointed. She glanced at

the doors and suddenly her face lit up. "Grandma!" she shouted, jumping to her feet.

Bethanne turned to see Ruth and Rooster walking into the hotel. "Rooster and I had the most wonderful day," Ruth said, hurrying toward them.

"Two shows, one right after the other, and both of them exceptional." Rooster looked delighted.

"I'm ready to get out of Missouri," Annie announced to anyone who cared to listen.

"What about dinner?" Bethanne asked once again. "All of us together. Max and Rooster are leaving tomorrow, and so are we."

"Count me out on dinner," Ruth said. "I'm exhausted and we've got a full day coming up."

"I'll go with Grandma," Annie said, as if she was glad of an excuse to escape. "We'll just get room service."

"You two are on your own," Rooster said as the three of them strolled over to the elevator a few minutes later.

Max looked at Bethanne. "Maybe we should say our goodbyes now, as well."

"How about a glass of wine?" she suggested instead.

He hesitated, then nodded slowly.

They found a vacant table in the lounge, and Bethanne studied the wine list. For the first time it felt awkward between them, as though they both feared what would happen next. In the morning they'd go their separate ways, and after that—she didn't know.

They each ordered a glass of red wine, an Australian shiraz, which was promptly delivered.

Bethanne gazed down at her wine, hardly noticing its rich ruby color.

"I have to be in California next week. I don't have a choice about that," Max said.

"I know."

Max's hand closed over hers. "My brother's handled the business ever since Kate died. It's time I went back."

"You're really going home?"

Max gave her a lopsided grin. "Luke was beginning to think I was never going to return. A lot has changed in the past three years—in the business, in his life, in mine. I'm ready now, only I didn't realize it until a few days ago. Until...you."

She met his gaze and held it.

"You'll go on to Florida, and we'll connect again later this summer. If that's what you decide."

Bethanne started to say that was too long to wait.

He shook his head. "No, you need to be with Ruth and Annie, with your son and his bride. With Grant."

Bethanne opened her mouth to protest, but again he stopped her.

"Make no mistake, I'd welcome the opportunity to explore where this relationship will take us, but I have things I need to attend to and so do you." His expression was determined. Unwavering. "While you're in Florida, you and Grant will have the chance to work this out—or not. Until you do, I'll stay out of your life. I'll abide by whatever decision you make."

"What if...what if Grant and I don't get back together?"

"Then let me know."

"You'll come to Seattle?"

"I'll come wherever you are. Anyplace. Anytime. All you have to do is contact me."

It sounded risky to Bethanne, scary, especially when

she wasn't sure of her own mind. She wanted Max to convince her they were meant to be together. He hadn't. She wanted him to fight for her. He wouldn't. The decision was hers.

"I don't like this," she confessed.

"Bethanne, we're both high on emotion." His hand cupped her cheek as if he felt the need to touch her, to hold on to her as long as he could.

They finished their wine, then returned to the front porch and sat in the swing, Max's arm possessively around her. She rested her head on his shoulder, closing her eyes. She wanted to keep these feelings with her forever.

Part of her wanted to argue with him, say she'd already made up her mind. Only she hadn't. Not really. Twenty years with Grant couldn't be easily shoved aside or forgotten. Max was right; they *were* high on emotion, on discovery. What they shared was fresh and new. Their feelings for each other had yet to be tested. All she had were these few days with Max. Seven days that had indelibly marked her. But could it be more than just a memory, significant though that memory was? *Should* it?

Max escorted her to her room and kissed her goodnight. Bethanne felt an urge to weep—but this time for reasons she understood far too well.

Twenty-Two

The next morning Annie was up at five-thirty, eager to hit the road. She turned on the bedside lamp and studied the road map. The day before had been a dead bore. Although she'd spent most of her time wandering from store to store and had even bought a few things, she'd grown tired of that.

The most interesting part of the day had been breakfast with her grandmother and Rooster. He seemed intent on letting them both know what a great guy Max was. She'd had some serious doubts about this biker. To all outward appearances, he was little more than a drifter. Her mother had hinted at the fact that Max owned a wine distribution business but she hadn't said much. Annie was convinced it was because her mother didn't *know* much.

But Rooster was obviously determined to fill in the blanks. He spent a good hour telling them about Max and his brother, Luke. He explained that Max had lost both his wife and his daughter and had gone off the deep end for a while.

Rooster turned every topic of conversation, every remark, into an opportunity to talk about Max.

When Grandma mentioned going to New Orleans, he'd said, "Max spent six months there."

"Doing what?" Annie had asked skeptically.

"Building homes with Habitat for Humanity. He also joined a group that reconnected pets with their owners."

"Oh." Annie had assumed he'd been drinking and gambling. The fact that he was helping victims of Hurricane Katrina quickly trampled her sense of indignation.

"So the two of you are heading home to California," Ruth said.

"We leave first thing tomorrow morning."

"Going back to do what?" Annie had asked.

"Max is stepping into the role he left three years ago," Rooster said. "He'll be working in the family business."

Annie made it clear that she wasn't impressed. She refused to even hint to Rooster that her views of Max were starting to change, much as she didn't want them to.

"I know you don't trust him," Rooster said.

"Plenty of reasons not to," Annie had muttered. "He's ruining everything between my mom and dad."

"Is he?" Rooster asked gently.

Annie nodded stubbornly, but her grandmother was evidently staying out of it.

"Kids want to see their parents together," Rooster said, reaching for his coffee mug and holding it out for the waitress to refill. "That's natural. But sometimes it isn't for the best."

"It is with my parents," Annie insisted. She looked across the table and met her grandmother's eyes, assuming Ruth would immediately agree. It came as a surprise when she didn't.

Hearing how Max had volunteered in New Orleans wasn't something Annie wanted to hear. She preferred to think of him as a drifter who'd taken advantage of her mother. Although she struggled to hold on to that image, she found it increasingly difficult, especially when she saw how happy he made her mother. Now that she knew that he had a good heart, it was even harder to dislike him.

But she wasn't ready to admit *that* yet, she told herself as she refolded the map. Both her grandmother and mother were still asleep.

Another minor complication had come her way in the past couple of days.

She'd emailed Vance back to let him know what a great time she was having and casually asked about his adventures in Europe. He replied right away. Matt and Jessie argued constantly. Everything cost more than they'd expected. At the rate they were going, they'd be out of money in a few weeks when they'd hoped it would last them a year. He hated hostels and had trouble making himself understood.

In Annie's opinion, if Vance was visiting a foreign country, he should make the effort to learn at least basic phrases in that language. She told him so, a comment he'd chosen to ignore. She hadn't heard from him since, and that was fine, although she did want Vance to know she was having the experience of her life...well, other than their last day in Branson. Unfortunately, she hadn't met anyone in Missouri the way she had in Vegas.

Jason had emailed her several times, as well. In fact, Annie hoped they'd keep in touch....

★ ★ ★

Bethanne didn't sleep well after Max dropped her off. There was so much more she'd wanted to say, so much more she wanted to know. He'd be traveling for several days, which would make communication difficult. She'd be on the road, too, heading in the opposite direction. Once she arrived in Vero Beach, Grant would meet her. She didn't want to think about her ex-husband, not when she was preoccupied by another man. Above all, Bethanne longed to be fair to both men. She wouldn't mislead Grant into believing a reconciliation was possible if she decided it wasn't. At the same time, she couldn't help wondering if what she felt for Max would diminish in the days ahead.

"We're ten hours from New Orleans," Annie said as Bethanne stepped out of the bathroom, dressed and ready to go. She said this as if it were little more than a Sunday drive in the country. "It's just six hundred miles."

"Six hundred miles." Ruth groaned as she completed her morning stretches. "You don't expect to make that in a single day, do you?"

"We can." Annie sounded completely confident as she tucked the map in her bag. "Especially if we get an early start." Hopping off the bed, she clapped her hands. "Come on, Mom. And, Grandma, just think—every day brings you closer to Vero Beach—and Royce."

Hearing that was all the incentive Ruth needed. Although Bethanne hadn't pried, she knew this trip had more to do with seeing Royce than with the actual reunion.

"And what about all the knitting you'll accomplish in ten hours, Mom?"

Because she'd spent so much time with Max, Bethanne

had neglected her project. Annie had a point; she could use the long hours on the road to knit…and think. She'd only completed the first glove so far. Her goal had been to finish the pair before they returned to Seattle.

They dressed and finished packing their suitcases. While Ruth directed the bellman with their luggage, Annie arranged to have the car brought to the front of the hotel. Bethanne checked out. After she'd put their expenses on her credit card, she handed the woman behind the counter a short note for Max, thanking him for a wonderful day. In a postscript, she'd added that she was going to miss him.

"Would you please give this to Max Scranton when he checks out?" she said.

The woman looked up. "Mr. Scranton's already left."

Already? Max was gone? Silly as it sounded, Bethanne wasn't prepared to hear that.

Bethanne drove, with Ruth in the passenger seat. "I don't mind telling you I enjoyed Branson," her mother-in-law said. "It was everything I'd dreamed it would be."

"You enjoyed attending the shows?"

"Yes, and Rooster wasn't half bad." She glanced at Bethanne. "I might have misjudged him. He's actually quite a nice man. A bit young for me, but a gentleman at heart."

"I'm glad you had a good time."

"Rooster." She shook her head. "I don't understand why he insists on using such a ridiculous name, but that's his business. He said—"

"Onward to New Orleans," Annie broke in. "I can hardly wait."

"Me, too." Ruth grinned. "My mouth's watering for that Cajun food Emeril's always talking about. Give me some shrimp étouffée and filé gumbo."

"Grandma, I thought you didn't like spicy food."

"Normally I don't, but I'm not about to pass this up. Besides, why did they invent antacid tablets if it wasn't for times like this?"

"I've heard so much about Bourbon Street…" Annie said dreamily.

"And apparently the French Quarter is quite a shopping experience," Bethanne added.

They stopped in Little Rock, Arkansas, for a late breakfast. Annie took over the driving after that, while Bethanne sat in the back and worked on her knitting. She was distracted by thoughts of Max and ended up ripping out several rows.

"We should call Dad," Annie said just outside Jackson, Mississippi, early that afternoon.

"We should," Ruth agreed.

Grant hadn't called in a couple of days, which was unusual. He seemed to be following his own advice and giving her the space she needed. But Bethanne suspected he was nervously waiting for her to get in touch with him.

"I'll call him," Ruth volunteered, and reached for Annie's cell phone, which rested on the console between them. She'd come to use it quite a bit this trip. Bethanne wouldn't be surprised if she bought one of her own.

Mother and son spoke about the trip for a few minutes before she turned around to hand the phone to Bethanne.

"Hello, Grant," Bethanne said.

"Hi," he said back. "How was Branson?" He sounded tentative, unlike his usual confident self.

"Wonderful." If he was waiting for her to fill him in about her time with Max, then he'd be disappointed.

"When do you plan to get to Vero Beach?" Grant asked.

"No later than Monday, although it depends on how many stops we make along the way," Bethanne told him.

"I've always wanted to visit New Orleans," Grant said. "It would mean more if I could see it with you." He paused. "Do you think that might be possible some-day?"

"I don't know…" And she didn't. Rather than dwell on that, she asked, "When do you fly into Orlando?"

"Monday afternoon."

"Great."

"Do you mean that, Bethanne?" he asked in a husky whisper. "Do you honestly mean that?"

"I do," she said. Being away from the demands of her business and the wedding plans would give her a chance to assess their relationship and decide if it was possible to step back in time. She wondered if she'd changed too much—and if Grant had changed enough.

"Tell Dad hello for me," Annie said.

"I will," Bethanne promised, and she did. She was grateful for the closeness father and daughter shared. She hoped that one day Andrew and Grant would find a common bond, too, and that her son would be able to forgive his father.

They spoke for a few more minutes and then Bethanne passed the phone back to Ruth.

They arrived in New Orleans around five-thirty that afternoon. For the past three or four hours, Ruth and Annie had traded off driving. By the time they got to their hotel on Canal Street, Bethanne was more than willing to call it a day. She was tired and uncharacteristically cranky.

After they'd checked in and had their suitcases brought up to the room, Annie and Ruth convinced her to explore the French Quarter with them, despite her protests.

"You'll feel better once we have something to eat," Ruth said.

They had no difficulty finding a fabulous restaurant. New Orleans was legendary for its food, and anyone they asked was willing to make recommendations. Bethanne loved the bistro's shaded courtyard and enjoyed every bite of her pecan-coated catfish and every sip of her Sazerac, a classic New Orleans cocktail. And the bread pudding with bourbon sauce… As Annie said, it was to die for.

Afterward, although she was tired and eager to get back to the room, Bethanne wandered into an antiques store in the Quarter and studied the cameos. She owned a couple of them, which she treasured, but didn't intend to collect more.

"May I help you?" a pleasant clerk inquired.

"Just looking, thanks," Bethanne said as she continued down the aisle. Both Annie and Ruth had followed her inside. They each found a different area to explore. The wooden floors creaked with age as Bethanne examined the contents of a display case.

"We recently got in something quite unusual, if you're interested in a memento that's out of the ordinary," the clerk said. She moved behind a glass counter and brought out a small box.

Inside was a plain fabric button. Bethanne couldn't see anything special about this particular button, other than its obvious age.

"This was sewn in the collar of a Confederate uniform," the woman said as she reverently took the button from its protective box and held it in the palm of her hand. "I have a photograph of it here." The clerk laid a picture of a tattered gray uniform beside the now-empty box. "When young men left for the War Between the States, their sweethearts would often soak a button in perfume. Once it was dry they'd sew it into their loved one's uniform collar, reminding the soldier of all he'd left behind. That way, whenever he was lonely for his home and his sweetheart, all he had to do was breathe deeply."

"That's so romantic," Annie said, coming to stand next to her mother.

"How much is it?" Bethanne asked.

The clerk named a price that shocked her. "For a button? Thank you, but no. That's way out of my price range."

"Mom, you should get it," Annie urged.

Bethanne shook her head. "What would I do with it?"

"Keep it as a souvenir of our trip," Annie said. "It's different and historical and so romantic."

Bethanne considered it for a moment. "I think I'd rather buy something else."

"Something more reasonably priced, you mean," Ruth commented, having joined them, as well.

The three shopped a bit longer. Annie bought a number of small items for her girlfriends and Ruth purchased pralines to bring to her own friends at home. In the end, Bethanne didn't get anything; she wasn't in much of a buying mood. She missed Max.

As soon as they returned to their hotel room, Ruth changed into her pajamas and was asleep almost immediately.

Annie was busy on her iPhone, answering emails. Taking the opportunity to soak in the tub, Bethanne sought a quiet thirty minutes to herself. A bubble bath was a luxury she hadn't enjoyed in a while. As she lay in the hot bubbly water, she closed her eyes.

She was completely relaxed when Annie stepped into the bathroom and sat on the edge of the tub.

"Do you need anything, sweetie?" Bethanne asked.

Annie didn't say anything right away. "I'm glad Max isn't here," she mumbled.

"I know." Bethanne tried not to sound defensive.

"I can see how much you like him."

"I do." Bethanne understood her daughter's concerns. "You're afraid Max might ruin any chance of a reconciliation between your father and me. Look, Annie, I know how much you want me to get back with your father. But what you need to remember is that nothing's the same as it was six years ago. Our family will never return to the way it used to be. You and Andrew are adults now. I'd never attempt to convince either of you to enter a relationship you didn't feel was right. I expect the same courtesy and respect."

Her daughter blinked and then nodded.

"We understand each other?"

Annie nodded again. "Just promise me one thing."

"What is it?"

"Give Dad a chance. Just give my dad a chance."

Twenty-Three

"Mom," Annie whispered. She hadn't slept. The glowing digital alarm by her side told her it was a little after three. There was a strip of light under the door from the hallway, but except for that and the clock, the room was dark. Grandma Hamlin snored softly in the other bed.

"Hmm?" her mother returned groggily.

"Are you awake?"

"I am now," Bethanne said, and rolled onto her back.

Annie stared at the ceiling. "Are you mad at me?"

Her mother sat up, leaning against the pillows, and studied Annie. "Why would I be mad at you?"

"Because of what I said about Max," she whispered. "The thing is, I think I might really like him if it wasn't for Dad." Annie had lain awake, examining her feelings, and realized that Max and Rooster were good guys, kind and helpful. She had no idea what would've happened at the lake if they hadn't come by when they did.

"You really care about him, don't you?" Annie sighed. Her father could have put an end to this romance and he hadn't. More than that, he'd actually insisted they leave Bethanne alone to make her own decision. Annie admired his attitude, which she viewed as brave and selfless, but she wanted to shout at him to *do* something and fast. He wouldn't listen, though. Both her parents were such complicated people.

"I do care about Max." Her mother's voice was tender.

"It's kind of weird watching my mother fall in love with someone other than my father."

"I can't say I'm in love with him, Annie. It's too soon for that. I'm...infatuated with Max, but we haven't faced any real difficulties yet. I think it would be easy to fall in love with him one day. I like Max a lot, and I hope things work out so we can be together, but they might not."

"But you love Dad, too, right?" She felt as if the dream she held of seeing her parents reconcile was crumbling at her feet.

"I do care a great deal for your father. I can't dismiss our years together because of an error in judgment he made." Her mother lay down again. "However, I doubt that you woke me up to chat about your father and me. What's up, sweetie?"

Annie sighed, unsure where to start. "I heard from Vance again." She made it sound like he'd only emailed her a couple of times. The fact was, Vance had contacted her nearly every day since he'd left for Europe with Matt and Jessie. She hadn't answered most of his emails.

"You mentioned that he's homesick and wants to come back to Seattle."

"He can't. His ticket home isn't good until next year. When he tried to change it, the airlines wanted to charge him for a whole new ticket. He doesn't have that kind of money and he can't ask his parents. He says the airline's being unreasonable and I agree with him."

"He must have known that when he booked his flights."

"But he already paid for his return ticket!"

"He's had a pretty quick change of heart, hasn't he?" Bethanne commented. "He's only been in Europe a couple of weeks."

"Yes…"

"What aren't you telling me, Annie?"

That was the problem with her mother, Annie thought. She read between the lines far too easily.

"Okay." She closed her eyes tightly. "Vance wants me to meet him in France at the end of the month." There, she'd said it, and held her breath while she waited for her mother's reaction.

"What do *you* think about that?"

Annie should've known. Her mother always did this. She turned everything into a question. "I'm not sure," she admitted. "That's why I wanted to talk to you. I need advice."

"All right," her mother said. "Obviously, this is bothering you. Otherwise, you'd be fast asleep."

"And so would you," Annie added, smiling.

"True."

Her mother didn't sound upset, though, and that was reassuring.

"First, how do you feel about Vance?"

"Now or before we left?"

"Now."

"Well…I miss him. Before he decided to go to Europe, we talked practically every day. We were almost always together, which is one reason I was so upset when I found out he was going to Europe with Matt and Jessie."

"He kept it a secret."

"He wanted to tell me, or so he said, but Matt told him not to."

"And he listened to his friend instead of doing what he knew was right."

"Yeah."

"Did he say why he wants you to meet him in France?"

Annie folded her hands behind her head and stared up at the ceiling some more. "He said he's tired of being a third wheel. Matt and Jessie are having all these arguments and he's afraid he doesn't have enough money to last a year and—"

"In other words, nothing is turning out the way he thought it would," her mother finished for her. "And that's why he invited you to fly over and join him?"

Just the way her mother asked told Annie she thought it was a pretty selfish reason. "That's what he said, but you have to remember Vance isn't exactly a great communicator."

Annie wanted to believe he was lost and lonely without her and that he regretted everything. He hadn't said so, but she knew that was what he really meant. Or what she *hoped* he meant...

"Well, you'll have to decide if he's sincere," her mother whispered. "If he's asking because he wants to be with *you* or he just doesn't want to be alone."

Annie lowered her voice, too, not wanting to wake her grandmother. "He does want to be with me!"

"That's not what he said, though, is it?"

"Well, no, but it's what he *meant*."

Her mother was silent for several minutes. "It sounds to me like you want to be with Vance, too."

That was true, although Annie hated admitting it. "He really hurt me, Mom."

"I know, honey."

"I think he needs to work harder for me to put this behind us, don't you?"

"Are you saying you don't think he's suffered enough?"

Annie snickered in the dark. "You're funny, Mom."

"You *do* want him to suffer, though, right?"

"Well, he should. He went behind my back and planned this whole trip without telling me anything. I'm supposed to be his girlfriend—wouldn't you assume he'd want me to know? *I* shared everything with *him*. I thought I wanted to marry him and I believed he felt the same about me."

"I know."

"Not only does he hit me with the news that he's going to Europe with his two friends, but then he insults my intelligence by asking me to drive him to the airport."

"That does take gall," her mother agreed.

"Wouldn't *you* want him to suffer?"

"I'm afraid I would."

Annie knew she could count on her mother to be on her side.

"But when is it enough? It's hard to know when I should forgive and forget."

"True," her mother murmured.

"I can forgive him…in time."

"In time," her mother echoed. "Eventually, you'll be able to look past his behavior—if you choose to. Men can be completely oblivious to what matters most. When you think about it, Vance must've known how upset you'd be, and yet he wanted you to send him off with hugs and kisses."

Annie felt better talking this over with her mother. Everything was starting to seem a little clearer. "I heard from Jason, too. He called me the day I spent alone in Branson. We've kept in touch since Vegas."

"So, what do you think?"

"Well, to be honest, it felt good to have someone interested in me after Vance was such a jerk."

"Do you like Jason?"

Annie shrugged. "He's okay."

"That's not a glowing endorsement."

"I know. I tried to figure out why I feel this way. He's really nice and fun and we had a great time together. Another girl would be over the moon about meeting someone like him. Then I realized what's wrong. Jason didn't act like Vance. I'm so used to being with Vance that it felt sort of...wrong to be with someone else."

Her mother shifted onto her side. "I remember when Paul—Tiffany's ex—and I went to dinner after your father moved out."

"Yeah?" Annie didn't like to remember that. Her father and the *lovely* Tiffany had hurt and betrayed two people. Well, four, including her and Andrew.

"I hadn't been out with another man for so many years that I started to shake. I didn't know how to act or what to say, and when I did find my tongue, I was convinced I sounded like a nutcase."

This wasn't a fair comparison to her situation with Jason. Her mother had been close to a nervous collapse the first few weeks after Annie's father moved out. Those days had been dreadful for all of them.

Annie had been furious with both her parents, but especially Bethanne. If her father fell in love with another woman, it had to be her mother's fault. Bethanne was boring, Annie decided. Her mother's whole world revolved around the house and the family and those dinner parties she put on for her father's business associates. She'd let herself go, too. Her hair was too long and she didn't shop for herself often enough.

In the weeks that followed, Annie had done her utmost to bring her father home. She'd cried and pleaded and told him she'd make sure Bethanne did whatever was necessary to make him happy. In retrospect, Annie was embarrassed by her behavior. She understood now that nothing she'd said had put a dent in his determination.

What hurt the most was discovering that he didn't even want to talk to her anymore, although they'd always been so close. Annie was convinced it was all *lovely* Tiffany's fault.

After she'd finished blaming her mother, Annie had turned her anger on the new woman in her father's life. The divorce was completely her fault, and if Annie could show her dad the truth about Tiffany, Grant would change his mind and come back to the family.

Annie had pulled some nasty tricks on the *lovely* Tiffany, but they'd backfired. The only thing her efforts had accomplished was to upset her father and widen the rift between them.

With her mother a weakling and her father refusing to have anything to do with her, Annie had nearly self-destructed. Fortunately, Andrew had stepped in and, with

Courtney's help, gotten her away from the dangerous path she'd chosen.

"You're quiet all of a sudden," her mother whispered.

Not wanting to confess where her mind had wandered, Annie said, "I had a thought."

"Don't let it go to your head."

"Funny one, Mom." Annie smiled into the dark.

"And? Want to share that thought?"

"Jason's actually really nice." Jason was more than nice; she'd probably try to keep this going, see where it went, although he lived in California and long-distance relationships were a drag.

"Do you know what you're going to tell Vance?" her mother asked.

"I think so." She paused. "Vance should've thought about being a third wheel when he agreed to go to Europe with Matt and Jessie," she began. "I've got more to do with my life than give up a whole month just so he doesn't feel lonely while he's away. He had his chance and he blew it."

"But you'd still like to be with him, wouldn't you?"

"Yes, but for all the wrong reasons."

"Oh?"

"I want to be with him because we're comfortable together. Familiar. But that isn't a good enough basis for uprooting my whole life." The more Annie verbalized her thoughts, the more convinced she was that she'd made the right decision. And the more she felt that pursuing a relationship with Jason made sense. The very reason she'd had doubts about him—the fact that he wasn't Vance—

was now why she wanted to see where a connection between them might lead.

"Can we go back to sleep now?"

"Okay," Annie said, but she didn't think she would.

Twenty-Four

They stayed in New Orleans another day, and after a leisurely drive, got to Vero Beach late Monday afternoon. Bethanne hadn't heard from Max. She'd toyed with the idea of contacting him, but had resisted.

For now.

"I can't believe how much everything's changed," Ruth kept repeating as they made their way into town. On the drive down Route 60, she'd pointed left and right, shaking her head at what were once orange groves as far as the eye could see, but were now mostly housing developments and suburban sprawl.

"Call Royce," Annie said when they reached their hotel and had unpacked.

Ruth paced the room, nervously rubbing her palms. "You think I should?" she asked, looking at Bethanne. "I mean, so soon? We just got here."

"You said you would," Bethanne reminded her.

"Grandma," Annie groaned. "He's waiting to hear from you. Now call him!" Annie commanded, gesturing at the room's phone.

Ruth glanced uncertainly toward Bethanne, who nodded her encouragement.

"Okay…I will," Ruth declared, sounding more like a schoolgirl than a mature adult, "but if this turns out badly, I'll blame the two of you." She fixed them both with a shaky glare.

"It won't, I promise," Annie said with utter confidence.

Bethanne watched discreetly as Ruth sat on the bed and punched in Royce's number from a slip of paper in her purse. She held the receiver to her ear, clenching and unclenching her fist. In the silence Bethanne could hear the phone ring, followed by a man's voice answering.

"Royce, it's Ruth," she began, her own voice fluttering with anxiety. She rushed on. "My granddaughter thought I should let you know we made it here safely. We're in Vero Beach at the hotel the reunion committee recommended."

While Bethanne couldn't hear what Royce said, she saw from Ruth's reaction that he seemed pleased to have heard from her. Ruth hunched over, and Bethanne could see her smiling.

"Sure—but my daughter-in-law and granddaughter are with me. All right. Uh-huh…that would be very nice." She looked at Bethanne and Annie, who stood with their hands clasped as they awaited the outcome. "Okay, yes… that's very thoughtful. We'll see you soon." Ruth hung up the phone.

"Well?" Annie asked expectantly. She and Bethanne were staring at Ruth.

"He wants to take us all to dinner," Ruth said.

"*All* of us?" Bethanne asked to be sure she understood correctly.

"His grandson is with him, and he's bringing him along for you to meet."

Annie smiled, clearly intrigued by this unexpected turn of events. "Was he happy to hear from you?"

Ruth blushed. "I think so," she said.

"Told you," Annie crowed, collecting a fresh set of clothes and heading for the shower.

"I need to change, too." Ruth looked down at what she was wearing. She brushed an invisible speck of dirt from the front of her blouse. "I don't know if I'm ready to see Royce again," she muttered, her forehead wrinkling.

"Yes, you are," Bethanne insisted, amused and deeply touched at the sight of her mother-in-law in such a state.

Ruth immediately started riffling through her clothes, searching for the perfect outfit in which to rendezvous with her high school sweetheart. With both Annie and Ruth occupied, Bethanne grabbed her cell and stepped out onto the patio, closing the sliding glass door carefully behind her. The waves breaking on the beach were hypnotic, and the ocean breeze dispelled the intense heat and humidity of late afternoon.

Sitting in one of the patio chairs, Bethanne punched out Max's cell number. She had no idea if she'd reach him. If she didn't, she'd leave a message.

Max picked up on the fourth ring, just before the call went to voice mail.

"Max...it's Bethanne."

"Bethanne." His voice was low.

"Where are you?"

"On the way to California." He paused. "Are you in Florida yet?"

"We arrived about thirty minutes ago."

"Is Grant there?"

"Not yet. He's meeting us later." She didn't want to think about Grant right now. "How are you?"

"Miserable." He laughed hoarsely.

"Are you really?" Bethanne hugged the phone tighter.

He muttered something under his breath. "You don't need to sound so happy about it."

"I can't help it. I'm feeling exactly the same without you."

"How was New Orleans?"

"We ate beignets at Café du Monde yesterday morning. Last night we listened to jazz on Bourbon Street. After that, I ended up drinking some wicked alcoholic concoction in a hurricane glass. It knocked me for a loop."

"You three didn't get into any trouble, did you?"

"None that I care to mention," she joked. "I'd always heard that New Orleans was famous for its food, and it was fantastic." She found herself chattering on. "Annie talked Ruth and me into trying a mint julep—"

Max snorted in amusement. "Were you able to walk back to the hotel afterward?"

"No…" Bethanne giggled. "We had to get a taxi."

She paused as their laughter died away, then said quietly, "I wish you'd been there."

"I do, too," he told her. "Maybe one day we'll go back together." Grant had said that, too…. Just then, Annie opened the sliding glass door, wearing a sleeveless summer dress Bethanne had never seen before. She must have purchased it in Branson.

"I need to go," Bethanne said hurriedly.

"I'm glad you called."

"I am, too. Give my best to Rooster."

As she ended the call, she experienced a piercing sense of loss. Instead of feeling better, she felt worse.

"Was that Max?" Annie asked.

Bethanne nodded.

"Dad called," Annie continued. "His flight landed on time and he's on his way to Vero."

"Okay."

"Grandma suggested he join us for dinner," Annie said, leaning against the glass door.

Bethanne's voice was cool. "What about the conference? Won't he be missing that?"

Annie shrugged. "You'll have to ask him."

For a moment, Bethanne wondered if there even was a conference. It had certainly come up very conveniently.

"Aren't you going to get ready for dinner?" Annie prompted.

Reluctantly, Bethanne stood up and prepared to go back inside the room.

"Mom," Annie murmured, putting a hand on her arm. "Grandma's pretty nervous about seeing Royce. You might want to help her."

"How am I supposed to do that?" Bethanne searched Annie's face.

"I don't know. You always managed with me." Annie smiled.

"But...Ruth isn't my daughter."

"Pretend she is." Annie glanced over her shoulder. "Someone's got to do something. She's pacing back and forth, and I'm afraid if she sprays on any more cologne she might set off the fire alarm."

Sure enough, Bethanne found her pacing the length of the room, pausing only to gnaw on her cuticles.

"Give me fifteen minutes," she told Ruth.

"Fifteen minutes for what?"

"To take a quick shower and change clothes."

"Then what?"

"Then I'm taking you to the bar."

"I can't let Royce find me in the bar!" she cried.

"Yes, you can." Bethanne adopted her firmest parental tone. "Now, don't argue with me."

Ruth stared at her like a forest animal caught in the headlights of an oncoming car.

Shortly thereafter, Bethanne escorted her to the lounge, which was a cozy, unpretentious place, with an old-fashioned wooden U-shaped bar and a few mismatched tables and chairs. A cheerful bartender took their drink order. Bethanne asked for two glasses of white wine, which were brought to the table a few minutes later.

Ruth took one sip and nearly coughed her lungs out.

"Are you okay?" Bethanne pounded her on the back.

Ruth shook her head vigorously.

"What's wrong?" Bethanne asked, startled.

"Royce just came in," she whispered, while she dug in her purse for a tissue to wipe her eyes.

"Where?" Bethanne scanned the dimly lit room.

Ruth nodded toward the tall, silver-haired man who'd just slipped onto a bar stool with his back to them.

"Are you all right?" Bethanne whispered.

Ruth seemed paralyzed with fright. "I don't know if I can face him."

Bethanne was surprised to see Ruth's hands trembling.

"I hurt him so much…" she began in a broken voice that Bethanne had never heard before.

"Ruth, you were young…. I'm sure he's gotten over it—"

Ruth cut her off with a sharp shake of her head. "He might have, but I'm not sure I ever can." She sat for several minutes, clutching the now-tattered wisp of tissue. Then, as Bethanne watched, she slid out of her chair and squared her shoulders.

Bethanne gave her a smile of encouragement.

Ruth walked up behind Royce and placed her hand on his shoulder.

Royce whirled around. His face registered shock. For a long moment all they did was stare at each other. "Ruth... Ruth, is that really you?"

"Have I changed so much?" she asked, taking a step back, as if dreading the answer. She pressed her fingers to her lips, seemingly on the verge of tears.

"No, no..." He blinked, apparently to clear his vision. "You're even more beautiful now. More beautiful than I remembered."

"Royce..." she said, then faltered.

They embraced wordlessly, then he took Ruth's face in his hands as he gazed down at her.

Just then, Annie entered the bar, having updated her Facebook page with photos from the road. Taking in the reunion between Ruth and Royce, she broke into a huge smile and gave Bethanne a thumbs-up.

Royce's grandson, Craig, was the next to arrive; shortly after he joined the party and introductions were made, Bethanne noticed that he and Annie fell into animated conversation. Royce and Ruth hardly looked up, drowning in each other's eyes.

Leaning back in her seat, Bethanne savored her wine and surveyed the scene. In a few days' time they'd fly home to Seattle and Bethanne would return to her regular life, but she wouldn't be the same woman. The trip had changed her. It had changed them all. The three of them had grown close, sharing their secrets, confronting their fears. And despite some moments of tension, they'd come to understand and support one another in new ways.

She was so immersed in her thoughts that she almost missed Grant's entrance. He walked into the bar and glanced around, brightening when he saw her. To her surprise, Bethanne felt a surge of affection. Tall and lean, Grant still cut a striking figure, and his energy was palpable. They'd been a good match—partly because Bethanne had always been content to remain in the background, his silent partner in more ways than one.

His smile was electric, transforming his entire face. As he started toward her, she was reminded of his ability to make people feel they were the sole focus of his attention. Over the years, she'd heard many of his colleagues talk about his charisma and its effect on clients. He obviously still had it.

Ruth spotted her son before he reached Bethanne and pulled him over to make introductions. Grant caught her eye and winked, but when the three couples sat down together, he was trapped on the other side of the table. After sharing a bottle of wine, they all left for dinner at the restaurant beside the hotel.

The Ocean Grill boasted an interesting assortment of wrought iron, stained glass and other collectibles. While they were being seated at their table next to the window, Grant wangled a seat next to Bethanne. Outside, the surf roared against the sand and groups of tourists walked the beach, waves crashing at their feet.

Bethanne felt Grant's hand touch hers beneath the table. "I've missed you," he murmured.

She gave him a fleeting smile but kept her eyes on the menu. The truth was, he'd been in her thoughts more than she wanted to admit. Despite her reservations, his familiar presence brought back the glow of happier times. Grant slipped comfortably into his role as father and son—something that Max, for all his intensity, could never do. She studied him as he chatted effortlessly with Royce and Ruth, full of high spirits and completely at ease. Grant was family, and that was difficult to ignore or dismiss.

The wine flowed as the evening progressed, and Bethanne relaxed. At Royce's urging, she ordered the pompano with apricot sauce and found it outstanding. As was typical, Grant and Annie both ordered the same entrée—the stone crab claws—which they ate with gusto.

After dinner Annie and Craig went for a walk along the beach. Royce and Ruth did, too, leaving Grant and Bethanne alone at the table. Bethanne stirred her coffee, suddenly self-conscious.

"I brought you something," Grant said.

"From Seattle?"

"Not exactly." He reached inside his dinner jacket and took out a small wrapped package.

"You don't need to buy me gifts," she protested, although she couldn't suppress her curiosity. Grant had always been a generous and original gift-giver; it was one of his talents. He never once forgot an anniversary or her birthday, and outdid himself from year to year in the extravagance and thoughtfulness of his presents.

"I wanted you to have this," he said as she untied the bow and removed the paper.

The instant she saw the box, Bethanne knew.

Nestled inside was the button she'd seen in the antique

store in New Orleans. Annie had obviously mentioned it to him; he must have ordered it that same night.

"Do you like it?"

"Very much," she breathed, recalling the story about the soldiers and their sweethearts.

"Every time you look at that button," he said, his head close to hers, "I want you to think of me."

Twenty-Five

That evening with Royce, Ruth felt as if the years had evaporated, and they were eighteen again. They talked nonstop without a trace of awkwardness, until Ruth realized it was midnight—and they were alone.

Bethanne and Annie had turned in for the night. Craig must have gone home. Apparently, Grant had driven back to Orlando, although she didn't remember him leaving. All Ruth could see, the whole night long, was Royce. All she'd heard was what he said. Everything else was a blur.

Before he left her at the door of her room, Royce had asked if he could pick her up the next morning and take her to his home on the Indian River. Ruth had agreed. Not once had he mentioned the circumstances of their parting fifty years ago, but she felt its shadow, even in their happiest recollections. Ruth wished they could leave the past buried, but she knew that unless they confronted it now, it could destroy any hope of a future. All that shame and pain...

Unable to sleep with such thoughts chasing through her head, Ruth rose before Bethanne and Annie and dressed, taking special care with her hair and makeup. The humidity in Florida during summer was unrelenting. She didn't expect her hair to stay in place, but felt she had to make the effort.

For Royce.

"Grandma, what are you doing up so early?" Annie asked groggily as Ruth came out of the bathroom.

"It's almost eight."

"That's early for you," Annie observed. Generally, Ruth was the one who lingered in bed. "Have you done your exercises?"

"I did." Ruth smoothed a stray curl into place. "I'm seeing Royce this morning."

"That explains it," Bethanne murmured from the other side of the bed, next to Annie.

"Did you enjoy meeting Craig?" Ruth asked her granddaughter. While her attention had been focused mostly on Royce, she did notice the two young people talking, their heads close together.

"He's really nice." Annie's face shone with what looked like genuine enthusiasm.

"Are you seeing him again?" Ruth asked.

"He's taking me out on the river—he promised we'll see manatees and dolphins." Annie stretched contentedly. "You never told me Florida was so beautiful, Grandma."

"It has its own unique beauty, just like the Pacific Northwest."

"Do you know when you'll be back?" Bethanne pushed herself into a sitting position, running a hand through her tousled hair.

"No…I'll give you a call later. If Annie's with Craig, what are you going to do all day?" She hated the thought of Bethanne stuck in the hotel room or out on her own, and hoped Grant wouldn't be tied up in those boring Realtor meetings.

"Grant's stopping by," Bethanne assured her. "He's got a session this morning, but he should be finished by lunchtime. We're going to meet up around one o'clock."

"What will you do this morning?"

Bethanne climbed out of bed. "I thought I'd laze by the pool and read. I have my knitting, too, so I've got plenty to do. Don't worry about me." She waved a hand at Ruth. "Enjoy your day with Royce."

"I will." Ruth glanced at her watch.

"Everything all right between you?" Bethanne asked Ruth in a meaningful tone.

Ruth shifted uncomfortably. "I…I don't know yet. I haven't really had a chance to talk to him…about everything." She shot Bethanne an anxious look. "I'll call you this afternoon, okay?"

"Of course." Bethanne blew her a kiss and Annie sent her off with a big smile. Certain that she was a few minutes early, Ruth headed into the lobby in search of a newspaper and a cup of coffee. To her surprise, Royce was already waiting, his newspaper unfolded in front of him.

"Good morning," she said. Just seeing him made her pulse race uncontrollably. It seemed impossible that fifty years had passed. Being with him felt so familiar, like rediscovering a language she'd spoken as a child. But could he ever forgive what she'd done?

Royce refolded his newspaper and stood. "Ruth…" he began, and then fell silent.

"You're early," Ruth said nervously. "I hardly slept last night," she confessed, hoping he could read what was on her mind.

Royce frowned and looked away. "I didn't sleep much myself."

"I'm hoping we can really...talk this morning."

He nodded. "I suppose we should." Reaching for her hand, he tucked it in the crook of his arm. "We have a lot to discuss, but before we do, I want you to know what bliss it's been to see you again."

"I feel the same." Ruth had never expected to have a second chance with him, and this time she was determined not to ruin things between them.

He escorted her to his car, and opened her door the way he had when they were teenagers. Royce had always been a gentleman, even as an impoverished boy of eighteen.

Instead of driving to his home on the river, he went in the direction of Orchid Island.

"Where are we going?" Ruth asked.

"I thought we'd start the day with a glass of freshly squeezed Indian River orange juice."

She guessed he was taking her to his childhood home. "Your father sold the groves, didn't he?"

"He did." Royce grinned over at her. "My brother bought him out."

"Arnie?" She squinted at him in astonishment.

"Benny," Royce corrected. He was the oldest in the family. Arnie, she recalled, was the youngest.

When they got to the property, he drove right in, along a row of perfectly aligned orange trees, stopping at the end. "Remember our prom night?" he asked.

Ruth laughed. "How could I forget it?"

"Even my children and *their* children know the story of how we arrived at the dance looking like a pair of miserable water rats."

"Mine, too."

Royce glanced at her. "Did I understand you right? Didn't you say that Bethanne and Grant are divorced?"

"They are."

"They looked like a couple to me."

Ruth hugged herself. "They did, didn't they? I can't tell you how thrilled I am to see the two of them together again. We came upon some bikers—motorcyclists—on the road... Well, Bethanne seems to have taken a liking to one of them. I have to tell you how concerned I am that she might actually be falling for this guy."

"That didn't seem to be the case last night."

"From your lips to God's ear," Ruth said fervently. "Grant went through a midlife crisis," she said by way of explanation.

"Which led to the divorce, I take it?"

"It did, but thankfully he realized how foolish he's been. I'm grateful that he's smart enough to see what's truly important. He's doing everything he can to get his family back."

"I wish him well."

"Thank you." Ruth drew in a deep, fortifying breath and forged ahead, fearing that if she put this off any longer, she wouldn't have the courage to say it later. "Speaking of being foolish, I—I want to apologize for the way I ended things...." She turned in her seat to face him, twisting the strap of her handbag. "I've agonized over my actions all these years, wishing I could rewrite that part of our history...." She let her words trail off. A knot had formed in her throat. She didn't list her offenses; he knew them as well as she did. "More than anything, I regret causing you pain. I was young and so foolish and I wish—" Her voice cracked.

In the silence that followed, Royce placed his hand over Ruth's, which still clenched her purse strap.

"I forgave you a long time ago," he said slowly. His gaze flickered to hers, serious and tender. For a moment Ruth was speechless.

"But how could you?" she finally croaked out.

He smiled wistfully, staring at the orderly stretch of trees. "I won't say it was easy…" he began. "For a while I was convinced I'd never love any woman again." He shook his head at some unnamed memory. "Fortunately, I was wrong."

So he'd loved his wife. Ruth was relieved to know that.

"Life has a way of setting things right," he continued with a philosophical shrug. "I married Barbara, and we had three remarkable children. I have no regrets." He squeezed Ruth's hand lightly. "I don't want you to have any, either. You and Richard were happy, weren't you?"

She nodded. She *had* been happy—as happy as she'd made up her mind to be. She and Richard both had their faults, but they'd created a good life together. And while she'd often wondered what would've happened if she'd married Royce, she hadn't allowed herself to obsess over it.

"Do you think we can really put the past behind us?" she ventured. "Can you accept my apology?"

Royce looked over at her.

"Of course," he said. His eyes brimmed with forgiveness, and something more. Ruth released her death grip on her purse and let her fingers curl around Royce's. For long minutes, they sat there in silence, each afraid to break the spell.

Royce's brother Benny met them soon after. They exchanged greetings, and then Benny gave Ruth a short tour, which concluded with Benny pouring them each a glass of fresh-squeezed, extra-sweet orange juice.

Ruth sipped hers, savoring this reminder of her childhood. "I'd forgotten how good Indian River oranges are." She sighed. This was orange juice at its finest; after all, Floridians took pride in the fact that it had been served at the White House.

As they walked back to the car, Royce pointed to a gnarled, fruit-laden tree at the edge of the grove. "I kissed you there for the first time," he said, nostalgia coloring his voice.

"Not there," Ruth said. "It was the second tree back."

Royce stared at her in amazement. "You remember?"

"Of course I do." Royce had always been—and evidently still was—a hopeless romantic. "I'd dropped by on some pretext about bringing your homework to you or something equally inane." She rolled her eyes at the transparency of it. "You walked me out to the car and asked if I'd ever been in an orange grove before."

"You hadn't, so I offered to show you around," he went on. His face lit up at the memory.

"I lied," Ruth crowed. "Good grief, Royce, I'd grown up around the groves!"

"You lied?" He pretended to be shocked.

"I'm no dummy. I was hoping you were going to kiss me and I didn't want to ruin my chances."

Royce opened the car door for her. "As I recall, I was all teeth and no finesse."

"As I recall," she countered, "the minute your lips met mine, my toes curled up and I nearly swooned."

Royce laughed and Ruth did, too. He raised her hand to his lips and gently pressed a kiss against her knuckles. "I can assure you I'm a much better kisser these days."

"For that matter, so am I," she said archly.

They drove back across the Seventeenth Avenue bridge, heading south once they reached the island. Royce's home presided over a narrow strip of land, with a view of the Atlantic Ocean from the front door and the Indian River from the back. Parking in the circular driveway outside his two-story house, he led her up the brick steps. When he ushered her in, the first things she saw were the large French doors that offered an expansive view of the Indian River. It wasn't really a river, she knew—it was part of an inland waterway that stretched from Florida to Maine. Filled with brackish water, the waterway teemed with fish and fowl and was home to various marine animals. As a child she could remember lying on her belly on the dock, petting the manatees. Before the days when such contact was frowned upon, Ruth had discovered that manatees and dolphins were intensely curious creatures, apparently as eager to learn about humans as humans were to learn about them.

"Oh, Royce, this is magnificent." She stepped around the table in the center of the foyer, barely noticing the huge floral arrangement that dominated it. "How long have you lived here?"

"A while now..." Royce gestured around him. "Ten years, I'd say. Since I retired from the math department at the University of Florida."

"You always wanted a home on the river," she reminded him. In their teens they'd spent many afternoons talking about their future. Naturally they'd be married. They'd chosen to ignore the fact that her family disapproved of him. They'd blithely planned to have two children and had even chosen their names: Molly and Royce, Jr.

"You were going to be a stewardess, remember?" Royce stared out over the water. "Sorry, I guess these days they're called flight attendants."

"Oh, yes." That would've been a dream job, being able to travel around the world. "Instead, I stayed home and brought up my children. Richard was a good provider and wanted it that way," she said matter-of-factly. "Later, after they were grown, I did tons of volunteer work."

Following his father's example, Grant had wanted the same for his wife and children. Bethanne had only worked outside the home briefly, before Andrew was born. From then on, her daughter-in-law had been an energetic and committed homemaker. It had been a rather old-fashioned choice, perhaps, and at odds with the times, since those years were the height of the women's movement. Still, Bethanne had seemed content, throwing herself into supporting Grant's career and being an ultra-attentive mother. Oh, how Ruth wished Grant had appreciated his wife more.

"What are you thinking?" Royce asked, moving to stand close beside her.

"Oh, nothing...just getting caught up in memories."

She shrugged, the silk of her blouse whispering against Royce's arm.

"Of us?" he asked quietly.

"No...my son. What Grant failed to realize when he left Bethanne was that she was the secret behind his success. She filled the same role for him that I did for Richard." Ruth shook her head. "It's easy to take a wife for granted, I suppose." She raised her eyes to meet Royce's. "Bethanne gave everything she had to my son, and he tossed her aside for a younger woman."

"He wouldn't be the first man to make that mistake," Royce said.

"And I doubt he'll be the last." Ruth sighed.

Royce wrapped his arm around her and pulled her close. "We still worry about our children, don't we?" he murmured in her ear. "No matter what their ages."

"I can't help myself," Ruth admitted miserably, leaning into Royce's comforting bulk. Grant wasn't her only concern. Robin was so similar to her father, and Ruth often feared her daughter would end up just like Richard, consumed by her job. In her darkest moments, Ruth imagined Robin dying young from a heart attack, without ever having really *lived*.

"Tell me about your children," she said, hungry to learn everything about him.

"Well...Peter, my oldest, is an attorney. He's married and has two children. Maureen is a pharmacist who was playing doctor with her dolls from the time she was two years old. She was constantly scribbling prescriptions and taking them to the drugstore. Our youngest son, Kent, went into the ministry, serving God in Haiti."

"Oh, Royce, it sounds like you have an incredible family." Ruth looked up at him.

He nodded. "I'm truly blessed."

"You had a good wife," Ruth said.

"I did," he agreed. "The kids turned out well, mostly because of Barbara—I miss her every single day."

"Who does Craig belong to?" Ruth asked.

"He's Maureen's son. He works with Kent part of the year in Haiti. He's still got a year of medical school. He has a true commitment to serving those who are suffering and in need of healing."

"He seems like a wonderful young man."

"He is, and he was quite taken with Annie." Royce winked as he said it.

Ruth beamed. "She liked him, too."

"Last night when I asked Craig to join us for dinner, he said yes, but I could tell he wasn't keen on the idea. When I woke up this morning, he'd left a message on my phone, thanking me for introducing him to Annie."

Ruth laughed delightedly. Annie was going to have plenty of male choices, she thought. That boy in Europe had some real competition now.

Royce turned to her, smiling. "Would you like a ride down the river?"

Ruth clutched at his hand, her face alight with pleasure. "Oh, Royce, could we really?"

"Maybe we could take a stroll down memory lane, as well."

"That sounds heavenly."

"Do you remember John Bolinger?" he asked as he led the way to the river dock.

"Of course. He was a good friend of yours."

"Still is. He'll be at the reunion."

"What about Connie Keenan?" Ruth wondered.

"Last I heard, she'd signed up, too."

Ruth clung to Royce's arm as they stepped carefully across the planks of the dock. He stopped just short of the motorboat anchored at the end of the walkway. Turning to face her, he lifted his free hand to touch her cheek.

"For me, the most important name on that list was yours. Oh, Ruth, I can't tell you how happy I am to see you again."

Ruth couldn't speak for the emotions that flooded her. Tears pricked her eyes and she lowered her face so Royce wouldn't see.

"So am I," she finally managed. "So am I."

Twenty-Six

Bethanne spent a lazy morning at the hotel, sleeping in late, while both Annie and Ruth went out for the day. Annie took off early with Craig, and Ruth was with Royce. Those two had been inseparable almost from the moment they'd seen each other the night before. Bethanne hoped they could resolve the past. It seemed promising because they obviously both wanted the same thing.

Young love, first love. Grant had been Bethanne's first love, and Ruth was right. There was indeed something special about giving your heart away for the first time. While it might not be possible to recapture what they'd once shared, she'd always have her memories of loving Grant.

Grant.

Max.

All at once Bethanne was too confused to know what she wanted. With Max everything was fresh and new. With Grant she carried—and would always carry—the baggage of his infidelity. Someone looking at the situation from outside might feel a decision between the two men was simple because of that painful history. It wasn't. She and Max hadn't even had their first disagreement. To this point all was bliss, but she was mature enough to understand that wouldn't last.

Bethanne had the whole morning to herself. After a leisurely breakfast of orange juice and toast by the pool, she took a long walk on the beach. She'd purposely left her cell phone behind, hoping to duck any and all responsibilities for the next hour or so.

The surf pounded the shore as she strolled down the sandy shoreline, which was nearly deserted. The breeze offered a respite from the heat and humidity. She wore a large straw hat she'd bought at the hotel gift shop and walked barefoot, her feet making soft indentations in the wet sand.

Mainly, her mind was occupied with thoughts of Max. Other than their brief conversation the day before, they hadn't spoken again. She realized he was giving her this time with her family, in much the same way Grant had given her time with Max. Was respect between rivals like honor among thieves? That concept made her smile, even if the comparison didn't *quite* work.

She tried to be sensible and realistic about Max, and yet whenever she thought about never talking to him again, never seeing him again, an instant sadness settled over her. It didn't seem possible that she'd come to care for a man so quickly and yet she had.

No one had made her feel the way Max did—at least not since the divorce. After six years of grief and anger, six years of forgettable relationships, Bethanne felt she might be incapable of giving her heart to another man...ever.

She'd loved Grant completely, totally. When she spoke her wedding vows she'd meant them to be forever. *Until death do us part...* Not *until someone better, cuter, younger or sexier comes along.* Forever.

Grant.

Last evening he'd been so good with both Annie and Ruth, and yes, with her, too. He seemed sincere in his desire to make amends. As Ruth had said more than once, it took a big man to admit when he was wrong. Grant wanted her back and yet she had to ask herself: Could he still bring her happiness? Could they be happy together again? She'd forgiven him to the best of her ability, but she wasn't confident she could trust him. Whenever he came home late, how would she know he hadn't been with another woman? She'd never asked if there'd been anyone before Tiffany. In truth, she didn't want to know, and chose to believe Tiffany had been his only indiscretion.

Sitting on the beach, she brought her knees up and dragged her fingers through the sand while her thoughts darted like bumblebees, flitting in one direction and then another. This decision was the most difficult she'd ever had to make.

Giving Grant hope for a reconciliation meant she'd have to forget about Max. If they were to have any chance of being a couple again, she'd have to give the relationship one hundred percent. That probably required counseling, for him *and* for her.

Bethanne wasn't so naive that she didn't realize she'd played a role in the breakdown of their marriage, too. She'd become complacent, too involved in her children and their activities. Grant left it up to her to arrange their social outings and she'd grown lax about setting aside time for just the two of them. They hadn't done anything to nurture their marriage. The blame for that, she knew, should be equally divided.

Another flaw on her part was her inability to recognize what was happening in Grant's life. In retrospect she must've been blind not to have noticed the signs. They'd all been there, as blatant as could be—almost as if Grant had *wanted* her to know. Perhaps he did, so she'd do something to stop him, something to show how much she loved him. But Bethanne had been oblivious to it all. She'd ignored the significance of countless late nights at the office and some imaginary big deal that never took place. Ignored the extra time Grant spent on his grooming each morning. She'd taken everything at face value, including the small unexpected gifts he brought home for no particular reason, gifts no doubt motivated by guilt. She'd ignored all of these signs, content to go blindly about her life, wrapped up in her daily routines.

Andrew had pitched for his high school baseball team that spring and Grant had attended only one game. Not once did she question his excuses. Their son was about to head into his senior year of high school and she was working on the grad night committee and—

Oh, what good did it do to dredge up ancient history? Closing her eyes, Bethanne fought back waves of regret, determined not to let them drown her in sadness and confusion. She was past this, past Grant.

Wasn't she?

"Bethanne?"

At the sound of her name, she turned to find her ex-husband walking toward her. He looked relaxed and fit and—all right, she'd admit it—handsome. He wore white cotton pants and a printed floral shirt that showed off his tanned arms.

Bethanne glanced at her watch. It couldn't possibly be one o'clock yet. Wrong. It was almost one-thirty.

Grant sat down in the sand next to her. "I didn't know what to think when I couldn't get ahold of you."

"I had no idea so much time had passed." She'd been on the beach for more than two hours. Thankfully, she'd lathered on sunscreen; otherwise, she would've burned to a crisp.

"Have you had lunch?"

She shook her head.

"There's a fish-and-chip place down the beach. Royce mentioned it yesterday. How about that?"

"Sure." She wasn't hungry but he probably was.

Grant helped her to her feet, and they started walking along the beach in the opposite direction. He took her hand, intertwining their fingers.

"Do you remember our first date?" he said.

Of course she did. "We had fish and chips on the Seattle waterfront."

"And I didn't have enough money for two orders so we shared the one," he said, grinning down at her.

"And the seagull stole your french fry." She smiled at the memory of Grant chasing after the bird, demanding his french fry back. She'd laughed herself silly and recalled thinking she could really fall for this guy. "We were so young."

Grant's eyes smiled back at her. They reached the small restaurant and chose to eat indoors in the cool, air-conditioned room. The tables were mismatched but the aromas that filled the place were enough to convince Bethanne she had more of an appetite than she realized.

They shared an order of fish and fries, for old times' sake. When their meal was delivered, Grant said, "That wasn't the only time I was short on cash. Remember the night Andrew was born?"

As if she could ever forget. "What I remember is your panic when I told you I might be in labor. You immediately started doing the breathing exercises *I* was supposed to do until I thought you were about to hyperventilate." Bethanne had been afraid they'd have to call an Aid Car for her husband.

"What you didn't know was that I hadn't paid the doctor everything we owed him and I was worried he wouldn't deliver the baby without being paid."

"Dr. McMahon never said a word."

"Thank goodness." Grant slathered a french fry with ketchup and popped it in his mouth.

"You so badly wanted a son," she reminded him.

"I did not," he insisted. "I would've been happy with either."

"So you said," she muttered, and picked up a fry, dipping it in a pool of ketchup. "But when the doctor announced we had a son, you gave the loudest whoop I'd ever heard and high-fived the nurse."

"I most certainly did not."

"I was there. I remember it clearly, Grant Hamlin."

"I expected another boy when you had Annie." He smiled, his gaze turned inward. "I fell head over heels for that baby girl."

Bethanne had to agree. Annie held her daddy's heart

in the palm of her hand the first moment he laid eyes on her. The only time their relationship had been strained was shortly before and then after the divorce. Everything seemed back to normal between them now, and for that Bethanne was grateful. Annie needed her father's love and approval perhaps even more than she did Bethanne's.

"Do you remember when Andrew got pneumonia?"

Bethanne set down her fork and reached for a napkin to wipe the grease from her fingers. Their son had been just eighteen months old and she'd already taken him to the pediatrician twice that week. The nurse had made her feel she was being overprotective and a bother. That night Andrew wasn't any better and she'd held her son in her arms for hours as he struggled to breathe. First thing the next morning, she drove him to the doctor again, ready to face down that dragon of a nurse, only to have the doctor explode in anger at her for not getting Andrew to the hospital. Bethanne had burst into tears. She'd phoned Grant, who met her at Emergency and gently took her in his arms. He'd been her strength when their son was put in an oxygen tent.

"There were some hard times when the kids were growing up, weren't there?" Bethanne said. She swore Annie had the worst case of chicken pox of any child she knew. They went down her throat and into her stomach. The poor child had been miserable for days. No one else had slept, either.

"We had plenty of good memories, too."

Bethanne had to agree they did. "Like our tenth wedding anniversary."

"Rome."

"And you were so confident your high school Italian would be enough for us to get around by ourselves," Bethanne said, wondering if he recalled some of their adventures.

"We could afford the plane fare and that cheap hotel and food, of course, but not much else," Grant was quick to add.

Not that Bethanne needed any reminders. Their budget had been squeaky tight and they were unable to afford any tours. All at once she began to laugh. When Grant gave her an odd look, she covered her mouth and muttered, "The cheese. Don't you remember the cheese?"

Grant stared at her blankly.

"You *can't* have forgotten the cheese."

"We bought cheese?" he asked, his eyes widening.

Still laughing, Bethanne nudged him. "You're kidding—you really don't remember? You were so sure you could make yourself understood. The Englishman at the hotel suggested a cheese shop, but somehow we got the directions wrong."

Grant shrugged; the story appeared to have been erased from his memory.

"We stopped in another store to ask about the cheese shop, and the owner kept shaking her head as you chatted away, looking for directions."

"No doubt in brilliant Italian."

"No doubt," she echoed. "Then the owner smiled, went into the back room and returned with two candlesticks."

"Leave it to you to remember that," Grant said with a grin. "We did eventually find the cheese shop, didn't we?"

"Eventually, after we stopped laughing."

Grant's eyes darkened then, and he grew serious as he reached for a paper napkin and dabbed the edges of his mouth. "We were happy, Bethanne."

"Yes," she said, as her amusement faded. "We were." He'd told her that more than once, and these reminiscences had confirmed the truth of it.

"We can be again."

Their eyes held. She longed to believe him, longed for some reassurance that the possibility was as real as it felt in that moment. Life during the past six years had taught her that the future didn't come with any guarantees.

"I want to believe that, Grant."

"I hope you'll give me the opportunity to make you happy." He took her hand. "All I'm asking is that we put the past behind us and try again."

She nodded, unsure how to respond. Being with Max had felt so right but he remained a mystery. When it came down to it, she knew shockingly little about him. He kept everything close to his chest, almost as if he was afraid to share too much of himself with her…with anyone.

Grant was safe, a known quantity. Yes, his betrayal had come between them, damaged them; despite that they knew each other as well as any two people who'd spent twenty years as husband and wife possibly could.

Or did they? She couldn't help wondering if Grant recognized the changes in her.

"Why the frown?" he asked.

"I was frowning?" Bethanne hadn't been aware that her uncertainty showed so easily on her face. "Do you *really* know me, Grant?" she asked. "The woman I am today isn't the woman I was when we divorced."

"I realize that. I'll admit you surprised me, Bethanne. You have an uncanny mind for business."

"I had a good teacher." She doubted that Grant knew how much she'd learned from him.

"You did?" he asked, astonishment reflected in his eyes.

"Yes," she told him. "You. When I hosted those dinner parties," she elaborated, "I socialized with your business associates, listened to their stories—and yours. You're good with people, Grant. They like and trust you right away. That's a gift."

"I never understood how much of a team we were until...until I was on my own," Grant said. "You did far more than arrange those social events. You were my emotional support, my encourager. I owed a great deal of my success to you and I was too self-absorbed to see it."

Hearing him admit her importance to his career felt good. More than good. His acknowledgment validated her in ways she hadn't expected.

"Thank you," she whispered, hardly able to speak.

"I realize now that I didn't appreciate you nearly enough. Fool that I am, I walked away from the one person in this world who complemented me better than anyone else ever could."

He leaned toward her and she toward him, and their lips met in a sweet, gentle kiss.

Bethanne drew back. If she thought this time in Florida, away from Max, would clear her head, she was wrong. She stood abruptly and grabbed her purse, ready to go. Their kiss had been...comfortable. And that had unsettled her.

Watching her closely, Grant stood, too. He'd paid for their lunch when he'd placed the order, so they were free to leave. They walked back to the hotel, side by side. He didn't reach for her hand and Bethanne was grateful. She wasn't sure what she felt. No, that wasn't it. She felt too *much*. Too many different emotions. Contradictory emotions. She longed to call Max and tell him what had happened, discuss it with him. But they'd made no promises to each other, no commitments. In fact, everything had been left unresolved.

As they walked, Grant peered down the beach. "Is that Annie and Craig?" he asked.

Bethanne looked up and nodded.

Annie saw them and waved, and then, with Craig at her side, she raced toward Bethanne and Grant.

"Mom, Dad," Annie said, sounding breathless and excited. "Craig and I have the most fantastic idea."

"Which is?" Bethanne asked.

Still gasping, Annie pressed her hand over her heart. "We want to redo prom night for Grandma and Royce."

"The whole thing," Craig said, equally excited. "From beginning to end."

"What do you mean? How exactly?"

"The dinner and photos, a limo and a dance and everything," Annie explained.

"I've already talked to the manager of the restaurant at your hotel and there's a private room we can use," Craig said.

Annie exchanged a smile with Royce's grandson. "Craig has a friend who drives part-time for a limo company, and he checked and they have a car available Saturday night…."

"I know Gramps would love to redo that night."

"Can we?" Annie's eyes seemed twice their normal size as she implored them to consider the idea.

Grant looked at Bethanne and she looked at him. She'd had enough experience throwing parties that this one wouldn't be a problem.

"We'll make it happen," she said.

Grant nodded. "Just tell me what you need me to do."

Twenty-Seven

"What are we doing?" Ruth asked in a bewildered voice. Her eyes shot to Bethanne, who merely shrugged. They wouldn't be able to keep the secret much longer, but she knew Annie wanted to play this out to the last possible second.

"We're going shopping, Grandma," Annie said, steering her grandmother out of the hotel room and down the hallway toward the lobby.

"But why? I brought everything I need. Will you two kindly tell me what you've got up your sleeves? And don't you say it's nothing, because I know better."

"You *don't* have everything you need," Annie insisted.

"Surely you've learned not to argue with Annie," Bethanne said, closing the door to their room and hurrying after them.

"Just where are you taking me?" Ruth demanded.

"Shopping."

"I found a perfect store right here on the beach that I want to show you," Annie said. "We can walk there. Come on, Grandma."

"I don't know what you two are up to," Ruth muttered, clearly confused but curious nonetheless.

"What makes you think we're up to anything?" Bethanne asked innocently. She'd done her best to arrange everything without raising Ruth's suspicions, but it'd been difficult. For the past twenty-four hours she'd met with florists, musicians and photographers. She'd run herself ragged and worked a miracle. Or what she hoped would be a miracle. Grant had talked to Royce and he'd agreed to do whatever he could to pull this off.

Royce had contacted a number of their high school friends in town, including Jane and Diane. Meanwhile, Annie, Craig and Grant had been busy decorating the hotel restaurant's private room, recreating prom night with the theme of *Breakfast at Tiffany's,* the same as it'd been fifty years earlier.

"I think it's time you spilled the beans," Ruth said, planting her feet squarely on the sidewalk and refusing to budge.

Annie's shoulders heaved in a sigh. "I guess we might as well," she said, glancing at Bethanne.

"I suppose you're right," Bethanne agreed, trying not to smile.

"Okay," Annie said, looking at her grandmother. "Craig and I were talking and I asked him if he knew what happened the night of your senior prom."

"He did," Bethanne added, "because he was well aware of what a disaster it turned out to be."

"And I was thinking," Annie said, picking up the story, "what a shame it was that the two of you were so disappointed. Then Craig said it was too bad we couldn't turn back the clock and do it all over again."

Annie threw her hands in the air as if that was explanation enough.

"That's when the two of them came to Grant and me," Bethanne said.

"With the idea of redoing prom night for you and Royce." Annie's face glowed with pride. "Only this time we're going to make sure everything goes perfectly."

"Redoing prom night," Ruth repeated.

"So right now we're taking you to pick up your prom dress."

"Pick it up? My goodness, I can't imagine where that old dress went…. The rain must have ruined it. In any case, I don't recall ever seeing it again. And need I mention that it most likely wouldn't fit even if I *could* locate it?"

"Royce had a picture your mother took that night. Apparently, you'd given it to him."

What he didn't know was that Bethanne and Grant had that photograph blown up so the couple would see themselves at seventeen and eighteen as they walked into the prom.

"I found a dress shop here in Vero," Annie said. "I showed them the photo and asked if they had any dresses similar to the one in the photograph."

"They couldn't have anything close to that dress." Ruth shook her head. "Fashion's changed a lot over the years."

"You're right, they didn't." Bethanne was eager to fill in the details. "But they knew of a secondhand shop that had high-end wear at reasonable prices and, well, I found a gown with an empire waist and took it to the seamstress who works at that dress shop…and all I can say is that she's *very* talented."

Ruth looked stunned.

"Come on, Grandma," Annie said, urging her grandmother along the sidewalk. "We haven't got all afternoon, you know."

"We need you to try on the dress first," Bethanne told her.

"First?"

"Yes. You have a hair and nail appointment next."

"Hair and nails," Ruth echoed as though in a trance. "I feel like someone needs to pinch me. Is this really happening?"

"It's really happening," Annie said gleefully.

"And Royce knows about this?"

"Yes, some of it, but only because we needed his cooperation. We didn't tell him until we had everything in place."

"Royce *wants* to do this?"

"He does." Bethanne slipped an arm around her and guided Ruth toward the dress shop. "He knows and approves."

"He's excited, Grandma. He always felt bad about how that night turned out."

"It wasn't his fault."

"He told me how wonderful you were," Bethanne said. "You could've been really unpleasant about it but you weren't."

The owner of the dress shop met them at the door and held it open. "I think this is a delightful idea," she said, welcoming them inside. She led them to the back where the seamstress stood waiting.

"This way," she said, and gestured toward one of the dressing rooms.

Ruth started inside—and stopped. Then, looking over

her shoulder, she stared at Bethanne and Annie. "Why, it's almost identical to my dress the night of the prom. Even the bow is the same." The lavender, floor-length empire-waist dress with its straight skirt and cap sleeves resembled the dress in the photograph to a remarkable degree. The seamstress had done exquisite work.

"Oh, Ruth," Bethanne breathed once her mother-in-law had tried on the dress. "You're absolutely gorgeous."

Annie nodded. "Grandma, this is going to be a night you'll remember for the rest of your life."

"I can't believe you'd do this for Royce and me," Ruth said tearfully.

"Mom and Dad worked really hard on this," Annie told her.

Rarely had Bethanne seen her daughter happier. It wasn't until she'd overheard Annie talking to Grant the day before that she understood why. In Annie's eyes the fact that Grant and Bethanne were getting along so well meant a reconciliation was imminent.

Until then, Bethanne hadn't fully accepted that her attitude toward Grant had changed. Without realizing it, she'd lowered her guard and allowed herself to become vulnerable to him. That recognition gave her pause. They'd worked together, running all over town, and had frequent "strategy" discussions. They'd laughed until they were giddy, and sipped wine until she felt light-headed. When Grant kissed her goodbye she could almost believe the divorce had never happened.

If it was possible to turn back the clock for Ruth, could she do it for herself and Grant, too? Bethanne didn't know.

Glancing at her watch, she clapped her hands. "We

have places to go and people to see," she said, dismissing her thoughts. She couldn't let herself get sidetracked. Not right now. She had too much to do.

By seven on Saturday, just six days before the actual reunion, all the preparations for the prom had been made. Royce and Grant were at his house, where the car was due to arrive any minute, while Bethanne kept Ruth company at the hotel.

Bethanne had purchased a party dress of her own at the secondhand shop. A frilly dress that was the kind of outfit Brenda Lee or Connie Francis might have worn, with a short skirt flaring out from the waist. A wide silk ribbon belted around her middle set off the strapless top.

"I feel seventeen all over again," Ruth said, running a hand along the front of her gown.

"Good," Bethanne said. "We want you to feel young and in love for your senior prom."

"Oh, Bethanne, I do. I really do. Royce is just the way I remember him…and so much more. I think I'm falling in love again."

"All we want is for you to be happy, Ruth."

"I know, and I appreciate that more than I can say."

Bethanne couldn't recall a time she'd seen Ruth this excited.

A knock sounded at the door, and Bethanne answered it to find Royce standing on the other side, dressed in a tuxedo and holding a wrist corsage in his hand.

"Is Ruth here?" he asked.

Ruth stepped forward and Royce's jaw sagged. "Ruth, my goodness, that's the same dress you wore the night of our prom."

"It isn't the same dress. It's a re-creation…. Annie and Bethanne arranged this."

He couldn't seem to take his eyes off her. "There's a car waiting for us outside," he mumbled.

"A car?" Ruth asked. She gave Bethanne a puzzled look. "I thought you said the prom was taking place right here at the hotel."

"It is," Bethanne responded in a whisper. "Just go with him."

"Okay," Ruth whispered back.

Royce helped her with her corsage, and Ruth pinned on the boutonniere Bethanne had ordered earlier. She walked them through the lobby and out the door, where the young chauffeur stood by the limousine. As soon as they appeared, he made a sweeping motion with his arm and held the back door open.

Royce handed Ruth inside and then hurried around the car. When they'd driven off, Grant showed up. "Where are they going?" Bethanne asked.

"For a ride down Ocean Drive," he said. "Things weren't quite ready yet, so we needed them to kill about fifteen minutes. Besides, the limo ride is part of the experience."

Bethanne followed Grant through the restaurant, where they attracted quite a few curious glances. With Grant attired in a suit and jacket, and she in her short, frilly dress, they must have looked like actors who'd stepped off the stage of a Broadway play about the 1960s.

Annie dashed toward her when Bethanne entered the room. "What do you think, Mom?" she asked eagerly.

Bethanne drew in her breath as she proceeded through an archway of colorful balloons. Annie, Grant and Craig had done a marvelous job. The band—five musicians and a lead singer—were off to one side behind a waist-high barrier of red velvet with "Class of 1961" emblazoned in gold lettering across the front. Several small tables, with lamps on each one, were artfully arranged around the room.

Other couples started to arrive, and the photographer came forward to snap their pictures.

Annie greeted each couple, giving them a printed program and offering the women a dance card.

"Everything looks so real," Bethanne told Grant. "I feel like a time traveler." The life-size photograph of Royce and Ruth was propped against one wall, framed by tiny twinkling lights.

"Just wait until the king and queen are crowned."

"Oh-h." Bethanne brought one hand to her mouth. She hadn't thought of that, but Grant had. They'd worked together to make this happen for Ruth and Royce, put aside their differences and become a team again. Even a few months ago, she wouldn't have believed it possible, wouldn't have believed they were capable of accomplishing this evening.

When the starring couple arrived, the band began to play, and almost before she was aware of it, Bethanne found herself in Grant's arms as he led her onto the small, makeshift dance floor.

"That's 'Moon River.' It's the theme song from *Breakfast at Tiffany's*. Andy Williams sang it the night I went to the concert with Grandma in Branson," Annie said as she and Royce's grandson glided past Bethanne and Grant.

"Apparently, Andy made an impression on our daughter," Grant said, smiling down at her.

"So it seems."

"Does it feel like high school all over again?" he asked, his head close to hers.

Bethanne nodded. "It's an amazing night."

"And it's only just begun," Grant murmured.

She couldn't imagine what else he had planned. But she was about to find out....

About an hour into the night, the band paused and Grant walked to the stage and reached for the microphone.

"The time has come to crown the king and queen of prom night," he said, sounding every bit the professional spokesperson. "I know the suspense is almost more than we can bear."

There was polite laughter. Jane and Diane and their dates—their husbands—gathered around Ruth and Royce.

"The ballots have been tallied and the decision made." When he announced Royce's name, a loud round of applause was followed by shouts and cheers.

"Speech, speech," the crowd chanted.

Royce stepped forward, and Grant placed a crown on his head, then handed him the microphone. "There's only one woman I want by my side this evening, and that's Ruth," he said.

"Then so be it." Grant held a second crown as Craig escorted Ruth to the small stage. Grant carefully set the crown on her head as tears glistened in her eyes. Then, right in front of everyone, Royce kissed her full on the lips.

The crowd loved it. So did Bethanne, who exchanged a warm look with Grant. They'd done this. It hadn't been easy, but all their effort was worth seeing the joy on Ruth's face. And on Royce's...

The music started again, and the "royal" couple walked

onto the dance floor, soon to be joined by others. Without conscious thought, Bethanne moved toward Grant.

He slipped his arms around her as if they'd never been apart. As if they were still a couple. A team. The two of them against the world.

"I can't thank you enough," Grant whispered as he drew her close.

"You worked as hard as I did."

"I wasn't talking about redoing Mom's prom night."

"Oh?" Bethanne wasn't sure what he did mean, then.

"I want to thank you for being the incredible woman you are, for giving my life meaning and for offering me hope that there's a chance for the two of us again."

She smiled up at him and closed her eyes as she allowed the rhythm of the music to carry her. Their steps matched easily, smoothly, as innate as breathing. They used to dance together like this, but that was in another lifetime….

Twenty-Eight

Max Scranton pulled his motorcycle into the driveway of the home he'd once shared with Kate and their daughter. He hadn't been here in more than three years. This was the first time he'd come back to Monterey since climbing on his Harley. He'd never intended to stay away this long, but there'd been no reason to return.

Until now. Until he'd met Bethanne.

Time lost all meaning as he sat on the bike in his driveway and stared at the house. He'd expected a flood of grief and regrets, but he felt almost nothing. No guilt, no heartache, no melancholy. His overwhelming emotion was sadness for what no longer existed. The life he'd known here was gone. He'd handed the business over to his brother and had lost touch with the majority of his friends.

Shutting down the engine, he climbed off the bike and removed his helmet. The key to the house was hidden under a fake rock near the front door. His brother and Rooster routinely stopped by to check on the place and give him updates, although he wasn't all that interested. He'd wanted to put the house on the market, but that would've meant returning and cleaning it out. He'd found the task too daunting.

The car pulling in behind him took him by surprise. Rooster.

He should've realized his friend would show up. Rooster looked quite different in slacks and a shirt with a button-down collar than he did in his leather vest and chaps. Max wondered what Ruth and Annie would think if they could see Rooster now. They probably wouldn't recognize him; the biker bore little resemblance to the successful advertising executive he was for most of the year.

Rooster got out of his car and closed the door, the sound reverberating in the stillness of the late afternoon. His friend joined him on the porch.

"What are you doing here?" Max demanded.

Max had phoned Rooster a few hours earlier, when he'd arrived in town. They'd parted ways the week before because of Rooster's business commitments. He should've known his friend wouldn't leave it at a simple call. "I was in the neighborhood."

Max didn't bother to respond to the obvious lie.

"Okay, I wasn't. I figured you might need some company."

"I'm fine."

Rooster's skeptical look revealed his doubt. "Do you want me to go in with you?"

Max studied the locked door as he considered his reply. He wasn't ready to face this alone. He appreciated the fact that Rooster was with him, although he'd be hard-pressed to admit it.

He finally inserted the key and opened the door. For an instant he stood there paralyzed. Moving forward required an effort so great he began to sweat. He went in and, after three steps, again stood motionless.

Noticing that Rooster was watching him intently, Max advanced another step. The house was exactly as he'd left it, exactly as he remembered. Directly in front of him was a stunning view of the Pacific Ocean through the floor-to-ceiling windows. White leather furniture was taste-fully displayed; a black grand piano rested in one corner of the living room and a huge natural-rock fireplace took up the far wall. The original artwork was worth ten times what Kate had paid for it. She'd always had an eye for talent.

"What are you thinking?" Rooster asked. "How do you feel?"

Max heard the hesitation in his friend's voice. He didn't know what he was *supposed* to think, what he should feel. Closing his eyes he tried to remember what it was like when he'd lived here with Kate and their daughter. Happy. He'd always love Kate, but she was gone and he was alive. He hadn't realized how much life he was capable of until he'd met Bethanne and discovered he could feel again, love again.

"This is a beautiful house," Rooster commented.

"Kate loved it," Max said. And so had he. Their home had been a place where friends and family gathered, where they enjoyed good food and wine and one another's com-pany. "I did, too."

He moved into the kitchen, and then the family room.

Portraits of Katherine at different ages lined one wall; her wheelchair and special computer had been stored in her bedroom.

"I kept an eye on the wine cellar," Rooster said.

Despite himself, Max grinned. "I assumed you would."

"Do you want me to get us a bottle?"

That sounded like a good idea. "Go ahead."

Rooster disappeared, and Max found two wineglasses in the alcove off the kitchen and brought them out. One day he'd share a bottle of exquisite wine with Bethanne....

The minute she came to mind, he experienced a burning need to hear her voice. He missed her smile, her scent, missed being with her. Before he could continue with these thoughts Rooster returned with a bottle of expensive French Bordeaux.

"Are we celebrating?" Max had to ask. The wine wholesaled for one hundred and fifty dollars, or it had three years ago. It was probably more now.

"Yes, we are. We're celebrating the fact that you're home."

"Home," Max repeated. He hadn't expected to feel this sense of welcome. He was really, truly back, and it felt damn good.

Rooster opened the wine and left it to breathe as they wandered from room to room, inspecting the house.

Max paused just inside the master bedroom door. The walk-in closet was filled with Kate's things—her clothes, shoes, jewelry. Seeing it gave him an emotional jolt. Automatically, he turned and walked away. He'd deal with that later. It was still too soon.

By the time he returned to the living room, Rooster had poured the wine. They sat across from each other in a comfortable silence. With a friend as good as Rooster, words weren't necessary. They savored the wine; Max decided it was worth every penny.

"Have you heard from Bethanne?" Rooster asked after a while.

"No, have you?"

Rooster chuckled. "Not lately."

"She's with her ex."

His friend's eyebrow arched. "You worried?"

Max could brush off his concern but Rooster would see through that easily enough. "I'd be lying if I said I wasn't." He tried not to think of Grant and Bethanne together. No one needed to tell him that the ex would do everything in his power to persuade Bethanne to give him another chance. For that matter, maybe she should. They had plenty of reason to try again.

"Are you going to do anything?"

"Like what?" Max reached for his wine goblet, holding the stem as he studied the dark purplish liquid. It helped if he focused on something like the rich color of the wine rather than his feelings for Bethanne.

"You could always call her. It wouldn't hurt to keep in touch, you know. Her ex phoned her every day, sometimes more than once. Fair is fair."

Max didn't remember it that way and said so.

"Okay, so Grant talked to the daughter, but you can bet Annie relayed every message."

Annie was definitely Grant's ally, as she should be. With Max out of the picture and Grant pleading his case, Max had to wonder if he stood a chance. "There's a good possibility I'll lose her."

"You okay to sit back and let that happen?"

"I don't have any choice." Before they parted, Max had told her he'd give her breathing room, and he was keeping his word.

"What do you mean?" Rooster argued. "The least you can do is tell her how you feel. Fight fire with fire."

Max mulled over his friend's advice. "I'll take it under consideration."

"Do."

Rooster left a little while later. Max remained in his chair, the wineglass in his hand. His cell phone was attached to his belt, within easy reach. Not once since they'd parted had he called her, although she'd phoned him that one time. Their conversation had been far too short— and then silence. And he knew why. Grant was being persuasive. No doubt about it, the ex had the advantage.

He unclipped his phone, punched out the number and closed his eyes as he waited for her to answer.

"Hello."

She sounded busy, harried.

Background noise made it difficult to hear. "It's Max."

"Max. Oh, Max…"

This wasn't the warm reception he'd been hoping for. The tension between his shoulders increased.

"Can you talk?" he asked.

"Give me a minute," she said. "I need to go out on the patio. I'm in a restaurant and it's hard to hear you."

The background clatter died down as Bethanne apparently stepped outside. "Where are you?" she asked.

"Monterey, California. At the house where Kate and I lived."

"Are you okay?"

Funny how that was the first question everyone seemed to have.

"So far. What about you?"

"I'm fine. Everything's good. Annie, Grant and I threw prom night for Ruth and Royce yesterday evening—they're out with friends right now. We fly home next Sunday, after the reunion."

"Prom night?" He frowned. "You arranged a prom night for your ex-mother-in-law and her high school boyfriend?"

"It's a long story. I'll explain later."

So there'd be a later for them. Or at least it sounded that way. "Bethanne, listen, there are things I need to tell you, things I should've told you before."

"Please don't say anything—it isn't necessary."

A chill went through him. "Are you telling me you've made a decision and you and Grant are getting back together?" That seemed the only logical explanation.

"Yes…no. I don't know… He's been so wonderful and…well, I didn't think it was possible, but after the past few days I'm wondering if maybe we should give it a shot."

Max couldn't blame her, although his disappointment was devastating. "Are you *sure* this is what you want?"

"No…no. Oh, Max, the minute I heard your voice my heart went crazy. Grant's here and everything seems idyllic. But I'm afraid this won't last." She sighed. "Try as I might, I can't get you out of my mind."

He relaxed a little. "I can't get you out of mine, either." He couldn't lose her so soon after he'd found her. "There's no need to decide anything now," he said. "You have time."

"Andrew and Courtney's wedding. I have to get through my son's wedding." Her voice was frantic. "I have to—"

"Bethanne." He murmured her name. "Stop. Take a deep breath and listen to me."

"Okay."

He heard her soft intake of air. "Everything's going to work out. I'm not going to pressure you one way or the other. This is up to you, and if you want to reconcile with Grant, then I'll abide by your decision and get out of your life."

"You'd do that? You'd walk away without a word?"

He would. He hated the thought of it, but he would. "Yes. I'd respect your wishes."

"But…" She sounded hurt, confused.

"Bethanne," he said. "That's what people do when they love the other person. Your happiness is paramount to me."

"Do you love me, Max? Is it possible to love someone after such a short time?"

These weren't questions Max felt qualified to answer. "I don't know." Anything less than total honesty would be wrong. "What I do know is that I feel alive when I'm with you. You inspire me to open my eyes and accept the past and not worry about the future."

"Oh, Max."

"If that's love, then that's what I feel. If you think Grant's the man who'll make you happy, then I'll remove myself from the equation."

"Max, hold on a minute."

She'd lowered the phone, but Max could still hear. "Tell everyone I'll be back in a minute." Someone else spoke, although Max couldn't tell who it was. "I'm not being rude. I'll be inside when I'm finished."

This wasn't a good time. He shouldn't have phoned.

"I'm back now. I'm sorry," Bethanne said.

"It's all right—I understand. I'll let you return to your meal." If he'd been smart enough to remember the three-hour time difference, he would've realized it was the dinner hour.

"I...want to see you," she whispered as though it was a weakness of character. "I know I'm being completely unfair and that you deserve so much more than to be left hanging. I'll be able to think more clearly once I'm back in Seattle and Andrew and Courtney are married. I... apologize that I can't be more definite than that."

At this point Max was willing to take whatever she was willing to offer. "Get through your son's wedding and then we'll talk. I'll fly up to Seattle and we can meet face-to-face."

"Does this mean we won't talk until after the wedding?" she asked.

"I'll leave that up to you."

"What do you mean?"

"I mean it would be better if you phoned me instead of the other way around."

"Okay." She seemed uncertain. "Do you *want* to hear from me?"

That was an understatement. "Yes, very much."

"Okay."

"I'll wait for your call."

"All right."

"Now go back inside that restaurant and enjoy your dinner."

"I will. Bye, Max."

"Bye." He didn't want the conversation to end, didn't want to break the connection. So he continued to hold the cell phone against his ear. He heard the click and knew she'd terminated the call.

He was losing Bethanne. He felt it and was powerless to do anything more than hope.

Twenty-Nine

Annie's suitcase was packed, and while her mother and grandmother ran a few last-minute errands, she stayed at the hotel. Her father would be picking the three of them up early that afternoon for the evening flight to Seattle.

While she waited, she sat in the restaurant that overlooked the Atlantic and read through her emails. Vance sent her as many as five a day. He said basically the same thing in each one.

He was miserable.

As he should be!

He wanted to come back to Seattle.

He should've thought of that before he took off without me.

He wanted her to join him.

Fat chance of that.

Annie wasn't willing to forgive and forget. Okay, deep down maybe she could be talked into letting bygones be bygones. Eventually. But as her mother had pointed out, she wanted Vance to admit he was wrong, which was something he seemed incapable of doing. That being the case, she ignored his pleas. If she sent him one email a day, he should consider himself lucky. Maybe it was petty and immature, but she made sure he knew she wasn't sitting around pining for him. In fact, she mentioned Craig's and Jason's names at every opportunity.

To be honest, the thought of joining him in Europe did appeal to her, but she'd never let him know that. Besides, she had a year of school left before she got her MBA and she wasn't going to drop out now just to spend a month or two on vacation. As Vance had so incisively said, she had *responsibilities*. He would no doubt realize soon enough that *everyone* had responsibilities.

Annie opened today's first email from Vance, read it and then settled back to mull over this latest bit of news. Vance was returning home at the end of August. His parents had deposited money in his account so he could get his ticket changed. He was heading home.

Annie's first reaction was sarcastic. *Isn't that wonderful?* At the same time, she couldn't help feeling kind of good, knowing that Vance would be in Seattle again. However, she was determined that their relationship wasn't going to slip back to what it had been. For that matter, she wasn't sure she wanted to be with him at all.

Vance had been secretive, insensitive and a jerk, and that was just the beginning of the list of character defects she'd compiled. If he assumed everything would remain status quo between them, he was in for a shock.

Annie generally waited a day or two before she replied to any of Vance's emails. She carefully composed a response and then reviewed every word before she pressed the send button.

She decided not to reply yet. Instead, she emailed Jason.

She planned to stay in touch with Royce's grandson, Craig, too; he'd been a lot of fun this past week. They had a great time putting together the prom for their grandparents. She thought it was really cool that Craig's grandfather and her grandmother had gotten together again after fifty years. Those two were crazy about each other. It reminded her of the way Max looked at her mother—and her mother at him.

She almost felt sorry for Max because after the past week it was pretty obvious that her parents would reunite. The truth was, she actually liked Max. Her problem with him was simple—he stood, or used to stand, between her mother and father.

"I figured I'd find you here."

Annie looked up to see her father. She checked her watch. "Hi, Dad."

"Hi," he said, and slid into the booth across from her.

Annie closed her computer. "I didn't think we were leaving for another couple of hours."

"We aren't. I was hoping you'd be alone so we could chat."

The waiter approached, and her father waved him off with a grin.

"What's up?" she asked. Reaching for her glass of iced tea, she sipped through the straw.

Her father crossed his arms on the table and leaned forward. "Did you notice how well things are going between your mother and me?"

Annie nodded.

"I think we might make a go of it."

"I hope so." However, Annie didn't discount her mother's feelings for Max. "Don't get overconfident, Dad," she warned.

"I won't. All I want is a second chance." He shifted uncomfortably. "I know I shouldn't be asking you this."

"What?"

He shook his head. "Never mind."

"Dad. Just ask me, okay?"

He didn't speak right away. "I know your mother got a phone call from Max the other night while we were at dinner," he finally said.

"Everyone knew about that."

"You went outside and talked to her."

It wasn't one of Annie's smarter moves. "Yeah, I told her she was being rude, which she didn't appreciate."

"Has..." He hesitated. "Has Max called again?" He frowned. "Forget I asked that. I shouldn't put you in the middle. I apologize."

"Dad!" She could so understand his wanting to know.

"I shouldn't have asked."

"You're right."

He exhaled slowly. "The problem is, I feel your mother and I are very close to patching things up, and yet I don't know exactly where I stand."

"Because of Max."

"You saw the two of them together—did you get a feel for what's going on between them?"

"Yeah, and, Dad, I don't want this to shake you or anything, but Max is hot."

"Hot as in...sexy?"

"Yeah. He's the strong, silent type. The kind of man most women notice."

"Oh."

"Not to worry—you are, too. Well, sort of."

He laughed. "Thanks. That's encouraging."

"Oh, Dad, quit worrying. Mom will do what's best for her, and that's what we all want, right?" Of course, what *she* thought was best for her mom was her dad.

"Right," he echoed. "I wish I knew what your mother was thinking, though."

Annie did, too. That morning she'd caught her mother staring at her cell phone as though torn by indecision. She'd stared at it for so long that Annie was about to comment. Before she could say anything, Bethanne closed it abruptly, and dropped the cell inside her purse.

Leaning back, her father raked his hands through his hair. "No matter what happens, I'll always love her. I was an idiot."

"We all are at one time or another." Annie wanted to wrap her arms around her father. She wanted to reassure him that life was filled with mistakes and that the key was to learn from our errors in judgment.

That thought made her sit up straighter. She was willing to look past her father's mistakes but not Vance's. Maybe she was being unfair to him. Maybe she should give him a second chance.

"The thing is," her father said, "if your mother decides we're finished, I don't know if I'll be able to love anyone else."

"Oh, Daddy." Hearing him say that made Annie want to weep. This was the kind of love she hoped to find one day. A forever kind of love.

"Also, before I forget, I wanted to thank you for telling me how much your mother admired that Civil War button. If there's anything else she likes, please pass the information along. I'm looking for ways to spoil her. I have six years to make up for."

"Oh, Daddy, you can be so thoughtful."

"Not always," he muttered. "I want your mother to realize how much I love her."

"If I think of anything else, I'll let you know."

"Great. I appreciate it."

He seemed in an optimistic mood and that pleased Annie. She glanced down at her computer. "Can I talk to you about something else?" she asked. "I could use your advice."

"Sure, baby, anything."

Annie flattened the paper napkin in her lap. "You remember Vance, don't you?"

"He's the guy you were dating."

She nodded. "The one I thought was about to propose."

"Oh, right." He frowned as if he'd welcome the opportunity to give Vance a piece of his mind.

"But instead," she went on, "he told me he was taking off for Europe. For a year."

"That was a real disappointment, wasn't it, honey?"

The sympathy in his voice soothed her hurt feelings. "I was devastated," she said. "I cried buckets."

"He doesn't deserve you, Annie. No one treats my daughter like that and gets away with it."

Annie loved the way her father rushed to her defense. "Vance is coming home at the end of August."

"So this European adventure didn't work out the way he planned, huh?" Her father's eyes flashed with satisfaction, as if to say this was what Vance got for hurting Annie.

"Apparently, Europe wasn't what he expected." She

tried to hide the pleasure it gave her to tell him so. "Now he seems to think everything will go back to the way it was before he left."

"You've got to be kidding!" His voice rang with righteous indignation.

"The problem is, I don't know how I feel about Vance anymore. I've gone out with a couple of other guys during this trip, but it isn't the same as being with him. He was more than my boyfriend. Vance was my best friend, too." She sighed. "For a while I thought I missed him so much because I was just so used to being with him. I decided that wasn't a good enough reason to get back together. But now…"

"You'll get over him, honey. Vance needs to know he isn't the only bird in the flock."

"I couldn't wait to tell him about Jason. He's the guy I met in Vegas. Jason was nice, and so is Craig. I talked to Mom about it and, well…"

"What did she say?"

It'd been a really helpful conversation. "We discussed me wanting Vance to be sorry for the way he treated me. Mom said—" Annie paused "—she said the real problem is that I wanted to make sure Vance understood that what he did was wrong. If he'd told me about this trip, it would've been different but to hide it from me and then expect me to be okay with it was too much."

"I couldn't agree with your mother more. Like I said, Vance doesn't deserve you. You aren't really going back with him, are you?"

"That's just it. I…I don't know."

"Don't, honey. If he's making plans behind your back now, that behavior isn't going to change."

"What do you mean? Are you saying that even if he apologizes I shouldn't give him another chance?" Annie was surprised to find herself sticking up for Vance, but she felt compelled to be his champion.

"Annie, you're smarter than this."

Annie stared at her dad.

"Once the pattern's set, nothing will change. Save yourself a lot of grief."

She continued to stare.

"Why are you looking at me like that?" he asked.

"So I shouldn't forgive him?"

"No way."

Annie blinked, more confused now than before. "But, Dad, you want Mom to forgive you."

Her father's eyes narrowed slightly. "That's different."

"Is it?"

"Yes! Listen, you can forgive Vance, if that's what you want. But can you trust him?"

Annie sucked in her breath. "Don't you think that's the same thing Mom's asking herself? Can she trust *you*, Dad?"

He blinked as though the question had caught him unawares. "Yes, she can. I've learned my lesson. I promise you before God and man that I will remain faithful to your mother. Never, ever again will I take her for granted."

Annie hoped that was true. She believed him—she had to—and prayed her mother did, as well.

Thirty

Bethanne, Annie and Grant drove to the airport in his rental, while Royce was taking Ruth in his own car. It was obvious to Bethanne, and no doubt everyone else, that the older couple had picked up where they'd left off fifty years earlier. All the resentments and regrets had apparently been laid to rest. Ever since the night of the prom, they'd spent nearly every minute together. And the class reunion the other evening had been, according to Ruth, the second-best event of the year.

Plans were already in motion for Royce to visit Seattle the following month. Andrew and Courtney's wedding was the perfect reason. Bethanne wouldn't be surprised if they decided to marry before the end of the summer. That would mean one of them would need to move and she wondered how they'd handle it.

"Did you enjoy your stay in Florida?" Grant asked as they approached the Orlando airport. The direct flight into Seattle would have them back in familiar territory within five and a half hours.

"Very much," Bethanne told him. The highlight for her had been prom night, when she'd felt so close to Grant.

"That was a lovely thing you did for my mother," Grant said. "You and Annie. It meant the world to Mom."

Grant had played no small part, although he was eager to give her the credit.

"I had a great time, too." Annie leaned forward from the backseat. "Even in Branson."

"Ah, yes, you and Andy Williams," Bethanne said, teasing her.

"Mom, promise you won't tell anyone about that, okay?"

Bethanne tried not to smile. "Don't worry, my lips are sealed."

"Thank you."

"I hope you'll let me drive you home," Grant said as they took the exit to the airport off the Bee Line Expressway.

"Andrew said he'd pick us up," Bethanne told him. "We planned that before we left." She'd missed her son and there seemed to be a hundred things she needed to discuss with him. Now that the wedding was just a few weeks away, they had to go over all the details for the rehearsal dinner.

"We can call him from the airport," Grant said. "There's no need for him to go out of his way when I have a car arranged."

Bethanne shrugged. She didn't want to make an issue of this, although she'd looked forward to reconnecting with their son. They'd talked while she was on the road, but nothing compared with a face-to-face conversation.

"Well, what do you think?" Grant pressed.

"It's fine, if that's what you want." She made an effort to disguise her lack of enthusiasm.

Grant didn't speak for several minutes. "I guess what I'm saying is that I want to be with you for as long as I can. If you'd rather ride home with Andrew, I understand."

Bethanne offered him a brief smile. "I'm happy to spend time with you, too."

He smiled and held her look. "Are you, Bethanne?"

"What do you mean?" she asked. She noticed that his hands tightened around the steering wheel.

"Annie and I had a short conversation earlier. She wanted my opinion of Vance and whether she should forgive him. I more or less told her to ditch him. Any man who'd treat my daughter the way he did isn't worthy of dating her."

"Daddy," Annie protested from the backseat.

"Then she reminded me that I was asking *you* to forgive *me*."

"I forgave you a long time ago," Bethanne said.

"But do you trust me?"

She hesitated. "I think so."

"I don't want there to be a single doubt in your mind. I told Annie and I'm telling you that there'll never be a repeat of what happened with Tiffany. I give you my word."

Bethanne looked straight ahead. He'd given his word before, standing in front of the minister at her family church; he'd promised to love and protect her, to remain faithful until death. She wished she could block out the doubt and tell him what he wanted to hear. It would be so easy to claim she trusted Grant. So easy to assure him that the thought of his cheating again had never entered her mind. Only, she'd be lying.

"Do you believe me?" he asked.

"I believe you're sincere," she said, not quite answering his question.

"You can trust me, Bethanne."

She smiled, hoping that would provide him with the reassurance he seemed to need.

She tried to concentrate on their relationship, on giving them another chance. Yet she couldn't dismiss her feelings for Max. She wanted to be with him. But she was with Grant, who so clearly loved her.

Grant placed his hand on her knee and Bethanne smiled over at him again, a noncommittal smile. He was trying so hard. But she couldn't give him the answer he was asking for, not now and maybe not ever. As she kept telling him, she was very different from the woman he'd once loved; the changes in her life had been dramatic. One thing was sure—she'd meet this challenge the way she'd met every other one in the past six years.

When they boarded the plane without Ruth, Bethanne was afraid her mother-in-law would miss the flight. Ruth was the last person to walk on, having waited outside security as long as she could in order to be with Royce. When she settled into her seat next to Bethanne, her face glowed with happiness.

"Royce is booking his flight to Seattle right this minute," she said, fastening her seat belt.

"So you'll be together again soon."

Ruth nodded. "Bethanne," she whispered, "am I an old fool? Is it possible to fall in love again at my age?"

"Ruth, good grief, you're not old! Besides, age shouldn't matter. Does Royce make you happy?"

"Oh, yes, but, well, there are complications. His family's in Florida and mine is in Washington."

"Your family's grown," Bethanne continued. "You can come for visits and vice versa."

"My friends are in Seattle."

"Same goes for them. Plus you'll make new friends and reconnect with old ones." Bethanne leaned over and squeezed her arm. "Do you love Royce?"

"With all my heart, and he loves me."

"Then you'll work something out."

Ruth went very still. "I wish it was that simple. I think these weeks apart will be good for us. They'll give us time to mull over some decisions."

"They will," Bethanne agreed, although she hoped Ruth would be more successful at reaching a conclusion than she'd been.

Grant sat with Annie across the aisle, and they had their heads close together almost the entire flight. More than once Grant laughed out loud at something Annie said, and she basked in her father's approval. There was no sign of the angry, rebellious girl Annie had been at sixteen.

Bethanne took the opportunity to knit, while Ruth watched a movie. When they landed in Seattle, Andrew was waiting in baggage claim. Bethanne's spirits rose the instant she saw her son.

"Andrew," she said, rushing forward. Her six-foot-tall son threw his arms around her and lifted her from the ground.

"Welcome home," he said.

"It's good to be back." Bethanne felt as though she'd

been away far longer than eighteen days. She wanted to unpack her suitcase the minute she stepped into the house and start a load of laundry. And then she'd walk from room to room in a small private ritual she had, something she did whenever she'd been traveling. She'd touch all the things she loved the most, the objects and pictures and mementos that made this house her *home,* the one place on earth where she truly belonged and that belonged to her.

"I thought your father phoned and told you he was giving me a ride." Bethanne slipped her arm around Andrew's waist.

"He did and I told him if he'd ordered a car, he should take care of Grandma and Annie. I said I'd drive you home. He didn't mention it?"

"No." But they'd barely spoken once they arrived at the Orlando airport. Bethanne had bought a Sudoku puzzle book and a couple of magazines after they'd checked their luggage and gone through security. She'd read the magazines while they waited at the gate, and on the plane he'd sat with Annie. As soon as they were airborne, Bethanne had taken out her knitting and finished her project.

Grant hugged his son, too, and although Andrew hugged him back, Bethanne noticed a decided coolness in her son's attitude toward his father. Grant still had work to do if he hoped to repair that relationship.

Father and son collected the suitcases from the baggage carousel, while Annie sought out the driver Grant had arranged.

"Bethanne," Ruth said, clasping Bethanne's elbows. "I can't thank you enough. This was the trip of a lifetime for me."

"I'm grateful, too," Grant told Bethanne. He hugged

her before they parted. "Would you like to go to dinner Tuesday night?"

After all the meals out, she'd prefer to stay in but hated to disappoint Grant. "That would be nice."

"We still have things to talk about."

She nodded. "I'll see you Tuesday, then."

"Perfect. I'll call first."

As Bethanne and Andrew started toward the parking garage, Annie found them. "Mom, I had a great time. Thanks so much."

"Thank your grandmother."

"I will. I'll see you Tuesday at the office, okay? Bye, Andrew. Talk soon."

Bethanne had decided they should take Monday off to deal with chores and relax before going back to work. She nodded, readjusted her purse strap across her shoulder. "Bye, sweetie."

Andrew was quiet on the way to the car. It wasn't until they'd driven out of the parking garage that he spoke. "Are you okay, Mom?"

"Of course."

He glanced at her. "Frankly, you don't look that good."

"Thanks a lot," she said humorously. Leave it to her son to be that blunt. "I'm fine… Oh, Andrew, I'm afraid I've met someone I…really like."

"Believe me, I've heard all about Max from Annie. Even Dad called me because he was worried. I'm glad. He could use a bit of competition."

"Have I lost my mind?" she asked. "Just when it looks like everything's coming together for your dad and me, I meet Max." She valued her son's opinion; Andrew knew her better than anyone.

"You haven't lost your mind, Mom. You're too down-to-earth for that."

She immediately felt a sense of relief. "What seems to bother everyone is that I know so little about him. The crazy part is that it doesn't seem to matter. I know what's important—that he loved his wife and that he's a good person, a really good person with a big heart."

"Then that's enough for me, too."

"Thank you." She meant that in the most profound way. She was grateful for his kindness and his faith in her.

"So, what about you and Dad?" Andrew asked next.

If Bethanne had an answer, she wouldn't be in this emotional mess. "He was wonderful the whole time I spent with him. He realizes what he did was wrong. Now he wants to…start over again."

"Is that possible, Mom?"

For years she'd been convinced a reconciliation was completely out of the question. Yet over the course of the past week, Grant had proven that he was willing to do whatever it took.

"Is it?" Andrew repeated.

Bethanne couldn't be anything but honest. "I'm beginning to think it might be."

Her son exhaled slowly. "You can actually forgive Dad for what he did to you? To all of us?"

"I'll never be able to completely erase the pain he brought into our lives," she admitted, "but I think I can let go of the bitterness."

"What about your feelings for Max?"

She shrugged helplessly. "I wish I knew what to do. In some ways I wish I'd never met him."

"But you did."

"I know." Max had seriously complicated her life. But before she could give that any further thought, Andrew turned onto her street.

This was the home she loved, the one she'd been determined to keep after Grant left. It represented far more than a house in a nice neighborhood. It was a symbol of her determination to rise above what Grant had done. She felt its welcome the minute Andrew pulled into the driveway.

She unlocked the front door and walked inside while her son dealt with her luggage. As he carried her bags upstairs to the master bedroom, she scooped the mail off the floor.

"You need me to do anything else?" he asked, walking back downstairs where Bethanne was sorting through her mail. Other than bills and a letter from an elderly aunt, there didn't seem to be anything of importance.

"No, I'm fine. Thank you for everything."

Andrew kissed her cheek, then headed for the front door.

"Can you and Courtney stop by on Thursday?" she called after him. "We should discuss the rehearsal dinner."

"Sure," he said, turning toward her. "What time?"

"How about six? I'll put something in the Crock-Pot."

"Courtney's got a bridesmaid thing, so she'll come later, but six works for me." He paused.

"Mom, I know you're troubled about this situation with Dad. I doubt I could give you any pearls of wisdom, but I'm sure you'll make the right decision."

"I'd appreciate hearing your opinion." She set the mail down and looked at her son.

"First, I want you to know that whatever you decide is fine by me. As far as I'm concerned, Dad doesn't deserve a second chance, but that's neither here nor there. All I really want to say is that you should go with your gut instinct. You did that when you started Parties and it's never failed you yet. It won't now."

"But I don't know what my instinct's saying," she muttered.

"Yes, you do. Just relax, sit back and listen to your inner voice."

He made it sound easier than it was. She walked him to the door, hugged him one last time and watched him pull out of the driveway. As soon as the car disappeared around the corner, Bethanne decided unpacking and laundry could wait. She visited each of the downstairs rooms, performing her coming-home ritual, before going up to her bedroom. Halfway there, she stopped and closed her eyes. Andrew had advised her to listen to her inner self. She concentrated hard and made a genuine effort to hear whatever message her intuition was trying to send. She heard her pulse roaring in her ears, but the message, unfortunately, wasn't clear.

Once in her room, she sat on the bed and, after debating for a couple of minutes, reached for the phone. Her hand closed around the receiver, and without further hesitation, she punched out the cell number that was engraved in her memory.

Thirty-One

Bethanne pressed the receiver to her ear and held her breath with each ring. She was nearly gasping by the time Max picked up.

"It's Bethanne," she said, struggling to talk. "Don't say anything, please. This isn't going to work. I'm so sorry." She was on the verge of sobbing. "Grant is trying so hard and he wants us to reconcile and…and I owe him that. We were married all those years and until the affair he was a good husband, a good father. He's sorry and I can't be confusing myself with you…so I won't be talking to you again." Despite her effort to make this as quick as possible, to say what she had to say and be done with it, a sob escaped.

She brought her hand to her mouth and managed to stifle a second one.

"Are you finished?" Max asked.

"Yes…I don't have anything more to say. I'm sorry, Max, so sorry. At any other time, I really think we could've made this work."

"This is your final decision."

She knew this break had to be definite. "Yes."

"You don't want to wait until after Andrew's wedding?"

Drawing this out any longer would make it even more difficult. "No."

"Why did you change your mind?"

If she confessed that she hadn't stopped thinking about him all the while she was in Florida with Grant, she'd only confuse matters. She couldn't let Max know that she had to get him out of her head if she intended to work things out with Grant.

"Bethanne?"

She couldn't answer for the lump in her throat.

"Bethanne," he said softly. "Are you crying?"

"No."

"Liar."

She laughed then, and the sound mingled with that of a sniff so it sounded almost as though someone was strangling her.

"If I could hug you right now, I would."

She wished it was possible. She needed to feel his arms around her, needed the comfort of his embrace.

"Are you sorry we met?" he asked.

"No." Away from him, she'd wavered. But now that she heard his voice, she knew she didn't have a single regret.

"I'm not, either."

"I need to go now." She couldn't talk to him because she was afraid she'd reverse her decision.

"All right, but I have to tell you something first."

"Okay." It probably wasn't a good idea to listen, but she couldn't help herself.

"When we last spoke, you said you couldn't think about any of this, about Grant or me, until after your son's wedding. I agreed. I'm holding you to that, Bethanne. Whatever decision you make needs to wait until after July 16—that's when the ceremony is, right?"

"But…"

"I won't call you. But you should understand that I'm not giving up easily. I'm here for the long haul."

"But… Grant's trying so hard," she said again.

"So would I if I were in his shoes. The fact is, I'm trying, too. I care about you, Bethanne. I didn't think I could fall in love again. You proved me wrong."

With every word he spoke, her resolve seemed to melt.

"Like I said, you won't hear from me, but I want to see you after the sixteenth. If, at that time, you feel a relationship between us won't work I'll accept that. But you're going to have to tell me to my face and not over the phone."

"Don't, Max, please don't."

"Don't what?"

"Don't love me. This is hard enough."

Her plea was met with silence.

"I wish I could be more accommodating," he finally said. "But I'm not a man who loves easily or often. I can't turn my feelings on and off like a faucet. This is what I feel, and it's not going to change no matter what you decide."

"I've got to give Grant a chance."

"Then you should."

He didn't offer a single argument. "Why are you being so amenable about this?"

"Am I? I was kicking myself for being too hard on you."

"You *want* me to let Grant try to persuade me?"

"Yes, because that's the only way you can decide. We'll meet after Andrew's wedding," he continued. "The two of us are going to sit down and you're going to tell me then what your decision is. Not now. Not when you just got off a flight and you're feeling tired and pressured."

"Yes," she whispered. She knew now that she'd been unfair to him. "You're right...I should never have called."

"I'm glad you did. Just hearing from you gives me hope."

She had to talk about something else before she started crying again. "Did everything go well with you and your brother?"

"Extremely well. I'm resuming my position in the business. What's your email address? I'll send you a link so you can check it out."

She rattled it off before she could change her mind.

"I'll talk to you in a few weeks."

"Goodbye, Max."

"Goodbye, my love."

She hung up the phone and fell onto the thick down comforter. Reaching for a pillow, she bunched it up under her head and closed her eyes, thinking she'd rest for a few minutes. The next time she stirred, it was dark outside and she felt chilled.

When she realized she'd been asleep, Bethanne sat up and waited for her vision to adjust to the dark. She'd had no idea she was this tired. True, she hadn't slept well in several nights...

Oh, no. Had she really phoned Max or was that part of some weird dream? Her stomach tensed. It felt far too real to have been a dream.

Bethanne dragged herself off the bed and took a hot bath, got into her pajamas and returned to her bedroom, peeling back the covers. She climbed into bed and didn't wake until early Monday morning.

Once she was up and dressed, she brewed coffee and put a load of clothes in the washer. Then she sat at her home office computer to check her email.

As the messages appeared, the most current at the top, she saw Max's name and inhaled sharply. He'd said he would forward a link to his company website, but she hadn't expected him to do it this soon.

She read the release and, smiling, picked up the phone.

"I called you last night, didn't I?" she said when he answered.

"Yes. Are you feeling better now?"

"Yes. I...I'm sorry."

"I mean what I said, Bethanne."

"Good."

She heard Rooster's voice in the background.

"I'm interrupting you," she said.

"Not really. Rooster's helping me clean out the house. I've got an appointment with a real estate agent this afternoon."

This was the house he'd lived in with Kate and their daughter. He must be dealing with a lot of difficult emotional issues. "Where will you move?" she asked.

"That depends."

"On what?"

He didn't hesitate. "You."

"Oh, Max." Her shoulders slumped. Guilt, never very far away, came to hover near her.

"Are you still upset?"

"No."

"I'm glad." He chuckled. "I thought you weren't going to call me again," he teased.

"I shouldn't."

"Yes, you should," he said. "Call me anytime you want, day or night, understand?"

"I won't," she told him adamantly. "Not until after Andrew and Courtney's wedding. That's what we agreed."

The doorbell chimed. She was in no mood for company. The bell chimed again and she groaned. Whoever was there didn't seem inclined to leave. "Hold on, someone's at the door," she said, putting down the phone.

Before she could get to the foyer, she heard the front door open. It was Grant.

"Grant?" she said, shocked that he'd just walk into the house. "What are you doing here?"

He shrugged. "I thought I'd stop by to see that you were doing okay after the flight and—"

"This is my home now! You don't have the right to let yourself in without an invitation."

He blinked as though her words offended him. "I apologize," he said stiffly. "The front door was unlocked and I wasn't sure you heard the doorbell."

As tired as she was the night before, Bethanne must have forgotten to lock it.

"Would you rather I left?" he asked, looking sufficiently

chastened. "I certainly didn't mean to upset you and I can see that I have."

Bethanne exhaled, torn between irritation and apprehension. She didn't want Grant to know Max was on the phone and, at the same time, she didn't want Max to know Grant was in the house.

"I've made a pot of coffee. Help yourself. I'm just finishing a phone call. I'll be there in a minute."

"Thanks."

She waited until Grant was on his way to the kitchen before she returned to her home office and closed the door.

Sitting at her desk, she propped her elbow on it and rested her forehead in her hand. "I have to go," she told Max.

"Remember, if there's anything else you want to know about me, all you have to do is ask."

Despite her discomfort, Bethanne smiled. "I'll remember."

"Call me anytime."

"I won't be calling," she said. This was becoming a litany, repeated time after time.

"That's a pity."

Grumbling under her breath, she replaced the receiver, then joined her ex-husband in the kitchen. Grant had poured himself a cup of coffee; he looked relaxed and at home.

"I apologize again, Bethanne. Walking into the house was presumptuous of me."

She wasn't going to argue. She crossed her arms and leaned against the counter. "As you can see, I'm safe and sound."

"Did you sleep well?"

"Very well." She didn't fill in the details.

He stirred sugar into his coffee. "Do you have plans for tonight?"

Seeing that she'd already agreed to have dinner with him on Tuesday, she couldn't imagine what he had in mind for tonight. "Not really. What are you thinking?"

"There's something I want to show you." He gave her a rather self-satisfied smile, which made her wonder. Still, she'd hoped for a quiet Monday evening.

"Today?" she asked. "Can't we do it later in the week?"

"Ah, sure." He was clearly disappointed.

"Could you tell me what it is?"

Grant cradled his mug of coffee. "It's a house, a lovely one that's been on the market for a while. The owners are ready to bargain—and so am I."

Thirty-Two

Bethanne didn't really want to see this house Grant was so excited about. She knew from the years they were married that he'd dreamed of one day buying a home on Lake Washington. Waterfront property was highly sought after and, in a word, expensive.

By Wednesday afternoon, Bethanne regretted ever having consented to this. She hadn't been back in the office long and had barely had time to do more than answer emails and catch up with a few pressing items that required her immediate attention. Julia Hayden had done a masterful job but there were a number of decisions only Bethanne could make. Her day was harried enough without this appointment.

He phoned at noon to confirm their meeting time. She almost told him that he should arrange the viewing for another evening. What changed her mind was how excited he seemed. She hadn't heard that kind of enthusiasm from him in a very long while.

A half hour before she planned to leave, Annie wandered

into her office. "Has your day been as hectic as mine?" her daughter asked.

"Yes," Bethanne said, glancing up from her computer screen.

Annie sat down in the chair across from her desk. "Did you and Dad get together last night?"

"We did." Grant had taken Bethanne to an old favorite of theirs. Zorba's was a family-owned Greek restaurant where they used to dine every year on their birthdays. Bethanne enjoyed Mediterranean-style cuisine, and so did Grant. Back then, it had been a real treat to splurge on a couple of special nights.

As Grant's career advanced they were able to dine out more often and they'd expanded their repertoire of restaurants. Bethanne hadn't gone to Zorba's since the divorce. Their meal on Tuesday evening had been pleasant and, not surprisingly, led to reminiscences of previous dinners there. The original owners, whom they remembered fondly, had retired and their children now ran Zorba's. While the recipes were the same, or so they were told, the food didn't taste quite as good.

"Dad said he was taking you to your favorite place."

"We had several favorite restaurants."

"You can't throw away all those years, Mom! You just can't."

Bethanne didn't comment. Instead, she changed the subject. "Did your father mention that he wants us to see a house this afternoon?"

"Yeah, I think that's great, don't you?"

Bethanne was a little startled by her daughter's reaction. "I'm not selling the house, Annie. I told your father that when he brought up this idea, but he insisted I at least look."

"It doesn't cost anything to do a walk-through, does it?"

Bethanne knew Andrew would appreciate her feelings about their family home. And she'd expected Annie to display some emotion regarding it. Annie had been four when they'd moved there and Bethanne doubted she had any memories of the apartment they'd lived in before that.

"Dad emailed me pictures of the Lake Washington house, and, Mom, it's really beautiful."

Over dinner at Zorba's, Grant had shown her brochures for cruises to the Greek isles, a trip they'd once antici-pated for their twenty-fifth wedding anniversary. Only, there hadn't been any anniversary and no trip. Bethanne had scanned the flyers while sipping a small glass of ouzo. The implication was that if they did remarry, they'd take one of these cruises—a second honeymoon.

Everything seemed to be moving so quickly. Too quickly for Bethanne. Grant was obviously trying to give her reasons to reconcile. He'd always been persuasive, a deal-maker, and he was using all his skills to sway her decision.

"Your father's trying *too* hard," Bethanne felt obliged to tell her daughter. "It isn't material things I want. There's so much more involved here."

Annie's eyes widened. "Mom, Dad's afraid." She hes-itated briefly. "Were you on the phone with Max the other morning when Dad came by?"

"What makes you ask?" She'd been careful not to let

Grant know she was speaking to Max. He might have overheard but she doubted it.

"Dad said he thought you might've been."

Bethanne didn't respond.

"It really threw him after the week in Florida."

"Oh?" So all this house business had to do with Grant's insecurities. But until Andrew's wedding, her decision was on hold. Her first priority was seeing their son happily married. Only then would she address these uncomfortable issues.

"The cruise, the house—it's all a bit much," she said.

Annie smiled. "Dad means well."

Bethanne nodded. "I know." She kept thinking about their meal at Zorba's. The recipes were the same as they'd been years ago, but the experience wasn't. Grant had wanted to recapture the past and his attempt had fallen short. Neither of them had acknowledged it, though. It might not be a good analogy, but Bethanne feared the same thing would happen with their relationship. Even if they both wanted a reconciliation to work, it might not. Too much time had passed. They no longer had the same interests or, she suspected, the same values. Bethanne liked quiet evenings at home, reading and knitting. From what Grant had told her, he often went out nights, to network, meet with clients and make connections. She, too, was required to spend a certain number of evenings at work-related occasions, but more and more she preferred to be by herself or with family and friends.

Another thought had come involuntarily when Grant suggested Zorba's. Had he dined there with Tiffany? She didn't ask. For a moment, she'd felt a fresh stab of pain but then shoved it from her mind, determined to enjoy the dinner.

During their conversation, she'd realized that the Bethanne he wanted back was the old Bethanne, the woman who'd supported and encouraged him. She couldn't slip into that role again, nor did she want to. She had her own business now. Grant was ambitious; so was she. Frankly, she didn't know if there was enough room in a marriage for that much ambition.

"What are you thinking about?" Annie murmured.

Bethanne sighed. "I want it to work with your father, but I don't know if it will. Five or six years ago, I would've moved to the moon if Grant asked it of me. Not anymore, Annie. Seeing this house is a waste of time. I know it and so do you."

Her daughter didn't say anything for a long moment. "You're right. I do."

Still, some part of Bethanne must have been trying to please Grant; she'd agreed to view this property simply because he'd been excited about it.

"Do you want me to call Dad and tell him you're too busy?"

"No." She weighed her options. Checking the time, she realized Grant was probably at his office already, waiting for her. "I'll go. Do you want to come with us?"

Annie's face instantly lit up. "I'd love it. Are you sure you don't mind?"

"I'm more than sure." In truth, Bethanne welcomed the company. With Annie accompanying her, she might be able to avoid an awkward discussion with Grant.

They drove to Grant's office in their own cars. He greeted Annie and introduced the listing agent, Jonathan

Randolph, who was going to show them the property. Annie rode with Jonathan, and Bethanne and Grant followed in his car.

"How was your day?" Grant asked as soon as they were alone.

"Frantic," she said. "What about yours?"

"Also busy." He glanced away from the road and smiled at her.

"You're going to love this house," he said as they entered the circular driveway that led to the double front doors.

Just looking at it from the outside, Bethanne had to admit this was a stunning home. "This has got to be way beyond anything you…either of us could afford."

Bethanne understood what Grant was doing. She hadn't been married to him all that time without knowing how his mind worked. He hoped once she saw the house she'd have a change of heart. He was counting on it.

And yet, after those same twenty years of marriage, Bethanne was astonished that he didn't know *her* better. She'd never longed for things. What mattered to her were the emotions and experiences they represented. Family night playing board games with their children, or a vacation that included Andrew and Annie, meant more than a diamond tennis bracelet or a pricey dinner.

"I know you love the old house," Grant said, coming to stand at her side. "I realize you have no intention of moving. All I want you to do is look at this place."

Annie was already out of Jonathan's car and eager to explore. Bethanne wished she shared Grant and Annie's enthusiasm.

True to her word, Bethanne toured the house. She had

to agree it was everything Grant had claimed and more. The views of the lake and surrounding area were breathtaking. And the inside—had she designed a dream home it would have looked almost exactly like this. A huge walk-in closet, the washer and dryer on the second floor and a deck off the master bedroom.

Grant hardly said a word as Jonathan escorted them from room to room, detailing the unique features, of which there were many. He waited until they were back in the car before he spoke.

"Well, what did you think?"

Bethanne took a moment to collect her thoughts. "You're right. It's perfect—"

"I knew you'd feel that way once you saw it," he said, nearly exploding with enthusiasm.

"But—" she continued.

It was as if he hadn't heard her. "I could see your eyes light up every time Jonathan showed us another room, especially the kitchen. Didn't you love that huge gas stove? I have to tell you, Bethanne, I could just see you roasting our Thanksgiving turkey in that oven. Plus, the house is a steal and—"

"A steal?"

"Yes, the owner's been transferred and is anxious to sell. The house has been on the market nearly six months and he wants it to move. He's making double house payments, so he wouldn't reject any reasonable offer."

Bethanne sympathized with the owner's predicament.

"I figure we could get the price down another ten percent," Grant said. "Jonathan suggests, and I agree, that we go in low and be willing to dicker. Banks prefer twenty-five percent down, and I can handle that. I'll have to sell a few of my stocks, but I feel this house might be an even better investment than what I can expect to do in the market."

"Then you should make that offer."

"I plan to, but living here on my own won't mean a thing if you aren't with me."

"Grant, please..."

"I'm not trying to pressure you, and I apologize if it feels that way."

"I'd rather not discuss this now, all right?"

He looked crestfallen. "Okay. I hope we can start over, Bethanne, and I thought a complete break with the past would be best."

"I'm not saying I don't want us to have a second chance," she clarified, "but it's premature to make that decision. I told Max, and I'm telling you, I want to wait until after Andrew's wedding."

"The old house is filled with memories," Grant argued. "Some of them must be painful, particularly for you. The only reason I wanted you to see this house is so you'd know I'm willing to invest everything in creating a new life with you."

"What you don't seem to understand," Bethanne said, speaking slowly, hoping he'd listen and understand, "is that I risked everything when you left so I could keep the house. I was the one who held our family together. I kept up the house payments and started a business. At the beginning of each month I calculated how many parties I'd have to hold in order to get the mortgage payment in on time."

"I know the first couple of years were rocky for you."

"Rocky?" The man didn't have a clue.

"Okay, I can see I stepped on a hornet's nest. How many times do I have to tell you I'm sorry?" he muttered, and she could see how difficult this was for him. Well, it was for her, too.

"So you don't want to move and start fresh," he said. "Fine. We won't."

She didn't know if he meant they wouldn't move or wouldn't start over, and she didn't ask. They drove back to his office in silence. The tension in the car was so high she almost expected the windows to shatter under the weight of it. Maybe he was right. Maybe she was incapable of freeing herself from the bitterness of his betrayal. She thought she had; she hoped she had. Apparently not.

Grant pulled into his assigned parking spot at the office and the two of them sat in the car. Neither seemed capable of moving. Bethanne hated the fact that they were fighting. When they were married, she was invariably the one who sought a reconciliation when they'd disagreed. Discord had always upset her.

"Bethanne," Grant said after an awkward moment. "I spoke out of turn. I apologize."

She took a shaky breath and forced herself to relax. "I do, too. I don't know why we lashed out at each other like that."

He reached for her fingers and wrapped his own hand around hers. "I'll do whatever makes you happy. I thought—well, it doesn't matter what I thought. What's important is your happiness. If you're still dealing with issues about me, then that's understandable. I deserve it."

"It isn't that…" Maybe it was, but only to a degree. "I don't want to give up my home."

"Then we won't," he said softly. He leaned over and kissed her cheek.

Thirty-Three

Andrew got to the house early on Thursday evening, the day after Bethanne had seen the Lake Washington house with Grant. Courtney would be joining them later. She had a dinner meeting with her bridesmaids, including Annie, who'd most likely come to the house with her afterward.

Bethanne had Andrew's favorite made-from-scratch black bean soup simmering in the Crock-Pot and corn bread baking in the oven. She'd purposely put on the apron Andrew had sewed in his high school Family and Consumer Science Education class. When she was in school, the class had been called Home Ec and it was for girls only. Times had definitely changed. Andrew had done a good job on the apron and she wore it with pride.

Her son breezed into the house, hugged her and then immediately lifted the lid on the Crock-Pot. "I was hoping you'd make the black bean soup."

"I've already passed the recipe on to Courtney."

"What about the one for rhubarb crunch?"

"That, too," Bethanne said, unable to hold back a smile. In fact, she'd put together a small family cookbook of recipes for every season. The black bean was Andrew's all-time favorite, and she used to have a huge batch going every college break. That soup alone was practically enough to bring him home.

He slid onto a stool at the kitchen counter and watched her for several seconds. "I got a surprise phone call on Monday."

"Oh? Who from?" she asked absently as she stirred the soup.

"Your friend Max."

Bethanne dropped the spoon, which clanged against the side of the ceramic pot. "*Max* called you?" She wondered how he'd gotten Andrew's number, then realized it wouldn't have been difficult.

"He wanted to send a case of champagne for the wedding."

Bethanne's mouth went dry. She tried to speak but couldn't get her tongue to cooperate.

"First, I told him I'd talk it over with you, but then I went ahead and made a decision. I hope you don't mind."

"Of course I don't mind. Whatever you decide is up to you and Courtney." Bethanne managed to speak, although her voice echoed oddly in her ears.

"It's really generous of him to offer. We haven't met, but I like him, Mom. He sounds like a cool guy."

Bethanne just nodded.

"When I mentioned that you and I were getting together tonight to discuss the rehearsal dinner, he offered to send a couple cases of wine for that, too."

Bethanne paid an inordinate amount of attention to the soup. "Your father might not appreciate your accepting either offer."

Andrew considered that for a minute, then shrugged. "I say if Max wants to send us wine as a wedding gift, we should let him. Courtney agrees. I wouldn't turn down anyone else's gift—why should I reject his?"

He had a point.

"Does it bother *you*, Mom?"

"No...I think it's a wonderful gesture."

"Me, too." Andrew slid off the stool and got two bowls, which he carried to the kitchen table, setting them on the quilted place mats.

"Did...did Max ask about me?"

Andrew appeared to find her question highly amusing. "He did."

Apparently, her son was going to force her to beg for every scrap of information. Andrew pretended interest in collecting silverware from the drawer.

"Are you going to make me ask?" she demanded.

He grinned. "I shouldn't be so cruel, should I?"

"No, you shouldn't," she said, placing her hands on her hips. She waited impatiently for him to fill her in on their conversation.

"He told me some more about how the two of you met."

She smiled at the memory.

"You didn't tell me you rode on the back of his bike."

"More than once," she admitted proudly.

"Now that's something I'd like to see."

In the beginning she'd been terrified by every bump and curve in the road, but gradually she'd learned to relax and enjoy the sensation of freedom. If the relationship be-tween Max and her developed, and that remained a huge question, she might eventually learn to ride herself.

"He didn't ask how it's going with you and Dad, if that's what you're wondering," Andrew said. "I think it's been difficult for him not knowing, but he said he prom-ised you this time with Dad and that he's a man of his word."

"Your father gave him the same opportunity," she re-minded Andrew.

"Well, sure, but he had Annie reporting to him every ten minutes. Max doesn't have anyone feeding him information."

That was true—and probably just as well.

"We only spoke for a few minutes. I told him I'd dis-cuss the wine and champagne with Courtney and get back to him in the morning. But basically we've decided to accept."

She felt her son's scrutiny as if he expected her to weigh in with an opinion. Like she'd already said, the decision was up to him and Courtney.

"You're sure you don't have anything to say about this?" he pressed.

The doorbell chimed just then, and to her surprise it was Grant. Andrew tensed as his father followed Bethanne into the kitchen. She returned to the other side of the counter while Grant leaned against it.

Father and son eyed each other, and Bethanne sensed the sadness in Grant. He missed his son and wanted the situation to be different.

"I hope you don't mind my dropping in like this,"

Grant said casually. "Annie told me you were discussing the rehearsal dinner tonight and I thought I should be here, too. I'd like to be part of this wedding." He risked a glance in Andrew's direction. "If that's all right."

Andrew didn't comment. "Mom and I were just talking about the wine."

Bethanne sent him a warning look, which he ignored.

"I have a couple of friends who are familiar with wine varieties. Should I check with them?" Grant asked.

"I believe we've already got the drinks covered, Grant," Bethanne said pointedly. "Thanks for offering, though."

"Oh." Grant looked somewhat taken aback. "I thought you two were about to discuss the menu. How do you know if you want white wine or red? Actually, it might be a good idea to order a case of each."

"Like Mom said," Andrew told him. "We've got that covered."

"It isn't that we don't value your input," Bethanne was quick to add, wanting to avoid a disagreement.

"What kind is it? Sauvignon blanc? Merlot for the red? That's what I'd recommend."

Bethanne looked to her son for help.

"I'm not sure yet, but I know it's going to be the best wine available," Andrew said. "Along with the wine, the same person's giving us three cases of champagne for the reception."

"Someone's *giving* you wine and champagne?"

Bethanne nodded.

"Really?" Grant's eyebrows rose slightly. "That's no small expense. Who's being so generous?" He rested his hands on the counter behind him. "Is it one of my clients?"

Since he obviously wasn't letting this go, Bethanne left it to her son to explain.

"It's Max Scranton," Andrew said after a brief hesitation.

"Who?" Grant asked, and then comprehension came into his eyes. "Max? That biker? You've got to be kidding!"

"Max owns a wine distribution company," Andrew informed his father.

"His brother's a partner," Bethanne corrected.

"True," Andrew said with a shrug, "but Max owns the larger part of the business."

This was news to Bethanne. Max and Andrew's conversation had obviously been longer than her son had implied.

"You aren't going to accept it, are you?" Grant frowned at Andrew, then Bethanne. "How do you think that would look?" he asked. "The two of us are working on a reconciliation and another man gives our son all the wine for the wedding. This has the potential to be embarrassing. What are you going to tell people?" He seemed to expect Bethanne to second his objection.

"I wasn't going to tell anyone anything," Bethanne said. "It's no one's business."

"Son," Grant said, looking at Andrew, "are you *really* going to accept this?"

Bethanne couldn't remember the last time Grant had addressed Andrew as "son."

"Well, Dad, I did talk to Mom and she said the decision was mine and Courtney's."

Grant glanced at Bethanne.

"The wine and champagne were given to them, not me," she said.

Grant blinked. "So...you're taking the wine."

"And the champagne." Andrew shrugged again. "It's a gift. Courtney and I were offered a nice gift by a friend of Mom, Grandma and Annie, so we're saying yes. This has nothing to do with you."

"All right," Grant said, attempting to disguise his wounded pride. Seeing the two soup bowls set on the kitchen table, he shoved his hands in his pockets. "It looks like you two have everything under control here. If you need me for anything, give me a call."

"Sure," Andrew muttered.

Wearing an expression of both hurt and disappointment, Grant walked out of the house.

Bethanne waited until the front door closed before she confronted her son. "Andrew, was it really necessary to say that the wine's from Max?"

"Yes, as a matter of fact, it was. Dad would find out about it sooner or later, and frankly I'd rather tell him now than have him discover it the day of the wedding."

She sighed, regretting the hostility between father and son, as she removed the corn bread from the oven and set it on the stove top to cool.

"Annie said earlier that you and Dad looked at a house on Lake Washington yesterday," Andrew commented.

"He wanted me to see it."

"So things between you and Dad are going okay?"

Bethanne didn't answer. Instead, she picked up the bowls, filled them and brought them back to the table. Andrew took the sour cream from the refrigerator and spooned it into a small serving dish.

"Your father is making every effort." She sliced the corn bread, not meeting his eyes.

"Sure he is. Dad wants you back because you flattered his ego. He needs that. He needs *you*. It took him long enough to realize he was never going to find anyone who'd do anything close to what you did for him."

"Andrew…I know you and your father have problems that need to be resolved, but Grant isn't that mercenary."

Her son laughed outright. "Mom, don't you believe it. Dad's always been about Dad. I'm not championing Max. I've only spoken to him the one time, so I don't know him. What I do know is the way you react whenever I mention his name. You get flustered—"

"I most certainly do not."

"There," he said, pointing his finger at her. "You're doing it now."

Embarrassed, Bethanne raised her hands to her face.

"It's been six years since the divorce and I've never seen you react to any man like you do to Max. You're crazy about him and I have to tell you I think it's great. I don't want Dad stepping in now and ruining it for you."

"But I don't *know* what I want," she said, sitting down and reaching for her napkin. Although she made a pretense of eating, she hardly swallowed a single bite.

"Yes, you do," Andrew countered softly. "You do know."

"Your father and I have talked about this and maybe he's right… I'd gotten so wrapped up in you kids and all the volunteer work I did with—"

"Mom," Andrew said, cutting her off. "You're a good mother. You always were."

"But was I a good wife?"

"Yes," he said emphatically, "and don't let anyone convince you otherwise. You did everything for Dad. You staged homes and ran errands and organized parties."

"Well, yes, I helped where I could."

"Trust me, you were a good wife."

"I played a role in the divorce, too, Andrew. I didn't see it right away but I wasn't completely innocent. I allowed our marriage to grow stale. Your father was manipulated by a woman out to advance her career and the shortest path came through using Grant. Yes, he let her do it, but he paid a high price for that. I wish you'd stop being so hard on him."

Andrew stared at her as if seeing her with new eyes. "I can't believe you're defending him."

"Think about it, Andrew. Your father's alone. Really alone. Oh, he talks to Annie but until recently the two of us hardly ever spoke. You don't have much contact with him, either. He isn't fond of his sister and—"

"And he doesn't visit his mother nearly as often as he should."

"Okay, I agree. Not only that, I believe your grandmother might be moving to Florida."

"Yeah, I got that feeling when I talked to her. She's head over heels for this old boyfriend of hers, isn't she?"

"Yes." Bethanne smiled. "But getting back to your father..."

"Okay, Mom, I see what you mean. Dad's out in the cold, but frankly he put himself there. It isn't like we shoved him out the door and then turned the lock. He chose to leave."

"It takes a big man to admit when he's been wrong," she said, consciously quoting Ruth. "Your father would give anything to undo the harm he did. I admire him for that. Look at it from his point of view."

Andrew slowly shook his head. "I wish I could. You and Annie might be willing to forgive and forget, but I can't. Dad was heartless and calculating. He couldn't dump us fast enough when he left. I tried to talk to him, tried to get him to see reason. I begged him to reconsider, and you know what?" Her son's voice rose with emotion. "He hung up on me. And you know what else? He doesn't even remember doing it. My coming to him meant nothing. *Nothing*. Well, he can come to me now and I'll give him the same treatment and we'll see how much he likes being ignored."

"Oh, Andrew…" Bethanne had no idea her son had ever tried to reason with Grant.

His jaw was clenched as she reached across the table and laid her hand over his wrist. "I wish I knew what to say."

He grew even more intense. "Don't ask me to forgive him, Mom, because I don't think I can."

Thirty-Four

"Where's Dad?" Annie asked anxiously, turning to Bethanne as if she could supply the answer. Annie and the other bridesmaids were lined up at the back of the church. Everyone was there for the wedding rehearsal—everyone except Grant. Courtney carried a paper-plate bouquet comprising the ribbons from her two wedding showers; her grandmother, Vera Pulanski, had created it. Her father, along with her brother, his wife and their two children, were seated in a pew. Her sister, Juliana, was her matron of honor, so she, too, waited with Annie.

"Dad should be here," Annie said. "Grandma and Royce were asking where he is."

"I'm sure he's on his way," Bethanne whispered reassuringly. The rehearsal was about to start and he hadn't shown up yet. This wasn't like Grant, who was rarely late for anything. The last time they'd spoken he'd said he'd be at the church by five, but it was quarter past now. She glanced at her watch again, fighting down her concern.

"Ms. Hamlin," Pastor Hudson said, smiling over at Bethanne. "I need you to sit here."

"Okay." She moved to the spot he indicated.

"Your husband isn't here?" he asked.

"Apparently, my ex-husband has been delayed," Beth-anne said, and looked at her watch again.

"Your ex-husband," Pastor Hudson repeated. "In that case we should make other arrangements."

Bethanne was about to mention that Grant wanted the two of them to sit in the same pew. She couldn't decide whether she should. Grant would be disappointed if they took separate pews, but she was afraid their family and friends would read too much into their sitting together.

In the end, she didn't say anything to the pastor; she'd explain it to Grant later.

The rehearsal was almost over before he arrived—breathless and contrite. "I got held up in traffic. There was an accident and everything came to a standstill," he said as he rushed through the church doors. "I tried to phone but everyone's cell is turned off."

"It's all right, Dad," Annie assured him.

"I'm sorry," he said again, and looked at Andrew, who ignored him. "I would've been here if it was humanly possible."

"We understand, Grant," Bethanne murmured.

He seemed to appreciate that, but it was several minutes before he calmed down. Pastor Hudson reviewed the procedures a second time. When he pointed out that Grant wouldn't be sitting with Bethanne, Grant's eyes shot to hers.

His look of chagrin nearly undid her, but she was impressed by his quick recovery. He nodded and silently took his place. Bethanne felt bad about it, but she'd never agreed that they'd sit together as a married couple.

"What happened?" Ruth asked when the rehearsal was over. "Everyone was worried."

"Traffic," Bethanne explained, coming to stand beside Grant.

"It's my own fault," he said. "I left the office later than I intended."

Royce joined them, slipping his arm around Ruth. The couple were charming together—a reminder to everyone that love is ageless.

"We're heading out for the rehearsal dinner," Annie said, approaching the group. "Grandma and Royce, do you want to ride with me?"

"Sure."

"I'll take them," Grant offered. "I need to spend as much time with my mother as I can."

"Why, Grandma?" Annie asked. "Are you going somewhere?" She exchanged a smile with Bethanne.

"Florida," Royce answered. "And the sooner, the better."

"Royce," Ruth protested, but not too much. "We weren't going to say anything until after Andrew's wedding."

"Are you and Royce engaged?" Bethanne asked.

Royce raised Ruth's hand to his lips while she blushed. "We are," he said. "No ring yet, but I didn't want even one more day to go by without making it official."

"Congratulations, Mom," Grant said, hugging her, then shaking hands with Royce. "So you're moving to Florida."

"I am," she said as she looked up at Royce. "You won't miss me."

"Don't be so sure about that, but I can see you're in good hands."

"You're welcome to visit as often as you like," Royce told him.

"Within reason," Ruth added. "We're going to be newlyweds and we might not be interested in company for some time."

Grant laughed. "You'll definitely see me in Vero," he said. His eyes met Bethanne's and he smiled.

Bethanne kissed the older woman's cheek. "I couldn't be happier for you, Ruth."

"Thank you, sweetie."

The church had started to empty; the wedding party, plus assorted family members, were on their way to the Blue Moon, where the rehearsal dinner was being held.

Grant led his mother and Royce outside. "Don't worry," he joked, "I won't be late for dinner." He pulled out his keys and pushed the remote to unlock the car door.

Bethanne waved and walked toward her own car.

The Blue Moon was a restaurant Bethanne had often worked with through the years. She had a good relationship with the manager, who'd been accommodating and helpful.

When she got there, Grant caught up with her just as she was about to enter the banquet room. "Before we go in, I have a question."

"Yes?" Bethanne said, although she would've preferred to put off a conversation with him until after dinner. She had a number of last-minute things she needed to check.

"Did Andrew decide to serve the wine…Max sent?"

"Yes." No point in prevaricating or dodging the truth. Grant stiffened at her answer.

"It was up to Andrew and Courtney."

"If someone asks about the wine, what will you tell them?"

"I'll say it came from a family friend—but why would anyone ask?"

Grant held her look for a long moment before he lowered his eyes. "You're right," he mumbled. "No one will."

Bethanne reached for his hand and gently squeezed it. "Tonight and tomorrow aren't about us. This time is for our son and Courtney. Agreed?"

Grant nodded. "I shouldn't have said anything. I can't seem to keep my foot out of my mouth, can I?"

Bethanne patted him on the shoulder. "Grant, it's fine." His evening had begun badly with that traffic accident and then arriving late for the rehearsal. She could see how tense he was throughout dinner, not really connecting with anyone, which was uncharacteristic for him. He stayed close to his mother and Royce and made eye contact with Bethanne several times, but she was busy organizing the dinner and greeting family and friends.

By the time she was ready to leave, he'd disappeared.

The wedding was taking place on Saturday afternoon at three. Bethanne helped Courtney dress, as did Courtney's sister, Juliana, her matron of honor. In her beautiful slim-fitting gown, with the wedding purse their friend Anne Marie Roche had knit and wearing Bethanne's gloves, she looked elegant. Lovely. Her beauty came from more than simply her appearance; so much love and happiness shone from her face that Bethanne was nearly brought to tears.

The photographers showed up around one and everyone gathered for the big photo shoot. Bethanne noticed that Grant remained in the background as much as possible, although he did spend some time talking to her father and his lady friend, Suzette, who'd arrived in Seattle that very morning and had rushed to the church.

Fifteen minutes before the ceremony was to begin, Bethanne, Courtney and the matron of honor, along with the three bridesmaids, assembled in a small room off the church foyer. Bethanne could hear the guests arriving.

If she survived this day it would be a miracle. Of all the hundreds of events she'd worked on through the years, the one that frayed her nerves the most was her own son's wedding.

"There's something you should know," Courtney said as Bethanne adjusted her veil.

Her future daughter-in-law looked so serious that Bethanne paused and lowered her hands. "Oh?"

"Andrew sent Max an invitation to the wedding. He felt it was the least we could do after he gave us the wine."

"And he didn't think to tell *me?*"

"He was going to, but, well, he wasn't sure how you'd react. We knew Grant wouldn't be pleased but Andrew said he really didn't care."

Bethanne inhaled a calming breath. If she was nervous before, this news set her completely on edge. Max could very well be in the church right now!

"Mom?" Annie stepped toward her. "You okay?"

She forced herself to nod. "Andrew invited Max to the wedding."

"He did?"

Bethanne clasped her hands.

"Are you glad?"

Bethanne suddenly broke into a huge smile. "Yes... very glad. I know that disappoints you, Annie...."

"No," her daughter said, stopping her. "It doesn't. I could see it wasn't really working with you and Dad. You both wanted it to, especially Dad, but it's too late."

Her daughter had recognized that almost before Bethanne did. "I'll talk to your father after the wedding."

"All I ever really wanted was for you to be happy, Mom."

"I know."

"Don't worry about Dad. He'll be fine."

Bethanne was convinced of that, as well.

Just knowing Max would probably appear at some point during the day filled her with a sense of joy, of anticipation and excitement—and it did nothing to calm her nerves.

To her delight, the wedding ceremony went perfectly. Bethanne dabbed at her eyes when Andrew and Courtney promised to love and cherish each other for the rest of their lives. Grant looked over at her as if remembering the day he'd spoken those same vows. She saw the pain in his eyes and knew how deeply he regretted having broken that promise. She smiled at him, telling him he was forgiven. And this time she meant that wholeheartedly, without reservations or lingering resentments.

Annie rode with Bethanne to the reception, which was being held at the Century Club. Years earlier, Bethanne had been a member and supporter of the club and, because of her association with it, was able to secure the hall. It was a Victorian building in the middle of the city, with five acres of manicured gardens and lawns. As far as she could tell, Max hadn't attended the ceremony, although she'd looked for him.

"Mom, did you see how happy Grandma is with Royce?" Annie asked.

"How can anyone avoid seeing it? I'm so pleased for your grandmother." Robin, however, hadn't taken the news of her mother's impending nuptials with good grace. Suspicious by nature, she'd demanded a background check, an idea Ruth had bluntly rejected.

Although she was preoccupied with keeping an eye out for Max, Bethanne managed to smile and exchange greetings throughout the meal. She moved from table to table, welcoming their guests. She lost track of Grant, but later noticed him making the rounds, too. When she could, she'd find a moment to talk to him about Max's invitation.

The best man offered the toast and the band began to play. Andrew had just escorted his bride onto the dance floor when Bethanne saw a figure standing in the back of the room.

Max.

She blinked, excitement mingling with joy.

This wasn't the Max she knew who wore chaps and a leather jacket. This wasn't the Max of simple needs and simple tastes, content to live life on the road. This was Max in a suit and tie. A man of sophistication and finesse and power. And yet...he was still Max. The Max she loved.

Drawn as if by invisible strings, she walked toward him.

He walked toward her.

They met halfway across the room, which was now

crowded with dancing couples. They stood motionless, facing each other.

"You did come," she whispered, hardly able to believe he was there.

"Would you rather I left and we talked later?"

"No…stay, please stay." She reached for his hand and held it in both of hers.

Thirty-Five

Grant saw Bethanne approach the other man and instinctively realized he must be Max Scranton. Anger surged through him but as he started across the room his son placed one hand on his shoulder.

"What are you doing, Dad?"

"That's Max! How dare he show up here." The anger burned even hotter inside him.

"I sent him an invitation."

Grant felt as if his own son had thrust a knife in his back. He stared at Andrew, shocked that he'd betrayed him in this way.

"Why?" He choked out the question. Did Andrew hate him that much?

"Dad," Andrew said, locking eyes with him. "Look at them. Take a good, long look at them."

Grant did and in that instant he knew with absolute certainty that it was too late. It didn't matter if Andrew had mailed Max an invitation or not. Grant had already lost Bethanne. He'd sealed his own fate the day he'd abandoned his family.

Without another word he turned and hurried out. Not knowing where else he could go, he went into the men's room. Pain overwhelmed him and, fearing he was about to collapse, he braced both hands against the wall, head down. He closed his eyes and struggled to breathe normally.

Despite all his efforts, his folly had cost him everything. He'd hoped to win back Bethanne. God help him, he loved her; he hadn't known how much until it was too late.

"Dad?" Andrew stepped into the room and stood directly behind him.

Grant didn't respond.

"It's going to be all right."

No, it wasn't. Nothing would ever be all right again. He was without hope. "I've lost your mother."

"Yes, I believe you have."

"She's going with Max."

"She's falling in love with him," Andrew said.

Grant straightened, fists clenched at his sides. He fought to hold on to his composure, although tears scalded his eyes.

"You're going to be all right," Andrew told him again.

Grant snickered. "Like you care what happens to me."

"Actually, I do," Andrew whispered. "I didn't think I did, and I'd rather not, but you're still my father."

Grant turned to face his son. His vision blurred as his eyes filled with tears. He'd thought he'd lost his son completely. With a wrenching sob he reached for Andrew and drew him into his arms and hugged him close, as though his very life depended on this moment. Perhaps it did.

"I'm so sorry," he sobbed. "So sorry. I need my son… please, I need my son."

It took Andrew a few seconds to return the hug. For a long time, they clung to each other.

"I need you, too," Andrew confessed. "I didn't want to, but I do."

They broke apart and after a few minutes Grant said in a husky voice, "Okay, I'm ready." He wiped the moisture from his cheeks with the back of his hand.

Andrew stared at him quizzically.

"I need to meet Max and wish your mother happiness." It wouldn't be easy but he'd told Bethanne he loved her enough to want her happiness above his own and he meant it.

Andrew nodded approvingly. "I'll come with you."

Grant regarded him for a few seconds. Although he'd lost Bethanne, he'd found the road back to his son. He put his hand on Andrew's shoulder, proud of the fine young attorney he'd become, and managed to say, "Thank you."

"I couldn't wait another second," Max whispered.

With a huge lump forming in her throat, Bethanne seemed incapable of doing anything other than gazing up at him. Not until she'd learned he might be at the wedding did she realize how desperately she'd missed him.

"I sincerely hope you're as glad to see me as I am to see you," he murmured.

Still in a trance she continued to stare. This was *Max*. Right here. Now. This minute.

Grinning boyishly, he added, "You don't need to give me your answer yet as long as you let me hold you."

Looking around her, Bethanne became aware that they stood in the middle of the dance floor with couples all around them. The music was slow and sultry, a love ballad.

"Maybe we should just dance," she suggested.

Max's grin widened. "I welcome any excuse to wrap my arms around you."

They moved a step closer and Max slipped his arms around her waist. Holding her tight against him, he lifted her feet off the floor, nearly crushing her in his embrace. Bethanne put both arms around his neck and buried her face in the curve of his shoulder. "I have missed you so much."

He snorted as though discounting her words. "You have no idea what I've been through."

"Probably not," she agreed. This time apart had been hard on her, too, but necessary. In the weeks they hadn't spoken, she'd been able to listen to her inner self and recognize what she wanted. Just as her son had said—once she listened, she knew.

What she wanted. Who she needed. Max.

Because of her twenty years with Grant and because of their children, she felt she had to give reconciliation an honest attempt, but it hadn't worked. It never really would, despite Grant's efforts to win her back.

Max's hold relaxed and she slid down his front until her feet were secure on the floor. Although they made a pretense of dancing, all they really did was shuffle their feet and gaze at each other. Bethanne was nearly giddy with joy.

Max pressed the side of his face against her temple and she closed her eyes. This must be what it felt like in heaven, she mused. This overwhelming sense of happiness, of being complete. This elation.

"Mom, Mom…" Annie's voice broke into her near-trance. Reluctantly, she pulled away from Max to look at her daughter, who'd hurried across the polished dance floor.

"Mom," Annie repeated, and stopped abruptly when she saw Max. Her jaw fell open. "Wow, you look…fabulous."

"Thank you." Max smiled down at Bethanne.

"I came to tell you Rooster's here."

"You brought Rooster?" Bethanne directed the question to Max.

He winked. "It's more a case of him bringing me."

"I owe him," Bethanne whispered.

"We both do."

"Rooster is talking to Grandma and Royce," Annie said. "And Dad's—"

"Oh, boy." Bethanne wasn't so sure what Grant's reaction would be, although she sensed that he knew it was over. Really over.

Annie shook her head. "Don't worry. I've already talked to Dad. He and Andrew…well, you'll see."

"I'll talk to your father myself." Bethanne couldn't leave this to anyone else. He had to hear it from her; she was about to explain that when Andrew and Grant approached them.

Grant stepped forward and the two men eyed each other intently. Andrew clasped his dad's shoulder and after a momentary hesitation Grant extended his hand. "I'm Grant."

"Max."

His gaze shifted to Bethanne, and he hugged her, then looked back at Max. "Love her."

"I intend to do exactly that," Max said. "Thank you."

Grant nodded and they exchanged handshakes. Grant turned to face Bethanne.

She met his look and saw the pain in his eyes. He held her gaze a moment longer and whispered, "Be happy."

She swallowed tightly. "I will." Then her eyes met Andrew's and she realized that the wall between her son and his father was gone.

Grant moved away and greeted an old friend as if nothing of importance had taken place.

Andrew came forward. "You're Max." The comment was more statement than question.

"I take it I have you to thank for the invitation," Max said as they shook hands.

Courtney joined them, and Andrew slipped his arm around her waist. "And this is Courtney, my wife. I imagine we'll be seeing a lot more of you in the future."

Max turned to Bethanne, his eyes full of warmth. "That's certainly my intention. By the way, congratulations."

"Thank you." Courtney smiled at him. "Andrew and I also wanted to thank you for the wine."

"And the champagne," Andrew added. "I'd offer you a glass but it disappeared pretty quickly after the toast."

Max seemed touched by their appreciation. "I wanted to do something for you. I hope your guests enjoyed it."

"We all did," Andrew assured him. Then, looking from

him to Bethanne, he said, "I hope you intend to make my mother blissfully happy."

Max took Bethanne's hand in his. "I plan to see to it at my earliest opportunity."

"And when will that be?" Bethanne asked.

"How about right now?"

"Celebrate, Mom," her son whispered. "This is a festive occasion."

"I am happy." How could she not be? Max drew her back into his embrace and they resumed dancing, held close in each other's arms. They passed her father and Suzette on the dance floor; he smiled and gave them an outrageous wink.

Annie left soon after, and Andrew and Courtney continued to mingle with their guests. Bethanne noticed that Max's appearance had caused a stir. She could almost hear the speculation as to who he might be and how she knew this handsome stranger.

"So that *is* you." Ruth marched up to Max and Bethanne, with Royce at her side.

"Hello, Ruth," Max greeted her, releasing Bethanne yet again.

With one hand on her hip, Ruth said, "If you'd been dressed like that when we first met you, you would've saved me a lot of grief."

"Sorry about that."

"As you should be."

Max laughed out loud. "And this has to be the famous Royce."

Royce thrust out his hand. "Glad to make your acquaintance," he said.

"Likewise."

"We were talking to Rooster a few minutes ago," Ruth said. "He was wearing a *suit*. And a tie."

Bethanne nodded. "He cleans up pretty well, too, doesn't he?"

"You two certainly played me for a fool."

"Ah, Ruth, would we do that?" Max teased.

"It appears so. Now, you listen to me, young man. For whatever reason, this girl loves you. I can't understand it myself. She was married to my son and I have to tell you, she—"

"Ruth," Bethanne interrupted, convinced Ruth had had one glass of champagne too many.

"She deserves a man who'll love and appreciate her," Ruth went on. "If that isn't you, then I suggest you leave now before I make a fuss and embarrass my grandson and his bride on their wedding day."

"I'm your man," Max said. "I plan to love Bethanne for the rest of my life."

"I can shorten that life if you fail me."

"What's going on here?" Robin, Grant's sister, rushed over to them, reading the situation all wrong. "Should I contact the authorities?"

"Oh, hardly," Ruth told her. "This doesn't concern you." She planted her hands on her daughter's back and steered Robin away. "By the way," Ruth said over her shoulder, "Max, this is Robin. Robin, Max."

He sent her a small wave.

"Is there anyone else I should meet before I take you someplace private and show you how much I've missed you?"

"I'm not sure." Bethanne looked around, conscious of all the people watching her and Max.

"Well, I am." With one sweep of his arms, he lifted her completely off her feet.

Bethanne gave a cry of surprise as she slipped her own arms around his neck. His right arm was around her waist and the other supported her legs. He started toward the exit.

It was such an outrageous, romantic thing to do, Bethanne didn't know how to respond. "Put me down," she gasped.

"Not on your life."

"Then at least tell me where we're going!"

"We're headed," Max whispered, his eyes brimming with love, "for the rest of our lives."

★ ★ ★ ★ ★

*If you enjoy Debbie Macomber's gift for storytelling and
heart-warming charm, you're sure to love*

SHERRYL WOODS

Read on for an exclusive extract from Sherryl's new novel
THE INN AT EAGLE POINT
*and fall in love with Chesapeake Shores.
Coming soon from MIRA Books.*

Prologue

The arguing had gone on most of the night. In her room just three doors down the hall from her parents' master suite, Abby had been able to hear the sound of raised voices, but not the words. It wasn't the first time they'd fought recently, yet this time something felt different. The noisy exchange itself and fretting about it kept her awake most of the night.

Until she walked downstairs just after dawn and saw suitcases in the front hallway, Abby hoped she'd only imagined the difference, that the knot of dread that had formed in her stomach was no more than her overactive imagination making something out of nothing. Now she knew better. Someone was leaving this time—quite possibly forever, judging from the pile of luggage by the door.

She tried to quiet her panic, reminding herself that her dad, Mick O'Brien, left all the time. An internationally acclaimed architect, he was always going someplace for a new job, a new adventure. Again, though, this felt different. He'd only been home a couple of days from his last trip. He rarely turned right around and left again.

"Abby!" Her mother sounded startled and just a little edgy. "What are you doing up so early?"

Abby wasn't surprised that her mother was caught off

guard. Most teenagers, including Abby and her brothers, hated getting up early on the weekends. Most Saturdays it was close to noon when she finally made her way downstairs.

Abby met her mother's gaze, saw the dismay in her eyes and knew instinctively that Megan had hoped to be gone before anyone got up, before anyone could confront her with uncomfortable questions.

"You're leaving, aren't you?" Abby said flatly, trying not to cry. She was seventeen, and if she was right about what was going on, she was the one who was going to have to be strong for her younger brothers and sisters.

Megan's eyes filled with tears. She opened her mouth to speak, but no words came out. Finally, she nodded.

"Why, Mom?" Abby began, a torrent of questions following. "Where are you going? What about us? Me, Bree, Jess, Connor and Kevin? Are you walking out on us, too?"

"Oh, sweetie, I could never do that," Megan said, reaching for her. "You're my babies. As soon as I'm settled, I'll be back for you. I promise."

Though her declaration was strong, Abby saw through it to the fear underlying her words. Wherever Megan was going, she was scared and filled with uncertainty. How could she not be? She and Mick O'Brien had been married for nearly twenty years. They'd had five children together, and a life they'd built right here in Chesapeake Shores, the town that Mick himself had designed and constructed with his brothers. And now Megan was going off all alone, starting over— How could she not be terrified?

"Mom, is this really what you want?" Abby asked, trying to make sense of such a drastic decision. She knew plenty of kids whose parents were divorced, but their moms hadn't just packed up and left. If anyone had gone, it had been the dads. This seemed a thousand times worse.

"Of course it's not what I want," Megan said fiercely. "But things can't go on as they have been." She started to say more, than waved it off. "That's between your father and me. I just know I have to make a change. I need a fresh start."

In a way, Abby was relieved that Megan hadn't said more. Abby didn't want the burden of knowing what had driven her mother to go. She loved and respected both of her parents, and she wasn't sure how she would have handled careless, heated words capable of destroying that love she felt for either one of them.

"But where will you go?" she asked again. Surely it wouldn't be far. Surely her mother wouldn't leave her all alone to cope with the fallout. Mick was helpless with emotions. He could handle all the rest—providing for them, loving them, even going to the occasional ball game or science fair—but when it came to everyday bumps and bruises and hurt feelings, it was Megan they all relied on.

Then again, why wouldn't Megan assume Abby could handle all the rest? Everyone in the family knew that Abby took her responsibility as the oldest seriously. She'd always known that her parents counted on her as backup. Bree, who'd just turned twelve-going-on-thirty, and her brothers would be okay. With Megan gone, Bree might retreat into herself at first, but, mature and self-contained, she would find her own way of coping. Kevin and Connor were teenage guys. They were pretty much oblivious to everything except sports and girls. More often than not, they found their exuberant, affectionate mother to be an embarrassment.

That left Jess. She was only a baby. Okay, she'd just turned seven last week, Abby reminded herself, but that was still way too young not to have her mom around. Abby had no idea how to fill that role, even temporarily.

"I won't be that far away," Megan assured her. "As soon

as I've found a job and a place for all of us, I'll come back for you. It won't take long." Then, almost to herself, she added, "I won't *let* it take long."

Abby wanted to scream at her that any amount of time would be too long, any distance too far. How could her mother not see that? But she looked so sad. Lost and alone, really. Her cheeks were damp with tears, too. How could Abby yell at her and make her feel even worse? Abby knew she would simply have to find a way to cope, a way to make the others understand.

Then she was struck by another, more terrifying thought. "What about when Dad goes away on business? Who'll look out for us then?"

Megan's expression faltered for just an instant, probably at the very real fear she must have heard in Abby's voice. "Your grandmother will move in. Mick's already spoken to her. She'll be here later today."

At the realization that this was real, that if they'd made arrangements for Gram to move in, then this separation was permanent and not some temporary separation that would end as soon as her parents came to their senses, Abby began to shake. "No," she whispered. "This is so wrong, Mom."

Megan seemed taken aback by her vehemence. "But you all love Gram! It'll be wonderful for you having her right here with you."

"That's not the point," Abby said. "She's not *you!* You can't do this to us."

Megan pulled Abby into her arms, but Abby yanked herself free. She refused to be comforted when her mother was about to walk out the door and tear their lives apart.

"I'm not doing this *to* you," Megan said, her expression pleading for understanding. "I'm doing it *for* me. Try to understand. In the long run it's going to be best for all of us."

She touched Abby's tearstained cheek. "You'll love New York, Abby. You especially. We'll go to the theater, the ballet, the art galleries."

Abby stared at her with renewed shock. "You're moving to New York?" Forgetting for a moment her own dream of someday working there, making a name for herself in the financial world, all she could think about now was that it was hours away from their home in Chesapeake Shores, Maryland. A tiny part of her had apparently hoped that her mother would be going no farther away than across town, or maybe to Baltimore or Annapolis. Wasn't that far enough to escape her problems with Mick without abandoning her children?

"What are we supposed to do if we need you?" she demanded.

"You'll call me, of course," Megan said.

"And then wait hours for you to get here? Mom, that's crazy."

"Sweetie, it won't be for long, a few weeks at most, and then you'll be with me. I'm going to find a wonderful place for us. I'll find the best private schools. Mick and I have agreed to that."

Abby desperately wanted to believe it would all work out. At the same time she wanted to keep her right here answering questions until she forgot all about this crazy plan, but just then a taxi pulled up outside. Abby stared from the taxi to her mother in horror. "You're leaving right this minute, without even saying goodbye?" She'd guessed as much earlier, but now it seemed too cruel.

Tears streamed down Megan's cheeks. "Believe me, it's better this way. It'll be easier. I've left notes for everyone under their bedroom doors, and I'll call tonight. We'll be together again before you know it."

As Abby stood there, frozen with shock, Megan picked up the first two bags and carried them across the porch and down the front steps to the waiting cab. The driver came back for the rest, followed by Megan.

Standing in the empty foyer, she tucked a finger under Abby's chin. "I love you, sweetheart. And I know how strong you are. You'll be here for your brothers and sisters. It's the only thing that makes this separation okay."

"It is *not* okay!" Abby replied vehemently, her voice starting to climb. Until now, she'd mostly kept it together, but the realization that her mom wasn't even sticking around to handle the initial fallout from this made her want to scream. She wasn't an adult. This wasn't her mess to solve.

"I hate you!" she shouted as Megan walked down the steps, her spine straight. She shouted it again just to make sure her mother heard the anger in her voice, but Megan never looked back.

Abby would have gone on shouting until the taxi was out of sight, but just then she caught a movement out of the corner of her eye and turned to see Jess, her eyes wide with confusion and dismay.

"Mommy," Jess whispered, her chin wobbling as she stared through the open doorway at the disappearing taxi. Her strawberry-blond hair was tangled, her feet bare, the imprint of her old-fashioned chenille bedspread on her cheek. "Where's Mommy going?"

Calling on that inner strength everyone believed she had, Abby steeled herself against her own fear, tamped down all the anger and forced a smile for her little sister. "Mommy's going on a trip."

Tears welled in Jess's eyes. "When's she coming back?"

Abby gathered her sister in her arms. "I'm not sure," she said, then added with a confidence she was far from feeling, "She promised it won't be long."

But, of course, that turned out to be a lie.

Welcome to Cedar Cove— a small town with a big heart!

Guess what? I'm falling in love! With Mack McAfee.

My baby daughter, Noelle, and I have been living next door to Mack since the spring. I'm still a little wary about our relationship, because I haven't always made good decisions when it comes to men. My baby's father, David Rhodes, is testament to *that*.

Come by sometime for a glass of iced tea. Oh, and maybe Mack can join us…

Mary Jo Wyse

Make time for friends.
Make time for Debbie Macomber.

You are invited to a Manning family wedding...

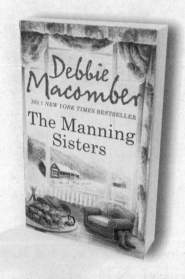

When Taylor Manning meets Russ Palmer, she thinks he's stuck in the past when it comes to women and she's just itching to teach him a lesson...

Christy Manning is on a flying visit to see her sister, Taylor. But when she sees Cody Franklin, it looks as if everything's going to change. Christy knows her feelings can't be real, because she's engaged to someone else. But Cody won't let the love of his life walk away again.

www.mirabooks.co.uk

M242_TMS

Join the Manning family for weddings to remember!

Jamie Warren's biological clock is ticking. There is one hope—her tall, dark, gorgeous best friend Rich Manning. Much to her surprise he says he'll help, but has one unexpected condition—they're legally married before the baby is born...

Paul's wife recently passed away, leaving him devastated. So when Diane's sister Leah arrives every night to take care of the dinner she saves him from the verge of collapse. Will grief be allowed to turn to happiness?

Make time for friends.
Make time for Debbie Macomber.

www.mirabooks.co.uk

M248_TMB

MIRA   MIRA

I want you to marry again...

On the anniversary of his wife's death,
Dr Michael Everett receives a letter Hannah had
written him. In it she makes one final request:
I want you to marry again – and she's chosen
three women he should consider.

Each of them has her own heartache, but
during the months that follow, Michael spends
time with and learns more about each of
them…and about himself.

www.mirabooks.co.uk

Finding a soul-mate for a mother who deserves to be loved!

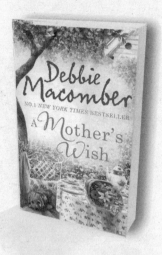

Meg's teenage daughter, Lindsey, had the nerve to place a personal ad on her behalf—worse, Steve Conlan, who answered the ad, *was* perfect, according to Lindsey…

Robin Masterton's young son, Jeff, thinks he needs a dog more than anything in the world. And there just happens to be one next door!

Perhaps there's a chance he'll have a dog, and a dad in time for Father's Day…

Make time for friends.
Make time for Debbie Macomber.

www.mirabooks.co.uk

M246_AMW

**If you had one wish
this Christmas...**

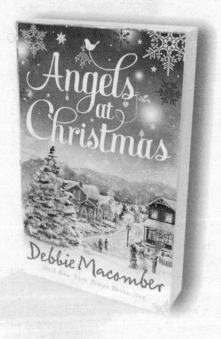

*Make time for friends.
Make time for Debbie Macomber.*

www.mirabooks.co.uk